Jesse McMinn is a writer, gamer, and Canadian with a love for fantasy in all of its forms. After graduating from Dalhousie University in the fall of 2014, he embarked on a five-month trip through Europe and Asia. After moving back to his home province of Ontario, Canada, he was married in October of 2018. He currently lives and writes in Toronto, Ontario with his wife, betta fish and crested gecko.

The Tower Series

Book 1 Loria
Book 2 Trials
Book 3 Archsage

Book 3 of the *Tower* series

Archsage

by
Jesse McMinn

This is a work of fiction. The events and characters portrayed herein are imaginary and are not intended to refer to specific places, events or living persons. The opinions expressed in this manuscript are solely the opinions of the author and do not necessarily represent the opinions of the publisher.

Archsage

All Rights Reserved

ISBN-13: 978-0-9945229-8-6

Copyright ©2019 Jesse McMinn

This book may not be reproduced, transmitted, or stored in whole or in part by any means, including graphic, electronic, or mechanical without the express written consent of the publisher except in the case of brief quotations embodied in critical articles and reviews.

Printed in Garamond and Footlight MT Light font types

IFWG Publishing International
Melbourne

www.ifwgpublishing.com

To Mom and Dad, to Nanny and Em, to Nicole, and to everyone who's been following Kyle on his journey since the beginning.

Loria

Buoria
Citadel

Eastia
Rhian
Proks

Nimelheim
Santrauss
Mist

Renir
Lafarr
Lundir

Centralia
Elfland
Reno
Donno
Kena
Kyle

Great
Plains
Harkoof clan
Oasis
Ar'ac
Morn's Rock

Westia
Impact
site
Timberfall
Skralingsgrad

Yeuda

N
W · E
S

It was twilight in the swamps of northern Ren'r.

Here, where vine-wrapped, moss-covered trees gorged themselves on the majority of the sun's rays, and legions of smaller plants survived on whatever remained, the difference between twilight and full noon was difficult to tell. Anyone walking on the forest floor would be doing so in near-total darkness, and for light would have to rely on the myriad of tigoreh lamps that lined the swamp's pathways, filling the air with their soft blue glow.

Presently, a man came walking down one such path. His manner and pace were at odds with his surroundings: he was advancing at a leisurely walk, his hands in his pockets and his one eye nearly closed. He paid no attention to the sounds of the swamp erupting all around him—the rustling of leaves, the chittering of insects, a distant cry that might have been animal or monster—and the darkness that surrounded him appeared not to bother him at all.

He was a tall man, over six and a half feet if one included his enormous, shaggy mane of blond hair. He wore a suit of leather armor over his clothes, and had a composite weapon, two swords and a shield combined into one unit, slung to his back. A disc of stone was tied over his left eye, concealing it from view.

Lughenor MacAlden carried on his walk, resisting the urge to open his good eye and look around. The only thing that kept it shut was his trust he had in his companion. Fortunately, he was good at trust. He focused on keeping his pace steady and deliberate, making sure not to stray off the path marked by the tigoreh lamps.

Every so often, his sensitive ears told him of a noise that did not fit in with the usual backdrop of the forest: a snapping twig, a vine scraping against the ground, a soft footfall. The noises had been faint at first, but now they were getting closer, and coming more often.

Any minute now, he thought.

It was as sudden as it was silent. A creature rose from the undergrowth of the swamp, twenty paces back from Lugh. Its body was thin and lithe, rubbery smooth and slick with moisture. Its face was dominated by two protuberant eyes and a pink mouth lined with small, nipping teeth.

It was barely five feet tall, but it watched Lugh with the rigid intensity of a predator. It carried a makeshift sword of wood and bone in one hand, and as it dove towards Lugh's unprotected back with an uncanny turn of speed, it raised its arm to strike.

Lugh heard the monster's footfalls a fraction of a second before its blade fell, striking him on the back of the head. His soul shield absorbed the worst of the blow, but the force of it still sent him sprawling to the ground, bolts of lightning dancing in front of his eye.

Lugh's heart pounded as he sensed the creature's sword rising once more. His instincts were telling him to jump to his feet, to roll sideways, to *react*, but he had to fight them until the last possible second.

Timing has to be perfect, he thought. *Otherwise we won't get them all.*

Just as the creature struck, Lugh threw himself to one side, rolling onto his back. The sword fell wide, and the monster hissed in anger. Lugh smiled in response. The sahagin had given up on stealth; this was now a fight, not a hunt.

At the sound of the hiss, more sahagin emerged from the darkness. They watched, but didn't come close. Cowardly creatures, none of them wanted to be the first to come to the aid of their brood brother.

The first sahagin swung again, a vertical chop. Lugh twisted his body, letting it scrape against his breastplate, refusing to regain his feet. The sahagin snarled and struck with sword and open hand, its movements quick and spasmodic. Lugh blocked what he could with his hands and let the other blows strike home; his soul shield was still whole, and for the moment the beatdown just barely hurt.

Becoming more and more convinced that Lugh was easy prey, the other sahagin finally moved closer. Lugh could see five in front of him, which would mean at least that many more behind. *No problem.*

The sahagin bobbed back and forth in a cautious advance, their eyes fixated on Lugh. Soon the circle around him would close, and all would strike at once.

Suddenly, another figure came charging down the path. He wore a light black coat, open in the front, which streamed out behind him as he ran, and he was gripping a silver sword in his hands. He raised his sword and bowled into the cluster of sahagin, his first strike killing one and wounding another. He spun and leapt over Lugh's prone form, flashing sword cutting into the ranks beyond him.

Confusion reigned. Some of the sahagin broke from the circle to attack the newcomer, while others bore down on Lugh, hoping to engage what they thought of as the lesser threat.

Lugh, however, was done acting as bait. He threw off his attacker and leapt to his feet, drawing his twin swords. He parried a blow coming from his left and cut down the sahagin that had dealt it, then dodged to the side, breaking free from the ring that surrounded him. The sahagin slashed and clawed at him, their caution dissolving as rage took its place. Lugh parried and then answered with his own rain of blows, his swords slicing through air and flesh. The sahagin were fast, but weak, and their makeshift weapons were no match for Lugh's silversteel swords. He bore down on them, forcing those in front into those behind.

His companion, meanwhile, was fighting on the other side of the ring. His silver sword clicked and hissed, growing and shrinking with each blow, adapting moment by moment. Swung in wide arcs, his heavy weapon knocked the sahagin's bone swords aside and delivered brutal slashes.

The newcomer was human, a head shorter than Lugh, with pale skin that contrasted sharply with his black hair and beard. His brow was furrowed in concentration, though there was also a smile playing about his lips.

Sensing an increase of energy inside his body, Kyle Campbell jumped backwards and prepared to vent his pent-up magic into one of the combat techniques that Lugh had taught him. A sahagin ran after him, slashing diagonally; Kyle, his reflexes bolstered by magic, shifted his stance and let the blade whistle past his ear. He called his built-up energy to the surface and retaliated with a horizontal blow that exploded in a wave of force, felling his attacker and the two behind it at once.

Now there were only two of the monsters left. As Lugh cut one of them down, the other suddenly croaked, dropped its weapon, and began to flee.

Lugh cursed, trying to pull his sword free of the sahagin he'd just slain. "Kyle!" he shouted. "Get the last one or we'll never see the end of it!"

Kyle sprinted after the monster, his eyes glued to its glistening back. He saw at once that it was hopeless; try as he might, he couldn't match the creature's pace. Acting on a sudden inspiration, he drew his arm back, willing his sword to retract into its smallest and lightest shape. As soon as it had, he planted his feet and threw. The sword whistled through the air and struck the monster squarely. Kyle saw it stumble and fall, then begin to crawl away, the sword still protruding from its back.

The sahagin was still crawling, hissing and spitting wetly when Kyle caught up with it. Kyle, bile rising in his throat, stepped on the sahagin's back, drew his knife and plunged it quickly into the creature's neck. The hissing stopped, and the sahagin's body went limp.

Kyle pulled his sword free from the monster, noting how well the sleek blade resisted any kind of damage or impurity. It had been a gift to him from King Azanhein of Buoria, as Lugh's swords had been, and was a marked improvement over any weapon Kyle had used thus far. Lately he had even found himself relishing the opportunity to use it—though this might have been due to the fact that combat was coming more and more naturally to him.

Lugh came strolling up behind him, cleaning the blood off of his swords.

"Saints be you got that one," he said, gesturing with his sword tip. "For a moment I thought he was going to get away from you." He laughed. "My mistake, right? You're becoming a real show-off, you know that?"

Kyle sheathed his sword. "I must have had a real show-off of a teacher."

"Right, right. Let's go get our stuff," Lugh said, and he started back in the direction they'd came.

Kyle fell into step beside him. "What would've happened if he *had* gotten away?"

"He'd have been back later with all of his friends—and we'd have been right back where we started."

"Wouldn't they leave us alone after all that?" Kyle nodded towards the gristly result of their battle as they passed by.

Lugh took one last look at the sword he'd been working on, then reached behind his back and let it slide home. "Nah. Sahagin might be cowards but they're tenacious little bastards too. We'd have been sleeping with one eye open all the way to the village."

Kyle understood. To hear Lugh talk about them, the sahagin were devious little opportunists. They wouldn't dare attack two men head-on; instead, they would follow, for days if need be, until their targets went to sleep or fell prey to one of the swamp's other dangers.

Now that the sahagin were gone, Kyle had time to examine his surroundings properly. There wasn't much to see: everything but the path picked out by the tigoreh lights was in complete darkness. Intellectually, Kyle knew that the sun would just now be going down, but it had been swallowed ever since he and Lugh had entered this patch of the swamp.

They reached a tree with a tigoreh lamp entwined in its roots; the tree behind which they'd hidden their travel packs. Lugh stepped behind it, reached down with a grunt, and threw Kyle's pack at him before slinging his own over one shoulder. That done, they switched direction again and set off down the path.

It took a while for Kyle's nerves, jangled from the fight with the sahagin, to calm down again. Walking the dimly-lit path had a kind of serenity to it, but Kyle's mind had a habit of picking out the small sounds that emerged from the darkness and amplifying them. The buzzing and chirping of insects he could deal with, and the rustling of leaves and lapping of water in the wind didn't bother him either. It was the snapping of twigs, the unknown animal cries that made him reach for the hilt of his sword. But he told himself that all was well as long as Lugh wasn't concerned. His companion had grown up in the swamps, and knew how to separate the signs that could be safely ignored from those that could not.

Kyle glanced sidelong at his friend. It was because of Lugh that they were making this expedition through the swamp, their destination the village where Lugh had been raised. Kyle didn't know why the trip had to be made—yet. All he knew was that if Lugh was to attain promotion, he had to first return to his homeland.

Promotion. A magical phenomenon, triggered by a certain event, that unlocked the true potential of an individual and granted them amazing power. As Kyle understood it, the triggering event differed from person to person, and could range from a near-death struggle to a formal ceremony. For Lugh, it clearly had something to do with his childhood, and with the swamp in which it had been spent.

Kyle thought back on the events that had led to this journey. At the start of it all had been the party's meeting with the mysterious Todd Wilder—a man that the world had known as Archmage Rosshku, before he had withdrawn from its history.

Kyle would always remember the days they had spent with Rosshku with fondness. When they had first encountered him in Proks, they had been directionless, weary, and mourning the loss of their comrade, Phundasa. Rosshku had injected them with a new energy and sense of purpose, helped them plan their next moves and prepare them for what lay ahead. Their ultimate goal: to hold council with the one being on Loria who might have the power to return Kyle back to his homeworld.

The Archsage.

Even after numerous discussions with Rosshku, Kyle had yet to obtain a clear picture of the man who'd once been the Archmage's master. Todd had often referred to him by his Kollic name, Vohrusien, which meant 'son of the void'.

Sometimes, he had instead called him 'the dread Archsage'.

In the end, it didn't matter what kind of a person Vohrusien was. Todd had claimed he was the only one with the power to send Kyle home, and Kyle was prepared to believe him. If there was even the slightest chance that they could enlist Vohrusien's aid, they had to take it.

However, before meeting with the Archsage, they would have to reach him. According to Rosshku, Vohrusien made his home in a tower in the northwest of Westia. It was the harshest landscape in the whole of Loria, the impact site of the meteor that had struck the planet over a thousand years ago. Though a millennium had passed since the meteor's impact, its crater was still saturated with volatile, alien magic, which twisted both landscape and wildlife.

It would be hard—very hard. In fact, it was practically a suicide mission. But Rosshku had faith in them, and they had faith in each other. Kyle's companions had refused to let him undertake the mission alone, and he was determined not to disappoint them.

Once Rosshku had seen their resolve, his mentorship had begun. He had taken each of them aside, tutoring them, counselling them, providing them with the tools they would need to survive. This was when Kyle's respect for the Archmage had grown the most. Todd always knew exactly what to do and say to work out the knots in Kyle's company. He had restored the morale they had enjoyed before Phundasa's death and then some, and had armed them against the trials they would soon be facing.

"Before you leave for Westia, there are other tasks you must undertake," he had said one day towards the end of their stay. They had all been together on the bridge of the *Aresa Bign*, Rosshku's airship, talking, enjoying each other's company, and listening to the Archmage's council. Todd, as always, had a halo of books floating around his head, covers facing the others as if they were eyes.

"What do you mean?" Lugh had asked.

"I have prepared you for your journey as best I can while you remain on the *Aresa*. But there are some preparations which have to be made in the outside world. To this end, I think it best if you split your party for the time being."

The thought of splitting their party had been shocking at first, and Kyle had been amazed that Todd would suggest it.

Nihs, who had come to defer to Todd with a respect bordering on reverence, said, "How should we be split, *Solrusien*? And where should we go?" *Solrusien* was an honorific of the Kol's invention, the twin of 'Vohrusien'—it meant 'son of the soul'.

"I believe that you, Nihs Ken, and you, Lughenor, know the answer to the second question already. I sense that the two of you are ready to achieve promotion. You have been delaying the process, but this must end now for the sake of your mission. So, why don't *you* answer *me*—where do you need to go in order to promote?"

Kyle had been confused by this exchange, and had looked to his companions for an explanation. Both of their faces had registered shock, followed by a kind of resignation.

"Here, in Proks," Nihs had said, after a moment. "That's where I need to be."

Lugh had followed with: "Lundir. It's a town in the north of Ren'r."

Todd had awarded them a simple smile in response. "Very well. Nihs Ken, you will stay here in Proks. Lugh and Kyle, you will travel to Ren'r. Miss Ilduetyr, *irushai* Deriahm…" he had addressed Meya and Deriahm, the last two members of their group. "One of you has already promoted and the other is not yet ready to promote, but I believe I have a task that is well-suited to your abilities. Once we have taken Lugh and Kyle to Ren'r, the three of us will travel to Ar'ac."

Kyle himself had often suspected that Lugh and Nihs had been putting off their promotion, but Todd had spoken with a certainty that brooked no argument. It was impossible to hide anything from the Archmage, just as it was impossible for a fish to hide in a glass bowl. To be in his company was to bare your soul to him; Lugh and Nihs both knew this, and they had accepted their missions without protest.

After they had bidden farewell to Nihs, the *Aresa Bign* had carried them with an uncanny speed to Ren'r, the landmass that, along with its southern counterpart Ar'ac, formed the greater continent of Centralia. Ren'r was the opposite of its brother in more than just location: while the Ar'ac was an arid land of deserts and savannahs, Ren'r was lush with greenery, streaked with rivers and dotted with lakes. In the far north of the continent were the infamous swamps of Ren'r, home to the hardy Lizardfolk and whichever Selks were brave enough to venture south from the coast.

Once the *Aresa* had dropped them off, Kyle and Lugh had gathered some supplies, and then carried on towards Lugh's old village on foot. Lugh had flatly refused the meagre transportation options that were available, claiming that the trek would be a learning opportunity for Kyle.

In the aftermath of their battle with the sahagin, Kyle thought, *he wasn't wrong.*

Now, the two of them walked in silence. Lugh's stride was relaxed, his hands in his pockets and his swords on his back. Kyle looked around as he walked. The path they were on was drifting upwards ever so slowly, and becoming brighter by inches. Soon, it was just possible to see the world beyond the tigoreh lamps. Grasses and reeds as tall as Kyle grew in thick clumps, covering every available surface. Enormous trees, their trunks green with moss and their branches heavy with flowers and vines, lurched unceremoniously from the swamp floor. Patches of water, completely grown over with algae, glowed with the faintest bioluminescence.

These were all common sights that Kyle could have seen in a swamp back home. Other, stranger plants grew here as well. One vine grew as a surrogate root to one or more trees, attaching itself to their trunks before snaking along the forest floor. There was a flower whose rigid leaves formed a perfect bowl over a foot wide—the liquid caught inside these bowls was a mixture of nectar and water, which lured and ensnared insects with its sticky sweetness. There was another plant still that looked like a string of balloons anchored to the forest floor; pouches of gas trapped within it gave it an edge in the ongoing battle for sunlight.

"Check this out," Lugh said, and cut one of the balloons free with his knife. It floated lazily upwards, soon getting lost in the lush canopy overhead.

There was wildlife here, too, but Kyle couldn't see it, only hear it. In a way he was thankful for this; the swarms of insects he had expected upon entering the swamp had yet to appear.

"It's the tigoreh lamps," Lugh said. "They've got a bit of magic that keeps the bugs away. The Selks who built these roads set it up that way."

"Nice of them," Kyle said.

"Nice doesn't have much to do with it. It's to keep disease down. There's all kinds of wonderful things you can catch from the bugs here."

"You said the first Selks lived on the coast," Kyle said. "Why would they ever choose to come down here?"

"Had to. Every coastline in the world flooded when the meteor hit. Our homes got wiped out and the fish vanished, so we had no choice but to pack up and move. Worked out all right for us, though. If we hadn't gone into the swamps we wouldn't have met the Lizardfolk."

Kyle looked around once more. He'd forgotten that the swamps were the home of the Lizardfolk. He'd met a few of their kind before; during the first adventuring mission he'd ever run, in fact. He thought of their colorful, scaled faces, their yellow eyes glowing with intelligence, and their cheerful, witty manner. He could see how they and the Selks would have gotten along.

By now, their path had turned into an incline, running along the side of a hill held together by a clump of trees at the top. It grew brighter with each step, and soon Kyle was amazed to see a purple-and-orange sunset breaking over the distant trees. He couldn't believe it had been daylight up here this entire time.

As Kyle took in the sunset, Lugh stared up at the hill to their left, his hands on his hips. He walked over to where Kyle was standing and jabbed his thumb back in its direction.

"Looks like a good spot," he said.

Kyle turned and leaned back, taking the hill in. It was quite large, more an earthen pillar than a hill. Anything not covered in greenery had been devoured by erosion; grass and the occasional tree gave way to sheer faces of loose rock and packed earth.

"A good spot for what?" he asked.

Kyle felt a rush of wind as Lugh ran past him, sprinting towards the hill. A second later, Lugh jumped, flying up and forward in a magically charged leap that carried him to one of the small outcroppings halfway up the pillar's face. Twenty feet above Kyle, he turned around and leaned over the edge, arms folded.

"You leapt off the *Ayger* when it was about to crash," he said. "So we know you can do it. But you never learned how to do it at will."

Kyle had to smile. Lugh was a great believer in hands-on learning.

"All right, then," he called up. "How do I do it?"

"Same way you do all the other tricks I taught you. You've got the ability, so all that's left is getting the mindset right. Once the feeling clicks in your brain you'll never forget how to do it. Best way to learn that feeling is to keep trying it."

That was another thing about having Lugh as a teacher; he never did very much teaching. Since most of the techniques Lorian fighters used in combat were fueled by magic, their mastery was governed by the nebulous rules of magic use—strength of will took precedence over all else.

Kyle faced the hill down, calling to mind what it felt like when the others leapt. There was always a sense of *pushing off*, being catapulted away from the ground by a pulse of magic. He imagined the smooth arc of flight, painting it in the air between him and Lugh.

Knowing that overthinking would only lead to failure, Kyle broke into a run and sprinted towards the hill. After a half-dozen strides, he flexed his muscles and jumped—a total distance of about six feet.

It took him a couple seconds to slow himself down and regain his balance. He could hear Lugh laughing above him.

"Shut up," he said, as he turned around and started to walk back.

"Sorry, sorry," Lugh called back, still laughing. "I forgot how funny it looks when a leap doesn't turn out. You're straining too much, you hear? You don't actually have to jump the whole distance, so don't try."

Right. Kyle knew that trying too hard was often his downfall. Magic was like quicksilver: exert too much force and it would slip between your fingers.

Back at his starting point, he turned to face the hill. Lugh was leaning against a tree, watching his progress. Kyle envisioned the leap once again. The initial pulse, the graceful flight, the shock-absorbing landing.

He ran towards the hill again, his focus bent on the ledge next to Lugh. He kicked off from the ground—and was launched into the sky with a *whoomph* of rushing air. A scream caught in his throat as he rose five, ten, twenty feet. His arms pinwheeled and he ran in the open air, fighting to keep himself upright and on-course.

The outcropping on which Lugh was standing came soaring towards him. He braced himself for his landing, stuck out one leg and hit the ground running, throwing up clods of earth as the ground absorbed his momentum. He ran forward to keep himself from falling over, and would have fallen off the far side of the ledge if Lugh hadn't grabbed him by the collar to steady him.

"There you go!" Lugh said, slapping him on the back. "No problem. Now you just have to keep it up until you can't get it wrong."

Kyle stood still for a moment, panting, trying to calm his beating heart. He wasn't normally afraid of heights, but the leap had left him shocked and light-headed. He tried not to look over the corner of the ledge as he recovered.

Lugh, however, already had his eye on another ledge farther up. He leapt over to it, and then turned back at Kyle, motioning for him to follow.

"Really?" Kyle called after him.

"Of course! You thought you'd leap once and we'd be done? Come on!"

"What if I fall?"

"Don't!"

Kyle eyed the distance between the ledges. It would be a relatively short leap, but he also had less room to get a running start. Then he thought, *I'm jumping using magic. I don't need a running start.*

He crouched down low, then took two steps and kicked off from the ground, praying that the leap would work. It did—he flew over to Lugh, the wind whistling in his ears. This time, he was able to stop himself short of falling off the ledge.

"Takes a while to learn how to steer yourself properly," Lugh said. "Probably feels a bit out of control right now, huh?"

"A little bit," said Kyle, who was leaning against the solid hillside for comfort.

"Right. Let's keep going!" And Lugh leapt again, this time almost straight up. Kyle watched as he rose up beyond the top of the hill, and came back down gently onto its summit.

Kyle had no choice but to follow. He braced himself and leapt straight upwards, mimicking Lugh's motions and trusting his instincts to fill in the gaps. He flew upwards and landed beside his friend, whose arms were again folded.

"Fancy seeing you up here," Lugh said, grinning. "Take a look."

Kyle looked. The hill they were standing on was the highest point in the swamp for a mile around; if it weren't for the copse of trees growing at the top, he would have a three-hundred-and-sixty-degree view of the area around it. Even as it was, the view was impressive. The sun was setting over the trees far in the distance, painting the sky orange and casting dramatic shadows over the landscape. In the darker patches where the sun never reached, it was possible to see an occasional glow of bioluminescence. Some were blue, while others still were green. The sight reminded Kyle of the hall of colors in Proks, with its giant, glowing mushrooms of all shapes and colors. Briefly he wondered about Nihs, and how he was getting along with his quest for promotion.

Lugh pointed northwards. "See the big clump of hills way in the distance? My old village is tucked away in there. Shouldn't take us too long to reach now that we can leap, right?"

Kyle followed Lugh's pointing arm with his eyes. The group of hills was miles away. "You've got to be kidding," he said.

Lugh laughed out loud. "I suppose so," he said. "Wouldn't want to kill ourselves leaping around at night."

"So we set up camp here?" Kyle asked.

Lugh looked around. "You know," he said, "now that I'm here, I'm not sure that I like this hill. I think we can do better, don't you?"

Kyle couldn't help but laugh when he realized what Lugh was suggesting. "It's possible," he said.

"We've got enough daylight to check out a few more before we decide. How about we start with that one?" Lugh pointed.

"Looks good to me," Kyle said. This time, he didn't wait to be left behind. He ran past Lugh and leapt off the edge of the hill, the cool night air rushing past him. His fear was already being consumed by exhilaration; his control was getting better and better. He landed on an outcropping of rock near the path they had been following, and immediately leapt again, marveling at how quickly he could cover ground with this newfound ability.

He had been foolish to think that he could outpace Lugh. After a couple leaps, his friend reappeared beside him, matching his pace, filling the spaces between jumps with magic-fueled dashes. Together they tore through the forest, jumping from vantage point to vantage point. Before long, they were atop the second hill, and Kyle collapsed to the ground, panting with exhaustion.

"See? That's what you get for being a show-off," Lugh said, waggling a finger at him. He himself was breathing quite heavily. "You can't get something for nothing. Leap for a couple miles and you'll feel the same as if you'd run them."

"Lesson learned," Kyle said, though in reality he couldn't have cared less. The longer he stayed in Loria, the more amazing discoveries he made—not just about the world, but about himself, and the abilities that this world granted him. He wanted to keep leaping, to get Lugh to teach him how to dash, to push the limits of his newfound strength.

"Let's call it for the night," Lugh said. "Tomorrow's a new day, right?"

"Yeah," Kyle replied. "It is."

Nihs Ken Dal Proks, fourth of Dari Ken Dal Proks' five children, made his way through the hall of colors en route to the home of Jire and Rehs, the family with which he was staying while in the city.

His family, of course, had its own home—an old stone house in eastern Proks. But Nihs had not been there in years, and had no desire to experience the questioning that would undoubtedly accompany his arrival there.

In fact, he would prefer if his family never found out that he had returned to Proks at all. But there was little chance of that; his younger sister, Kisi, had likely already told the others. The fact that none of them had tried to meet with him was proof that they felt the same way about his presence in Proks as he did.

Nihs shook his head. *I must clear my mind of such thoughts.* After all, he knew that he would have to face his family in order to accomplish the mission that the Archmage had assigned him.

Nihs reached the colorful curtain that marked the entrance to Jire and Rehs' home and brushed it aside, entering the warm space beyond. He was immediately greeted by Kisi, who dashed across the room and threw her arms around his stomach.

"*Nizu!*" she shouted in jubilation.

Nihs, despite himself, had to return her embrace. "I see you've managed to track me down, *Kisiren*," he said.

She pulled away from him slightly, glaring at him with her bright green eyes. "You said we could spend time together once I was done my studies, but you've been gone for *days!* Where have you been?"

"I'll explain later," Nihs reassured her, knowing that he could not under any circumstances do so. Kisi was brilliant, but she was absolutely terrible at keeping secrets. Bad enough that she was bound to tell the family that Nihs was back— if she found out about his meeting with the Archmage the news would spread through all of Proks.

Kisi continued to glare at him, her eyes comically narrowed, as he escaped from her embrace and moved further into the room. He nodded to Rehs, who was working in the kitchen, and then caught sight of Nella, another one of his sisters, who was rising from a nearby pile of cushions.

Nella, unlike Kisi, was not Nihs' blood relative. But the two of them had been friends since childhood, and the strength of the bond they shared was such that they were considered siblings.

Nihs had always relied on Nella's friendship and support; even though she rarely ventured outside of the Kol's homeland, she and Nihs spoke nearly every day via the overhead. Now that they were physically close together, Nihs found himself craving her presence even more.

She crossed the room to him, her ears unfolding at the sides of her head. Nihs' did the same, and when Nella reached him, the two of them locked forearms, and their ears wove around each other in a helix shape.

"You've returned," Nella said simply. "But the others are no longer with you. Why is this, *Nizu?*"

"The others have left for Centralia," Nihs said. "They've each been given work to do. As for myself…" he paused, realizing that Kisi had sidled over and was listening to every word.

"*Kisiren*," he said, "it's very late. Shouldn't you be getting to bed?"

Her reaction, as expected, was outraged. "You just got here!" she said. Then: "I'm not tired! I want to stay up and talk with you and *Nellazan!*"

"You need to sleep," Nihs said, "so you have a fresh mind for your lessons tomorrow. You know that."

Kisi blew her cheeks outward in a pout. "Lessons, lessons, lessons!" she shouted. "That's all mother and father ever talk about, and now that's all *you'll* talk about, too!"

Nihs was going to respond, but Kisi stormed out of the room before he had the chance. He heard the patter of her feet in the back rooms and then the *whump* of her throwing herself down on her bed.

Rehs clucked her tongue from the kitchen. "What a temper that one has," she said softly.

"Mm," Nihs hummed his agreement. "I can't imagine where she gets it from."

"I think she is frustrated," Nella said, as they walked together back to the sitting area. "She claims that her lessons bore her, but the more her teachers try to teach her the more she resists."

"She's not doing poorly, is she?" Nihs asked.

"Quite the contrary. She's far outstripped the others her age even though she won't apply herself. I've kept her on track as best I can."

"Thank you, Nella," Nihs said. "I dread to think of what would happen if you weren't there to corral her. Though it shouldn't be your responsibility."

"It can't be helped. She won't listen to anyone else. Save for you, of course."

That did little to inspire confidence. When it came to study of magic, Kisi was nothing short of a prodigy; even their father, Dari, could see that she had the potential to become the most talented of his children. But she was worryingly obtuse in many other ways. She could not, or would not, understand why Nihs distanced himself from the rest of the family, or why he resisted her attachment to him.

Not for the first time, Nihs thought, *it's a good thing she's so gifted, or her attitude would have gotten her dismissed as a lost cause long ago.*

He forced himself to push Kisi from his mind. His sister was a constant form of worry for him, but he couldn't let her distract him from the task at hand.

He could see from her expression that Nella felt the same way. "*Nizu,*" she said, "what news from the Archmage?" She had been with Nihs and the others when they had first met him, but had been forced to leave to avoid those in the city questioning her absence.

"He's given each of us a task to complete before we make the journey to Westia," Nihs said. "That's why the others have gone—Kyle and Lugh to Ren'r and Meya and Deriahm to Ar'ac."

"And what about you, *Nizu?*" Nella asked.

Nihs took a deep breath. Saying it would make it that much more real, and further increase the cost of failure.

"I'm to seek my promotion here in Proks," he said finally. "The Archmage believes that if we're to succeed in Westia, we all have to be at our full strength. Lugh and Kyle are in Ren'r for the same reason."

Nella drew a sharp breath, but said nothing. She searched Nihs' face, working out how to respond.

Rehs came over carrying a tray of drinks. She deposited two on the table before seating herself nearby. Nihs didn't mind her listening; after all, she and her partner Jire had housed Kyle and the others in Proks, and knew the significance of Kyle's origins.

"I see," Nella said at last. "The Archmage is right, of course. But securing your promotion will not be easy. You are strong of soul but far behind in your academic studies. The elders will require both before they will recognize you."

Nihs had spent some time thinking about this. "What if I were to appeal to an authority beyond that of the elders?" he said.

Nella's eyes grew wide. "You don't mean—"

"I will walk the dark path," he said, rising from his seat, "and submit myself to the judgement of the caves. If I succeed, then my claim to sagacity will be writ in stone…and I will have earned the right to don the sagecloak that King Azanhein has given me."

As he said this, he touched the satchel at his hip, inside which was carefully folded a beautiful red sagecloak. Kyle and Lugh might have already taken to wielding the gifts Azanhein had given them, but Nihs had vowed that he wouldn't so much look at his until he was worthy of wearing it.

He looked at Nella, realizing that she hadn't yet answered. She had risen, as well; her expression was pensive, calculating. Her own sagecloak, a deep, purplish blue, hung about her shoulders. She, unlike Nihs, had earned it in the usual manner, studying magic academically and only occasionally engaging in spellcasting as proof of concept. Her power stemmed from understanding and efficiency rather than brute strength. This was the only kind of power that the elders of the Kol respected.

The dark path was different. In the caves, the opinions of the elders didn't matter. Nothing did, but one's ability to communicate with the earth and bend it to their will. This was the kind of power that Nihs possessed.

He could tell from Nella's expression that she was coming to the same conclusion. Nihs did not have academic standing or the favor of the elders; his own father would be more likely to deny than vouch for his merit. The path would be his best, if not only, hope of attaining sagacity.

But Nella would not be Nella if she couldn't see both sides of any issue, find the chinks in any argument.

"There will be nothing left for you in Proks if you fail," she said. "You will be made an outcast. Kisi will be left without a brother, and so will I."

"I won't let that happen," Nihs said.

Nella breathed out slowly, and put her hands on Nihs' shoulders. Her ears unraveled; Nihs' did the same, and the two wound around one another.

"I believe you, *Nizu*," Nella said. She closed her eyes, letting her thoughts and emotions spill into Nihs via the bridge created by their crossed ears. From this, Nihs could see that she truly did believe in him; at the forefront of her mind was a burning desire for the rest of the world to see his merit as she had always been able. Her desire was, however, mingled with fear, and Nihs knew that nothing he could say or do would dispel it entirely: the same fear was eating away at his own heart.

I won't let that happen, Nihs thought, knowing that Nella would be able to sense his resolve, if not the source of it. *It won't happen, because I will exit the caves a sage, or not at all.*

Every Lorian knew the tale of the origin, the simple and ancient poem that detailed the birthing order of the world's ten intelligent races, beginning with the Kol and ending with man. According to this legend, the first Kol had been born in the darkness of a mountain cave. Blind and nearly deaf, it had wandered aimlessly through the rocky maze, spiraling ever downwards towards the core of the earth. There, in the deepest part of the caves, it had heard the faintest of sounds—echoes of the gods' voices, preserved from a time when they had still walked the earth.

Enraptured, the first Kol sat and meditated for months as the echoes taught it the secrets of magic. As it waited in the darkness, its body began to change and adapt to what would become the ancestral home of their race. Its ears became long and flexible, so it might better taste the magic around it and bend it to its will. Its body shrank in size, and its eyes became large and sensitive to light. Finally, the first Kol emerged from the deep caves, evolved and enlightened, a being of knowledge and magic. Proks, the first city the world had ever known, was founded, and two thousand years later there the Kol still lived, working patiently to uncover more of magic's secrets.

The trial of the dark path was an homage to the struggle that the first Kol had endured. By undertaking it, one sought enlightenment in the same manner as their progenitor, navigating the caves below Proks deaf and blind, guided only by whispers of magic. It was possible to reach the deepest part of the caves only if one's soul was sufficiently attuned to the earth's rhythm. Those who could not hear the earth's whispers were doomed to wander forever…unless they forfeited the trial, a supreme insult which was guaranteed to make the Kol in question an outcast for the rest of their life. Any Kol who was held in high respect by their peers would never take such a risk.

For Nihs, it was his only chance of attaining sagacity.

Entrance to the trial was controlled by its keepers, a pair of Kol known as Xira and Kyen. They would be somewhere in Eastern Proks—exactly where could be easily discovered on the overhead. However, no conversation held on the overhead was completely private, and Nihs' request for an audience with the keepers would be bound to draw attention. The audience wouldn't be a private one.

Nihs turned into one of the many alcoves that lined the stone walls of Eastern Proks and sat down with his legs crossed. There were a few Kol here, but none would pay him any attention. He forced himself to breathe slowly and unraveled his ears. He closed his eyes as his ears began to undulate back and forth, picking up on the magical signals permeating the air.

Soon, a very different picture of reality than the one his eyes normally painted appeared before his mind's eye. He was a soul, a single point of light floating in a vast ocean of magic. There were others—the Kol of Proks, and the Kol living in the lands beyond, were all lights in their own right, a multitude of stars scattered throughout the world. Eddies and currents of magic swirled all around and through them, and thoughts and emotions flew like birds from soul to soul. Being part of that enormous collective was a breathtaking, rapturous experience, and one that the other races could never hope to experience. The overhead was the only place where a Kol could feel perfectly calm and safe, and among themselves they often wondered how the other races managed to carry on without such a refuge.

Nihs, however, had business to attend to. After sifting through some of the voices on the chance that he would hear something worth hearing, he cast a thought out to his fellow Kol:

I seek the keepers of the dark path.

He sensed others turning their minds toward him; lights shone brighter and tentative, half-formed thoughts were cast in his direction.

…Who…what…the keepers…why?…who…the path…

Then, a new voice, distinct and focused:

Who are you, and why do you seek the keepers?

Individual voices were difficult to discern on the overhead, but still Nihs thought that he did not know the speaker. He replied calmly, though his heart was beating:

I wish to walk the path. I am Nihs Ken Dal Proks.

Surprise greeted his words. Some two dozen Kol who were listening in contributed to a cascade of whispers that tickled Nihs' soul.

Nihs…son of Dari…he can't…scorn…brother of Vago…shame…who does he think he is?…brother of Alen…

You will find the keepers in Ata chamber, the voice replied. Its coldness, felt more deeply and fully than possible with spoken words, made Nihs' spine tingle.

Thank you. I am indebted to you.

The voice cut through the darkness like a lash. *I tell you this only because it is not my place to deem you worthy or unworthy to walk the path. That is the keepers' domain. Who will attend this audience? I cannot.*

Several voices made themselves apparent at once. *Attend…I will attend…and I will…son of Dari…*

I will go to Ata chamber, Nihs said, but the owner of the strange voice was already gone.

Slowly, Nihs wrapped his ears and opened his eyes. The overhead, the shared consciousness of the Kol, faded, and was replaced by the stark light of reality.

Nihs' throat was dry, and his hands, resting on his crossed legs, were trembling. He knew where he had to go, but the scorn his simple request had attracted unnerved him. He had had no idea that his favor with the people of Proks had fallen so far.

This may be more difficult than he thought.

A ta chamber was just one of hundreds that were scattered throughout Proks. The city, formed almost entirely of natural caves, had no pattern or reasoning to its physical structure. This was of little worry to its residents; any Kol who could sense the magic around them and had access the overhead could never be truly lost. Nihs might have visited the chamber before, or he might not. He had no reason to remember. He strode through the vaults and galleries of Proks, allowing his senses to guide him.

The chamber was a kettle-shaped cave with smooth, polished walls. Its ceiling was dominated by a huge crystalline structure that had been lit from inside by a cluster of colored lamps; patches of light covered the walls and floor like shards of colored glass.

The chamber's floor sloped sharply upwards from the entrance. Sometime in the past, a series of steps had been carved into the floor, creating a small auditorium. Some eight or nine Kol were speckled throughout the chamber, sitting or standing on the various levels, carrying on private conversations.

Several eyes turned to Nihs as he entered. Nerves jangling, he looked around, hoping to discern which of these Kol were the keepers of the path. He was spared the trouble, however, when one of the Kol near the entrance addressed him.

"You are Nihs, I assume?"

The speaker's arms were folded, and a luxurious yellow sagecloak was draped across his shoulders. Nihs noticed with apprehension that the Kol he had been talking to was cloaked, as well.

"I am," Nihs said. "Are you one of the path's keepers?"

The speaker grinned, exposing sharp teeth. "I am Nihs Sul Dal Proks, here to witness your audience. The keepers you seek are here." And he turned his head and called over his shoulder. "*Xirasi! Kyren!*"

A pair of Kol on the other side of the chamber broke from their conversation, looking around to see who had beckoned them. Nihs Sul caught their attention and they crossed the chamber to join him.

Nihs had never met the keepers before, and their appearance took him by surprise. They were both male, and dressed in robes and hats of black and purple. They were younger than Nihs had expected, and their movements were timid and unsure. Each gave the impression of wanting to hide behind the other, and their gazes were unfocused. Suddenly Nihs was reminded of Lian and Lacaster, the twin assassins who had been sent to capture Kyle not a half-month ago.

Are these two twins as well? he thought. *No; they're from separate families. Is this then the result of serving as a keeper of the path? Little wonder there are few who aspire to become one.*

"This boy wishes to walk the path," Nihs Sul was saying. "You must examine his worthiness—such as it is."

By this time, Nihs was the center of attention in Ata chamber. He could sense the eyes and thoughts turned towards him. His face burned, but he forced calmness upon himself. A single crack in his poise could be enough to undo him, particularly if this Nihs Sul, his namesake, had his way.

Xira, or perhaps Kyen, focused on Nihs with difficulty and said, "The worthy do not walk the path; those who walk the path are worthy. All are permitted to seek. The path accepts all into its embrace."

Not if you have anything to say about it, Nihs thought bitterly, and surely enough, Nihs Sul said,

"So there is nothing? No test? How do we even know that this boy is who he claims to be?" He sneered down at Nihs. "A son of *Darizot*. I am a friend of Alen and a contemporary of Vago; neither has spoken to me of any brother but the other. Did you think to adopt the prestigious name of Ken to increase your chances of being granted access to the path?"

Nihs felt his apprehension withering in the face of newfound anger. *You dare suggest I would lie about my own family?*

"I am the son of Dari Ken Dal Proks!" he snapped. "Son of Lese, younger brother of Vago, Alen and Suri, elder brother of Kisi. Do you claim to know my folk better than I?"

Nihs Sul bristled. "I do! Do you claim to know better than your elders?"

"Enough!"

This was a new voice, belonging to a Kol who sat at the back of the chamber. He rose now, and stepped forward. Nihs' lungs turned to ice. It was his father, Dari.

"Of his family, at least," Dari said, "he is telling the truth. Your skepticism is admirable, Nihs Sul, but misplaced. That is indeed my son."

For the first time Nihs Sul's confidence faltered. "I…did not know you were in attendance, Dari Ken. My apologies."

Dari ignored him. His eyes were fixed on his son's; both sets of eyes were the exact same shade of brown.

"I would, however, question my son's intentions," Dari said. "He disappears from the city and neglects his magical studies for several years. Now he returns to Proks unannounced, and immediately seeks the dark path. What manner of chicanery is this?"

Nihs stared into his father's face—the stern brow, the narrow, mistrusting eyes, the nostrils that flared whenever he was displeased, the thin-lipped mouth that Nihs had never once seen curl into a smile—and felt his resolve weaken. *Why is my father here? Why must everything and everyone stand in my way?*

"I seek ascension to sagacity," Nihs said. "For reasons of my own."

The nostrils flared. "So you can more effectively maim the world around you and slaughter your fellow creatures, no doubt. Are you so taken by your barbarous instincts that you must profane one of our sacred rituals to further your own power?"

His words clawed at Nihs' heart, threatening to tear it to shreds. His own father thought he was some kind of monster, and not completely without reason. How could he hope to defend his position when he himself was consumed by doubt?

"I have been given a great mission," he said, his voice nearly cracking. "I must deepen my understanding of magic in order to fulfill it."

Nihs Sul snorted. "A great mission! Have you ever heard such nonsense?"

"You will remain silent," Dari snapped at him. "I am perfectly capable of disciplining my son without your help."

Horror and shame consumed Nihs Sul's face, and silently he stepped back.

"Whatever reason you have for wishing to attempt the trial is none of my concern," Dari continued. "It is the keepers that will decide your worthiness to walk the path, and the path that will decide your worthiness to live. However, as always, you have neglected an important detail. You possess no sagecloak and no one to present it to you should you succeed."

That his father had even spoken the word 'succeed' was reason to give Nihs hope, but this presented another problem.

"I have a sagecloak," he said, touching the satchel at his hip. "But it is true that I have no one to present it to me."

The sting of Dari's reprimand must have worn off, for Nihs Sul laughed and said, "*You* have a sagecloak? Where is it? For if you are speaking the truth,

Nihs Ken, and if you emerge from the path enlightened, I will present it to you myself!"

Nihs' heart raced. Nihs Sul had been meaning to tease him, but his promise was still a promise. He would be honor-bound to keep it if Nihs attained sagacity.

Hands shaking, Nihs fumbled for the catch of his satchel and pulled out the dark red sagecloak. The fabric spilled into his hands in luxurious folds and ripples. It was the first time he'd looked upon it since it had been given to him in Buoria. He'd forgotten how exquisite it was.

This detail was clearly not lost on the others in the chamber. Nihs Sul's eyes bulged, and his father's lips tightened. Both of them had clearly noticed that this was one of the finest cloaks they'd ever seen; it put Nihs Sul's yellow cloak to shame and even stood up to Dari's cloak of midnight black.

"*Where did you get that?*" Nihs Sul spluttered, all composure lost.

"For the last time, you will be silent!" Dari barked at him. He flew down the steps toward Nihs, who stepped backwards, holding the cloak out before him like a protective talisman. Dari snatched it from his hands and held it up to his face for inspection.

"No Kol made this," he said. He glared at Nihs. "Another insult to our kind and ways. Who gave you this forgery?"

"It is of Buorish make," Nihs said. "It was given to me by King Azanhein of Buoria."

Shock crackled through the room. Nihs could already hear the whispers that would permeate the overhead following this audience: *King Azanhein...Buoria...a sagecloak...*

Conflict was apparent on Dari's face. King Azanhein was no Kol and thus held no sway in Kollic society, at least in theory. But even here in Proks the name of Loria's most powerful monarch was known and respected. And if this truly was a gift from Azanhein, then Nihs must have won his favor somehow.

"I suppose you can prove that Azanhein gave you this cloak?" Dari said.

Nihs swallowed. Up close, his father felt more real, more vulnerable, but also more overpowering a presence.

"My only proof is the cloak itself. You yourself said it was made by no Kol. Who other but King Azanhein would have the power to create a cloak to rival one of our own? It was woven by Buorish artisans, and imbued with the power of the Heart of Buoria."

Dari's nostrils flared. Nihs realized that his father knew he was telling the truth, and was struggling to process the information. Suddenly he turned away from Nihs, still clutching the sagecloak. He climbed the steps and thrust the cloak into Nihs Sul's unresisting arms.

"I...but..." Nihs Sul began.

"But what?" Dari snarled. "You swore to present my son with his sagecloak should he succeed; there it is. It is yours to keep until that time when Nihs emerges from the caves, if ever he does."

He turned back to Nihs. Undisguised hatred was burning in his eyes. "Since my son seems determined to make fools of us all, perhaps we could have our keepers judge his worthiness and be finished with this sorry charade. Well, Xira? Well, Kyen? Shall my son walk the path?"

Xira, who had remained silent throughout the entire argument, said, "Yes. Indeed. He must still be made blind and deaf. Once he is so, he will think and feel as our ancestor once did. This is the only necessity that must be observed. All else is trivial."

"Very well," Dari said. "See to the preparations. To perish or to thrive; his fate now rests with the spirits of the caves."

Kyen and Xira descended the steps, and each put a hand on one of Nihs' shoulders.

"Come with us," said Kyen. "We will take you to the path."

And so Nihs was turned around and led outside, away from his father's hateful gaze, away from Nihs Sul's dumbfounded stare, and away from the beautiful red sagecloak that the king of Buoria had given him.

Xira and Kyen led him down through the caves of Proks, then further down into the uninhabited chambers below the city. Though these caves were in reality not far from the city, there was no reason for any Kol to visit them regularly, and soon the world around them was as silent as it was swallowed by darkness.

The darkness held no secrets for Nihs, who was guided by the keepers as well as his own senses. His eyes opened wide, and his ears, even curled at the sides of his head, twitched and squirmed, sampling every meager sound and current of magic that the caves offered.

Finally they came to a chamber much like every other they'd traversed so far. Xira and Kyen released Nihs' arms and stood before him.

"Two thousand years ago," Xira said, "our ancestor stumbled through these very caves, deaf, blind, and ignorant of magic. Even in this state, he heard and heeded the whispers of the earth around him as they guided him to enlightenment. This, Nihs of the Ken folk, is your task: follow the way of our ancestor and you will be rewarded in the same manner as he. Open your soul to the earth, and let it guide you towards magic, understanding, and sagacity. Do you accept this trial?"

"I do."

Kyen stepped forward, and pulled a long silken scarf from his satchel. Grabbing it by one end, he began to wind it around and around Nihs' head, covering his eyes and pinning down his sensitive ears. Nihs trembled, fighting down his instinct to throw Kyen from him and rip the bandage off. With every turn around his head the scarf took, his senses became duller, and the world around him more distant. Soon he would indeed be blind and deaf, in a way only a Kol could truly appreciate. Sight and sound were one thing, but once his ears could no longer twitch and taste, he would have no sense of the currents of magic around him, and would be truly cut off from the earth's rhythm.

"Once your senses are stifled, we will leave you," Kyen said. "Reach the chamber of the gods and you will be enlightened. Fail to do so, and your fate will be to wander the caves forever. Remove your bandage and your life will be saved, but you will have profaned the trial and your honor will be forfeit."

Kyen's voice was nearly inaudible by the time he had finished talking—or perhaps he was talking still, but Nihs could no longer hear, see or sense him. The bandage pressed in from all sides, relentless and complete in its oppression of his mind. The silk was soft and warm against his skin, but it might as well have been a manacle of cold iron for the way Nihs felt as he wore it.

He stood there in the darkness for fully a minute before he realized that Kyen and Xira had already left. The trial had begun, and Nihs hadn't even known.

He pressed his lips together and swallowed. He flexed his fingers, grateful for even this meager sensation, then ran his hands across the bandage that covered his head. It was incredibly tight, but the way that it pressed in on his ears, collapsing his soul into itself, was worst of all.

This is it, Nihs thought. *No more elders, no more family, no more seeking approval. Only one thing matters now, and that is the strength of my soul. Whatever happens next is entirely up to me.*

He stretched his arms out in front of him and took his first faltering step. His foot came down later than expected, and his clawed toes grabbed at the stony ground, barely managing to keep him upright. Even his balance was thrown with this cursed bandage on.

The first step is always the hardest. Isn't that so?

He took another step, then another. Each was surer than the last, and by the time he passed into the first tunnel he was walking steadily. He strained his senses, as would someone willing their pupils to grow larger in a darkened room. He still had a feel for the air around him; he knew that there were walls to both sides, a ceiling above, and nothing but blackness ahead. And in the darkness of his mind, the faintest of magical currents, an eddy as thin as a string of gossamer. If he moved, it spun to pieces and disappeared from his mind's eye. But if he stood still, calmed his breathing, and yearned outwards with his soul, he could catch a sense of it.

That is what I must follow, if ever I'm to see the light of day again.

And Nihs walked on.

The next day dawned bright and chilly, and Kyle rose from his sleep refreshed and exhilarated. He had dreamed of home last night, as he had nearly every night since his fall into Loria. In the past, these dreams had been cold and vivid, leaving him with a sense of sadness and dread upon awakening. But these days they were disjointed and half-formed, scratching harmlessly at his psyche.

Absently, he touched at the silver necklace he now always wore under his shirt. It had been given to him by Rosshku the Archmage, as a defense against the mysterious enemy who'd been following him ever since his arrival.

"I don't care for the way this person is able to track you wherever you go," the Archmage had said. "I doubt even I would be able to do so without marking you in some way, and I sense no such mark imprinted on your soul. I can't rob your enemy of his ability to go searching for you, but I can conceal you from sight." And he had given to Kyle a delicate silver necklace, a thin chain adorned with a single pendant. The sight of the pendant made Kyle want to turn it over and over in his hand, coming to terms with its odd shape. The twisted and folded silver gave the impression of hiding something within it, of secretly being a coin with three sides.

"Wear this, and your soul will be invisible to any prying eyes," Rosshku had said. "Don't remove it for one second, as I have a feeling that your opponent is searching constantly for you."

As soon as Kyle had slipped the strange necklace on, he had been engulfed by a feeling of *otherness*, a sense that his mind and body were no longer one. His sight had gone black and he had nearly lost consciousness. After a few seconds, however, the feeling faded, and now Kyle no longer even noticed the necklace's presence. He had done as the Archmage said, and hadn't removed it once since that moment. It gave him great comfort to know that his enemy could no longer find him, particularly after what had happened with the twins, Lian and Lacaster. Their attack had cost Lugh his ship and his eye, and Phundasa the Orc his life.

At the thought of Phundasa, Kyle's throat tightened and his hand fell from his neck. He'd been told a hundred times that Phundasa's death wasn't his fault, but not once had he believed it, and he was convinced that this would never change. Lian and Lacaster were dead now, which was well and good, but it had been thanks to his companions, not him. His only choice now was to find a way to return to where he belonged, and leave Loria behind. Only then would his remaining friends be completely safe.

He heard a stirring behind him and turned to see Lugh emerging from their tent, combing his hair out of his face with one hand. He blinked his one eye blearily, then joined Kyle at the lip of the hill.

"Nice morning," he said, yawning and stretching.

"Yeah."

"Want breakfast? Or think you can wait a while?"

"Why?" Kyle asked. "What did you have in mind?"

Lugh pointed across the swamp at his village, tucked away in the distant hills. "If we get a move on we can reach Lundir in an hour. I happen to know someone there who could make the wait for breakfast more than worthwhile."

"An hour?" Kyle said, shielding his eyes with one hand to get a better view of the swamp below. "We can't make it that fast, even with leaping."

"Not if we keep standing around talking about it," Lugh said. "Come on, help me strike the tent."

There was no arguing with Lugh, and before long the two of them were leaping across the countryside, bringing Lundir closer with each bound. Apart from the occasional misfire, Kyle found that leaping was now coming to him as naturally as any other motion. The only problem that remained was the exhaustion that set in after only a dozen leaps, but Lugh promised that this would change as Kyle got stronger.

Once Kyle could leap no longer, they spent some time walking, following the same winding path that they'd taken through the swamp the previous day. It was rising steadily, and the crawling, snagging greenery was giving way to trees rooted in firm earth. The difference brought on by the morning sun and lack of undergrowth was astounding. The forest now seemed bright, cheerful, and friendly. The chirping of birds was constant, and Kyle saw many a strange creature scurrying about the forest floor.

"See that thing?" Lugh pointed at a squirrel-like creature who was watching them nervously from a low-hanging branch. It had a lanky body with large, crooked hind legs and ears twice the size of its head. "That's a nuck. You know, the thing that Nihs is always calling me."

Kyle laughed. He had indeed heard Nihs call Lugh a 'nuck' several times throughout their journey. Seeing one in the flesh was something like meeting a celebrity.

Once Kyle had rested, they resumed leaping, skipping over large sections of the path by jumping over ponds, gullies, and patches of foliage. Kyle couldn't remember when last he'd had so much fun. He could go wherever he wanted, whenever he wanted; nothing could stand in his way. In a single stroke, the world had gotten so much smaller, but so much more interesting, as well. If something caught his eye in the distance, it was the work of a moment to leap towards it and catch a closer look.

As Kyle and Lugh made their way, the town of Lundir grew ever larger in the distance. It was nestled between two peaks that stood out from the swamp around them. Free of the moisture of the swamp, but still benefiting from its constant rain, the peaks were completely covered in greenery, and at first it was difficult to tell where the forest ended and the town began.

As they drew closer, Kyle realized that the task of telling forest and town apart would not be getting any easier, for one blended into the other without any sort of preamble. The houses here were made of wood, though unlike those of the Kol in western Proks, their foundations were firmly rooted in earth, and their roofs were of thatch. Sturdy wooden walkways connected the houses over uneven or waterlogged ground, but other than this there was no suggestion that the town had been planned at all, or was in any way permanent. Smoke curled from every chimney—judging from the smell, they must have been burning some kind of peat rather than wood.

At Lugh's suggestion, they leapt back down to the path and entered Lundir from the main gate. A Selk was lounging by the town's entrance, though whether he was an official gatekeeper or merely looking for a good place to smoke Kyle had no way of knowing. He was nearly as tall as Lugh, though his frame was much thinner. He was wearing a sleeveless vest and a cap that looked like half a deflated bladder, and his eyes nearly bulged out of his head when his eye caught Lugh's.

"Ey! Countryman!" He vaulted to his feet and immediately took Lugh by the hand, grinning from ear to ear. "Lookit you so fine with yor sword o'silver an' locks o' gold! Whatsa citty boy like yew doin' in good ol' Lundir?"

The gatekeeper's accent was so strong that at first Kyle thought he was speaking a different language. Lugh, however, acted as though he'd understood every word.

"You don't know me?" he said, grinning as well. The two Selks' expressions were eerily alike, and Lugh's own accent had already started to slip. "I'm Lugh Alden, aren't I?"

The other Selk's eyes grew even wider. "You don't mean Hael's brother, Saints rest him? Ol' Por Amam's ward?"

"The same!"

"Well I'll be a jabberin' loon! I know Por Amam said yew'd gone off to the city to be a great fine adventurer after what'd happened to dear ol' Hael, never said nothin' 'bout you ever comin' back!"

"She doesn't know," Lugh said. "Is she home now?"

"Well o'course! Not too many chillin's fer her to look affer these days, none o' that age where'n they can't yet help they mums and dads at work. But let me walk you there, I'm wantin' to see the look on Por Amam's face fer meself when 'er young ward shows up at 'er doorstep pretty as you like affer all these years!"

Kyle was lucky if he caught one word in two of everything to come after. Lugh and the newcomer fed off each other's energy, each becoming more and more incomprehensible as time went on. After Kyle was introduced ("An' who's yer friend, a pleasure o'course, name's Yorendell, call me Yoren if y'like, how long yew been knowin' Lugh fer then?"), they were marched through the streets of Lundir by their enthusiastic guide. Judging from Yoren's excitement and the attention the three of them attracted, Lugh's appearance was the one of the more interesting events to strike Lundir for some time.

They eventually came to a large cottage of wood and stone that overlooked the village. A flagstone path led to the front porch, which was home to two rocking chairs and a table between them. Decorations and knick-knacks were everywhere: earthen jugs, wind chimes of glass and metal, and wooden carvings clearly made by several different artists. It seemed at first like utter disorganization, but some details weren't quite right. The front porch was swept clean, and the garden at the front of the house was meticulously kept. Overall, Kyle got the impression that someone inside the house was fighting a bitter war against the encroaching chaos, and had grudgingly yielded certain locations to its enemy while staunchly keeping others clean.

As they made their way up the path, Lugh's pace slowed, and his head turned in all directions.

"Exactly as I remember it," he said softly. "Makes sense, really, it's only been a few years. Feels like a lot longer."

Yoren strode forwards to knock on the cottage's door, but it opened before he could get two blows in. He looked up at the woman who had opened the door—for she was a very tall woman indeed—and said, "Lookit who's here, Por! Ol' Lugh what came back from the citty!"

Grinning from ear to ear, Yoren stood to one side so the cottage's owner could get a clear look at Lugh. She was, as Kyle had noticed, a very large woman. She was at least three inches taller than Lugh, who himself nearly had a foot on Kyle. She had a long curtain of strawberry blonde hair that fell well past her hips, and her four ears framed her face like a crown. Her dress was plain, her hair was touched with grey, and a delicate spider's web of wrinkles had settled upon her face; but she still retained most of what once must have been a ravishing beauty.

For a moment, she stared at Lugh, unable to speak. He spread his arms, his eyes twinkling. Then, just as it looked as though she might regain her composure, he dashed at her, arms still outstretched, and caught her in a massive embrace that lifted her off her feet. She cried out and Lugh, laughing, lowered her to the ground, peppering her cheek with kisses.

"Por Amam!" he cried out.

Finding her voice at last, the woman said, "Lughen! Let go of me, you troublemaker, before I throw you off! Where have you been all this time?"

She broke free of Lugh's embrace and held him at arm's length, hands on his shoulders. He was dancing from foot to foot with excitement, but her face was critical as she looked him over.

"And what's happened to your eye?" she demanded, reaching for the stone disc he wore over his wound. "Unless this is one of your strange city fashions?"

Lugh pulled his head away from her questing hand. "Pora! Couldn't that wait for a second? Aren't you glad to see me?"

She struggled for a moment, then her face melted into a warm smile. "Of course I'm glad to see you, you little rogue. It's been far too long."

"Ain't that somethin', Pora?" Yoren said. He had grabbed onto his cap and was bouncing on the balls of his feet.

Por Amam shot him a shrewd look. "Something indeed, Yoren Tallow. Almost as remarkable as would be your chores getting done before the winter sets in, wouldn't you say?"

"Owps!" Yoren said at once, and squashing his cap onto his head he went bounding back down the flagstone path, hooting with laughter.

Por Amam watched him go with a long-suffering look on her face, her arm linked in Lugh's. Then she said: "Well! Are we going to stand here letting the heat out, or will you come inside and tell me what's going on?"

"Of course!" Lugh said.

"But you'll introduce me to your friend first, since you always remember your manners?"

"Of course!" Lugh said, not missing a beat. "Por Amam, this is Kyle, a fellow adventurer. Kyle, this is Por Amam, my group-mother!"

"A pleasure to meet you, Kyle," said Por Amam, inclining her head to him. "Now, why don't you come in and have some food before Lughen eats it all?"

The inside of Por Amam's cottage was as warm and inviting a place as Kyle had ever seen. Most of it was a single round room dominated by a large stone fireplace and an extensive kitchen. Pots, pans, and plates were stacked on every surface, and cups and cutlery dangled from hooks attached to the beamed ceiling. Dried herbs, some familiar and some not, were tied in bundles and hung on the walls. It smelled wonderful, and looked more like a kitchen fit for a restaurant than a single person. Every surface was spotless, and the copper pans gleamed.

Beyond the kitchen was a large round table surrounded by chairs of every size, height, and color, and beyond that, underneath a large sunny window that overlooked the side garden, was what could only be called a play area. A large chest was literally overflowing with toys, and more still were strewn about the floor nearby.

Kyle's mental picture was starting to come together. *Group-mother*, he thought. *Is this some kind of orphanage?* He realized that he'd never heard Lugh mention any parents.

"I suppose you'll be wanting breakfast," Por Amam said as soon as they were inside.

Lugh endeavored to look coy. "If you wouldn't mind…"

Amam was already bustling about the kitchen, fetching cookware down from the walls. "You'll be through half my pantry before the day is out," she said. "You might as well let me cook it all first. Now pull up a chair and keep me company as I work."

Lugh chose a tall, spindly stool from the table and dragged it over, hitching it up on two feet as he leaned his elbows on the counter. Por Amam swatted at him with a spoon as she walked past, and he obediently sat back, the stool's feet settling to the floor with a *thunk*. He watched her as she busied about with a dreamy look on his face.

"Por Amam," he said, "you are still the most beautiful woman in Ren'r, do you know that?"

She shot him a venomous look. "Don't you start with me, young man. Now, am I going to have to wring my story out of you?"

"Which story was that again?"

"All of it! Where have you been, what have you been doing? And why have you come back?"

"That's obvious, I missed your cooking!"

Por Amam pointed a sharp kitchen knife at him. "Lughen, if you don't stop fooling around…"

"All right, all right!" Lugh brushed the hair out of his face. "Where do I start?"

Kyle had heard bits and pieces of Lugh's story before, but this was the first time it all came together into one picture. Some of the names and places Lugh mentioned were familiar to him, though many were not. As he spoke, Kyle realized that here in Loria, he'd gotten used to everything being about *him*; Lugh's story was a sobering reminder that this world was full of people living out their lives in complete ignorance of his existence.

"As you surely know, it all started about four years ago…"

"Five," Por Amam said.

"Really? Has it been so long?"

"Yes, Lughen."

"Huh. Well, in any case…"

After leaving Lundir, Lugh had traveled south, towards the big city of Reno. He'd made stops along the way to join the adventurer's guild and pick up some work. Early on, he'd paired with a human hero who, after promising to mentor him, had signed them up for a job that had nearly gotten Lugh killed, and taken all the resulting pay for himself.

"So that's why you hate heroes," Kyle said.

"Just the bastard ones. Our friend Reldan from the goblin mine reminded me a little too much of that guy, I'll admit. Anyway, it's in the past now."

Lugh's luck had improved as he drew closer to Reno. He joined a party of adventurers four strong, and his skill and experience developed rapidly. He started to make friends and connections in the guild, and before long he was enjoying a steady stream of work. Where before he had been scraping by, he was now living comfortably. His original party broke apart, but the five of them remained in contact, doing the odd job together.

"Those were the good old days," Lugh said wistfully.

"What happened?" Kyle asked.

"Nothing. That was the problem. It went on for over a year: go out, do an easy job, get paid, go home, spend your money. It was boring. I'd heard all these stories of the world outside but I'd barely seen any of it. I started to think, 'I'm an adventurer, so how come I never go on any adventures?' The last thing someone in our profession should be is bored, don't you think?"

"Sure," said Kyle.

"So I left. Packed up my things, had a last party with all my friends, and then kept moving south. Still hadn't been to Reno after all that; everyone had told me I'd never find a job there. But I figured I'd try my luck."

Kyle smirked. Relentless optimism had always been one of Lugh's defining traits.

"And?" said Por Amam. "How did that go?"

"Not too great. Two months in and I'd burned through nearly all my money, and picked up maybe half a job in the meantime. I was starting to think I'd have to move on. That's when I met Nihs."

That caught Kyle by surprise. "You two met in Reno?"

Lugh nodded. "Funny…Reno's the farthest place in the world from Proks, but it seems like every Kol who leaves one ends up in the other. In fact, I'd bet there's nearly as many Kol in Reno as in Proks."

"Who's this Nihs?" Por Amam asked.

Lugh smacked his forehead. "Saints! You haven't met him, have you? That's no good. I'll have to drag him out here once we're done with our mission. He's a Kol friend of mine," he added to Por Amam. "Nasty temper, complete know-it-all, but he's probably the best friend I've ever had. And you didn't hear me say that. Anyway, where was I?"

The beginnings of Nihs and Lugh's partnership had been rocky, but they had quickly realized that they would need each other's skills in order to survive. Lugh was good at making friends, and Nihs was skilled at finding jobs. Lugh was strong in combat, Nihs was strong in magic. Nihs' smarts were fueled by his endless love for books, whereas Lugh had a practical sensibility about him and an instinct that Nihs couldn't match. Soon, they were taking on jobs that neither would have been able to complete on their own, and their careers took off.

Somewhere along the line, Lugh befriended a rich Selk named Ellander and made the infamous bet that would ultimately win him the *Ayger*. Kyle was still burning to know what the bet had been, but Por Amam was more interested in the *Ayger* itself.

"You won an airship in a bet?" she asked incredulously. "Where is it?"

Lugh's face fell. "I'm afraid it's gone, Pora. Such a shame…I would have loved to take you out in it. Most beautiful thing I've ever seen—apart from you, of course."

"Lughen—you—rascal!" Por Amam punctuated each word with a smack on the arm. "And what do you mean, it's gone?"

Lugh sighed. "I'll get to that."

With the *Ayger*, Lugh and Nihs' range increased immensely. All of Centralia was now no more than a day's flight away, and even Westia and Eastia were within reach. Thanks to the overhead, the pair could chase after promising jobs wherever they happened to crop up. They made a good deal of money, Lugh spending most of his on equipment and the *Ayger*, Nihs squirreling most of his away.

"Of course, the money's just there to fill in the gaps between adventures," Lugh said. "The adventures, that's what it's always been about." Kyle believed him. From what he had seen, Lugh enjoyed spending money and acquiring it in equal measure; it was the holding onto it that he didn't care for.

By this time, both he and Lugh had been given something hot to drink, and the first of what Kyle could only imagine was going to be a thirty-course breakfast was ready to be served. Por Amam's frenzied cooking had filled the entire cottage with warmth and a delicious smell, and Kyle's stomach growled as she filled two plates with food and set them down on the table.

Kyle stared. On the plate before him was bread, meat pudding, broiled fish, freshly-cut vegetables, scrambled eggs and diced potato, all steaming hot and heavily seasoned. It was the best-looking breakfast he had ever seen.

Lugh nudged him. "You going to let all that get cold?" he said around a mouthful of food.

The rest of Lugh's story would have to wait. Kyle hadn't realized how hungry all of their leaping had made him, or how much he'd missed good food in general. He'd never had a breakfast quite like this one before—cereal and toast were much more likely to appear on his morning plate than roast fish—but Por Amam's masterful cooking made up for any strangeness and then some. He doubted if even Artisan Ishmaal, Azanhein's personal cook, could conjure a meal so appealing.

Kyle, for all his enthusiasm, was no match for Lugh. The bread took him three mouthfuls to finish off, the pudding took two, and the fish might have been a single one were it not for Por Amam's acidic glare. He downed a glass of juice all at once, then used the wide cap of a fresh mushroom as a shovel for his potatoes. Por Amam's face was disapproving, but it was clear that she had given up on teaching him table manners long ago.

"Delicious," he said, leaning back in his chair. "Is there any more?"

When Lugh was informed that no, of course there wasn't any more, and if he hadn't wanted to watch Kyle eat, he shouldn't have finished so quickly, and *don't you dare steal from his plate*, he decided to continue his story.

"Me and Nihs went at it like that for quite a while," he said. "That took a long time to get boring. It's different when you're in a new city almost every day. But after a while we realized we weren't improving very fast, and the jobs were starting to get a little easy. So we flew back to Reno to pick up someone else for our merry band."

"Rogan?" Kyle said.

"The very same. You'd have liked him, Pora. Minotaur, huge guy, could punch through a wall if he wanted. Met at a hideout one night and hit it off right away. Nihs liked him since he was sensible, I liked him because he knew how to keep the *Ayger* running."

"Where is *he*, now?" Por Amam asked.

Lugh scratched his chin. "Had to head back to the plains just a month or so ago. Some kind of trouble with his clan down there. I'll admit, I have no idea how the Minotaur work. I hope we run into him again, though. He was a good friend.

"Anyway, after we picked Rogan up it was the same story again for a while, only more. More jobs, more money... We pooled everything we had together and soon we were living pretty well. Hit up all four continents in a halfmonth, saw cities, forests, mines, even Elfland for a little while, and that's not something you forget easily."

"And at *no* point during any of this did you think of stopping back home, and seeing all the people who missed you so much?"

"I wasn't ready yet," Lugh said, distantly.

"Ready for what?" Por Amam demanded. "Did you think you could only come home once you were rich and famous?"

"Not exactly." There was a pause, then Lugh said, "Pora, I'm going to try and find Hael's sword."

Por Amam's reaction was as fast as it was unexpected. "No," she said. "I forbid it."

"Pora—"

"Bringing the sword back won't bring your brother back. All it will do is put you in danger. Is that what Haelin would have wanted?"

"I'm not trying to bring him back, Pora," Lugh said. "It's just that—"

"Just what? What is so important about that sword that makes it worth it to risk your life?"

Lugh was calm in the face of Por Amam's fire. "Do you know what promotion is, Por Amam?"

"I've heard, yes. And?"

"It's my time to promote," Lugh said. "In fact, I think it was my time years ago. But no matter how many jobs I do, no matter how many monsters I kill, it doesn't happen. That sword is holding me back, I can feel it. Every time I think about promotion I think about the swamp, and the grave…I have to go there, or I'll never get any stronger."

Por Amam's expression was cold, and her voice was quiet. "And what if you get killed out in the swamps? What then? Will we build another grave next to your brother's, and another again when the next foolish young Selk takes up your quest?"

"I won't get killed. I'm stronger than Hael was back in the day. And I'll have Kyle with me."

Kyle was treated to a menacing look. "And I suppose that nothing I say will change your mind."

"I'm sorry, Pora, but this is something I have to do. For Hael and for myself."

Por Amam shook her head softly. A few wisps of gray-gold hair fell across her cheek, and suddenly she seemed very old.

"Oh, Lughen…There is nothing a strong young man must do but build—his house, his roads, and his family. Your brother was a wild sort, dark of hair and heart. The swamp took him, but you, with your sunny hair and happy face…I prayed you would not go the same way. And now, look at you, you've become even fiercer than Haelin was."

It wasn't often that Kyle saw Lugh with anything but a smile on his face, and now that it was gone, he barely recognized his friend. Lugh got up, circled the table and put his arms around Por Amam.

"I won't go the same way," he said. "I promise. I'll be back, and I'll bring Hael with me. You'll see."

"I guess you'll be wanting an explanation for all that," Lugh said later. They were walking through the streets of Lundir, weaving between homesteads and trees. The air was cool and clean, the world wet with mist. They were heading north, their destination the swamps beyond the city. Lugh was walking at a casual pace with his thumbs in his belt. His polished stone eye glinted in the sun whenever it found a gap in the forest canopy.

"A little bit, yeah," Kyle admitted.

"What first?"

Kyle wanted to ask Lugh about his brother, but the words stuck in his throat. Instead he said, "What exactly is Por Amam?"

"You mean other than the best cook you'll ever meet? She's what we call a group-mother. It's an old Selkic tradition that goes back to the days of the valkyrie. You ever hear about them?"

"No."

"Well, you might have noticed that Sea Selk women aren't the cute little things that town Selk women are. They're bigger and stronger than the men, and once upon a time, they made up some of the fiercest warriors in the world. It was their job to go and fight wars while the men hunted and built homes and roads. With the women fighting and the men building, there were a lot of little ones running around with no parents to raise them. So, we left them in the care of the group-mothers—women who were too old to fight, or had been injured in battle. By the time the valkyrie disappeared, we'd gotten used to it. Not too many group-mothers left these days, but out in little villages like these you still see them around."

"What happened to the valkyrie?" Kyle asked.

"Wyvern died, the war against humanity ended, and the sun came out. After that, it was a long, long time before anybody felt like fighting again. Things changed, and a lot of old ideas didn't make it through."

Kyle was spared the effort of speaking when Lugh added, "You might as well ask me about Haelin while we're at it."

"All right, then. He was your brother."

"Older by six years. Por Amam raised us together. If you want to know what he was like, take everything you know about me and flip it on its head. In all the years I knew him, I saw him smile about as many times as I have eyes."

"You didn't get along?"

"The opposite, actually. He was my hero growing up. While I was eating and playing and causing mischief, he was breaking his back working, and as soon as he got his first sword he was out training with it night and day. Once he hit sixteen he became a caravanner, and after that I was lucky to see him once in a month."

"Caravanner?"

"Selks who take supplies between villages and keep monsters off the roads. The original adventurers, you might say."

Normal people don't become adventurers. That was one of Lugh's favorite sayings, and it was Haelinor who'd taught it to him.

"Long story short, Hael got himself killed one year when he was out with the caravan. They lost the road and got bogged down, and he was one of the ones who stayed back while the others went to a nearby village for help. That nearby village just so happened to be Lundir."

Kyle felt his throat constrict. He could see the shape that Lugh's story was taking.

"You must have been terrified," he said.

Lugh snorted. "You don't understand how much I thought of Haelin. I was never afraid for him for a second. In fact, I was excited that he'd be home soon and have more stories to tell me. I wanted to go out with the others and help bring the caravan back, but they told me to stay home—then I wanted to stay up and wait for them. Hours later, we hadn't heard from them, and Por Amam forced me to go to bed. I woke up the next morning and…"

Lugh looked up at the sky, and his chest swelled with a long, drawn-out breath. "Well, that's it, really. The caravan had come in a few hours after I fell asleep, but Hael was still out in the swamp. Monsters had attacked while they were bogged down. Everyone but Hael made it out."

"I'm sorry."

"Don't be. It happens; a lot more often with caravanners than adventurers, since caravanners don't get to pick their work. The swamps are a rough place, and there are a million and one things that can go wrong. Too many things go wrong and you can lose your life. I know that now. But I didn't take it too well at the time. Everyone was telling me how brave and strong Haelin had been, but I hadn't thought he was brave and strong. I'd thought he was the *strongest*. You know what I mean?"

Kyle nodded. "Yeah."

"Hael's fellow caravanners threw a grave together for him, somewhere off the path north of here. Found a patch of solid ground and jabbed his sword into it. Can't be more than a few hours' walk from here, but I've never gone to visit it. I tried, when I was younger. But my legs would freeze up as soon as I reached the village gate. Wouldn't take me any farther north, no matter how hard I tried. Guess that's why I finally ended up heading south, once I decided to become an adventurer. Anyway, that's where we're headed now. Let's see if I can get my legs working this time, huh?"

They reached the outskirts of Lundir not too long after. The ground sloped slowly downwards, and the trees thinned. A tall wooden gate separated the village from the swamps beyond. The gate was shut, but gravity swung it open when Lugh lifted the heavy wooden bar.

Lugh and Kyle stood at the threshold, Lugh with his hands on his hips, Kyle resting one palm on the hilt of his changearm. He stole a glance at his companion. In his hard leather armor, with his silversteel swords on his back, and his stone eyepatch covering one eye, Lugh looked more fearsome than Kyle had ever seen him. For the first time, the fact that Lugh was older than him truly sunk in. He'd always seen Lugh as a friend and mentor, but never as an elder. Now, it was as if adulthood had settled around his shoulders like a mantle.

"Well," Lugh said, "here we go."

And he took one long stride forwards, bringing both feet together smartly on the other side of the threshold. He looked back at Kyle.

"Piece of cake," Kyle said.

Lugh's brow furrowed. "What's that supposed to mean?"

Kyle started to laugh. "It means something that's easy to do."

Lugh soundlessly formed the words *piece of cake* with his mouth. He shook his head.

"Your world must be a strange, strange place. Are you sure you want to go back there?"

"Pretty sure," Kyle said, joining Lugh on the other side of the gate. "That's if I can get back, of course."

"Won't know until we try. Speaking of which, I think it's time we get moving."

Nihs moved through the darkness.

Though the bandage around his head allowed no light to enter his eyes and no sound to enter his ears, the void that surrounded him was anything but empty of feeling. It was a textured, layered nothingness, a maze of barely perceptible sensation. His feet felt a change in the ground's texture, his outstretched arms lost the cave wall and cold air brushed his cheek—he had entered a large chamber. Then, the ground sloped downwards, his footing faltered, and he felt rather than heard the pops and snaps of sound as a multitude of small rocks fell in a miniature landslide around him.

As he had done several times since the trial had begun, he sat down cross-legged on the cave floor and rested. The activity soothed him; never before had taking a simple step been such an ordeal. Twice now he had set a foot down only to find that there was nothing beneath it; both times he had strangled a cry in the back of his throat as his stomach pitched and swooped.

He wetted his lips with a quick flick of his tongue. Panic was starting to rise within him. He'd walked for at least an hour by his estimate, but was either no closer to his goal than when he started or was unable to tell the difference. The eddy of magic he had felt at the start of the trial had been promising, but it had soon tattered and twisted apart only to be replaced by a hundred others. Each was as soft and as invisible as a breath of air. They would lick his cheek, get snagged in his seashell ears, then disappear a split-second later when he jerked his head to follow them. He couldn't pick one out from the others if he tried, and would have no way of knowing which to follow even if he could.

His heart fluttered as despair overwhelmed him. It knew the truth that his mind refused to face: he was failing this trial. A grim view of his future began to eclipse his thoughts. He would have to throw the bandage off and wallow in shame for the rest of life. He would live as a fugitive, banished from Proks, never to see his sisters again. His father, his elders, all who had ever thought ill of him, would be vindicated.

No. Better to die down here than choose that path. Death is quick and kind. Shame is a wound that cuts again and again for the rest of one's life. I have enough honor in me to choose rightly should it come to that.

Feeling bizarrely comforted by this thought, he allowed his panic to wash away, then turned his mind to the task at hand. He sat and meditated for some time, allowing his thoughts to wander where they may.

The hour he'd spent walking had been wasted; that much was clear. He recalled a piece of wisdom that he'd once shared with Kyle: *you can't return to where you've been if you don't know where it was you left.* Of course, he'd had to butcher the saying for Kyle's sake. No one who could not speak Kollic, or who had never visited the overhead, could comprehend its true nature. Nihs knew that it applied to many things in life: to physical journeys, to threads of thought, to knowledge of one's own strengths and limitations. It applied to this cave, where Nihs was blind and deaf in more ways than one. He did not fully understand from where he'd come or where he was going, and without that knowledge he had no hope of passing from one to the other.

These caves were like his thoughts. Let yourself wander for too long, and you could lose yourself forever. He would do no more walking, not until he knew which path was the proper one to take.

I'm lost, he said to himself. He often held conversations within the recesses of his own mind; so far, he'd managed to keep this a secret from Lugh.

Long before you entered this cave, I think you'll agree, he answered himself. *But that is the beauty of the path. The lost enter, and the found emerge.*

Those who emerge at all, that is.

Why do you doubt your abilities? You've faced far more daunting tasks than this in your travels. Do you think Nihs Sul would stand a chance against the eyrioda alpha, or the elemental you fought in the plains of Buoria?

That's not the same.

It is exactly the same. The Kol's understanding of magic runs deep, but it has been warped over the ages by dogmatism and pedantry. Magic is wild and free. The most learned sage in Proks has no greater understanding of magic than you, you who have conquered the evils of the world by twisting fire through your fingers. And that is because magic cannot be learned. It can only be felt.

Nihs hesitated. Could it be true? His years of learning resisted. Who was he to claim greater knowledge of magic than his elders and betters? But the thought spread through his mind, converting it, uniting tattered half-thoughts and weaving them into a strong resistance against his lifelong indoctrination. Was he the wisest Kol who had ever lived? Certainly not. But he was as wise as any other—and stronger of soul than many. He was already a sage in heart and soul; in everything, in fact, but the cloak on his back. And that cloak was waiting for him at the end of this tunnel.

Stop thinking, and start feeling. Open your soul and let the magic guide you. The wrapping around your head isn't there to blind you. It's there to shut out distraction, to grant you a sight greater than your eyes have ever known.

Nihs rose, and spread his arms wide. His mind cleared, relinquishing its tight control over his soul. His own magic drifted outside his corporeal self and mingled with the magic in the air around him. Suddenly, what had been thin cobwebs of light in his mind's eye became fireworks, their every twist and eddy laid bare before him. How had he ever thought himself lost? It was all there for him to see.

You don't belong in these caves. You've always thought it to be a curse. This world is so much grander and more beautiful than the city of Proks. You are fortunate, in that you are destined to travel wherever there is magic. You will never be lost again.

Nihs started to walk.

It was a long journey to the end of the path, and the way was fraught with danger—fissures, lakes of frigid water, tunnels that twisted endlessly in on themselves. Nihs' throat was dry, his palms and knees were scraped and bleeding, and stepping down on one of his clawed toes sent spasms of pain shooting up his leg. But he walked on and on, with a smile on his face and confidence in his step. He had never known such elation, such surety of purpose.

It was all so obvious to him now! He realized he'd known it for years, but had always before shied away from the truth. Why was it that so many young Kol left the halls of their ancestors to live in Reno city? Why were the most magically talented Kol those that lived like outcasts far from Eastia? It was not they who had lost their way. It was the Elders, the scholars, the Dari Ken Dal Prokses who had forgotten the true nature of magic. It was wild, exciting and unfathomable. Attempting to understand it only chased it away.

The magic was guiding him forwards. Bright bands of it danced before his mind's eye and filled his soul with warmth. He walked, skipped, and finally ran, half-crawling, as it called him.

He entered a chamber with many exits—no matter. He ran straight ahead, crawled upwards, turned right and skirted a cave with a pockmarked floor. He was still lost, in a sense, but knew now that it was only a matter of time before he emerged.

Another passage, a long, wide slope that rose steadily. The magic was so strong that Nihs almost had to close his soul to its influence. His sight was consumed by light. It warmed not just his soul, but his skin, touching it like droplets of dew. He ran on, enraptured.

A final burst of light and joy. He'd emerged into a massive cave, larger than any he'd ever seen. He could feel magic all around him, stretching into the distance for what seemed like an eternity. He had arrived at the chamber of the gods; he knew he had. He needed neither Xira nor Kyen to tell him he'd made it.

He reached behind his head and fetched at his blindfold. His whole body was shaking with emotion. He was aware of his heart beating inside his chest, his mind firing off its electrical impulses, his lungs filling and emptying of air... And if he reached his soul outwards, he could feel the same feelings in all of the creatures living in the earth around him, from the microscopic insects to the unfathomable beasts that lurked deep below.

But more than anything, he was happy. He had done it, he had made it. He was no failure; he was a sage. The spirits of the earth had confirmed it, and no Kol could deny it now.

The binding, tight as it was, came apart under the assault of his clawed fingers. Feverishly he undid the wrappings, unwinding it until it was loose enough to fall from his head of its own accord. His ears unraveled, and his senses tripled again as they undulated through the cool air, free once more.

He opened his eyes—and was nearly blinded by the stunning light of the sun.

Nihs gasped. There was nothing else to do.

He was standing in a large valley surrounded by the mountains of Eastia. Birds chirped in the distance. Autumn had not yet touched this place; the trees' leaves were green, and the grass in which he was standing was waist-deep, lush and wet with dew.

He should have felt horrified, but to his own surprise he found that he didn't feel much of anything. He reached out and ran a hand through the flowing stalks around him. It came back cold and covered in droplets of clear water.

Nihs looked around. The valley was beautiful. The sky was blue, the mountains were white, and the earth below was green. How long had it been since he had walked, alone, under the light of the sun? He took a step forward, then another, as all thought of the trial was wiped from his mind.

He set off, headed nowhere in particular, pushing through the verdant grass. Soon he was shivering, soaked from the chest down, but the cold was somehow enjoyable. His eyes were glowing, and after-images of magic still danced in front of them. The world was bursting with life.

The grass thinned, and Nihs came to the edge of a small lake. Its bed was lined with small stones, and a few solitary trees grew on the far side. It was an idyllic scene, and it came naturally to Nihs to sit down by its edge, fold his legs, and stare into the calm water.

The revelations he had experienced in the caves came rushing back to him. Magic—everything, all of this, came down to magic in the end. For millennia the Kol had devoted themselves to unraveling its secrets, to peering deeper and deeper into its true nature. But its most profound and perfect secret, the only one that needed remembering, had been the first to be discovered.

Magic had no rules; it could not be explained or measured. The Kol had tried, and in doing so, had only slipped farther and farther away from the truth. Understanding and purity were at odds with one another. The truest, most powerful magic was that which was woven by the unlearned.

Nihs let his eyelids flutter closed as these thoughts washed over him. There was more, much more to think about, but he resisted. After all, that was the pitfall that the Kol of Proks had fallen into. What use was thought for one who could reach out and touch the essence of the universe, and feel the truth in a way that could never be rationally known?

A strange, euphoric sensation enveloped him as he sat meditating by the edge of the lake. Magic, more than he had ever gathered before, was flowing towards him, climbing upwards into him from the earth below. It filled every pore until he felt full to overflowing, and still the tide edged upwards, through his legs, then his chest, spilling down into his arms and setting his mind afire. It was frightening; he had never known such magic, and felt as if the fire inside him would continue to grow until it burst violently from him.

A single, disconnected thought formed in his mind:

This is promotion. I don't know how, or why, but…I am becoming a sage.

Promotion: magical metamorphosis. He had been judged worthy after all, though by whom he was no longer sure.

Still afraid, but armed with knowledge, Nihs drew deep breaths and let the sensation engulf him. Every fiber of his being was consumed by energy, and still magic flowed into him from all directions. It made itself known to each of his senses; sound, light, and a burning fire in his chest all grew in intensity until he could bear it no longer. His fists clenched, his feet tore up clods of earth as his toes flexed.

Then, just as the frightful energy inside of him began to pass into the realm of terror and pain, Nihs felt his soul wrench open, and take all of the unconverted magic around him unto itself. It billowed outwards, stretching and straining to control the new power it had absorbed. The excess magic flowed into his body and mind, into his organs and sinews, his nerves and synapses, feeding them as they had never been fed before, growing and expanding them, teaching them, evolving them. Nihs could actually feel his body changing, his bones grinding to make way for new muscles and arteries; he gasped and would have cried out if he had been able to muster such control over his body. His heart pumped furiously and his mind crackled as new pathways were formed.

Finally, his soul, having finished its work, settled proudly into the new form it had sculpted. It was twice the volume it had ever been before, and its new home was a polished, perfected version of what it had been before.

Shaking, Nihs rose to his feet. He had grown at least an inch, and his own body felt alien to him. He stared at his palms and flexed his fingers. He was still the same person—and yet everything about him had changed. The way his joints bent, the way his eyes focused; even his thoughts formed more swiftly, and out of their usual order. But most different of all was his soul. He could feel it burning away inside him, vaster and more powerful than he had ever imagined it could be.

The grass around him, affected by his overflowing magic, had grown taller, as well. Some of the longer stalks had bloomed spontaneously at the moment of Nihs' promotion. He eyed them with amusement.

He heard footfalls behind him, and turned to see Kyen and Xira running towards him, following the path he had carved out of the grass. Both were wincing in the sun's light, and their purple-black robes were rumpled and soaked.

"What—what have you done?" Kyen said, as his companion wheezed and shielded his eyes. "How did you come to be here?"

Nihs looked around him. He was bemused. "The magic guided me here."

"But...you...the surface..." Kyen was at a loss for words, his face twisted in confusion. "Why? How?"

Try as he might, Nihs could not empathize with Kyen's distress. He felt incredibly calm, as if the grass around him were a sea, and he was caught up in its gentle waves. The breeze teased at his cheek, and even without focusing he could feel the tendrils of magic inherent in it.

"I did as you asked," he said. "I followed the whispers of magic in the caves. They led me here. There's nothing more or less to it than that."

Kyen was agonized. "No one has ever done this before. We thought it impossible. We did not even know of this exit from the caves."

"And?"

Kyen's mouth moved, but no words came. Finally, he said, "We must consult the others—"

"You must do nothing of the sort. You and Xira are the keepers of the trial, are you not? You are the only ones that may decide whether or not I have completed it."

The two guardians shared a glance. Nihs felt a couple of half-formed thoughts pass between them. Never before would he have been able to sense such subtle magic.

"We…You must give us some time, Nihs of the Ken folk," Xira said at last. "We must talk of this."

A ghost of irritation touched Nihs' soul, but the elation that promotion had brought upon him had far from faded. He watched with disinterest as Kyen and Xira walked a way off, touched their foreheads together and began to talk hurriedly.

Nihs breathed slowly. His strength and control were returning already. He wanted to stretch his body, mind and spirit, and discover his new limits—but there would be plenty of time for that later.

Instead, he sank once more to the ground and crossed his legs. He closed his eyes and unraveled his ears, and soon he was drifting bodiless through the overhead. Most of the Kol of Proks were below him, now; he could see the lights of their souls scattered beneath him like a city at night. There was one soul in particular he was looking for. He could only hope that she was connected to the overhead at this moment.

*Nellazan…*He cast the thought out into the void.

After only a brief moment, the reply came. *Nizu? Is it really you?*

Nihs could feel her apprehension, though she tried to mask it. *It is. Nellazan, I have walked the path. I am a sage now.*

Exultation, tinged with only a slight disbelief. *Nizu! That is wonderful. But…why is there doubt in your mind? Where are you? What has happened?*

That is…well…

Then, a new voice, incredibly close, loud as a thunderclap and knife-sharp: *An intriguing tale, no doubt, but premature. Your sagacity is in question yet, Nihs Ken. Open your eyes and face us. As for you, Nella Ran…I would speak no more of this until we have determined just what my son has managed to accomplish.*

Nihs' eyes opened with a snap, and his world flooded with color once more. He saw that his audience had grown since entering the overhead: Kyen and Xira had been joined by Nihs Sul, a handful of others from Ata chamber, and Dari, Nihs' father.

Nihs felt fear rise in his throat like bile as he beheld his father. Darizot was standing directly in front of him, arms crossed, his face set in the dour, puckered grimace with which Nihs was all too familiar. His black sagecloak seemed to absorb the morning sun.

"Well," he said, "I see you've decided to join us. I don't suppose you'd care to explain yourself?"

Nihs rose, brushing the grass and dew from his suit. It had been a long, long time since he had spoken to Dari face to face, but already he was remembering how to deal with his father. It was better to claim complete ignorance than try to muddle through with imperfect knowledge; much like Nella, Dari could pinpoint the flaw in any argument.

"I cannot," Nihs said.

Dari's nostrils flared. "Of course not. Who could try to rationalize your behavior?" A gout of air escaped from his lips like steam from a valve.

"He has failed, hasn't he?" Nihs Sul asked. His voice was reedy and uncertain; clearly this hadn't been a good day for him. "He never reached the chamber of the gods."

In other circumstances, Nihs might have felt a certain kinship for his namesake—no one should have to feel the brunt of his father's anger. As it was, the way that he withered in the face of Dari's stare was almost comical.

"That," came the clipped response, "is not my authority, nor anyone else's here, save for the keepers of the path. Their judgment is as sound as it is imminent, I am sure."

Nihs followed Dari's gaze to see that Kyen and Xira were still huddled off to one side, whispering frantically between themselves. They looked up when they sensed the others' attention, and made their way across the intervening space, each trying to hide behind the other.

"Well?" Dari said.

Kyen took a step forward. "We…that is…Nihs Ken…he has completed the trial."

A horrified gasp from Nihs Sul, a flaring of the nostrils by Dari. And Nihs, silent and unnoticed, felt his heart soar.

"And how do you figure that?" Dari said, each word dropping from his mouth like a slug.

"The…the path is a test of one's affinity for magic. The chamber of the gods, it…it is a place of concentrated magic, suitable for the trial, but it in and of itself is not the trial's purpose. Your son…Nihs Ken…he walked far, far further than any Kol has been made to walk. He…his feat of magic, sensing the surface…it is far beyond the trial's demands. And his legitimacy is evidenced by his promotion. He is a sage now, in all but cloak and title."

Whispers and murmurs broke out in earnest. Finally someone spoke, and Nihs realized that it was he.

"But Kol are meant to be of the caves," he said. "Why was I able to promote by reaching the surface?"

Xira met his eyes gravely. "We do not know. Perhaps the young Kol of future generations are not meant for the caves. The pull of the surface is strong in you, so strong that it called you to itself even when you were deaf and blind."

What did I tell you? said the voice in Nihs' mind.

Dari clenched his jaw. Nihs had never seen him so angry. "And is that your final word?" he said.

"It is," Xira said.

For a moment Nihs was actually afraid that his father might lash out, might uncross his arms and unleash all of his pent-up fury and disgust in the form of magic. But then he turned to Nihs Sul and said, "I believe you promised something to my son."

It was all Nihs Sul could do to reach into his satchel and pull out Azanhein's red sagecloak. Hands shaking, he reached out and draped it around Nihs' shoulders. The presenting of the cloak was a simple ceremony and no words were required, though the friend, family member or elder who performed it often took the opportunity to speak a few words of praise for the benefit of whomever might be watching. Nihs had expected his namesake get the process over as quickly and painlessly as possible, but to his surprise Nihs Sul turned and addressed the small crowd once the cloak was fastened.

"I have been humbled by this experience," he said. "For today my namesake has taught me that there is always more to learn of magic, and that presuming to know all of its moods and motives leaves one vulnerable to...lapses in judgment. Thank you, Nihs Ken."

A few noises of assent and appreciation, but Dari's scowl was enough to keep most of the onlookers silent.

Humbled he may be, but Nihs Sul's scheming certainly hasn't stopped, Nihs thought. *He still knows how to make the best of an embarrassing situation. Having failed to ridicule me, he now hopes to cultivate a reputation for humility.*

But he was satisfied. Everything had gone far better than he had dared hope. Azanhein's cloak was heavy and warm against his back; the strength of the Heart of Buoria was at his command. His father wasn't happy with him—Nihs had come to terms with the fact that this may never be so—but at least his third son had failed to become an even greater source of shame.

Nella will be proud, Nihs thought, *and little Kisi will be thrilled. And now if my father disapproves of her affection for me, he'll have to keep it to himself.* And at the thought of his sisters, Nihs' heart filled with joy, and suddenly he couldn't wait to be in their presence.

Tomorrow, he would catch an airship to Ar'ac, where the party had promised to meet once their personal quests were done. But he would spend one more night in Proks.

He awoke from his reverie to find that Dari had already left, sweeping up most of the others in his wake. Only Kyen and Xira remained, and once they caught Nihs' eye they bowed silently to him and left.

For now, Nihs was in no hurry to follow them. He looked up at the sky, and everything that those Kol who dwelled in caves never had the chance to see: the clouds, the birds, and most importantly, the sun. He closed his eyes and cast a thought out into the air.

Thank you. I would have failed were it not for your guidance.

You're very welcome, said the voice of Archmage Rosshku in his mind.

M eya squinted her eyes nearly shut as a cloud of dust, borne by the high prairie winds, climbed the ridge of the hill upon which she stood and barreled towards her. The grains of sand felt like minuscule bugs nipping at the exposed parts of her body, but she had no trouble ignoring them. The plains held no shortage of real bugs, and given the choice, Meya would much rather take the wind.

Behind her, Deriahm was finishing his morning exercises. He performed these every single day without fail, waking up early to get them over with before the sun rose. Meya, who had spent most of her childhood in church, was used to regimen, but the sheer, unflinching discipline of the Buorish mind still shocked her. Deriahm's exercises, like most of the habits that made him who he was, had been learned in the military, a military in which all young Buors were forced to serve. Meya found this practice barbaric, but she kept the thought to herself. There were far greater evils in the world than the way Buors treated their children.

Deriahm, finished, drew up beside her. Though he'd been exercising for at least half an hour, there was no sound or rise and fall of the chest to show that he was breathing heavily.

"Do you see anything of note, miss Ilduetyr?" he asked.

She sighed—half amusement, half exasperation. "You can call me 'Meya', Deriahm," she said.

"My apologies, Meya. Informality does not come easily to us."

Meya believed him, particularly because he still choked on her first name whenever she could get him to use it. It wasn't even her real one; like many adventurers, she had adopted a new one when coming into her career.

"Don't worry about it. And the answer's no—if I didn't know we were headed in the right direction, I might start going insane."

Deriahm shifted in his armor. "Perhaps we should reassess our strategy. If we seek higher ground, we may catch sight of a settlement where we can acquire newer information."

"They'll just tell us what we already know: that the herd passed by some time ago, headed further south. We just have to catch up."

Deriahm nodded. "I believe you are right. In which case, our way is clear. Are you prepared to break camp?"

Meya was, so they walked back to the golden vehicle they had called home for the last three days of their lives. It was called a drifter, a wide, flat tigoreh vehicle designed to skip over the dust and scrub of the plains. It was parked in the shade of a rocky outcropping to keep the heat at bay, but the leather seats still burned when Meya sat down.

Every day was the same routine; Meya would drive for the first few hours, at which point they would find some shelter and stop to eat lunch—or at least, Meya would eat lunch while Deriahm completed his afternoon exercises. Then, Deriahm would take the second shift while Meya sat or dozed in the back. They had been chasing the herd this way for days, but so far had seen no sign that they were getting any closer.

The drifter's key had been left in place overnight; it wasn't as if anyone was going to ride away in it. Meya switched on the Ephicer engine and the machine hummed into life, lifting itself a few inches off the sandy ground. She brought it about until was facing south across the plains, then opened the magic intake. It leapt forward at once, kicking dust and gravel out from under it.

They sped across the plains, the wind whipping around Meya's head—the drifter had a canopy, but they would have boiled alive under it. It was hot, but they were still far enough north to avoid the crushing heat of the deserts and plateaus of southern Ar'ac. This land, at least, still had definition, and hardy plants and grasses eked out a living wherever they could.

Meya wasn't much one for Ephicer machines, but even she had enjoyed their first day of skimming over hills in the drifter. It was a tough vehicle, nearly impossible to flip, and the wide-open space they had to ride around in had seemed full of promise. Now, she couldn't wait to be back in civilization. Deriahm was as polite and helpful as a travelling companion could be, but his company lacked the human warmth that Meya had always found to be the best quality of people as a whole.

They came across a wide riverbed, and followed it to a valley that had been carved out by water long ago. There was shade and greenery here, and even a bit of muddy water sitting in the deepest part of the valley. They stopped for lunch, and this time Deriahm decided to join Meya in her meal. He pulled out his travel *rouk* pipe and inserted a cake smaller than Meya's palm. He lit it, and then sat inhaling the smoke through a thin, flexible hose.

Meya, who was on travel rations, ate with boredom and stared down the length of the valley. A huge bird—a monster known as a gricks—was drinking from the sludgy water a few hundred feet away.

"Are you well, miss Ilduetyr?" Deriahm asked her suddenly.

"Hmm?" Meya said. "Yes, I'm fine."

Deriahm was puffing at his pipe, his visored helmet giving no clue as to his expression. "I am sorry to pry, but I notice that you seem fatigued of late. I worry that you are not receiving enough food."

"We brought enough food to last a halfmonth," she said.

"Of course. My apologies."

Meya didn't know much about Deriahm, but she did know that he was a terrible liar, and about as subtle as a bag of rocks. She pinned him down with her red eyes and said, "Deriahm, I wish you would say whatever you're trying to get at."

He laid down his pipe and sighed, smoke curling from his helmet. "I must apologize once again, miss Ilduetyr. My approach of delicate matters is unskillful at best. It is your mental health, rather than your physical health, about which I am concerned."

This was so unexpected that Meya could only say, "What? Why?"

"You have recently suffered a significant personal loss. And you are under a great amount of emotional stress besides."

"Oh." The way Deriahm framed it should have sounded ridiculous, *did* sound ridiculous, but Meya found herself looking away from him, brushing the hair out of her eyes.

"I only hope that you are coping well," he continued. "I cannot say I have experienced a similar loss myself, but I do know how profound the impact of such losses can be."

"No, you don't," Meya said.

"You may be right—"

"I *am* right," she said, glaring at him. "You can't know what it feels like until it happens to you. You just can't."

She wanted to be angry at him, but she could sense his empathy even through his iron mask.

"I am sorry," he said. "You are right, of course. But if I cannot understand, I can at least promise you my unwavering support. We are companions now, and I wish for you to know that my strength is yours."

Meya found herself at a loss for words. She searched the slats in his visor for a hint of human expression, but of course there was none. But his voice had sounded as raw and earnest as a child's.

"Thank you, Deriahm," she said finally. "I appreciate it."

Deriahm bobbed his head and raised his pipe to his visor. "I am glad," he said. "And as it so happens, there is something I may tell you already that will raise your spirits."

Meya's brow creased. "What's that?"

Deriahm lifted his arm, and Meya followed his pointing finger down the length of the valley. Her eyes alighted on the muddy water at the valley's floor. The gricks had flapped away a few minutes before, and now she saw why. A multitude of tiny ripples were peppering the water's surface. Now that she was paying attention, she could feel it as well—the constant thrumming of the ground beneath her.

She gasped. "The herd!"

"Indeed. Shall we break camp? I believe we have an acquaintance to make."

Darkness had fallen once more. The sun was blazing in the sky above, but to Kyle and Lugh, trekking through the swamp, it might as well have gone out hours ago.

The swamps beyond the village of Lundir were, if possible, even more sinister than those before it. The trees here grew so thickly together that they formed into twisting curtains of wood and leaves, impossible for a human to navigate. The route's only saving grace was the wooden walkway that carved a winding path through the swamp.

Any territory not taken up by trees was drowned in turbid, foul-smelling water. Lugh had said it was poisonous, and Kyle was not entirely sure if he had been joking.

There was still light, in the form of the tigoreh lamps that lined the walkway, and there was still sound, in the occasional chirp of an insect or the wet *slop* of a shift in the water's surface. But other than this, Kyle was blind and deaf, and the swamp around him was filled with unseen terror. He rested his hand on the hilt of his silver sword, and eyed the foliage around him for signs of movement.

Lugh, for his part, was watching the left side of the path with intensity. According to him, his brother's caravan had lost the path when it had reached one of the swamp's occasional patches of dry land. With no wooden walkway to mark their direction, they had headed straight for the next tigoreh lamp, accidentally cutting away from the safety of the trail and becoming bogged down in the swamp. Lugh had never seen the area before, but assured Kyle he would know it when he saw it.

Lugh had been with Kyle ever since his fall into Loria, and there was no one in this world that Kyle trusted more, but these assurances still did little to inspire his confidence. The fact that they were searching the swamps blindly for the remains of a man who had perished within them was not lost on him.

For hours they walked. The going was tense, but at least it was easy; they had past generations of caravanners to thank for the ramshackle wooden walkway that kept them above the swamp. It was a simple task of keeping an eye on the ground, minding the slippery wooden surface, and moving carefully from lamp to lamp.

More than once a sound burst forth from the darkness around them, and once it was even the distinct hiss of a sahagin—but nothing came into Kyle's limited field of view, for all the times he nearly drew his sword in fear.

Then, a new sound emerged: an inhuman wail coming from the path ahead. Kyle's guts knotted instantly, but Lugh put a calming hand on his arm. The sound drew clearer and closer, and Kyle realized that it was singing—horrible, off-key singing, accompanied by the jangle of metal.

A feeling of warm relief melted away his fear. Whatever creature was making that pitiful sound, it couldn't be too threatening.

They crossed paths with the perpetrator not two seconds later, as a light emerged from a bend in the walkway and they found themselves faced by a slim figure. It was a Lizardman, a rail-thin, ocher-colored specimen with a long, narrow face, so unlike the Snakes Kyle had met near Reno city. He had an enormous travel pack slung across his back which clattered and jangled with every step. Tools, containers, and tigoreh lanterns were fastened to it wherever they would fit.

The newcomer actually yelped when he caught sight of Lugh and Kyle, his reedy singing cutting short. The pack wobbled, threatening to pull him off-balance. He righted himself and said: "Such a scare you gave Sersi! So rare does he share the road. Nothing but sahagin and scamps, most usual."

"No sahagin here," Lugh said, folding his arms. "Just a couple of adventures. I'm Lugh, and this is Kyle. Where are you headed?"

Sersi blinked one eye and then the other. "Adventurers? Oooh. Sersi headed here and there. He wanders, and trades, his bits and bobs, yes, very useful many find them."

Lugh was surprised. "By yourself?"

Sersi adjusted his pack, and his 'bits and bobs' clanged loudly. "Oh, yes. The noise scares away the sahagin, you know, and the singing. I am one, but they think me ten! Sersi marches with an army on his back, he does. Say, care you to buy a soldier? A lantern, or some food? We do business?"

Lugh gave a short laugh. "Thanks, but no thanks, friend. Not unless you can tell me where a caravan went off the road near here some years ago."

"A caravan? Oooh." Sersi tapped at his long snout with an equally long finger. "No wrecks near here, no, or Sersi would know. Years ago?"

"They went off this side of the path between two lamps, over a patch of dry ground."

"Oooh, oooh, yes, some dry ground near here. Big enough for a caravan, yes." Sersi turned back the way he'd come. "Seventeen lanterns, or so, thattaway. Sersi knows. Sahagin country, that. Not even Sersi's army keep him safe." He turned back, and with the polished instinct of a master trader, added, "but perhaps a nice lantern, light your way, find your caravan, yes?"

Lugh started to laugh. "Tell you what, Sersi, I'll take one, as thanks for that info."

The scrawny Lizardman positively cooed with pleasure. "You will not regret it, sir!"

They parted ways soon after, each heading off down the way the other had come. As Sersi disappeared down the path, they heard his awful singing drifting out of the darkness, the *clang-clang-clang* of his pack serving as accompaniment.

"Strange little fellow," Lugh said, hitching his new lantern to his belt.

"Yeah," Kyle said. "Hard to believe he makes a living out here, selling things like that."

"I doubt if he does," Lugh said.

"What do you mean?"

"Ever heard the phrase 'skin of stone, head of cotton'? Probably not, so let's say there's a reason why Lizardfolk are known for being friendly and leave it at that. Sersi struck me as the kind of man who wouldn't be able to help but sample his own merchandise from time to time."

Kyle had the mind of a cynic, and he caught Lugh's meaning immediately. "You think he was a drug dealer?"

"Not *just* a drug dealer," Lugh said fairly. "But I'd bet that's how he makes most of his money. Doesn't make much sense to focus on bits and bobs when there's so many interesting herbs and mushrooms growing in the swamp, does it? The money's better, and the merchandise is free, if you know where to find it."

Kyle was starting to see their encounter with Sersi in a whole new light. "He didn't try to sell *us* anything strange."

"We aren't Lizardfolk, so he didn't bother. Most of the drugs they take are poisonous to us weaker folk. Remember that if a Lizardman ever offers you something—their friendliness can end up killing you."

"I'll keep that mind."

Cotton-headed as Sersi might have been, they decided to follow his advice. They started counting the lanterns that lined the side of the boardwalk; as soon as they hit fifteen, they slowed their pace, watching for a sign that this was the stretch of road they were looking for.

"Why don't you use your lantern?" Kyle whispered at one point.

"Don't want to lose my night eyes—well—eye, anyway. And I don't want to draw the sahagin's attention. Sersi might put his faith in his singing, but I prefer a bit more stealth."

They came to a small hummock, and Lugh leapt off the path to investigate. Kyle stood and waited, watching Lugh's ill-defined form move about at the edge of sight. Once or twice he thought Lugh had disappeared completely, but then his friend reemerged, sliding down the hillside and vaulting back onto the path.

He shook his head at Kyle's inquisitive stare. "Can't be the place. Not big enough, and too steep to take a caravan across."

"Think Sersi could have been wrong?" Kyle asked.

"Could be. But we've got a ways to go before we can say for sure."

They carried on. The path climbed and curved to the right, then passed through a dense patch of reeds. Crowding in on either side of the path, they threatened to swallow it entirely, and their spindly stalks felt like fingers brushing against Kyle's arms as he slipped between them. More than once he was tempted to draw his sword and hack a path through them.

Then they were on the other side, and the wooden walkway disappeared. Instead, long, straight poles of wood laid end-to-end marked the way forward. Though the ground was firmer here, it was still clogged with water, and Kyle's boots sucked and squelched with each step he took.

Lugh's face was contemplative. "They don't often make paths this way," he said. "Saves wood, but it doesn't last long…One of these markers rolls off, and it's gone."

Kyle knew what Lugh was getting at. Not long after the path had changed, he noticed that the logs which formed it had become cleaner and brighter in color.

"This part of the path is new," he said.

Lugh nodded. "You're right. Can't be more than a couple years old. Let's keep our eyes open."

There was a twist in the path, and there it was: to their right, the path continued, marked by the newly placed logs and a tigoreh lamp. To their left, a rising trail that lead upwards along dry earth, wide enough to be mistaken for the path itself were it not for the markers leading the other way.

Lugh put his hands on his hips. Kyle could feel his excitement.

"This is it," he said in a low voice. "The markers must have been missing when Hael's caravan came this way. Come and look at this."

Kyle stepped forward, and when he squinted through the darkness, he saw the faint glow of a lamp far in the distance, just visible down the leftmost path.

"Of course, they were coming from the other direction," Lugh said, his voice now shaking. "But the view was probably exactly the same. They saw this lamp, thought it was next in line, and made right for it. But they were cutting across sahagin territory."

Kyle nodded. Lugh was right, he could feel it. On Earth this would have meant little, but here in Loria, feeling was everything. There was something drawing them down the leftmost path, something more than the distant lantern. This was the place.

"Let's go," he said.

"Yeah," Lugh said. "Let's."

Kyle had been prepared for the worst, but shockingly, he and Lugh found their path completely free of obstruction. In fact, the quietness around them only became more pronounced as they walked, until the only sounds that reached their ears were their own footfalls.

Kyle kept his eye on the far lantern, worried that they would get lost once they left the path. At first, the going was easy, but then the uneven ground soon forced them in a new direction and Kyle lost sight of the blue glow. Lugh forged ahead, unworried. Kyle grit his teeth, held onto his sword, and followed.

The ground here was firm, held together by large clumps of grass and some of the swamp's huge, rambling trees. They stepped over snaking roots and odd mushrooms smeared bioluminescent sludge on their footwear.

Finally, Lugh stopped. He put his hands on his hips and looked around. Mist was condensing on his stone eyepatch; a droplet formed, ran down its carved surface, and landed on his cheek.

"Stay here," he said to Kyle after a moment. "I'm going to see if I can look around."

He leapt straight upwards, and Kyle heard him come down a moment later. He craned his neck, but couldn't see where Lugh had landed. After a moment Lugh fell back down to the path with a *whump*.

"No luck?" Kyle guessed.

"I can see the lamp well enough," Lugh replied. "That's what worries me. They're too close together to get lost, even out here. I'm starting to think the caravan went further off course than we thought."

Kyle looked down the path in both directions. "Keep going and look for a place it might have gone off?"

"Not a bad idea. If we reach the lamp without seeing anything promising, we'll just have to think of something else."

They were spared the trouble. They came to a bend in the path, with a moss-covered hill to their right and an open space to their left. There, in the distance beyond a minefield of poisonous water, was another lamp.

They stood for a moment, taking in the blue glow. Kyle was trying to figure out the significance of what they had just seen. The path leading to the new lamp was bright; the pools of water and the air above them glowed blue with a million pinpricks of light. Was it possible that Haelinor and the others had tried to cross over this watery plain with the caravan?

"What do we do?" he asked.

There was a strange expression on Lugh's face. "I don't know," he said, "but I do know that the swamp doesn't play fair. Things aren't always as they seem. That's why the caravanners are risking their lives every time they go out here. That's why the Selks care so much about roads. Stick to the road and you'll be fine. Stray off the path and…"

He stepped forward, and his boot came down on a stone poking out from the ground. There was a *clop* that sounded unnaturally loud in the still air, and the thousands of points of light instantly scattered, disappearing into the ground, the trees, and the air. Suddenly, they were once again in darkness.

Kyle swallowed, and it stuck in his throat. The strange feeling he had sensed before was getting stronger. They were getting closer. There was something here that was more than it seemed.

Slowly, Lugh unhooked Sersi's lantern from his belt and switched it on. The Ephicer inside glowed to life, and he started forward carefully, each step calculated. Kyle followed, and they picked their way across the waterlogged ground towards the path-marker in the distance.

It went out.

Kyle caught his breath. He had never seen an Ephicer light go out of its own accord before. His heart pounded, and he started to hear snatches of sound at the edge of hearing. He was afraid, and he couldn't tell which, if any, were real.

A hand clapped him on the shoulder, and he jumped. Then Lugh's face swam into vision, pale and eerie in the light of his lantern. He said, "Listen. Don't let this place get to you, all right? But do keep your sword handy. I have a feeling we're almost there."

Kyle nodded, and quietly drew his sword. Its familiar heft and silver sheen gave him strength. *There's nothing out here I can't face, as long as I can keep myself from killing Lugh by accident.*

They pressed on, and the ground began to rise. There were no more patches of water, and soon they crested a low, wide hill. Beyond the hill was a shallow valley, featuring two small pools of water on either side.

Kyle caught a glint of something in the valley's center. At first, he thought his eyes were playing tricks, but when Lugh raised his lantern he saw it again. They walked forward, and Kyle saw what it was.

A squared-off block of gray stone was jutting out of the ground. It had been jammed in on its long end, and was leaning slightly to one side. A long strap of leather had been wrapped around it and tied off two-thirds of the way up, and three simple runes were carved vertically into its surface.

Lugh sank to his knees. There was no expression on his face, no sadness or joy, but a faint surprise, an incredulity that had set in before other emotions could take its place. He reached out, and with his index finger traced the runes from top to bottom.

"Hael-in-or," he said. "That's what these mean. This is him."

Kyle didn't know what to say. "I'm sorry, Lugh."

Lugh pulled his lips back in a smirk. "Don't be. I just…can't believe I'm finally seeing it, after all these years. I don't know what I expected."

He knelt there for a moment longer, and then rose slowly to his feet. He heaved a sigh, then turned and looked at Kyle.

"There's one problem," he said. "His sword is gone."

Kyle, stunned for a moment, looked down and saw that this was true. "Someone stole it?" he said.

"Maybe," was all Lugh said in reply.

Kyle looked at his companion. Lugh's brow was creased, and his normal smile had disappeared. At first Kyle assumed he must have been angry at the unknown thief, but this did not seem to be the case. Not for the first time, he got the sense that there was more going on here than he could understand.

"What should we do?" he asked.

Lugh didn't answer right away. He paused, looking at the grave, then cast his eyes over the swamp around them.

"Let's stay here for the night," he said.

Kyle gaped at him. "You can't be serious."

Lugh smiled faintly. "Don't worry," he said, "we'll be fine, I promise. Nothing will hurt us here."

"Why not?"

"I just know. Can't you feel it? There's something special about this place."

Kyle *could* feel it, but what disturbed him was that he still couldn't understand. Was this something that all Lorians did, or just Lugh? Make decisions based on sudden feelings? He knew that Loria worked by different rules than his own Earth, but that didn't make it any easier to accept.

Lugh put a hand on his shoulder. "I understand you're worried, all right? But trust me on this. I'm the one being tested here, not you. You're not in any danger."

Kyle just shook his head. "One day I hope I can figure out what all of you see that I don't."

"I know you will. By the end of tonight, you might understand a little more." He gestured toward the side of the valley. "Let's roll out our beds and get a canvas hung up between those trees. That should keep most of the damp out."

At first, Kyle was convinced that he would never catch a minute of sleep out here. The air was cold and damp, and every sound pricked at his ears and made his pupils stretch themselves wide. But shivering and staying alert was exhausting, and fatigue crept up on him without warning. Even so, his sleep was shallow and unsatisfying. Figures danced in front of his mind's eye, ill-formed but always present. His dreams had been strange ever since the assassin Lacaster had hit him with the cursed arrow; it was as if a wall of smoke were separating him from his memories. He tossed and turned, sat up, beat the bundle of clothes he was using as a pillow, and slammed his head back down.

He surfaced from his sleep once more to see a figure walking slowly away from him. At first, he thought it was another dream; then he blinked the fog from his eyes and saw that it was Lugh. His friend was creeping slowly away from their camp and towards Haelinor's grave. His silversteel swords were slung to his back.

Kyle wanted to get up and ask Lugh what he was doing, but something held him back. He watched Lugh walk over to his brother's grave and sit down cross-legged before it. He pulled out Sersi's tiny lantern and lit it before placing it on the ground next to him. He drew one of his swords and held it balanced across his lap. His good eye, visible to Kyle, was fixed on Haelinor's grave.

Kyle watched for five, ten minutes more, but nothing happened. Finally his fatigue won him over, and he fell back into sleep.

Lugh waited to get out of bed until he heard Kyle's rhythmic breathing coming from the bedroll opposite him. Once he was sure Kyle was asleep, he rolled silently out of bed and went groping for his weapon. He rose and walked over to his brother's grave.

It's going to happen tonight, he thought. *I'm not sure exactly what it will be, but I'll be ready for it.*

How had Haelinor's caravan gone so horribly astray? Why had the tigoreh lamp gone out as soon as he and Kyle had approached it? He couldn't be sure, but in his experience, intuition was usually enough.

The swamp didn't play fair. Sure, even skilled caravanners made mistakes from time to time, but they'd be much more prone to it if something was helping them on their way.

There had been more than just an innocent mistake behind Haelinor's death. Lugh was sure of it. There were two things that marked the Selk's roads through the swamp. The planks themselves, and the tigoreh lamps. If the planks were gone, you had to trust the lamps, and follow.

But if one of the lamps was gone...

Or had been snuffed out...

Or had been moved...

A cry rang out through the darkness. Lugh's ears twitched; but the cry had been distant. He ignored it and turned back to the task at hand.

He would be a hero by the end of the night. He knew it. He had been ready to face his brother's grave, and that meant he was ready to promote. He'd reached the proper place. Now all that was left was to wait for the proper time.

He sat down, unhooked his lantern, lit it and set it down. Then he drew one of his swords from his back, and held it across his lap. His good eye traced over the dimly-lit runes etched into the grave before him. His thoughts turned to Haelin's companions, the caravanners who had traveled with him, fought with him, and laid him to rest here.

You could have just written 'Hael', or even nothing at all—you must have known that anyone who found this grave would already know whose it was. Saints, you didn't need to make a grave at all. But you did. You found just the right spot of land, and you stuck a rock in the ground and you carved his entire name into it. You probably thought it was stupid at the time… that it didn't matter. But it matters to me. Thank you.

Now, if only the thing who had taken Hael's sword would show its ugly face.

Lugh waited and tried to meditate. He'd never found much use in it, despite Nihs' constant championing of its benefits. Trying to clear his mind was an exercise in futility. As soon as he had it all nice and empty, a slew of new thoughts would rush in to fill the void. Besides, wasn't that what meditation should be about? Chasing all of your little thoughts to the edges of your mind, clearing them out, getting them out of the way? It made sense to Lugh, but whenever he shared that with Nihs the little Kol looked at him as though he'd committed high treason.

He spared a few thoughts for Nihs. Was his quest for promotion going well? Nihs was strong and smart, but he spent far too much of his time thinking up problems for himself—and magic was all about conviction. Really, it was a miracle that Nihs could use magic at all with that family of his breathing down his neck.

Hopefully that Nella girl can slap some sense into him. Funny—she reminds me a lot of Meya. We seem to attract a certain kind of woman into our lives.

And then he was thinking about Meya and Deriahm, down in Ar'ac doing, well, whatever they were doing. The Archmage Rosshku hadn't told the rest of them why those two had to go south. Very mysterious. But if the Archmage thought it was a good idea, then Lugh wasn't about to argue.

Meya and Deriahm…We barely know either of them, really. And they know Kyle even less. Funny how they're giving everything up to help him get home. But that's what adventurers do. We stick our noses in other people's business, fix their problems, travel halfway around the world to get a job done. That's just the kind of people we are.

And now he was thinking about Kyle. *Good kid. Lost, though. And not just because he's trapped in Loria. Doesn't know who he is or what he wants to be. I know how he feels. I think we all do. Maybe that's why we all want to help him so much. He's the adventurer to end all adventurers.*

But Kyle was changing and growing faster than anyone Lugh had ever met. Lugh could hardly believe that the man he knew now was the same one that he, Nihs and Rogan had found barely a month ago. That Kyle had been pale, weak, and above all, miserable. It had shown in everything about him—his clothes, his face, the way he barely bothered to hold himself up. Now he was strong and capable, and becoming more so every day. Whenever Lugh stole a glance at him, his eyes were narrowed in thought, and Lugh could practically hear his brain churning away as it processed all of the lessons Loria was teaching him. At some point Kyle had decided that it was worth trying after all, and Lugh had a sneaking suspicion that he would leave them all far behind if he stayed in Loria long enough.

Of course, getting Kyle out of Loria was why he, Lugh, was here in the first place. If there was ever a reason to be thankful for Kyle's existence, this was it. How long would Lugh have avoided this moment if Kyle hadn't appeared? It had already been far too long.

Sorry, Hael. I just wasn't ready. It's different now.

There came a noise behind him. It was a short croak, low enough to be mistaken for the sound of a bubble bursting on the swamp's surface. But to Lugh it might as well have been a voice speaking his name.

Lugh opened his eye, stood up, and turned around. Blue light washed over him as he did so. It glinted off the polished surface of his eyepatch and gave his face a ghostly hue.

In front of him stood a sahagin as big as himself. The soft blue flesh of its stomach was protected by limbs of hard, scaly hide. A large frilled crest protruded from a rudimentary helm made from some monster's skull. There was a shield of bone strapped to its left arm, and in its right was a curved sword that looked like the talon of a massive bird. It had a dull bronze surface flecked with black, and Lugh had last seen it five years ago in the hands of his brother.

Like all of its fellows, this sahagin had a long, flexible tail that ended with a fin used for swimming. But unlike any other sahagin Lugh had ever seen, this one kept its tail curved upwards behind it, its tip level with its head. There was a small tigoreh lantern tied to the tip.

Lugh should have been furious, but all he could think in this moment was: *I understand.*

The sahagin croaked for a second time. Lugh had no idea what the croaks meant, if anything, but he interpreted this one as, "I killed your brother. Now I'm going to kill you."

Lugh drew his second sword and leveled it at the monster. His heart was pounding, and his hands were shaking. His eyepatch felt cold against his skin. To his surprise, he realized that he was deathly afraid. Not even Hael had survived this creature. What hope did he have?

But more importantly, what choice did he have? The answer was none. He was doing this for his brother, for Kyle, and for himself. He couldn't turn his back on all three of them.

"Come get me, you slimy bastard," he growled.

Half-asleep, it might have been one minute or ten before Kyle realized that the sound he was hearing was the ring of steel on steel. As soon as he did, he vaulted out of his bedroll, grabbed his sword and dashed off into the swamp without wasting a single moment on thought. It didn't even cross his mind to check Lugh's bedroll. He knew it was his friend out there and knew there wasn't a moment to waste.

He crested the hill that overlooked Haelinor's grave and saw Lugh locked in battle with a massive sahagin. Lugh was dancing around his enemy, trying to slide his twin swords though the monster's defenses. But the sahagin's tough, scaled limbs got in the way of every strike, and it had the same sinewy, eel-like grace that made all sahagin such slippery foes.

Kyle had always felt that there was something terrifying about watching his companions fight. In battle, there was never any time to worry about the danger they were all in, but when he was nothing but an onlooker every blow made him wince.

He ran forward, then kicked off the ground as Lugh had taught him. As he flew across the intervening space, he willed his sword into its larger shape and wound up a huge, baseball-swing strike. Lugh saw him coming and dove out of the way, just before he swung full-force into the sahagin's back and sent it flying into a nearby tree.

Kyle landed on his feet after spinning nearly full-circle. The sahagin was incredibly strong—it was a matter of seconds before it was on its feet once again, rearing back up to its full height. Kyle wasn't afraid; the taste of blood was in his mouth and he knew that no monster was a match for him and Lugh.

He felt Lugh put a hand his shoulder. His friend was laughing, but it was resigned rather than pleased.

"I should have known you'd do that," he said.

"What do you mean?" Kyle said.

Lugh's face became serious. "Listen, Kyle. I know you want to help. But this is something I have to do myself. It's my promotion test, understand? That's the sahagin that killed Haelinor. Or maybe he's Haelinor come back to life—I'm not sure. Either way, I have to be the one to kill it."

Kyle looked from Lugh to the monster and back. It was rallying, and had started advancing on the two of them. He wanted to argue, but couldn't make himself do it. Lugh was always giving, and never asked anything for himself. If he was doing it now, it must be for a good reason.

He clapped Lugh on the arm. "All right," he said. "But my soul sword's coming out if it starts winning."

Lugh laughed again, and this time it was genuine. "I wouldn't expect anything less," he said.

Kyle leapt away, and Lugh turned his focus back to the battle. He couldn't be angry; Kyle had no way of knowing that this fight was special. In fact, Lugh found that he was happy for the interruption. It did him good to know that Kyle was close, even if he wasn't fighting.

The sahagin was bearing down on him with the deliberate slowness of a predator. It was as tall as Lugh, but the frills on its head and limbs made it look bigger. Not only that, they were distracting. He was going to have a merry time keeping track of what it was doing.

Realizing that his back was to Haelinor's grave and the slope of the valley, Lugh started to circle. He kept his off-hand sword pointed forwards, ready to stab or parry, and his other raised, ready to strike. Normally he wasn't so careful, but something told him that this was one battle where he couldn't afford to make any mistakes.

The sahagin wasn't so concerned. It advanced at a fast walk, hissing under its breath. It drew close, and then suddenly dashed forwards, sword scything through the air. Lugh blocked quickly, started to strike back, then realized a second swing was coming and blocked again. His aim was wild, and for a moment his guard was knocked aside, but the sahagin had already distanced itself from him. Lugh's hands shook as he regained his balance. The creature had just been testing him— if it had been playing more aggressively, he would have lost his life.

Don't worry about that. Just focus.

The sahagin's mouth hung open as it circled. Its shield was half-raised, ready to block. Lugh's good eye was glued to it, watching for any hint of motion.

Slowly, the sahagin raised its shield and started to push at him, testing his strength, seeing if it could catch him off-balance. He decided not to give it the chance. He sprang backwards, then circled. The sahagin pivoted, tracking his movement, keeping its shield raised. Lugh hadn't had much hope that he could get around it, but now he knew for sure. It was fighting much more defensively than any sahagin Lugh had ever seen—then again, it wasn't like any sahagin he'd ever seen.

He dashed forward instead. He feinted, then struck; the sahagin blocked easily. He circled to the right and struck again. The sahagin's response was to turn violently, trying to hit him with the swinging butt of its shield. Lugh force blocked—spent some of his magical potential to scatter the blow and replace impact with distance. Unscathed, he flew backwards, but his foot caught on the marshy ground and he flipped over onto his back. He heard Kyle shout out just as the monster leapt at him, limbs flailing. Lugh spent more magic, cutting sideways with both swords just as the creature was about to land on top of him. It was knocked aside, and Lugh jumped to his feet.

Strong as the sahagin was, it couldn't use metamagic—that was a privilege reserved for the intelligent races of Loria and to some of the higher classes of monster. Funneling magic into blows and blocks was the adventurer's key to fighting, but it had to be used strategically. Use too much energy in attacking, and you'd leave yourself open for the inevitable counterattack. Stretch a battle by blocking for too long, and you would tire yourself out. Though the sahagin was only a monster, it was still more than a match for him. Its natural weapons—claws, teeth, tail—and the violent instincts that came with them easily made up for Lugh's magical ability.

As they circled each other once more, Lugh realized that there was one area in which the sahagin couldn't hope to match him: equipment. Haelinor's sword was sturdy, for certain, but the sahagin's shield was simple wood and bone. If Lugh hacked at it with his silversteel swords, it would fall to pieces. The question was how long that would take, and whether Lugh could pull it off without getting a sword stuck in the shield.

It's my best chance. I've got to break its guard somehow.

The next time the sahagin lunged forward, Lugh sidestepped into its shield and struck solidly with both swords. He was rewarded with flying chunks of wood. The sahagin swung its shield arm out, bashing at him, then followed up with a cut at chest height. Lugh backed off, let Haelinor's sword whistle by, then lunged again with both swords. The sahagin blocked, and there came two *thoks* of wood as the swords buried themselves deeply in the rim of its shield. Lugh sucked in his breath—*not good*—and made a split-second decision. He lifted a leg and kicked at the shield just as the sahagin pushed forwards to unbalance him. The swords came loose, but Lugh fell over backwards. He rolled out of the way as the sahagin tried to impale him, and regained his feet.

Lugh hacked again, and again, then started to kick at the shield as chunks of it came loose. The sahagin made no attempt to stop him at first, and by the time it realized what he was doing, the shield was coming apart. Finally it hissed in disgust and shook its arm to dislodge it. It fell to the ground in tatters, and the sahagin flexed the claws of its now-open hand.

Lugh wasn't afraid. The sahagin's claws wouldn't be able to get through his armor, and Lugh wasn't planning on giving it the time or space to swipe at him anyway. He had two swords, and he could swing either faster than the sahagin could block. If he kept a cool head, the fight was his.

They clashed again, and this time it was Lugh who tested his opponent's ability to block. The sahagin was fast, but Lugh knew that he could overwhelm it. He started to vent more metamagic, his blows coming faster and harder. Blood blossomed on the sahagin's arm, then leg, then hip, then leg again. It hissed and snapped, then started to flail, clawing and biting; whatever strange intelligence it had been granted was withering away, and animal instinct was shining through. It was more dangerous now than before, but Lugh was dangerous, too. He might have been friendly and cheerful outside of battle, but he had spent the last five years of his life slaying monsters for money, and this monster was holding his brother's sword hostage.

In a way, the sahagin had sealed its own fate. If it hadn't killed Haelinor, Lugh never would have ventured away from home. He would have grown up like Yoren, living a peaceful life of drinking, laughing, and road building. He never would have become an adventurer, and accumulated the dozens of scars that marked him as a slayer of monsters. And now, five years later, he wouldn't have delivered the crushing blow that knocked its weakened guard aside and buried his sword in its neck.

Blood spattered from the wound, and the sahagin's mouth opened and closed like a fish gasping for water. Its knees buckled, and as it fell it looked at up at Lugh with something like supplication. Lugh just reached out and took Haelinor's sword from its unresisting hand.

"Sorry," he said, "but that's mine."

He kicked the creature off of his sword, then turned away and walked back up the hill where Kyle was waiting. His breathing was ragged, but his heartbeat was slow and strong, and Haelinor's sword felt warm and familiar in his hand.

The walk back to Lundir was as long and as dark as the walk out had been, but to Lugh, it was a jaunt in the sunshine. There was an old Selkic saying, *the shortest road is the one that leads home*, and now, the thought of Por Amam's kitchen drew him forward.

Kyle had been silent at first, giving him nothing but a nod as if to say that was all that was needed. Now he said,

"Congratulations."

Lugh nodded. "How many times did you think you'd have to step in?"

Kyle flashed a quick smile. "Trusted you all along," he said. It was an obvious lie, but Lugh could forgive him that. Kyle was the kind of person who always assumed the worst, a helpful trait to have when danger was afoot. *He's like Nihs in that way*, Lugh thought. *Helps balance me out.*

Kyle had something else on his mind. "So…is that it?" he said.

Lugh caught his meaning, and the question made him realize that no, that was not it—he hadn't promoted yet. He lifted Haelinor's sword to his eyes and searched the bronzed blade for answers.

"No," he said, drawing the word out. "I'm not quite done yet."

"What do you have to do?" Kyle asked.

Lugh tapped the flat of the blade against his fingers. The answer came to him at the same time as Kyle's question. "I think I know," he said. "Let's see if I'm right."

Kyle seemed confused but, being Kyle, he didn't want to show it. "Sure," he said.

They walked on. Lugh, no longer afraid of sahagin, or anything else for that matter, reached for his belt and turned Sersi's lantern on. Light, friendly and calming, bathed the trees around them.

"So that thing had been luring caravanners into the swamp," Kyle said.

"Seems like it. I've never heard of sahagin doing that—they're usually not too bright. There was something special about that one, that's for sure."

Kyle nodded, and the next hour or so was spent in silence. Lugh was tired and hungry, but he felt better than he had in a long time. The light from Sersi's lantern may as well have been bursting from his own chest. He held Haelinor's sword in the way one might hold the hand of an old friend.

Finally, the canopy receded, light flowed into the world, and Lundir came into view. Lugh had never seen the northern gates from this side; for some reason, that simple realization struck him.

They passed through the gates and into the town beyond with little fanfare. Part of Lugh had been hoping for some recognition, even a bug-eyed look of amazement from Yoren, but another part of him knew that this way was best. Lundir was not really his home, not anymore; this mission was as much about letting go as it was about honoring his brother's memory.

Por Amam's cottage looked as tranquil as it had the day before, at least from the outside. Lugh knocked, and Por Amam's voice came through the door: "Come in!"

Lugh shrugged and ducked his way through, Kyle following closely behind. When they passed through the threshold, they saw at once why Por Amam had been too preoccupied to answer her door. She was seated in her living room surrounded by a circle of children. A large book bound in leather was perched on her lap; she had been reading to her wards.

Every pair of eyes turned on Lugh and Kyle as they came in. Lugh saw Kyle's hesitation from the corner of his eye—he imagined that Kyle wasn't very good with human children, let alone Selkic ones. The young Selks looked at the two intruders with the wide-eyed stares of children to whom all unfamiliar adults are a spectacle. They must have sensed that Lugh's visit was an important one, because they stayed completely silent.

A flurry of emotions passed across Por Amam's face as Lugh stepped closer, holding Haelinor's sword out in front of him. She rose gracefully from her seat by the window, saying nothing, her eyes fixed on Lugh's. She held out her arms, and the children in front of her moved out of the way so Lugh could come closer and place the sword in her hands.

She lifted it up to her eyes, examining the hilt, looking for the runes that matched the ones Lugh had seen on Haelinor's grave the night before. She didn't speak or even move when she found them, but Lugh saw her eyes start to shine.

"What do you think?" Lugh said. "Hael's back to stay now."

At that, her tears finally spilled over, and she drew both of her sons into one embrace.

Kyle watched Lugh present the sword from a distance, sensing that he wasn't needed at this ceremony. As soon as Por Amam took the sword from Lugh, the atmosphere in the small cottage changed. Kyle heard a faint noise tickling his ears, and a subtle light grew in the corners of his vision. When Por Amam traced the runes on Hael's sword with her finger, the feeling swelled like an orchestra tuning up. And when she embraced Lugh, it burst forth, a blaze of light and sound that washed over Kyle and the circle of children in kind. It engulfed Lugh entirely, such that Por Amam's arms were wrapped around a column of light. She held for a moment, then backed away in surprise.

Still the energy flowed from Lugh in all directions, shooting out the windows of Por Amam's cottage and turning the pots and pans hanging in her kitchen into dazzling circles of light. Lugh's form was almost indistinguishable at the center of it, but Kyle saw him lifting his own hands to his eyes in amazement.

Finally the light tapered off, slowly, like a fire burning itself out, and Lugh reemerged. He looked at once exactly the same as he always had, and completely different from before. He had grown at least two inches and his hair half a foot. He stood straighter, larger, more solid, as if the Lugh Kyle had known before had been nothing but a reflection of the real thing.

Lugh was staring at his own hands as if he'd never seen them before. He looked up at Por Amam, his expression rapt, then looked back at Kyle.

"I did it," he said, as surprised as anyone.

Kyle raised his eyebrows and smiled. He couldn't help it after seeing Lugh's expression.

"Congratulations," he said.

Lugh nodded absently, then went back to staring at himself. He probably would have gone on forever if Por Amam hadn't put her hands on his cheeks and turned his head to face her.

"Well done, Lughen," she said softly, and hugged him again. Then she drew away and said, "Well! Given the circumstances, I don't think we need to finish our story today, do you?"

It took Kyle a moment to realize that she was addressing the circle of kids around her; he'd forgotten they were even there. They were staring up at Lugh with goggle-eyed amazement, and Por Amam had to physically place herself between him and the children to get their attention.

"Instead," she said, leaning down at them, "why don't we see if Lugh will tell us the story of how he got this sword?" And, clearly knowing her audience, she pulled out Haelinor's sword and set its tip into the ground with a *thunk*. "I'm sure he'll tell us if we ask him nicely."

As soon as this had the time to sink in, a chorus of small voices, most of them directed at the ground, started pleading for Lugh to share his story. Put on the spot, Lugh had no choice but to be ushered into Por Amam's chair and seated in front of his fascinated audience. Por Amam herself sat at the back of the group, cradling a girl (no, a boy, Kyle corrected himself, Selkic boys had long hair) who was slightly smaller than the others in her arms. Kyle stood at first, until Por Amam twisted her head around and invited him to sit. Knowing that he had as little choice as Lugh, he did.

Lugh sat at the edge of Por Amam's chair, his hands on his thighs. "Where do I start?" he said.

"At the beginning," Por Amam told him.

"All right. Well, I grew up in Lundir, same as all of you. When I was young, I had a brother named Haelinor, and he…"

Once the story was done, Por Amam allowed each of the kids to come forward and hold the sword for a moment. She made them thank Lugh for his time, then ushered them all out of her cottage, saying that it was time to play outside. Once the patter of footsteps had died away, she took up the sword and carried it to her fireplace mantle.

"I'll have one of the men in town build a mount for it," she said, "but for now, it will do fine here." She turned to Lugh. "Are you sure you don't want to take it with you?"

Lugh shook his head. "It belongs here," he said. "I wouldn't feel right using it anyway."

Por Amam nodded. "Then here it will stay," she said, "and the story of how it came to be here will be another for me to tell the children."

Lugh flashed a grin. "Your stories always did scare me, Pora."

"Good," she said firmly. "The world is filled with frightening things. Better to know them as stories when you're still young than meet the world a fool years later."

"Speaking of meeting the world," Lugh said, putting his hands on Por Amam's arms, "Kyle and I have to move on soon. We've got an important mission to get to."

Por Amam's face was sad, but understanding. "I won't try to stop you," she said. "Only beg you to be careful, and to come back to Lundir before too many years pass. Will you stay for one more meal?"

"Well," Lugh said, "since you insist…"

Por Amam set Kyle and Lugh to work chopping cheese and cured meat while she picked and washed vegetables from her garden. They dined on meat, cheese, vegetables and bread, and Por Amam opened three bottles of apple cider for them to drink. It was a hot day, and Kyle drank greedily. Soon he was feeling pleasantly light-headed.

He cast his eyes around the cottage and caught sight of Por Amam's face. She was watching Lugh eat with a tolerant expression on her face. The set of her eyes was strangely familiar, and even as Kyle watched, her face melted and changed. Her hair became dark, her clothes restitched themselves into new shapes, and then the changes blossomed outward. The table at which she was seated, the walls behind her, all molded and transformed before Kyle's eyes. Por Amam's Selkic dress had turned into a shirt and jeans; a light, not a tigoreh lamp but an electric light with a pear-shaped bulb, had hung itself from the ceiling above the table. Day had shifted into night, and what little light came through the windows of Por Amam's cottage was stark and artificial.

It all happened in seconds, and as soon as Kyle blinked, it was gone. He was back in Loria.

His eyes darted back and forth, but neither Lugh nor Por Amam had noticed. He opened his mouth to say something, then clamped it shut. It could wait—would have to wait—until they had left Por Amam's cottage.

They did so not too long after. Lugh had to turn down more than one offer to stay longer, and Kyle realized that whatever she said, Por Amam didn't want to say goodbye to him again. She gave in in the end, and walked them to her front step, where she drew Lugh into a lingering embrace. Then, to Kyle's surprise, it was his turn. Por Amam was tall enough to rest her chin on his head, and as she did, she said, "Take care of him, won't you?"

"I'll do my best," Kyle said, "but he's usually the one taking care of me."

Por Amam stood in her doorway to watch as they descended the path from her cottage, then turned south out of Lundir. Lugh kept twisting himself around to wave her goodbye. There was a smile on his face, but something deeper and less joyful in his eye.

Soon they were on the road again, and Kyle fell into step beside Lugh.

"Where to next?" he said.

"There's a town south of here with an airdock. Then it's just a day's flight from here to Ar'ac."

"Think the others are there yet?"

"Hard to say. Nihs got a head start, so I wouldn't be surprised if he's waiting for us already. Still no idea what Meya and Deriahm are up to, though."

Kyle nodded. Archmage Rosshku hadn't deigned to share Meya and Deriahm's mission with the rest of the party, only promised that it would be of help to them, and that everyone was to meet at a hideout in northwestern Ar'ac. Their rendezvous was a little too close to Reno city for Kyle's comfort, but he had to trust Rosshku's judgment. After all, this whole mission was about trusting Rosshku's judgment.

From Ar'ac, the reunited party would be heading to Westia. Then it would be a long, arduous trek to the impact crater where Archsage Vohrusien was said to live. Then—well, there was really no sense in thinking that far ahead. If there was a truth to be known about his presence in Loria, he would learn it then, and no sooner.

But Kyle's mind was still turning, orbiting around a single central thought: why, in Por Amam's kitchen, had he thought himself back in his childhood home, and why had Por Amam herself turned, for a flash of a second, into his mother?

The journey down to Ar'ac was made in two jumps by commercial airship, and to Kyle was little more than an opportunity to rest and think. Lugh, on the other hand, was fidgety and impatient; he didn't do well with waiting at the best of times, and Kyle thought he must be itching to test the limits of his new power. Unfortunately, with the *Ayger* gone, they had no personal training room to tear to shreds.

All of the biggest and fastest liners flew to Reno city, but Kyle and Lugh didn't want to risk stopping over. They flew instead to a small town down the coast west of the city. They arrived late at night, and had just a few hours to kill before their next ship left. This one flew straight south, cutting across Centralia Bay en route to Ar'ac's northwestern coast. Here was a city called Mjolsport, a halfway stop for many of the water-bound ships that hugged the coast of the Ar'ac as they headed north towards Reno city.

The two arrived in Mjolsport in late afternoon. It was a medium-sized town blessed by a hot sun and a cooling coastal breeze, a hive of activity with sailors, traders and adventurers constantly coming and going. There were a large number of Minotaur here, and Kyle had to adjust to streets, doorways and houses that were half again as large as he was used to.

Their meeting point, rather than an adventurer's hideout, was a regular inn called the Hungry Horn. This was another of Archmage Rosshku's suggestions. Kyle's pursuer knew that he was travelling with a band of adventurers, and was probably having their hideouts watched.

"The key is the Kol," Rosshku had said. "All that James Livaldi needs is a single Kol in his service, and any word spoken about you on the overhead will reach his ears. Be wary of any Kol you meet on your travels."

This seriously limited the party's options, as every hideout had at least one

Kol in its employ to pass news and missions to the others. Thus, the Hungry Horn.

It was a nice enough inn, but the simple fact that it was found several streets up from the waterfront kept it from becoming too busy. Kyle and Lugh found it without trouble; there was a swinging sign over the door that depicted a drinking horn overflowing with beer.

Lugh put a hand on the door and looked back at Kyle. "This is the place," he said. "Let's see what there is to see."

Kyle nodded. Best case, they were the last ones to arrive. Worst case, they were the first. *No,* Kyle thought, *worst case, we're the* only *ones.*

Lugh swung the door open, and Kyle's heart immediately swelled. His friends—all of them—were seated at a table in the dining hall. Meya was the first one he saw, with her distinct white clothes and red hair. Nihs was perched on her shoulder, and for the first time Kyle had seen was wearing his elegant red sagecloak. Deriahm was seated to Meya's right, straight-backed and dignified. His black armor blended somewhat with the dim light inside the hall.

Across the table from the three of them was a newcomer Kyle didn't recognize. He was a Minotaur with incredibly broad shoulders and a distinct fur coat, a pinkish red that was speckled with black spots. His back was to them and his head was hunched over, so of his face Kyle could only see a suggestion of curved horns.

"That's them!" Lugh said, laughing in relief and striding forward. Meya was the first to see them, and her serious and tired face broke into a radiant smile. Nihs' eyes flickered upwards, and the massive Minotaur twisted around in his seat with a groan of wood.

Kyle stopped short, stunned. As the Minotaur turned around, his pink coat was revealed as not its own, but rather a fur mantle that was draped around his shoulders. In reality, the Minotaur was a dark chestnut, and his jutting brow and deep-set red eyes were intensely familiar.

"Kyle, Lugh," Rogan Harhoof said amiably. "It's been some time."

The next few minutes were slightly confused. Lugh shouted Rogan's name before drawing him into a rough embrace, pounding him on the back and laughing; Rogan drilled his knuckles into Lugh's head before engulfing Kyle's hand in his own. Meya rose from behind the table, put her arms around Kyle and then did the same for Lugh. Kyle and Nihs shared a nod of acknowledgment, and Deriahm bowed and shook Kyle's hand while Lugh and Nihs congratulated each other on their promotions.

Kyle caught a morsel of this conversation, and the subject of promotion made him realize what was different about Rogan the Minotaur. Rogan was even larger than Kyle remembered him, and his weapon, an enormous and ornate battleaxe, was new. The next chance he had to speak with Rogan, he said, "You promoted too, didn't you?"

Rogan nodded. "That I did."

"How did it happen?" Kyle asked.

"It's a bit of a story." Rogan, unconsciously it seemed, touched the luxurious fur mantle he wore. "I know Lughenor will want to hear it, so I've held off to avoid telling it more than once."

"I think there's going to be a lot of stories going around today," Kyle said, watching the others make their greetings.

Rogan's bushy eyebrows met. "I think you might be right."

Kyle and Lugh took a few minutes to settle in, then met back with the others in the dining hall for food and drinks. The storytelling started even before the drinks arrived. Lugh went first, telling an only modestly embellished account of how he had recovered his brother's sword. Nihs went next; his story, and the way he told it, could not have been more different from the one that came before it. Kyle had learned from his lessons with Nihs that the little Kol could talk almost endlessly on the subject of magic, and he nearly did that night. Meanwhile, the details that the others were interested in—the politics leading up to the trial, and his father's reaction afterward—had to be wrung out of him.

By this time, they were into their second round of drinks, and their food had started to arrive. As they ate, the storytelling broke off into a number of smaller, disjointed conversations. Kyle thought that he had never been surrounded by a happier group of people. He didn't know what explained it; with the exception of Lugh, Nihs and Rogan, they had hardly known each other for a matter of weeks. But as Meya and Rogan chatted about the news from Reno and Lugh snickered at Deriahm's deadpan responses to his jokes, Kyle felt a fluidity within the group, an ease and comfort of being that he had only ever felt among his closest friends. He realized he was unbelievably glad, not to mention relieved, that the party had been reunited. With Rogan back, they were now six, and he, Lugh and Nihs had never seemed so formidable.

Suddenly Kyle remembered the morning after the first mission he had run with Lugh, Nihs and Rogan—the raid on the goblin-infested mine in Donno. Lugh had drawn his sword and pointed it at the sky, claiming that he would be a hero someday, and Nihs a sage. Rogan had laughed at them then, calling them children playing with wooden swords. But Lugh had made his dream come true, and Kyle had been there to witness it.

They had progressed onto their third round of drinks—or at least, Lugh, Rogan, and Kyle had—and Lugh was pressuring Rogan to begin his story, but Rogan was still champing on the massive haunch of meat that was his supper. He waved an enormous hand at Meya and Deriahm.

"Why don't you start instead?" he said.

"That's *right*," Lugh said. "We never found out what you two were up to."

"Fetching him," Meya said, nodding at Rogan. "That was the mission Rosshku gave us. He knew that he'd be out in the plains with his clan, and wanted us to track him down."

"How'd you pull that off?" Lugh asked. "It's a big continent down there."

Meya smiled. "People tend to notice when a herd of Minotaur gallop by. We bought a drifter and went asking from village to village."

"You bought a drifter?" Lust had awoken in Lugh's eyes. "Where is it?"

Meya gave him an indulgent look. "We sold it, Lugh."

"*What!* We could've ridden it all the way to the impact crater."

She ignored him. "Rosshku dropped us off southeast of here and told us where we should start looking. We bought the drifter and packed it full of food, then headed straight south. It took us three days to find the clan, then another to catch up with them."

Rogan laughed deeply. "It's not so easy to catch a herd of Minotaur on the move, not even with an Ephicer engine."

"Where were you all headed?" Kyle asked.

"Better hunting grounds." Rogan pulled a bone out of his mouth and plunked it down on his plate. "The bastard who'd taken over after my father died had everyone sitting in one place. Far too many ribs were showing by the time I arrived."

"Why'd they stay, then?"

"Honor. Respect. Stubbornness. Hate as I do to say it, in some ways we are stupid creatures."

Nihs sipped his drink. "I think we're getting a bit ahead of ourselves."

"Of course. Carry on, Meya."

"There's not much more to tell. By the time we reached the herd, Rogan had already taken over the clan. All we had to do was tell him that we needed him, and he dropped everything to come back with us."

Rogan's eyebrows creased. "Now, that's not fair," he said. "I didn't drop everything."

Meya folded her arms and treated him to the same look she'd given Lugh. "Graysa might disagree."

Rogan actually looked embarrassed. "I don't think we need to talk about that now, do you?"

Lugh looked back and forth between he and Meya. "What's that supposed to mean?"

"Shall you tell them, or shall I?" Meya said.

"Tell us *what?*"

Rogan's face was chiseled from stone, so Meya glanced sidelong at Lugh and said, "That he left his pregnant wife behind to go roaming the world with us."

That Rogan had a wife was news to Kyle, and apparently was to Lugh as well, because he slapped both palms on the table and shouted, "*What!?* You're married? Since when?"

Rogan, fuming, took a swig of his drink. "Married isn't exactly the right word," he grumbled.

"And she's *pregnant?*"

"We don't know that," Rogan said, glowering at Meya and speaking in the tones of a man whose last hope rested on the truth of his words.

"*You* don't know that," Meya said, sitting back and taking a drink herself. Her red eyes were twinkling. "*I* do."

Lugh was looking both pleased, and disgusted at being led on for so long. "I don't know about you," he said to the table at large, "but I need two things: another drink, and the rest of your story. From the beginning."

Finally finished with his enormous supper, Rogan pushed his plate to one side and leaned forward. The table creaked as he set his elbows down, knitting his fingers under his chin.

"Where to begin?" he said. "Back in Reno, I suppose. I stayed on when the rest of you left for Eastia."

"Feels like forever ago," Lugh said.

"That it does. Well, I had nothing else for me in the city once you left, so I stayed right there in the docks and asked around for the next ship headed to Westia. Found one headed to Oasis in less than ten minutes."

"Where's that?" Kyle asked.

"On the coast south of here," Lugh said. "Huge city, almost as big as Reno."

Rogan nodded. "If you have any business in Ar'ac, you go one of two ways. The short, hard one, straight south from Reno, or the scenic route: hug the coast, stop at Oasis, and then head east. Going the opposite way, you've got the same choice. A lot of Ar'akki are allergic to Reno; they prefer to do their business in Oasis, where the sights and smells are familiar. Of course, everything ends up touching Reno in the end.

"I knew that someone in Oasis would be able to tell me where the Harhoof clan had been seen last, so a flight there suited me fine. I found what I was looking for before the end of the first day, and I took off again the next morning."

"You were in a hurry," Meya commented.

Rogan grunted his agreement. "I said before that Minotaur are stubborn creatures, and our racial affliction only gets worse when we're together. My father's clan was large and powerful, and that made it all the more dangerous when he died without naming a successor. If we fell to fighting, you would have seen the dust kicked up from your village in Ren'r."

He directed that comment to Lugh, who said,

"Hard to imagine, really. And hard to imagine you could put a stop to it."

"I only knew I had to try. I thought that if I got there fast enough, and played everything just so, I might take my father's place before the clan could in collapse on itself."

"You're still here," Kyle said, "so obviously it worked."

"Better than I could have hoped, really. But I'm getting ahead of myself." Rogan stroked at the tuft of hair that hung from his chin. "From Oasis I flew straight east. It wasn't a commercial flight, so I had to work all the way there. Good thing I did—the ship was a wreck, and I'd be willing to bet we'd all be buried under the desert sand now if I hadn't been there to keep it in the air."

"That sounds familiar," Lugh said.

Rogan snorted with laughter as he reached for his drink. "We made it to a trader's outpost out in the middle of nowhere—can't even remember the name. I knew the clan was somewhere southeast of there. I had nothing left to do but start running and hope that I found them in time."

Meya was shaking her head. "You *ran*. Just like that." It was obvious she was thinking of her own grueling journey across the plains.

This time Rogan laughed out loud. "Of course! Running is what we're made for. I'm not the fittest of us, and I can run for days. I did, too; day and night, until I couldn't see for the sweat. That night I stopped by a patch of green, rested and drank, picked the rocks out of my hooves. Then I was on my feet again, running."

He paused for a moment. "I was happy. Happier than I'd been in a long time. No offence, Nihs, but you can keep your overhead. I would take the vast yellow earth and the great blue sky of the plains over anything else in the world."

"I suppose we can *all* claim at least one gift that the other races would kill to experience," Nihs said, rather graciously. "The Oblihari sing of the wonders of flight and the Chirpa titter on about the warm sun and cool shade of their homeland." Suddenly he turned to Deriahm. "Even the Buors have their addictions, I'm sure. What do you say, *irushai*?"

Deriahm's armor clinked softly as he shifted in his seat. "I cannot speak for the taste of all Buors," he said, "but I believe it is fair to say that most of us find an exquisite comfort in the process of bringing stability and order to a naturally chaotic world. We fancy ourselves caretakers to all things, from the march of our own thoughts to the streams of lava that flow from the Heart of Buoria. For many of us, this compulsion lies at the heart of our character."

"You know, I'm not quite surprised to hear that."

"Don't tease," Meya said. "There are worse things."

"How right you are."

Lugh sipped his drink. "So you ran and you ran and you ran. How did you manage to find your clan after all that?"

Rogan snorted. "It was much easier than it should have been. Usually if you're tracking a Minotaur clan the best you can do is aim for where they were last seen, and nine times out of ten they're long gone by the time you get there. But I told you that the gelding who'd taken over for my father had the clan stopped in its tracks."

"Why?" Kyle asked.

"Moving on is difficult, sitting still is easy. You see, clans like mine make our living off of the animals in the plains. We hunt down their herds, cull their numbers, and then eat the meat and sell the pelts, bones—whatever the traders in Oasis or the southern desert will buy. When I reached our clan, they'd just had a successful hunt; made a big score, you could say. At the orders of their chieftain, they were lounging about, eating and drinking, and counting up their earnings the way a merchant would count his gold."

"That doesn't sound so bad," Lugh said. "That's what *we* do when we finish a job."

"Yes, but your next job doesn't escape you while you're occupied with making a fool of yourself," Rogan growled. "The herd had moved on, you see, turned south into the desert, and my clan was in danger of losing their trail. They were spending so much time celebrating their scraps that the rest of the meal was about to run off on them.

"Come to think of it, I doubt Blackhorn intended on following the herd south at all. That would have been too difficult. Better to turn right around and sell everything they'd managed to scrape together, and never mind whatever happened next."

"Blackhorn," Lugh said. "Is this the fellow we've been hearing so much about?"

"The craven bastard," Rogan growled. "I should have lopped his head off long ago. Creatures like him grow and fester like weeds if you give them half a chance."

"Charming," Nihs said.

"So he's the one that took over after your dad died," Lugh said.

"Yes. And I would stake my life that he's the one who killed my father in the first place."

"*What?*" Meya said. "I thought it was an accident."

"Aye, that's what Blackhorn told everyone. And with no one to say otherwise, he got to be rid of my father without being branded as a murderer."

"Back up," Lugh said. "How did your dad die?"

Rogan nodded as if to acknowledge that the story was once again getting away from him. "He, Blackhorn, and another man named Rovik were out hunting. They were after a hyena that had made off with one of the clan's foals. A nasty piece of work named Gershel."

To confused looks, he added, "Monsters that make themselves known to a clan more than once are named. It's an old tradition that stretches back to the days when we believed that monsters were twisted and lost versions of ourselves. The plains are vast—what are the chances of seeing the same monster more than once? So, if you did, it meant that the monster's destiny was tied to your own, or at least to that of your clan."

Kyle suspected that 'hyena' carried a different meaning in Loria than it did on Earth, and he was proven right when Rogan said, "Gershel was no stranger to our clan. He was a cunning, vicious creature, twenty feet from head to tail. He was old, and tough. It didn't matter how many spears we put in him—by the end of his life he was missing an eye and half of one leg, but he would always slip away, lick his wounds, and be back to harry us the year next. The foal he carried off wasn't the first he'd stolen from our clan, but my father intended it to be the last. As soon as he heard what Gershel had done, he swore that he would bring back the beast's head to replace the child that had been lost."

Meya shook her head. "Some replacement. I would rather have my child back."

"There was that hope, but it was a slim one. If the child couldn't be saved, at the least they could put an end to Gershel for good. My father took up his axe and picked Rovik to come with him—a young lad, but a fast runner and the herd's best tracker. That's when Blackhorn volunteered to come along, as well.

"There was no love lost between my father and Blackhorn, but Blackhorn had never actually crossed him directly. He was that kind of creature, a Gershel himself, always testing the rules but never going so far as to break them. My father knew he was a coward and a liar, but to refuse his request would have been a great insult; the kind of insult a proper chieftain should be above making. So he and Rovik and Blackhorn set off after Gershel's trail to bring the beast to justice.

"They were on his trail for a day and a night. It went straight south, into the heart of the badlands, where Gershel made his home. Rovik nearly lost it more than once—in places where the wind never stops, there's nothing but bare rock for miles around. But they found him, sure enough, thanks to the drops of foal's blood they found along the way."

Kyle, caught up in the story as much as the rest of his friends, sucked in air through his teeth. In his mind's eye he could see the three Minotaur gathered around a small splotch of blood, knowing that it meant their enemy was close, but also that the foal's life was running out with each moment.

"Gershel's den was tucked halfway up a great mountain of rock, as cut-off and well-hidden as any dwelling place could be. It's no wonder they were never able to find him before. They were too late, though; by the time they got there the foal had already been eaten."

"Saints, Rogan," Lugh said, reaching for his drink. "This is supposed to be a good story."

"The story is what it is, and the poor mother who lost her child wouldn't think kindly of passing over the details. In any case, once he saw the foal was dead, my father didn't waste any time. He drew his axe and charged."

Rogan stopped there, leaning forward to grab his drink and then leaning back to take a massive gulp. He folded his arms, drink in hand, and stared straight ahead, long enough that Lugh finally said, "Then what?"

Rogan set his drink down once more. "He battled with Gershel," he said in a tone of finality, "and lost. At any rate, that's the story the rest of the clan heard."

"You think it was Blackhorn," Lugh said.

Rogan nodded. "I'm not sure exactly how, and it seems unlikely we'll ever know. Maybe they never found Gershel at all—but I doubt that. I think Blackhorn wounded him, and then let Gershel finish him off."

"What about Rovik?" Nihs said. "He would have seen the whole thing."

"He corroborated Blackhorn's story that Gershel got the best of him. I doubt the clan would have believed him otherwise."

"He was Blackhorn's henchman, then."

But Rogan shook his head. "Rovik wasn't the kind of Minotaur to follow Blackhorn of his own free will. I think Blackhorn threatened him into silence. Again, we'll never know for certain."

"Why not?"

"I'll get to that later." Rogan took another sip of his drink. "Blackhorn returned to the clan two days later. He was carrying my father's axe and had Rovik slung across his shoulders."

"Dead?" Lugh asked.

"Unconscious. Wounded by Gershel, or so he would have everyone believe. According to him, the three of them had fought Gershel together. Rovik had been wounded and my father killed. Blackhorn had pried my father's axe from Gershel's jaws, then wounded him in kind and escaped with Rovik once the creature was at bay. At first it looked as though Blackhorn's story wouldn't stick, but as soon as the clan shamans brought Rovik back from the brink of death, he confirmed everything.

"After that, it didn't take long for Blackhorn to become the new chieftain. He was a hero to anyone who believed his story, and those that didn't were soon silenced. Blackhorn could be fearsome when he wanted to, and he had allies within the clan—Hardskull and Whitemane, two of the biggest brutes you've ever laid eyes on. Some nasty looks and a bit of roughing around is all it took for him to silence the opposition.

"It was around this time that Grayarm sent his message. He had always been a friend of mine and of my father's, and he knew that there was trouble brewing. The next time the clan was close to civilization, he snuck off and sent the missive through the adventurer's guild. It was a wise move; Blackhorn was watching for any signs of unrest within the clan, but he had no reason to think of me—Ravigan's wayward son—as a threat. It was just the edge we needed to throw him over."

"How'd you pull that off?" Lugh asked.

"Not easily. You see, there are no rules of succession when it comes to Minotaur chieftains. Blood counts for something, but strength rules all. Some of the clan members would follow me out of respect for my father, but to overthrow Blackhorn, I would have to make my own claim stronger than his. At the time of my arrival, I had nothing to bolster my claim but my father's name. Blackhorn had his story, my father's axe, and his cronies Hardskull and Whitemane. I knew that he would win if I challenged him face to face.

"So, when I first found the clan, I kept my distance and waited for nightfall. Then I snuck into the camp, looking for Grayarm. I thought that he could help me figure out a plan to take Blackhorn down, and I was right. That night, we went around the camp in secret, looking for those that we knew were close to my father. I revealed myself to each of them, and made a promise: that I would soon leave the camp, and return with Gershel's pelt slung across my shoulders."

All of a sudden something clicked in Kyle's mind, something so obvious that he couldn't believe he hadn't realized it before. He put a hand on the blushing red fur collar that Rogan wore.

"That's him," he said. "That's Gershel right there."

Rogan's eyes glowed with pride. "Of course. I'm not the kind of man to go back on a promise, am I?"

"Well, go on, then!" Lugh said. "How'd you do it?"

"The first step was tracking him down. All I had to go off of was Grayarm's secondhand account of Blackhorn's story, and we didn't even know if the story was true."

"What about Rovik?" Meya asked. "You couldn't get him to help you?"

"He was already dead by the time I got there. Killed by accident in a 'tussle' with a fellow clanmate."

"I'm starting to see the pattern," Nihs said.

Rogan nodded. "Monsters like Blackhorn are all the same. They know of only one way of dealing with their problems—burying them."

"He should have met some of the Orcish warlords we dealt with in Eastia," Meya said. "He's starting to remind me of them."

Rogan shifted in his seat. "I didn't like my chances of finding Gershel, but it was the only lead I had. I set out that very night. First, I had to find the remains of the camp my clan had been using when Gershel took the foal. After that, I followed the tracks that my father, Blackhorn and Rovik had made on their hunt. Luck was with me—the wind hadn't yet taken all of them."

Rogan scratched at his wiry beard. "I found Gershel right where my father and the others had. His lair was nothing more than a cleft in the rocks. The ground was covered in bones, and the air stank of hyena. He was sleeping when I found him, but I wasn't about to try sneaking up on him. I walked straight up to him, bones crunching under my feet, and his good eye flipped open before I'd gone three paces. We faced each other down, and I drew my axe, staring into that glowing eye of his. It was a cruel, cunning eye, and there was an intelligence there that I didn't care for in the least. I realized that, sure as I recognized him, he recognized me. He knew I'd come to finish what my father started."

Rogan paused to take another pull from his drink, and Kyle realized that among his friend's hidden talents was a knack for storytelling. There was a quality to his low, rumbling voice that lent seriousness to everything he said, and he was leading them on as easily as Por Amam had done with the circle of children who sat around her chair.

And who in the group was closer to their inner child than Lugh, who said, "*Well?* What happened then?"

"Gershel and I battled," Rogan said, "and I won."

This was such an outrageous deflection that they all started shouting at once. Kyle and Meya banged on the table and Lugh punched at Rogan, who likely didn't even feel the blows but pretended to flinch away from them.

"You ass!" Lugh shouted. "Tell us the story already!"

"All right! All right!" Rogan was laughing now, the deep rumbling coming from his chest causing the surfaces of their drinks to quiver. Lugh stopped punching him and he settled back down.

"Let me see. Well, Gershel came to his feet once we were done staring at each other. He was missing one of his front paws, but his other was long and had claws like you wouldn't believe. He also had fangs, snaggled, sharp as razors, so vile and rotten that his bite was as poisonous as any snake's. I knew all this from the stories I'd heard about Gershel before I left, so I was wary from the start. We circled each other for a time, and just when I thought the old beast was too cowardly to make the first move, he…"

Rogan went on to describe a battle of astonishing viciousness and brutality. It was as far removed as could be from the fast-paced, skill-based fights Kyle was used to, and knowing that Rogan had been one half of it made it all the stranger to hear.

Gershel charged at Rogan, snapping, then ducked aside at the last moment and made a wide swipe with his claws. Rogan blocked, rammed into Gershel with his shoulder, then wrapped one massive arm around the creature's neck. Gershel thrashed about and gnashed his jaws while Rogan tried to pull him from his feet; he came free, and Rogan went over. Rogan blocked high just as Gershel lunged in to crush his skull between his jaws. Flecks of slobber landed on Rogan's face as he fought Gershel off. He got a kick in against one of Gershel's hind legs, and the massive beast yelped as he fell over on top of Rogan. Rogan threw him off, came of his feet, and hefted his axe, but Gershel had already circled to one side. Rogan swiped his axe left and Gershel dodged back; that gave Rogan the chance to brace himself and head into a charge. Gershel tried to dance around the charge and hamstring him as he went past, but Rogan's aim was true. He gored Gershel's neck and the hyena retaliated by snapping at his shoulder. Rogan threw him off, swung his other arm around, and slapped Gershel's face with the cheek of his axe. He followed up by jabbing at the creature, but Gershel batted his axe aside and came forward with another swipe. Rogan let his axe fall to the ground, ducked under Gershel's sweeping paw, and lifted the monster right off his forepaws onto his hind legs. Gershel went over sideways, his body twisting around like a fish, and Rogan leapt forward, kicking him square in the underbelly with a hoofed foot.

It went on and on, grapples and bites, swipes and chops, charges and leaps. Gershel got in a terrible bite at Rogan's side, but Rogan, in return, brought both fists down on his skull and nearly brained him. Gershel caught Rogan's axe in his teeth, and Rogan responded by yanking it, and several of Gershel's rotting teeth, free.

Finally, Gershel started to slow down. He was bleeding from multiple wounds and limping, an injury to his good forepaw leaving him nothing reliable on which to stand. Rogan was tasting fiery victory, hefting his axe and measuring Gershel up for a finishing blow when something made him pause.

"He was whimpering," Rogan said. "No—crying like a frightened child. He'd started to back away from me, his tail between his legs. He was beaten, and he knew it. In his last moment, he was trying to show submission, hoping that I would spare him."

Of course, they all knew that Rogan hadn't let Gershel live—the pelt around his neck was proof enough of that—but for a moment, they all believed that he might.

Then Rogan said, "I'd just started to lower my axe, realizing what was going on, wondering if I had it in me to kill him in cold blood, when he lunged at my neck."

Meya actually gasped. "He *tricked* you?"

Rogan nodded grimly. "He was smart, old Gershel, I'll give him that. And if I hadn't been as fast as I was, it would be he wearing my pelt to keep warm at night."

"What did you do?" Kyle asked.

"Followed instinct, nothing more. I put my axe between me and him." He held one hand out, fingers together, palm open to the floor. "Gershel's lunge carried him into it, and his open mouth went right around the blade. His skull all but split apart at the jaw. He killed himself with his last desperate attack."

Silence greeted his words. They stared into their drinks as if mourning the death of Rogan's old nemesis.

"What I would've given to see that fight firsthand," Lugh said finally.

"It was a fight to remember," Rogan agreed. "I wish you could have been there, all of you. As it was, there was no one there when Gershel died but me and him. I pulled my axe back and he fell to the ground, nothing more than a bag of bones. I was about ready to collapse myself, but I had work to do. I started a fire and then set to work skinning the beast. I fleshed the hide and strung it up next to the fire. I spent the next three days camped there, waiting for the hide to dry."

Meya was looking at him in mingled shock and disapproval. "You had just been nearly killed by that hyena and the first thing you did once he was dead was skin him?"

Rogan contrived to look a bit sheepish. "Well, not the very first," he said. "I did eat, and I patched myself up, too."

"You patched yourself up," Meya repeated, making it clear that whatever patching up he had done could not have been up to her standards as a cleric. "And what did you eat?"

Rogan made a vague gesture with one hand. "What was available," he said.

Meya's face grew even more shocked when she realized what he was saying. "*Rogan!*"

"What? Gershel ate that foal, and he probably ate most of my father, as well. Besides, we Minotaur aren't ones to waste good meat." He paused. "Though it wasn't good meat, come to think of it. Gershel was tough as nails, and tasted about as foul as you'd expect him to. Not that I had much of an appetite in any case."

"Why not?"

Rogan twisted in his seat and pulled up his shirt, exposing his side. There was an ugly, pockmarked scar there, nearly a foot across. "Gershel's bite festered while I was making camp. The poison in his teeth wormed its way into my brain, and I spent the first two nights shivering, sweating through my fur, and hallucinating that Gershel's hide was coming back to life to eat me."

Meya looked ready to murder him. "You realize you're lucky to be alive," she said.

Rogan shrugged. "After the first night, I knew the worst had passed. I ate more of Gershel and smoked my wound to cure it. I knew that I'd be able to head back to the clan and be healed properly once Gershel's hide dried out."

Meya shook her head violently to show her disapproval, and Kyle realized that, like the rest of them, she had probably had more to drink than was good for her.

"On the third day," Rogan went on, "I decided that I felt well enough to travel, and Gershel had dried out enough to keep for the journey. I kicked out my fire, slung him across my shoulders, and set out over the plains. But as I walked, my infection started to come back, and the hallucinations came with it."

His eyes were far away as he continued. "Sometimes I thought Gershel had come back to life and was stalking me. I would turn around and look behind me, again and again, expecting to see him behind every outcropping of rock. I kept reminding myself that he was dead, that I had his fur slung around my shoulders as proof—but then I started to believe that it wasn't just his fur, it was *all* of him, that he was still alive and wounded, and I was bringing him home to the clan as Blackhorn had done with Rovik.

"If I thought the hallucinations would get better from there, I was wrong. Before long I didn't believe that Gershel was stalking me, or that he was around my shoulders. I *was* Gershel. I had fused with the beast, and the fur around my neck was proof. I was a slavering, hungry hyena, and I was tracking down the Harhoof clan so I could sneak into their tents and devour their children."

Kyle shivered. The thought of Rogan overtaken by madness was not a pleasant one.

"By the time I reached the clan I was both Rogan the Minotaur and Gershel the hyena. I could be one or the other as easily as I liked—as easily as one could don or remove a fur mantle, I suppose. I feared nothing and no-one; I strode right into camp just as the sun was rising over the dunes, headed straight for the chieftain's tent.

"A following built around me as the others realized who I was and what I'd done. They could see the fearsomeness in my eyes, but none of the madness. Not only that, but Grayarm and those Minotaur loyal to me had been hard at work while I was away; they had been talking of Gershel, and of what a shame it was that he was still alive, and how we would still need to live in fear of him as Blackhorn hadn't been able to finish him off."

"*Oh,*" Lugh said. "That's wicked. You're a sneaky one, my friend."

"We're not entirely without subtlety. And it worked, too; by the time I was back, Blackhorn's support was eroding out from underneath him. It would only take one good blow to knock him down.

"Of course, I wasn't concerned with any of this when I came staggering into our camp. I was shouting Blackhorn down, calling him a coward and a murderer, demanding to be given my father's axe. I came right up to his tent, and Whitemane stepped out. I told him I wanted to see Blackhorn; he refused, and advised that I turn around and walk away unless I wanted trouble. I *did* want trouble—or rather, Gershel did—and he didn't waste any time. I charged at

Whitemane and clobbered him over the head, and he fell to the ground, out cold. That was it for Blackhorn's bodyguard.

"I kept shouting, knowing that Blackhorn would have to come out and face me—and the clan—sooner or later. Still, he took his sweet time. No doubt he was plotting, trying to figure a way to beat me with all the odds against him.

"Finally he did come out, and I knew what his last stand was going to be. His back was straight, and he held my father's axe. He looked, dressed, and spoke like a chieftain. He was going to try and beat me on merit, convince the clan that he was the rightful chieftain. He started to talk, and I knew exactly what he was going to say: that I was a wayward son who consorted with thin-skins; that I knew nothing about my own people and their ways; that I was an outcast who wasn't there to witness his own father's death, what have you. Well, I wasn't in the mood for any of it."

"You slugged him across the face, too," Lugh guessed.

"Not quite. I walked up till there wasn't a foot between us and shouted into his face." Suddenly Rogan launched into a terrible, booming voice: "'Blackhorn! I am the son of Ravigan. I am the slayer of Gershel. I am ten times the man you could ever hope to be. That axe is *my* axe, and this clan is *my* clan. You will leave both of them to me, now, or I will split you open and grind your carcass under my hooves!'"

"Damn," Lugh said. "What did Blackhorn do?"

"He wet himself," Rogan replied.

This was too much. Rogan's story had been carrying them all along for the better part of an hour, and now, at the thought of Blackhorn losing control of his bladder, their entire table burst into uproarious laughter. Lugh knocked his drink over and Meya started to cry with laughter as she moved her food away from the expanding puddle. Nihs joined in, and Kyle could even hear a few guffaws coming from behind Deriahm's visor.

Rogan continued, struggling to make himself heard. "I don't know what did it—the shouting, the madness in my eyes, or what else—but Blackhorn completely lost his will. He looked like I'd slapped him across the face, and when I reached forward to take the axe from him, he held it out to me like a present.

"It all went quickly from there. Blackhorn left the clan in disgrace, and Whitemane was cast out with him. Hardskull groveled at my feet until I was forced to forgive him—he was a stupid man, but not an evil one. Blackhorn's other supporters faded into mist as soon as I was made chieftain again.

"At some point I got around to having the clan shamans look at my infection. They cured me as best they could, but one of them warned that a part of Gershel's soul had been left inside me by his bite. I think he was right...you see, I had promoted somewhere out in the wilderness while I was carrying Gershel's hide back to the clan. Something about promoting in the midst of my madness, with the fur collar around me, tied my soul to Gershel's. I feel him every waking moment. He sits somewhere inside me, ready to stretch his legs as soon as I fall into a rage. Whenever I get angry, I feel the way I did back when I wandering the desert—that Rogan and Gershel are a hair's breadth apart, and I could become one or the other at a moment's notice."

A pall fell over the table as Rogan said this, and Rogan himself fell silent, perhaps realizing the frightfulness of what he'd just admitted.

Lugh said, "Rogan, you didn't go crazy just in time to go travelling with us, did you?"

Deriahm cleared his throat. "If I may," he said, "I believe the good Harhoof's condition aligns quite closely with our understanding of the berserk phenomenon. Berserk often manifests itself in individuals whose physical strength is so overwhelming that it can subvert the mind's control. Perhaps the good Harhoof's promotion unlocked this potential in him. Gershel the hyena, then, is simply a mental trigger that accompanies—or causes—the berserk state of mind."

Lugh's eye lit up with both fright and incredible excitement. He leaned toward Rogan.

"You're a *berserker* now?" he asked, as if Rogan knew. "Is it possible?"

Meya suddenly gasped. "It *is*," she said, "because when we were staying with Archmage Rosshku, one of the things he taught me was a calming spell. He must have known Rogan was going to promote—he taught me how to handle him before sending us down to Ar'ac to fetch him."

Lugh started to laugh. "Rosshku must have been worrying that Rogan would be going on a rampage down there."

Rogan harrumphed. "He needn't have. I'm well in control, thank you."

"So you say." Lugh looked at Meya. "I'm keeping *you* between *me* and *him* from now on."

"Ever the gentleman," Meya said.

Grinning, Lugh downed the dregs of his drink and set his glass down on the table.

"Well," he said, "is that it, then? The life and conquest of Rogan the Minotaur?"

Rogan's eyes twinkled as he, too, finished his drink. "I would say so," he said. "I took control of the clan, got them moving again. We found the herds—wasn't long after that that Meya and Deriahm showed up. I left the clan in Grayarm's charge, promising that my leave of absence would be shorter this time. And… that's all."

Lugh nodded, his eye down in the bottom of his glass. "Great, great," he said, "though I notice you did leave out one thing."

"Oh? What's that?"

Lugh clunked his glass down and leaned across the table. "The *pregnant wife* part, you oaf!"

"This is foolishness," Rogan growled. "Can't you leave well enough alone?"

"No," Lugh said, "I can't. Who's the lucky lady?"

Rogan simmered, but it was clear that he had decided it was best to get this over with quickly. "Graysa is her name. We've known each other since we were foals. She found me out when she heard that I had returned to Ar'ac." He shifted in his seat. "We had never been close…in that way, at least, when we were children. We might have made some foolish promises way back when, but I had completely forgotten about them. I was surprised to find that Graysa hadn't."

"You should have known better," Meya said.

Lugh was grinning from ear to ear. "So you *married* her?" he said. "Where did you find time to do that between all the shouting and killing?"

"I told you that 'married' wasn't the right word," Rogan said. "The child marks the union. We will be married once she's discovered to be pregnant. *If* she is pregnant at all," he added, glowering at Meya.

She propped her elbows on the table, rested her chin on knitted fingers, and looked at Rogan dreamily. "Poor, poor Rogan," she said. "Trust me; she is." She shifted her gaze to Lugh. "I could tell from the second I met her. I *am* a cleric, after all."

Rogan actually growled at her. "A witch, more like. It's far too early to tell."

"Not for me."

"So you *did* get her pregnant!" Lugh said.

"It's possible," Rogan begrudged.

"Yes," Meya said.

Lugh started to laugh. Kyle had heard him laugh many times before—Lugh was always the first to pick up a joke—but this laugh had a tone to it Kyle had never heard. Lugh laughed until it filled his whole being, and light glinted off his stone eyepatch and sunny golden hair. He laughed until they all laughed with him, jostling each other and crying on to each other's shoulders.

"I think that calls for another drink!" Lugh shouted.

King Azanhein of Buoria watched as the figure at the end of his throne room stepped forward, each footfall coming down with a sharp *rap* of metal. Every two paces, the man passed under a pair of lances held by Azanhein's royal guard. These were some of the most formidable warriors that Buoria had to offer, but the man who walked between them was a formidable warrior himself, and had made the walk to Azanhein's obsidian throne more than once. He paid them no attention, but kept his eyes on his king.

By Buorish standards, his appearance was plain; his black armor was nondescript and the sash he wore was a solid blue common in Buoria. If Kyle had been present in Azanhein's throne room at that moment, he wouldn't have recognized the man, even though they had just recently met. His name was Sardassan, and some days before, when Kyle had stood before the Buorish court of law, he had spoken eloquently in his defense. At the time, it had been his assignment to witness the trial and ensure that the court reached the proper verdict; happily, he had had to intervene but the once.

He reached Azanhein's throne, the last of his footsteps echoing into the corners of the great hall. He bowed deeply at the waist until his body was nearly perpendicular.

"Your majesty," he said to the marbled floor.

"Sardassan. It is good to see you. Please, rise."

He did so. As they had been since entering the throne room, his arms remained folded behind his back at the elbows. This pose was as functional as it was polite; it concealed Sardassan's forearms from view, which in turn ensured that the needle-thin daggers normally scabbarded along them remained hidden.

Sardassan's career was not primarily that of a fighter, but that didn't mean he was incapable of defending himself. Anyone who crossed swords with a member of Azanhein's secret service would soon understand just what a lifetime of extreme discipline and conditioning could accomplish.

"I bring news on the subject of Kyle Campbell, your majesty," Sardassan said.

"I am very glad to hear it. He is safe, I trust?"

"Indeed. *Irushai* Deriahm and miss Ilduetyr have reunited with the party proper, in a small town on the northwestern coast of Ar'ac. The purpose of their mission was to recruit the Minotaur known as Rogan Harhoof into the party."

"The very same man who left Kyle's company before his arrival in Buoria," Azanhein said in surprise. "Chosen, no doubt, for the bond of loyalty he must share with Kyle."

"That was my assessment as well, your majesty. The Archmage has so far greatly emphasized the need for secrecy in this mission."

"Then I am doubly glad he has decided to involve himself in this matter," Azanhein said. "Our values could not be more aligned. You have not been able to contact him thus far?"

Sardassan cleared his throat. "I believe he does not wish to be contacted, your majesty, and there is little we can do against the Archmage's will."

Azanhein dipped his head. "Frustrating, but unsurprising. What of Kyle's next action? Will the party make directly for Westia?"

"Tomorrow, your majesty."

Azanhein nodded. "Then Kyle's final trial will be completing the journey to Vohrusien's tower. And, despite all of our power, we will be unable to assist him in this."

Sardassan nodded himself in agreement. There was nothing more to be said.

Azanhein sighed. "Then let us prepare for both his eventual return and possible demise, and keep hope in our hearts that it is the first set of plans we will be executing."

Sardassan bowed. "Of course, your majesty."

The second floor of the Hungry Horn opened out onto a flat balcony whose floor was the ceiling of the common room. It was little more than a large wooden platform, but even from two stories up the view over Mjolsport was fantastic, a sea of twinkling lights that gave way to the true sea miles in the distance. The sun had set, but in the height of Lorian summer it rarely fell more than a few inches below the horizon—a dull red light still glowed from the southwest.

Lugh rested his elbows on the rough, untreated wooden railing, savoring the cool ocean air. A cup containing the remains of his last drink for the night was dangling from his fingers.

Most of the others were in bed already, but Lugh knew that, for him, turning in now would be a wasted effort. As a child, he'd never had any trouble falling asleep. In fact, one of his favorite times of every day had been its end. The setting of the sun, the slow bronzing of the earth followed by its descent into cool darkness; the pop of the fire, the warmth of Por Amam's arms as she carried him to bed; the sweet sound of her voice as she sang him to sleep, then the very different song of insects chirping outside his window. He would pass from Por Amam's embrace into that of his bed, then dip softly into the fantastical realm of sleep and dreams.

All of that had changed with Haelinor's death. To fall asleep had become to risk waking up to heartbreak. To dream was to re-live the demise of his brother in a way that surpassed even the worst of his waking grief. Years had gone by where Lugh could barely sleep at all; he would go days without it and would have gone more were it not so dangerous for someone in his profession to do so. Drinking had helped, as had smoking mint—that peculiar herb that was practically a staple of Selkic life. But Haelinor had been against both when alive, and that was enough to keep Lugh clean, for the most part. So he'd lain in bed, eyes wide open, learning more than he cared to know about the roofs beneath which he slept.

As everything, that too had changed with time. The painful memory of his brother faded, and he found himself sleeping more and dreaming less. By the time he and Nihs had met, he was sleeping full nights more often than not; by the time two of them had met Rogan, he hadn't carried any mint for months.

Now, with memories of Lundir once again fresh in his mind, Lugh knew that this night would be a hard one. If he waited long enough, and let the cool salt air wear away at his thoughts, he might at least escape dreamless—but no. There was no sense in putting it off. He would need all of his strength for what was to come next, and sleep, after all, was sleep.

He poured out the rest of his drink and turned to go back inside, and saw that Nihs had just come out from his room. He was massaging one seashell ear, and his red sagecloak was draped around him like a blanket.

First we couldn't get you to wear the thing, now we can't get you to take it off, Lugh thought. He could hardly blame Nihs: the sagecloak was one of the most beautiful pieces of clothing Lugh had ever seen.

"What are you doing out here so late?" he said.

Nihs looked at him with his head tilted back and his eyelids half-closed, contriving to appear sleepy, aloof and irritated all at once. "I could ask the same of you."

"Fair enough. Care to join me?"

Nihs sighed and scampered up the side of the railing so that the two of them could be face to face. The railing swayed dangerously beneath him, but his sharp nails dug in and found purchase. He folded his legs underneath him like a cat, and for a while the two of them sat in silence, watching the moon's rays dance across the waves.

"Are you worried?" Nihs asked suddenly.

Lugh brought himself back to the present. "Huh? Worried about what?"

Nihs treated him to a despairing look. "Have you forgotten what's coming next, or are you being willfully dim again?"

"Oh! That." Lugh waved a hand. "Why? Would it do any good if I was?"

"It might," Nihs said. "It would at least tell me that you've finally admitted to yourself you're not invincible."

Lugh tapped at his stone eyepatch. The dull *thud* of his finger reverberated through his skull. "If I needed any convincing, I got it here. Don't worry about me, Nihs. I know."

"And do you know that you—that all of us—have our limits, as well?" Nihs pressed.

"Yes."

"And that this mission is far beyond them?"

"It's risky," Lugh admitted.

"Lugh, it's insanity! The *adaragad* is the most dangerous place on earth. Squadrons of elite Buorish soldiers have perished trying to study it. Adventurers with decades of experience refuse to approach it."

Nihs' voice came to him so strongly, so desperately, that Lugh actually jumped back. He looked at his friend, and was shocked at what he saw. Nihs wasn't just being his usual nagging self—he wasn't speaking on behalf of practicality or pessimism. He was afraid. It was written naked on his face, all the more obvious for the fact that Lugh had never seen it there so plainly. Nihs' brown eyes were wide, and his mouth, usually tight-lipped, was hanging almost open. He looked incredibly young, and Lugh was reminded that, by Kol standards, he *was* young; the youngest of their group, in fact.

Lugh sighed. "You're right," he said. "It's more than risky. It's probably the most dangerous thing we'll ever do."

Relief swept over Nihs' face; he'd been hoping to hear that.

"But," Lugh added, "I don't think that changes anything. We have to go. We're as ready as we'll ever be, so it might as well be now."

"We don't *have* to go," Nihs said. "We don't *have* to do anything. The only reason we say that is because we told Kyle that we would."

"And?"

"What do you mean, 'and'? *And* that means that there's nothing stopping us from backing down! We don't have to give up, only bide our time—take a year to train and prepare, give Kyle time to promote, Deriahm too, if he's still with us. And who knows, after all that perhaps Kyle will decide that his Earth isn't worth the risk. He's thriving here in Loria, and don't tell me you haven't noticed. He won't recognize himself a year from now. What if he decides to stay?"

There was truth in all this, but it was a weak, deceptive truth that survived by deliberately avoiding the real truth. Lugh could see this, and he could tell that Nihs could, as well.

"That won't work," he said. "Kyle can't stay in Loria. You heard what Azanhein and Rosshku said; if he stays here, he'll keep growing more and more powerful until nothing can contain him. He'll keep gathering enemies, too, and the rest of us will get caught in the crossfire. But even *that's* not the real reason. He *needs* to go back, and it needs to happen soon. I'm not sure why, but I know it's true—you do, too."

Nihs' nostrils flared as he sucked in a deep breath of ocean air. For a moment, he looked quite like Darizot—then he exhaled, and his father left his frame, leaving only a frightened young Nihs behind. "Yes," he said finally. "I do. I just wish we didn't—" he shook his head. "I wish it were anywhere else. Just not there."

Lugh nodded slowly. "We'll get through it," he said, his one eye lost in the shimmering waves beyond the city. "We always do."

Kyle dreamt of home.

The dreams had come to him on and off ever since his fall into Loria, and at first, there had been a sort of cohesion to them. Each night he had grown older, reliving first his childhood, then his adolescence, and finally the beginning of his adulthood. But ever since Kyle had been struck by the cursed bolt fired by Lacaster the assassin, his mind and soul had been scrambled, and any sense of orientation had been lost. First, he was in Reno, then Cleveland; first he was talking to Rogan the Minotaur, then he was talking to his boss at work.

Tonight, the dreams were made even more disturbing by sights and sounds that Kyle knew belonged neither with Earth nor with Loria. He was rushing through the dark tunnels of the goblin-infested mine when they suddenly transformed into a large, opulent study. At the far end of the room was seated a man with a thunderous expression on his face; there was something familiar about him, and Kyle felt a flutter of fear in his stomach. Then the study fell to pieces, and he found himself staring up at a jagged, snow-covered mountain, incredibly high, beyond which rose a black tower bursting with orange light. As he beheld the tower, knowing that the orange light was the reason he'd come to this forsaken place, Kyle realized that a multitude of silver wires was stretched across the sky, like a series of rainbows leached of their color. He couldn't decide whether to be calmed or terrified by the wires—whether they were the supportive beams that kept his sanity intact, or the cage that kept him from greater understanding. Before he could solve this dilemma, he began to fly up into the sky to meet them. He flew faster and faster, soaring into space, burning past the stars towards the edges of the universe. A point of light appeared in the distance and he raced towards it. Faster and faster, closer and closer it grew—until Kyle woke violently, his eyes snapping open and his breath catching in his chest.

He sat up, pressing the heel of his hand against his temple. The room he shared with Nihs was still dark; he had no idea if he'd slept five hours or five minutes. He tried to make sense of what he'd just seen, but the meaning of his dream floated just out of reach, like the name of a familiar song that refuses to come to mind. Everything had seemed so familiar and yet so alien; so significant, and yet so meaningless.

He laid back down, but his mind was buzzing. He sat up again, debated for a moment, then threw his covers off and swung out of bed. He had no real idea of where he would go or what he would do. He only knew that trying to fall back asleep would be pointless.

He crept out into the hallway and looked left and right. All the doors were closed, and the building was silent. He found himself craving fresh air, and tiptoed down the stairs into the common room. It was completely deserted; he must have woken up in the dead middle of the night.

He stepped outside and was met by a cool ocean breeze. Many of the nights they had spent in Eastia had been cold and blustery; on that continent, autumn was approaching. But, due to Loria's crooked orbit, this meant that it was summer in Centralia, and it had grown warmer and warmer as they travelled west. Just one of the many things that Kyle was getting used to.

He stood just outside the doorway, wondering where to go next. He shouldn't go wandering around the city at night—his sense of direction was excellent, but he still didn't know enough about Loria not to raise suspicion if anyone were to question him. Besides, he didn't have his weapon, and he'd gotten used to carrying it around everywhere he went. He had just resigned himself to going back inside and trying to sleep when he heard the footsteps.

Kyle had a suspicious nature, and his time in Loria had honed his instinct for danger. The noise had come from off to his right. He didn't twist his head around, but tilted it ever so slightly, rolling his eye to see what he could in his peripherals. Nothing—but there came a sigh of wind that sounded like a voice saying *"Oh!"*. It could have been his imagination, but it wasn't.

More footsteps, hushed voices saying "It's him!" and "Now!"

He drew his soul sword and spun around, just as a half-dozen men spilled from the alleyway beside the Hungry Horn. They were all armed, some of them with swords, some of them with bizarre clubs that Kyle had never seen before, made of golden tigoreh and crackling with electricity. Kyle thought they might be some kind of Lorian stun stick.

The men rushed him, but the second they saw Kyle's soul sword they shrank back, those in the rear bumping against those in front. Several of the men uttered oaths and one looked ready to bolt outright. He was looking at the soul sword with an expression of pure terror on his face, and his mouth opened and closed in surprise.

"He-he's not supposed to have that!" he said.

"Who cares?" someone in the back said. "Get him!"

But the man in front stared as if hypnotized. "That's the thing that killed Havel!" he said, his voice quavering.

Kyle thought he understood. His soul sword was a keepsake from Earth, *his* Earth. It was made of nuclear energy, and anything in Loria that it touched was violently blown apart. Lorians seemed to understand this on an instinctive level—that was why this grown man, who was the size of a heavyweight boxer, was planting his feet and refusing to bring himself any closer to it.

That was all well and good, but Kyle had another problem. Lacaster's cursed bolt had sealed his ability to use his soul sword; the Archmage Rosshku had restored it, but not completely. Drawing his sword used to feel natural and invigorating; now, the sword burned angrily in his palms as if made of acid. Kyle could feel the remnants of the curse travelling up his arms like an infection from an untreated wound, and knew that he had a minute, maybe two before the pain became unbearable. He grit his teeth—he couldn't afford to let these men know that.

Kyle dropped into a battle-ready stance and advanced, keeping his eye on the man at the front of the pack. His eyes grew wider and wider as Kyle got closer, until finally his nerve broke and he split sideways from the group. One of the other men swore and ran after him, shouting "You handle Kyle!" over his shoulder.

Two down, Kyle thought. *Not bad.*

The remaining men fanned out. They were humans, all four of them, ranging from their twenties to forties, each as hard-eyed as the last. If they were afraid of Kyle's soul sword, they hid it well.

"Come quietly," one of them said in a low voice.

"I've got a better idea," Kyle said, and lunged. A second later, his world was obscured by a column of raging fire.

Lugh first heard the clash in the street when Havel's friend gasped, "He's not supposed to have that!" His brow creased and he looked at Nihs.

"Did you hear something?" he said. His head was buzzing with alcohol, but his instincts were still sharp, and they were warning him that something was wrong. Nihs felt it too, and started to cast his eyes up and down the street, looking for the source of the noise.

"Wait a moment," he said. "Look down there—that's Kyle!"

Lugh leaned over the railing, saw the unmistakable blue glow of Kyle's soul sword, and then caught sight of the men surrounding him. All traces of drunkenness were burned from his mind by a rush of adrenalin.

"Nihs!" he shouted.

Nihs had already spread his arms wide. His eyes were shining red, and his cloak was glowing to match. Magic flooded into him, and his cloak billowed as if stirred by a high wind. He braced one arm with the other and thrust it up and out. A massive soundless concussion rocked the night air, and a column of fire erupted from the ground between the four men. There were shouts of surprise; the two men in the center of the fan were blown off their feet, and one of them lost his soul shield. He shrieked and rolled around on the ground, slapping at the fires that had caught on his clothing.

"I need my weapon!" Lugh shouted at Nihs. "Help him!"

Nihs nodded once, his face set. He was already drawing in magic for a second spell.

Lugh sprinted inside and charged down the hallway to the room he shared with Rogan. He twisted the knob and shouldered his way in. Rogan sat up at once, immediately reaching for his axe.

"Who's there?" he growled.

"It's me!" Lugh shouted. He was already diving for the pile of equipment he'd left at the side of his bed. "Kyle's in trouble!"

"*What?*" Rogan boomed.

"No time. Get the others up and get outside. I've got to help Nihs."

He didn't waste time seeing if Rogan understood; there wasn't much to understand. He threw his composite weapon onto his back and slipped into his chestplate, the most vital part of his armor. He dashed back outside, pulling his twin swords into his hands.

He went out to the balcony to find Nihs still perched on the banister, raining magic down on the men attacking Kyle. He felt a grim satisfaction. Nihs couldn't have been better placed when the attack broke out. What were these men going to do against a magic user who had taken them by surprise?

He opened his mouth to tell Nihs that help was coming, and ended up shouting something completely different.

"*Nihs! Look out!*"

He was too late. A dark figure leapt onto the balcony, unsheathing a weapon in mid-air. As it landed behind Nihs, it swung, and the blow hit him squarely in the back. Nihs released a gut-wrenching cry of pain and surprise as he was ripped from the balcony. He flew like a green cannonball and smashed into a building on the opposite side of the street; fragments of blue magic exploded out from the point of impact as his soul shield broke. He fell limply to the ground and was still.

For a moment Lugh just stood there, horrified. Nihs wasn't dead, but after that he would surely be the closest thing to it. And the figure who had struck the blow was disturbingly familiar. Lugh had seen it plastered all over Reno city, with *WANTED* written below in red letters.

"Radisson," he said.

Michael Radisson, infamous criminal lord of Reno city, lifted his sword up onto his shoulder and turned to face him.

"What a joke," he said. "The first time I'm sent after this kid he hog-ties one of my men and kills two more. And now I have to kill a whole whack of adventurers to get at him." He smiled a smile that touched nothing on his face but his lips. "I'm going to beat him within an inch of his life once I get my hands on him. Little bastard is more trouble than he's worth."

Lugh wet his lips. "You'll have to get through me first," he said.

"And I'm going to have a good time doing it," Radisson agreed.

Lugh lunged. His swords flashed, but Radisson twisted and deflected both blows with a single sweep of his sword. Feet still planted, he swung his sword around, and Lugh just barely managed to get his own guard up in time. He force blocked, and the impact of Radisson's blow made him skid backwards on his feet.

He grit his teeth and appraised his enemy. Radisson was big for a human, nearly as tall as Lugh, and incredibly broad of shoulder. His composite weapon could be either a shield and a sword, or a single greatsword; this was the form he obviously preferred, and was what he had used to deal such a terrible strike to Nihs' back. As Lugh had already learned, he could swing it deceptively fast.

All of this insight came in the flash of an instant; that was all the time Lugh got. Radisson dashed forward, and struck down with an overhead chop. Lugh dodged sideways, closed in, and was nearly brained by a smashing fist. He ducked under it, but it was awkward, last-minute maneuver, and a second later his feet were kicked out from under him. He landed hard on his back and had the wherewithal to roll out of the way just before the huge sword came down again.

He's fast, Lugh thought. *And strong.* He was starting to understand why Radisson was one of Reno city's most feared criminals.

He jumped to his feet and backed away, expecting a moment's relief, but Radisson was already chasing after him. Radisson stabbed, the length of his greatsword devouring the distance between them. Lugh swatted the point away, went to follow up, and thought better of it as another fist came out to close the gap in Radisson's guard.

That's how he does it, Lugh thought. *Swing, then punch and kick until he can get his sword back up. Well, next time he sticks his arm out, I'm going to lop it off.*

Radisson grinned humorlessly when he saw Lugh back away. He sized him up for a second, then dashed back in. He swung horizontally and Lugh had no choice but to back up; he swung again and again, pushing Lugh back toward the entrance to the balcony. Finally Lugh had no choice but to run forward and leap right over him. He soared ten feet up into the air, then gasped in pain and surprise when the tip of the greatsword rose up and raked against his calf. He spun and landed hard on his side. He felt the wooden floor of the balcony shake, and before he could recover, Radisson ran up and kicked him full in the chest. He flew backwards, breaking the wooden railing, and tumbled off the side of the balcony. He fell fifteen feet and only half-managed to break his fall on the hard, stone street—his wrist gave out when he stuck out a hand, and his forehead clanged against the flagstones.

Stars popped in front of his eyes and his vision swam, but he shook his head and rolled to his feet. His soul shield had held, but barely. He couldn't afford to make another mistake.

Of the four men that had surrounded Kyle, one of them had been completely knocked out of commission by Nihs' fireball, and another was limping, hanging back while his two buddies tried to get Kyle stuck in a corner. Forgetting Radisson for a moment, Lugh took advantage of the confusion caused by his fall and lashed out at the man closest to him. The man blocked, but Kyle saw what was happening and struck from the front with his soul sword. There was an angry buzz of magic as the attacker's soul shield was burned away. A second later, it gave, and the man screamed as a hole half the size of his head opened up in his chest.

Lugh tasted victory, and the remaining attacker looked terrified out of his wits. A second later, Radisson dropped down on him from above, smashing him into the ground. Pain exploded in his head, and a tingling rush swept over his body. A split second later, his world flickered, then went out.

Kyle watched, horrified, as Radisson bore down on Lugh, striking him squarely across the head and shoulder with his massive sword. Lugh's mouth opened and his tongue lolled out. His good eye rolled back into his skull and he fell limply to the ground. The blue aura of his soul shield twinkled and shattered, falling in delicate tatters all around him.

A second later, pain exploded in Kyle's side. He gasped in surprise. It felt like hundreds of tiny claws were burrowing into his skin. He twisted around, and saw that the remaining man had seen his chance, and struck with his strange stun-stick.

Kyle tried to move, to swing his sword, but his limbs refused to obey him. His lungs tightened in his chest, and he started to gasp for air. The man was holding his stick against Kyle's side, letting it flicker and spark, watching Kyle's movements with a mixture of cruelty and fear. He knew he had caged a dangerous animal, one who could easily rip him limb from limb if it managed to escape.

Kyle was aware of Radisson approaching from behind him.

"Damn…" he said, or tried to say. His teeth had clamped shut and couldn't be parted.

There came a bellow like the roar of a giant, then a crash that felt like a minor earthquake. The quake nearly shook Kyle's legs out from under him, but the sound resonated through his soul. It was a blood-curdling, animal yell, and Kyle's first instinct upon hearing it was to run and run until he was as far away from what made it as possible.

The man who had been holding him in place gasped and stepped back; the stick detached from Kyle's side, and feeling came back to his limbs. He instantly struck out with his soul sword. The man, too confused and terrified to block, caught the blow on his shoulder. His soul shield held, but the impact knocked him sideways off his feet.

Absently, Kyle thought, *nothing used to be able to hold up against this sword. The curse has made it weaker.* In this moment, he didn't mind. The effects of his soul sword at full power had been terrifying to behold.

He turned around, and what he saw filled his heart with joy. The sound and the horrible crash suddenly made sense—it was Rogan the Minotaur. He was crouched in a battle stance, holding his father's axe in both hands. His red eyes looked like pools of blood, and his horns shone in the dim light of the Hungry Horn's lantern. It looked as though he had tried to do to Radisson what Radisson had done to Lugh, but the mercenary had been too quick to dodge. Now, Rogan and Radisson were circling one another, Radisson with his greatsword up on his shoulder, Rogan puffing steam through his nostrils.

Through his peripherals, Kyle noticed that the stun-stick man was getting to his feet. He backed away, trying to keep both him and Radisson in his line of sight. A second later, there was a streak of black and another of white. Kyle smiled openly. It was Meya and Deriahm.

Deriahm, in full armor as always (*does he sleep like that?* thought Kyle), rushed the stun-stick man, longsword striking methodically down, from the left, from the right. The man blocked the first two blows, lost his weapon to the third, then lost his soul shield to a bash from Deriahm's shield. Deriahm bashed again, and the man crumpled to the ground.

Meya, meanwhile, had run up to Kyle and grabbed his forearm to get his attention.

"Are you alright?" she asked. Kyle nodded.

"Good. I'm going to help Nihs and Lugh. Stay away from Rogan. He'll be just as dangerous as Radisson once he goes berserk."

That wasn't what Kyle was expecting to hear, and it sent a thrill of fear up his spine. He turned back around to watch the fight.

Rogan was huffing and puffing, steam shooting from his mouth and nose with each breath. Without being told, Kyle knew what was going on—Rogan was working himself into a rage. He and Radisson were testing each other, lashing out with their oversized weapons, sparks flying whenever they met. Radisson looked nearly as furious as Rogan—his chance at Kyle had been all but shot, and he was out for blood. His jaw was set, and his lips were parted in an angry snarl. He struck again and again with his greatsword, and Kyle realized that even massive Rogan might not be a match for him.

His fingers itched. He had retracted his soul sword almost without thinking; the searing pain in his forearms was still fading, but now he was preparing to inflict it upon himself again. His sword might not be as powerful as it once was, but he doubted if even Radisson could survive more than a few blows from it. That, and he would be willing to bet that it could break that massive greatsword. He put his palms together and began to gather his will.

He felt a hand on his arm. It was Deriahm.

"I would heed the good miss Ilduetyr's advice, mister Campbell," he said. "Soul sword or no, Radisson is a truly dangerous foe, and to put yourself in harm's way will do us little good. It is noble and natural to want to act, but you have already fought valiantly. It is now time for *us* to fulfill our promise to *you*."

Kyle, as he often was when Deriahm spoke, was stunned. He looked into the inscrutable black visor and nodded once. He pulled his hands apart.

Rogan and Radisson were now fighting full-force. It was terrifying and awe-inspiring to watch. Radisson was a blaze of metal and Rogan seemed to be growing larger and redder with each passing moment. The red fur he wore about his neck no longer seemed an ornament, but part of Rogan himself. Its shiny surface rippled as Rogan's muscles worked underneath it, swinging his axe to ward off each of Radisson's strikes.

Kyle realized that their tussle had started to draw the attention of the people of Mjolsport; windows were lighting up on both sides of the street and a few passersby had shouted in surprise and run off. *To fetch the police?* Kyle wondered. He couldn't remember seeing any Buorish policemen in town, and was wondering if they had a presence here.

Radisson had obviously noticed this, as well, and his face grew even more murderous. He redoubled his attack on Rogan, and with dismay Kyle saw that he was being pushed back. Fear crept into him. If Rogan couldn't handle Radisson, what hope did the rest of them have? Radisson's sword started to slip by Rogan's guard and hit home; it grazed him on the arm, then the leg, then the chest. The blows were barely scratches and Rogan's soul shield warded them off with ease, but the fact that they had gotten through was telling.

Rogan, on the other hand, clearly had no room in his mind for fear. The cuts he endured only angered him further, and he started to bellow. His head shuddered uncontrollably, and his body steamed. He began to speed up, and soon it was Radisson who was giving ground.

Deriahm reached an arm out and steered Kyle backwards. "Have a care, mister Campbell," he said. "Once Rogan becomes fully berserk, he will not be able to tell friend from foe. He is liable to harm you even by accident in this state."

Kyle took the advice to heart. The grave and wise animal that he knew had all but disappeared; Rogan was a blur of frothing, roaring fury. His fighting technique started to slip, his precise attacks becoming the swings of a wild animal.

Radisson hung back, watching his opponent with a calculating stare. Kyle knew nothing about the man—in fact, at that point he didn't even know it was Radisson they were facing—but he saw genuine experience at play here. There was a reason Radisson had survived in Reno when so many other criminals had failed, and too late Kyle thought to warn Rogan of what he saw. But even if he had spoken, would Rogan have listened?

Suddenly, Radisson dashed forward, ducked past Rogan's failing limbs, and struck at his unprotected side. Rogan howled and lashed out; Radisson dodged easily, swung his sword, and struck Rogan's head on the opposite side. He danced back, out of the way of a wild axe strike, and then dove in again, stabbing forward. Rogan's soul shield buzzed and then broke, and the sword buried itself in his stomach.

"*No!*" Kyle shouted, and he heard gasps from his companions around him. Dimly he realized that Meya was back, with Nihs on her shoulder. The tiny Kol was looking wan, but his eyes were open, and that he was able to keep his balance was cause for relief.

But that was of little comfort to Kyle as he watched Rogan burble and cough blood into Radisson's face, reaching along the length of his sword as if to throttle him. Radisson pulled his sword back and stepped out of reach as Rogan sank to his knees, clutching at his wounded stomach.

Radisson turned to look at the rest of them. His jaw jutted out, and he spat blood from his face.

"Who's next?" he said.

Meya shrieked in anger and thrust a hand forward. A blinding flash of red light erupted from her palm. Radisson dashed sideways; Meya followed with another bolt of hurting magic. Radisson growled and lunged, closing the distance between them. Kyle and Deriahm stepped away from each other, fanning out as Kyle has been taught. His soul sword hissed into his hand.

Radisson bore down on Meya, wanting to take out the most dangerous member of their group. She kept away from him nimbly, her face set in concentration as she cast spell after spell. The red light hit home as often as it missed, but Radisson ignored it.

Meya had once described her magic as 'pure hurt'. It travelled through weapons, armor and walls, and could slay any living thing with equal surety. But it wasn't as powerful as Nihs' elementalism, and had nothing like the same impact. If Meya could avoid being hit for long enough, she was sure to win—but could she?

Nihs dropped from her shoulder and rolled off in his own direction. He staggered with every step, but still launched the occasional spell at Radisson's chest and head. He was determined to make a nuisance of himself, enough to keep Meya safe from Radisson's fury.

Kyle and Deriahm closed in from behind, and for a second Kyle underestimated just how skilled Radisson was. One second, they were about to strike at his unprotected back; the next, his sword came whistling out of nowhere in a huge sweep, and both of them were forced to step back. Kyle blocked with his soul sword and it was forced backwards nearly into his own head.

Radisson chased after Nihs and Meya, blocking the attacks of the first and ignoring the second. He was panting now, but there was a wild look in his eyes, and he seemed more dangerous than ever. Kyle and Deriahm tried to engage him again and again, but every time his huge sword came around and opened up distance between them.

Time to test my theory, Kyle thought.

He closed distance again, waiting for Radisson to take notice and swing at him. He did, and Kyle planted his feet, vented all of his combat energy, and swung as hard as he could at Radisson's sword. The impact nearly blew him backwards, but he held fast as his sword sparked and gnawed away at the metal of Radisson's weapon. By the time Radisson realized what was going on, his sword was sheared through. The last two feet of it went spinning off into the street, clattering against the ground.

Radisson bellowed a terrible oath. He ducked to one side, and Kyle was taken by a momentary confusion. Radisson dove and rolled, circling around Kyle and Deriahm to their left. Kyle, with Deriahm's warning ringing in his ears, set his guard and stepped back, not knowing what was coming. He watched Radisson scramble away from him for a moment, and by the time he realized what was happening it was too late. Radisson rose to his feet, lifting Lugh's unconscious body with him. He set what was left of his sword against Lugh's neck, and faced them from across the street, breathing heavily.

"Right," he said. "I've had enough of this. Drop your weapons or I'll slit his throat."

A deep despair crawled into Kyle's chest. He felt sick to his stomach. How could everything have turned on them so quickly? Lugh's head lolled back and forth as Radisson held him up. A trickle of blood began to run from his neck.

"*Do it!*" Radisson snapped. He nodded at Kyle. "You. Suck that thing back in. If I see it again, your friend dies." To Deriahm: "You. Drop them. And you two—if I see one spark of magic, his head's coming off."

You haven't won, Kyle thought, but to bide his time—and because his sword was burning away at his palms—he did as asked.

There was a loud clang of metal as Deriahm's sword and shield fell to the ground. Radisson's face glowed cherry red with fury. "*Quiet!*" he hissed.

"I am sorry, sir," Deriahm said softly. "I only did as asked."

Radisson's nostrils flared, but it was obvious that he didn't want to waste time with this. "Right. Here's how this is going to work. Kyle, get your ass over here. Slowly."

Shaking with anger, Kyle stepped forward. *This is Rhian all over again*, he thought. *Damn it, damn it, damn it! Why can't I keep my friends safe?*

Suddenly he stopped. "No," he said.

Radisson's eyes bulged. "What?" he snapped.

"No," Kyle said, louder. "I'm not coming with you, and you can't make me."

"Kyle," Meya said urgently, but he ignored her.

"Let my friend go. You lay a hand on him, and you're dead."

Radisson's face split into a terrible, manic grin. "You must be even stupider than I thought," he said. "You don't understand how this works, do you?"

"More than you do," Kyle said. "Let's see. You're outnumbered, you have no weapon, and the police will be here in seconds. We've got a bishop on our side who can bring people back from the edge of death. I should know, because she did it to me.

"The way I see it, all I have to do is stall. You hurt Lugh, and we'll kill you. Take too long, and the police will be here. You don't have a chance of winning no matter what you do." Kyle drew his soul sword and levelled it at Radisson. "And I swear to God, if you hurt Lugh I'll run this sword through your damn heart. I'll rip you apart from the inside out until all that's left is jelly. *DO YOU HEAR ME!?*"

The shout was in part to give weight to his threat and in part to draw attention. Kyle had no idea if the police were in fact coming, but if they were, he wanted them to hurry the hell up.

Radisson regarded him, then turned to one side and spat blood.

"You know what?" he said. "You're right. I *don't* have a lot of time. So I'm done pissing around with you." And to Kyle's horror, he drew Lugh's neck back and started to draw his sword across it. Blood spurted.

"*NO!*" Nihs' shout was horrified and ear-splitting. He started to draw in magic, but before he could release his spell, a dark shape loomed behind Radisson. A pair of massive hands shot out and grabbed Radisson by the arms. They twisted the remains of the sword out of Radisson's hand, then lifted him straight off his feet. Lugh sank to the ground once more.

Rogan emerged from the shadows, lifting Radisson ever higher and squeezing ever tighter. Radisson yelled and thrashed, but his arms were pinned to his sides, and Rogan seemed possessed by an unbelievable strength. His furred body and curved horns looked hellish in the dim light. He growled and steamed as he crushed Radisson's ribs between his hands. Radisson shouted, then shrieked, then could only draw wet, ragged breaths. Finally Rogan lifted him full over his head, and with a mighty bellow smashed him against the ground. Radisson's soul shield flew to pieces, and he rolled and landed on his back. He had just managed to flip himself over and was trying to get his arms and legs under him when Rogan's massive hoof came down on his back. Radisson's limbs splayed out and blood shot from his mouth.

Rogan, howling, lifted his leg to bring it back down, but Meya shouted "*No!*" and dashed forward, holding both hands out, palms forward. White light glowed from her hands, and Kyle felt a wave of calm wash over him when he caught sight of it. There was a soft, pure quality to it, like the flame of a candle burning in a draftless room, and Kyle found himself hypnotized.

Rogan stared at the light dumbly, his hoof coming back down softly. His breathing calmed and the red rage boiling in him started to burn away. A few seconds later, Gershel was gone entirely, and Rogan the Minotaur had returned. He hung his head and shook it, as if to dislodge the last remnants of his fugue.

Slowly, Meya lowered her hands, and the light faded. Nihs came forward, still panting.

"*Why?*" he snapped.

"Because he has information," Meya said at once. "And he can't tell us who hired him if his guts are all over the street."

She turned to the others, and Kyle saw a terrifying coldness in her eyes. "Who wants to do the honors?" she said. "I need to help Lugh."

Nihs brushed past her at once, and Deriahm stepped forward as well. Kyle followed behind.

Nihs stood in front of Radisson, his arms folded across his chest. Rogan still had one hoof planted between his shoulders, but it was clear that Radisson wouldn't have been able to move regardless. He looked up at Nihs with pure hatred written on his face, but in this moment, Nihs, at his full height of less than two feet, looked more frightening than Radisson could have hoped to.

"I am angry," Nihs said. "I am angry because Phundasa is dead, the *Ayger* has been destroyed, and my best friend has lost an eye, all to your imbecilic attempts to kidnap Kyle. Who put you up to this? Why do they care so much about Kyle? And how do they keep managing to find us?"

Radisson coughed blood, and Kyle realized it was because he was laughing. He laughed for so long that Kyle worried they were going to use up all of their time listening to him do it.

Finally he spoke. "I thought you were stupid before," he said, "but now I'm sure. Why would I tell you anything?"

Nihs' face flared with anger, and the air darkened as he drew magic in. "Because I'll burn you to cinders you if you don't!" he snapped, and Kyle was shocked to realize that he was dead serious.

But Radisson only laughed his suppurating laugh. "So what? Go ahead. I'm dead meat anyway. I end up a pile of ash now or rot in a Buorish prison for the rest of my life. Tough choice."

"If I may interject, sir," Deriahm said, hunkering down, "that is not entirely correct. We Buors are a reasonable folk, and our justice system is not designed to punish the guilty so much as offer them the chance for redemption. Your redemption can begin now, if you allow it. If you assist us, I will ensure that your actions count in your favor when you stand before the Buorish court."

Good cop, bad cop, Kyle thought in wonder. *They didn't even plan it. How much is there to being an adventurer that I don't know about?*

Radisson was looking up at Deriahm as if seeing him for the first time. Then he said, "You think I'm going to believe that? I'll take my chances."

"Why?" Kyle said suddenly. Both Nihs and Deriahm turned in surprise. Kyle stepped forward and dropped to his haunches as Deriahm had done. He ignored his friends, and looked directly into Radisson's eyes.

"You don't owe him anything," he said. "The guy who hired you to kidnap me. He screwed you, over and over. He sent you after me and got your men killed. Now he's gotten you beat, and when you're arrested and thrown into prison he won't do anything to help you. Besides," he added, "we already know who it is. We just need you to tell us we're right. It's James Livaldi, isn't it? He's behind all of this."

Radisson didn't answer, but Kyle could see from his expression that he had been right.

"How do you figure that?" Radisson said.

"When you kidnapped me in Reno, you brought me to Sky Tower. I wasn't supposed to know that, but I got it from one of your men. But that's not the main reason—the main reason is weapons."

He nodded at the bodies strewn about the street. "Those sticks your men were using…they didn't match the rest of their equipment. Same with the guns they had in Reno. And the ship that the twins were piloting in Eastia had a cannon attached to it, even though everyone thought that Ephicer technology wasn't there yet. Livaldi's been giving you prototype weapons so you can chase me down, hasn't he?"

Radisson's expression had lost a great deal of its anger, and when he laughed again, Kyle could tell that it was at Livaldi's expense rather than his own.

"Not bad," he said. "That little shit thinks he's so smart—not smart enough to cover his tracks, though. But if you want to know why he's after you, you'll have to ask him yourself."

"What about the twins?" someone asked. It was Meya—she had joined the circle surrounding Radisson, Lugh limping along beside her, one arm wrapped around her shoulders. He was looking sickly and his eye would only open halfway, but he was awake and on his feet, and the wound on his throat had closed. Meya was supporting him with both arms, but her eyes were fixated on Radisson.

"Were they your men?" she pressed. "Who ordered them to shoot down the *Ayger* and kill Phundasa?"

With difficulty, Radisson craned his neck to look up at her. "Lady," he said flatly, "I have no idea what you're talking about."

It was obvious that he was telling the truth, and Meya glared at him but said nothing else.

"There's one more question," Nihs said quietly. "How is James able to find us time and time again? What magic does he have access to that allows him to track us?"

Contempt came back to Radisson's voice. "You think he shares all this stuff with me? He tells me where Kyle is and tells me to go grab him. I don't know how he finds out." The word *out* was consumed by a fit of coughing. When it passed, he added, "Are we done here? It's a little hard to talk with this big bastard crushing my spine."

Kyle and the others shared a glance, and the unspoken question *'What now?'* passed between them. Deriahm cleared his throat and said, "I believe, good sirs and madam, that we should depart from this place as soon as possible. It is only a matter of time before Mjolsport's watch arrives, and if they find us, we are certain to be waylaid for questioning."

Nihs was shocked. "Did I just hear a Buor suggest that we flee from the police?"

"Indeed, sir. Under the circumstances, I would consider it a reasonable course of action."

Another shared glance, then Lugh raised his head with difficulty and said, "Let's grab our stuff and then get out of here, yeah?"

"Let's," Rogan agreed, finally taking his hoof off of Radisson's back. The mercenary drew in a wheezing breath as soon as he did.

"Hey!" he snapped at their backs. "You're just gonna leave me here?"

Lugh limped past him, Meya still acting as his crutch. "If you manage to slip past the police in the state you're in, you deserve to escape," he said.

Radisson, unable to keep his head up any longer, slowly laid his cheek against the ground.

"Bastards," he said to the ground.

Though the Hungry Horn was mostly a Minotaur establishment, the landlord was a Selkic man. He was garrisoned behind the bar when they came in, and pointed a small Ephicer rifle at Lugh with a look of panic on his face.

"Don't move!" he yelped.

"Calm down," Lugh wheezed, not slowing his pace. "The fight's over. We'll just be grabbing our things and slipping out the back door. You do have one of those, don't you?"

The landlord was at a loss for words. "I...you..."

Lugh made it to the bar, fumbled for his wallet, and laid some money on the counter. "I broke your balcony," he said. "Sorry about that. Also, there's a crime lord bleeding out on your front step. The police will probably be by soon to mop him up."

They left the poor man to his distress and climbed the stairs to their rooms.

Since Meya was now healing the wound in Rogan's stomach, Kyle helped Lugh on the way up.

"You enjoyed that more than you should have," he said blandly.

Lugh smiled weakly. "Feeling a little giddy at the moment. Must be that."

"Must be."

They gathered their belongings as quickly as they could, Kyle, Meya and Deriahm splitting Lugh, Nihs and Rogan's packs between them. They left out the back way as Lugh had said, and soon were creeping through the dark streets of Mjolsport. They made a wide circle around the Hungry Horn, then headed northwest toward the waterfront. To their intense relief, they didn't meet a single policeman on their way.

Mjolsport's harbor was bustling most every time of day, but this was the very deepest part of the night, and the port was so quiet that Kyle could hear individual waves lapping against the stone quays. Airships and water-bound vessels alike lay silent in their berths.

"What now?" Nihs hissed. "There won't be any ships leaving at this time of night."

"Yes, there will," Lugh said grimly. "There always are. Split up?"

"Not on your life!"

Lugh nodded. "You're probably right. All right, let's get a move on, then."

They set off down the waterfront, looking for any sign of activity. Kyle didn't share Lugh's hope that they would find anything of use, and was casting around in his mind for any alternative.

"What would be so bad about letting the police find us?" he said to Lugh. "Every Buor in the world knows who we are. Couldn't we just explain ourselves?"

Lugh shook his head. "The police in this city aren't Buorish," he said. "That's the way with a lot of cities in Ar'ac."

"Oh," Kyle said, realization dawning. "Damn. If I'd known I wouldn't have shouted so loud."

Lugh smiled wanly. "No harm done, they didn't show up anyway. Useless…if the guard *had* been Buorish, they'd have been there before I was."

They crept along, Kyle now understanding the need for secrecy. For better or worse, the port was as devoid of guardsmen as it was of sailors and pilots.

After a while, they came across a trio of Orcs playing cards under the canopy of a tiny, dingy shelter that was half-open to the night air. A single Ephicer light was wedged in the corner of its supports, casting a dim light over their game.

"Hullo there," Lugh said, "what are you all waiting for?"

"None of your business," one of them said gruffly without looking around.

"We're looking for a ship headed for Westia," Lugh pressed.

"Then go find one."

Lugh looked back at the others, shrugged, and they carried on. As they were walking away, one of other Orcs said, "Try *Brass Ring Shipping*. That way," and he jerked his chin inland.

"Thanks," Lugh said.

The Orc grunted and went back to his game.

They found the Brass Ring office two streets in, though they very nearly missed it. It was a squat, grungy place. Two portly, elderly Orcs with wrinkled, dour faces were sitting outside, smoking. They were wearing vests open at the chest, and one of them had an ashtray perched on the bulge of his stomach.

"Ye've got a bit of a cut there," the smoker said as they approached. He lifted an arm with difficulty and pointed at Lugh's neck. Meya had taken the worst of the wound away, but it was still horribly scabbed, and Lugh's collar was stained with blood.

"I've had worse," he said vaguely. "This Brass Ring Shipping?"

"Yeah."

"Cheers."

Like the shelter that the three Orcs had been playing under, the Brass Ring was little more than a shack thrown together from shipping materials, with a bit of canvas stretched over for shelter. Kyle was amazed at how the stone buildings and walkways of Mjolsport had yielded to a place like this on the waterfront.

The place was dominated by a long table, behind which was seated an Orc reading some kind of magazine printed on flimsy paper. He was about as old as the men outside, and he was the first Orc Kyle had seen wearing a pair of glasses. He glanced at them with disinterest as they came in.

"Yes?" he said.

"Hullo," said Lugh. "We're wondering if you've got any airships leaving for Westia soon."

The Orc appeared to think about this. "Ehh," he said. He rose slowly from his chair, crossed over to a sheaf of papers stacked on the counter, and thumbed through them. He pulled one out, held it up for inspection, then slid it across the table toward Lugh.

"*Agartes*," he said, tapping the name with a finger. "Noon tomorrow."

Kyle's heart sank. *Noon?* he thought. *Way too late.*

"Anything sooner?" Lugh was saying.

The Orc thrust out his lower lip and gestured at the papers in front of him, as if to say, *what do you expect?*

Rogan shouldered his way forward. He was still clutching at his stomach where Radisson had stabbed him. "How about ships leaving for Ren'r or Ar'ac, then?" he asked. "Anything for Oasis, say?"

"Oasis, yes," the Orc said, nodding. Thumb-thumb-thumb, slide. "*Markuss*. Boat."

"A *boat?*" Lugh groaned, but Rogan turned and said, "If it's to Oasis, it won't take more than a few days. It'll get us away from here and we'll be able to find something for Westia from there."

"All right, all right," Lugh said, waving a hand. "When does the…*Markuss* leave?"

The Orc made a seesawing motion with one hand. "Less than two hour," he said.

"Great. We want to book passage."

If this caused the old proprietor any surprise, he didn't show it. He looked their group over. "Four hundred nell," he said.

"Done. Can you tell us where to find this boat of yours?"

They were led outside, the elderly Orc walking in big, waddling strides. They followed him down to and along the waterfront for about ten minutes, until they came across a large vessel being loaded by a team of Orcs and Minotaur. It was flat-bottomed like a barge, and had two large Ephicer engines mounted at the back. The golden tigoreh that formed its hull was tarnished, and everything that wasn't tigoreh looked very dirty indeed. It was certainly no *Ayger*.

An Orc much younger than their escort vaulted down from the deck when he saw them approach. Their guide gestured vaguely at their group.

"Passage," he said.

The younger Orc was taken aback. "Really?" he said, looking them over. Then he shrugged. "All right. None of my business. We're leaving as soon as we get loaded up."

"Great," Lugh said. He plunked himself down and leaned back against a wooden bollard. "We'd be delighted to help, but we've got some resting to do."

"You're not kidding," the Orc said, looking their sorry group over. He had his hands on his hips and was looking after the elderly Orc who had dropped them off, but this one was already waddling back to the comfort of his outpost.

"If you're worried that we're criminals, you can rest easy," Lugh said, eye closed. "We just ran into some men who were a little too pushy for our taste."

"If he wasn't worried before, he is now," Meya pointed out. She was finishing her healing job on Rogan, both hands flat against his stomach.

"It's none of my business," the young Orc repeated, but it was obvious that he felt it should be, and would be if there was any sign of trouble. Kyle was reminded of some of the characters he had met back in college—young men who would stand in the corner of the pub and glare at anyone who looked too rowdy, clenching and unclenching their fists and telling themselves they would get involved if anything happened. Luckily for them, it rarely did.

Mentally, Kyle relaxed. This young Orc would be no trouble once he decided that Kyle's party wasn't any.

"Are you the one in charge here?" he asked.

The Orc nodded. "Raghuz is my name."

"Kyle," and they shook hands.

"Awfully young lad to be in charge of such a big boat," Lugh said from his resting place.

Raghuz snorted. "We make this run half a dozen times every month. Any of us could do it with our eyes closed."

"Fair enough, but I'll ask politely that you don't. If it came between that rig and the coast, my money would be on the coast winning."

"Listen," Kyle said, "why don't Deriahm and I help you load? We can be off that much faster."

"A capital idea," Lugh said.

Raghuz was hesitant to accept their help at first, but once Kyle and Deriahm made a few trips without dropping cargo into the ocean, he relented. Kyle wasn't usually the sort to volunteer, but he was as anxious to get moving as he had ever been. The rest of the crew treated them with indifference—clearly, if they were all right with Raghuz they were all right with them.

The rest of the party hung back to recover, with Meya's help. Nihs had a deep bruise across the length of his back where Radisson had struck him, and was cut and scraped all over. Rogan had the wound in his stomach to contend with, and with Lugh it was his head, shoulder, and neck. Meya went from one to the other, healing the worst of the wounds first, then spending more magic to patch up what was left. By the end, she was pale and her skin was drawn—signs of magic overuse. Her subjects looked much better for wear, but already the bone-deep fatigue that was the side effect of healing magic was starting to show.

As Kyle carried boxes and watched his companions out of the corner of his eye, he felt mingled shame, relief, and pride. Once again, his presence had put everyone in danger—but they had risen above it, taken out Michael Radisson and escaped the police to boot. Most importantly, they had all gotten out of it alive.

That's all that matters, Kyle thought. *That's more important than getting home…that's more important than anything.*

First there were fifty boxes left to move, then twenty, then five. As one of Raghuz's crewmates hoisted the last up onto his shoulder, Raghuz sought them out and welcomed them aboard.

"The *Markuss,*" he said expansively.

It was a fairly large boat, and a fairly ugly one. Its wooden deck was molding in places, and slick with water and grease everywhere else. Crates of supplies and coils of rope were piled into every corner, and the twin Ephicer engines looked ready to burn out at any moment.

"Nice," Lugh said.

Raghuz snorted again. "It's a tub," he said flatly. "One of these days I'll be able to convince those old fools to invest in a half-decent ship. Until then...well, let me show you to your quarters."

There were only four rooms left on the Markuss, and they were pod-sized, containing tiny cots and nothing else.

"You'll have to make do, I'm afraid," Raghuz said unhelpfully.

Lugh looked down at the tiny bed and sighed. "Right. Rogan and Meya get their own. Nihs and I, Kyle and Deriahm?"

"Wonderful," Nihs said. "I've always wanted to know what it sounds like when you're trapped in a cave with the tide coming in."

"We're casting off," Raghuz said. "You can do as you please as long as you stay out of the crew's way."

Lugh sat down on the edge of his bed. "I'm going to sleep," he announced.

"And me," Rogan rumbled, still holding his stomach as if worried it would come undone.

Nihs dropped his pack in the corner and wrapped his sagecloak about himself. "I need something to eat, myself," he said.

Lugh sprang to his feet. "I changed my mind. Food, *then* sleep."

Meya started to laugh. "We should *all* eat," she said, "and then we should *all* sleep. We need to rest as much as we can while we have the chance."

"You'll have to wait for food," Raghuz said firmly. "We don't eat until we're well at sea."

Lugh sat down again. "All right, then. Sleep, then food, then more sleep. Final offer."

Their four-day trip on the *Markuss* was as uneventful as a trip could be. It couldn't have possibly made a starker contrast against the events in Mjolsport. Their days consisted of sitting around the deck, staying out of the crew's way, and watching the coast roll by whenever it was in view. Lugh, Nihs and Rogan, who were recovering for most of the voyage, slept for eighteen hours of each day's thirty-two, leaving Kyle, Meya and Deriahm alone for much of the trip. Kyle found himself growing closer to both of them, particularly Deriahm, with whom he also shared his nights. Once he had gotten used to having the smooth metal of Deriahm's chestplate pressed against his back—Buors *did* sleep in their armor—he'd come to find the *irusha's* presence somehow calming. At least Deriahm was completely still and silent when asleep, which was absolutely not the case with Lugh if Nihs' complaints were to be believed.

One day, the three of them were seated on the deck, taking part in their favorite pastime of watching the coast go by. Deriahm had set up his tiny *rouk* pipe and was blowing smoke into the calm ocean air.

"What would happen if one of us tried using that?" Kyle asked him.

Meya laughed. "I asked him the exact same thing when we were travelling together."

"I am afraid the results would be less than pleasant," Deriahm said. "Buorish lungs are acclimated to *rouk*, but a human such as yourself would be asphyxiated by it." He tilted his head thoughtfully. "That isn't to say there are none who have tried, of course. There are a number of gourmands of varying races who claim to take pleasure in smoking *rouk*."

"I'm not surprised," Kyle said. "Look far enough and you'll find someone who's into anything."

"Indeed, sir."

The conversation dwindled off. Meya sighed and cast her gaze out toward the coast. "I wish this ship would move a little faster," she said. "I keep thinking that someone is going to catch us up."

"Tell me about it," Kyle said.

There was a pause, then Meya added, "So it was Livaldi all along."

Kyle nodded. "Looks that way."

"You know," she said, "there's something about that that doesn't make any sense to me."

"What do you mean?"

"Livaldi is supposed to be a genius. So why is he doing such a terrible job at capturing you? He sent the twins after you once and Radisson after you twice... it's the same strategy over and over. If you're so important to him, why is he being so careless? It's like Radisson said—he can't even be bothered to cover his tracks."

Kyle had never thought about this before. "You're right," he said slowly. "It is strange. You'd think he'd come up with something more subtle."

Deriahm tapped the mouthpiece of his pipe against his chin. "Perhaps we are misinterpreting our foe's intentions," he said. "Doctor Livaldi could have an ulterior motive which his apparent blunders serve to mask."

"If so, what could it be?" Kyle said, more to himself than anything. "I don't even know what he wants from me in the first place."

"That's easy," Meya said. "He wants information about your world. He probably thinks he can steal your technology if he gets a hold of you."

Kyle managed to laugh. "If that's what he thinks, he's going to be disappointed. I don't have a damn clue how most of our technology works."

Meya and Deriahm both laughed at this, but Kyle's mind was elsewhere. What *did* Livaldi want from him? Where did his fascination with Kyle come from—and how had he found out about him in the first place?

D r. James Livaldi, President and CEO of Maida Weapons, was furious.
In normal circumstances, fury came about as easily to Livaldi Jr. as a lack of it had come to his late father. Livaldi Sr. had been a dark, brooding man with a booming voice and thunderous temper; his son, as if in defiance, had grown up small, slight, and reserved. But as Saul stepped into Livaldi's office on feet of velvet, he reflected that lately, the resemblance between the young master and his father was growing at an alarming rate.

Livaldi's study, found at the very highest floor of the now nearly-complete Sky Tower, was dominated by a massive window that offered a dizzying view of Reno city below. Before the window was Livaldi's desk, and behind the desk was the young master himself.

Saul stopped short fully ten paces from the desk, as he had been trained to do. Even from here, he could see the lines of worry on Livaldi's forehead and the deep bags under his eyes. Strands of loose hair hung down at the sides of his face, and his shirt collar, normally kept a blinding white, was rumpled and unwashed. James looked about ten years older than he ought to, but worse was the haunted look on his face.

The disorganization had spread to the rest of his office, as well. Books and papers had been left strewn about, and the sheer amount of them suggested that James was not getting his usual work done.

But worst of all was the coffee.

No fewer than half a dozen mugs crowded Livaldi's desk. A seventh was several feet away, lying on its side at the center of a brown stain on the carpet. The eighth mug in the set was sitting on the table to Saul's left, under an ornate Ephicer machine that sputtered and coughed constantly.

He's brewing a cup, Saul thought. *And I would wager my life that he's filled and emptied each of the others at least once today.*

It was distressing—no, it was heartbreaking—to see the young master this way. James Livaldi *was* Maida, he and his brilliant mind, and if it were to be brought low by…by *that*…then James himself would follow, and his empire with him.

Livaldi was staring straight ahead when Saul entered, his elbows on his desk and his knuckles drilling into his cheeks. His lips were peeled back in a slight snarl, and one eye was twitching.

Saul coughed politely and waited.

"You don't have to tell me," James said at last. "I already know."

Saul shivered. Even James' voice didn't sound right. It was low and gravelly, as if his throat had been stripped bare.

"Sir?" he said.

Livaldi's violet eyes flickered in his direction. "Kyle," he said, like a man dying of thirst asking for water. "He escaped again."

"Yes, sir."

"Radisson is dead."

"Of that I am not sure—"

"It doesn't matter!" Livaldi slammed a fist down on his desk. Six empty cups jangled in unison. "It's *over!* He *lost!*"

James looked pensive for a moment, as if he'd lost his train of thought, then leaned back.

"And Kyle got away," he finished. He picked up a pen from his desk, toyed with it for a moment, then threw it back down. He picked up an empty mug, glanced inside, then set that down as well. His gaze grew distant.

"Why can't I see him any more?" he said. "I don't understand. He's hiding from me…but *how?*"

You just found him, Saul wanted to say, *and it didn't make any difference. Why can't you see that this will never work?*

It had been not a full day ago that one of Livaldi's scouts—the travelling salesmen who preached the word of Maida throughout the world—had reported a Kyle sighting in the sea town of Mjolsport. He and his companions were staying at a local pub, drinking and telling stories, as loud and conspicuous as could be. Before this information arrived at Livaldi's desk, the young master had been as miserable as Saul had ever seen him, brooding about his office, tugging the hairs from his head and lamenting the fact that his second sight was showing him no sign of Kyle. The transformation that the news had brought on had been remarkable. Livaldi was galvanized, energetic, as excited as a child before On-Cross.

"Where's Radisson?" he asked at once. "Find him. Send him after them. He can use the *Aether.*"

Saul couldn't help himself—he gasped in surprise. The thought of entrusting the *Aether* to Radisson's band of ruffians was repellant.

"Sir, there must be—" he began.

"You're wasting time!" Livaldi shouted. "Kyle could move on at any minute! I want Radisson after him and I want it *now!*"

Saul knew from years of experience that attempting to dislodge a thought from Livaldi's mind once it had taken root was an exercise in futility. He dipped his head, pivoted on the ball of his foot, and left to make the necessary arrangements. It was a mistake, and Saul knew it from the first, but he would die before he disobeyed one of the young master's orders.

And only one hour ago, news of Radisson's defeat had made it back to Saul's ears, and, evidently, to Livaldi's. Despite himself, Saul was impressed. Radisson had been a frightfully powerful man. If Kyle and his party had defeated him even without Kyle's soul sword, it meant that they were getting stronger—much stronger.

But, if the two remaining men from Radisson's gang were to be believed, Kyle *did* have his soul sword. Was it possible that Lacaster had lied about hitting him with the arrow? Livaldi didn't seem to believe so. He was convinced that Kyle had somehow cheated—broken the rules of the deadly game that the two of them were playing.

Secretly, Saul wondered what Kyle would say if he heard that Livaldi considered all of this to be a game.

Saul brought himself back to the present. James was over at his coffee machine, pulling the finished cup from its golden clutches. He took a sip, stood still for a moment, then suddenly whirled around and flung the cup across the room. Pearls of black liquid flew everywhere; Saul raised an arm to shield himself and felt a few scalding drops hit the palm of his hand. The cup skimmed through the air and shattered against the far wall.

"*Nothing!*" Livaldi shouted. "*Nothing, nothing, nothing!*"

He grabbed the machine and started to shake. Reflections from the golden surface danced across the ceiling and the table underneath the machine rattled.

"*Why won't you tell me where he is!?*" he screamed. "*What's wrong? What changed? How is he hiding from me?*"

When no answer came, he threw the machine down in disgust and turned to Saul.

"Send everyone," he said. "Every salesman, every engineer, every secretary in the whole company! Send them to Ren'r, send them to Ar'ac, to Santrauss and Skralingsgrad! I want every single person on the Maida payroll to be out looking for Kyle! The first one to find him will become rich beyond his wildest dreams, on my name as a Livaldi."

He stormed back to his desk and threw himself down. Suddenly his anger cleared, and a smile broke out on his face.

"The *Wyvern*," he said. "What is our status?"

Saul was completely out of his depth. "Sir?" he said, mostly to bide time while his thoughts unscrambled.

"The *Wyvern*. Have the fools in engineering made any more progress?"

Ah…yes. Saul thought. *An update on the latest firearm.* It was almost, but not quite, a return to normalcy.

"I'm afraid not, sir," he said, folding his hands behind his back. "They are simply unable to provide the weapon with the power and accuracy you requested while keeping it to a manageable size. They suggest—"

Livaldi held up a hand, and Saul clamped his mouth shut at once. A dreamy look had come over the young master's face.

"Send me the latest prototype," he said. He tapped the wood in front of him. "Here, on my desk. I will finish it."

Once again, Saul felt like his world was falling to pieces around him. "But, I thought that Kyle—"

Livaldi waved the words away. "Kyle will take care of himself," he said breezily. "He'll resurface, sooner or later. I'll need to keep myself occupied in the meantime, won't I? If the engineers aren't able to finish the gun, I suppose I'll have to do it myself."

"I…yes, sir. I will have the latest prototype for you within the hour."

"See that you do. Oh, and Saul?"

Saul turned in the doorway. "Yes, sir?"

"Every salesman. Every engineer. Find him. I don't care how you do it."

"Yes, sir."

Saul stepped into the elevator, punched the button for floor zero, and stood stock still as the doors slid shut. His face remained impassive as the elevator began to slide downwards, but on the inside, his mind was roiling.

Enough, he thought. *It's gone too far. I have to put a stop to this, for the young master's sake.*

The very notion of going against Livaldi's wishes was almost enough to make him balk, but then he thought of the bags under the eyes, the tousled hair, and the coffee mug thrown across the room. He thought of Livaldi's insane, haunted face, and redoubled his resolve.

He would find Kyle, yes indeed. And when he did, he would confess everything.

The *SS Caribia* was not the prettiest cruise ship in the world. It only had room for two hundred passengers and its features did not include an indoor rock-climbing wall, but it did manage to sell tickets. It did so for two main reasons: one, because the berths were quite cheap, and two, because not everyone came specifically for luxury.

In Kyle Campbell's case, the *SS Caribia* represented an escape from his problems, which currently included unemployment and sobriety. The solution to at least one of these problems could conveniently be found on the *Caribia* itself, and so it was that during the ship's launch, Kyle could be found on deck, leaning on the rail, armed with a gin and tonic.

He was aware of someone walking up beside him. Through his peripheral vision he could see a young man with ginger hair, a few years younger than him, leaning on the railing of the boat. Although Kyle was trying not to tilt his head in the man's direction, since that could indicate interest, he did notice the circular beard and glint of glasses that just screamed 'student'.

Please don't say hello to me.

"Hey," said ginger beard.

Damn.

There was nothing for it. He turned to face the man that had penetrated his bubble of silence.

"Hey," he replied, trying to inject into that one syllable as much disinterest as possible. The man seemed not to notice.

"What're you in for?" ginger continued, looking concerned. "You look like you're a million miles away."

Something about this jangled against Kyle's mind. A sense of wrongness crept into the scene.

"What?" he said.

"I said, 'are you feeling alright?'"

"Yeah," Kyle said, although this was rapidly becoming untrue. "Why shouldn't I be?"

He turned to look at ginger beard. The young man was staring down at him with a frown on his face.

That's funny, Kyle thought, *I remember you being shorter than me.* Then: *Wait, why do I remember you at all? We've only just met.*

He stood up, peered closely at ginger beard's face, and as he did the man's skin began to fall off in tatters. No, it wasn't falling off—it was peeling away, and so was the deck underneath Kyle's feet and even the sunny sky above him. Kyle's world was reshaping itself piece by piece, a new scene emerging from behind the old. When it was finished, he found himself standing on the deck of the *Markuss,* staring up at Lugh. His friend as frowning and looking at him in concern, just as ginger beard had been.

"What just happened?" he said. "Are you alright? You looked like you were in a trance or something."

Kyle rubbed a knuckle against his brow. "I…I think I was," he said, too distracted to be anything but honest.

Lugh put a hand on his shoulder. "Don't move," he said. "I'll get Meya and Nihs. They'll want to hear about this."

"I'm fine, you don't need to—"

"Kyle?"

"Yeah?"

"Shut up."

It was in fact the whole of Kyle's party that came back with Lugh to the deck. Meya approached him at once and put her hands on his temples. There was a soft light, and Kyle felt his consciousness shift and sway. She drew back a moment later.

"It doesn't seem like there's anything wrong with you now," she said, sounding more frustrated than relieved.

Nihs scurried up onto her shoulder and peered closely at Kyle. "What, exactly, happened?" he asked.

"I'm not really sure," Kyle said, appealing to Lugh.

"We were just standing there, talking," Lugh said. "Then he got this look like he was dreaming. He wouldn't answer me properly when I asked him questions. It was like he was in a different world."

"And you, Kyle?" Nihs said. "What were *you* seeing and hearing when this was going on?"

Kyle looked down, not wanting to talk. For reasons he couldn't explain, he found all this embarrassing.

"I thought I was back on the *Caribia*," he said at last. "The ship I was on when I came here. Lugh was one of the other passengers I'd met."

For a moment, Nihs' face was puzzled and grave. Then he nodded, once, and said, "I think I understand."

"Mind sharing?" Lugh said.

"You told us once that you've been dreaming of your home ever since your fall into Loria."

Kyle nodded.

"Dreams take place when atmospheric magic permeates and influences the mind, causing a kind of hallucination. They reflect our recent thoughts as well as the atmosphere around us, and usually only strike when the mind is vulnerable. Dreams are, in fact, a naturally occurring magical illusion—the difference being, they're not powerful enough to affect us when we're awake."

"Except in my case," Kyle said, allowing a bit of gloom to creep into his voice. He was getting used to being the exception in most things.

"Yes," Nihs said. "Given enough influence—enough magical interference—there's no reason why a dream couldn't overwhelm a conscious mind. Regular atmospheric magic isn't powerful enough to do this, but as we've learned, particles of energy brought over from Terra are anything but regular."

"But there *are* no particles of Terra's atmosphere here," Kyle said. "The only ones that exist are in my soul sword."

Nihs, as he often did when his intellect ran away with him, was looking pleased. "Not quite," he said. Suddenly he extended a hand, palm up. "Give me your phone," he said to Kyle.

Kyle blinked in surprise. "What?"

"Your phone—the one we took from the monster in Buoria. You've been holding on to it, haven't you?"

His tone was slightly accusatory, and for a second Kyle wanted to snap back at him. *Of course I've been holding on to it. Why shouldn't I? For all we know another giant monster could come out of it if I don't.*

But he knew that Nihs meant well, just as he knew that the real reason he still carried his phone was because he wanted to. Poor as it was, it was the only memento he had from home, and even broken and useless, it comforted him.

He reached into a pocket with shaking hands and brought out the charred, twisted piece of metal. It was silly, really—it tore up the pocket of his pants and hurt his hands to grip. He should have been relieved to be rid of it, but it took a tremendous amount of willpower to drop it into Nihs' waiting hand.

"Thank you," Nihs said, his tiny green fingers closing around it.

"You really think that will help?" Rogan rumbled.

"It's worth a try," Nihs said, stashing the phone away. "We *think* that it was robbed of all its power when Kyle stabbed it in the ash plains, but perhaps it still holds a measure of influence. We can't have Kyle dropping into trances at random once we reach Westia, so we have to try whatever we can to stop them."

"What if it starts happening to *you?*" Meya pointed out. "Or whoever is close to it?"

"Then we'll seal it in a box and drop it into the ocean," Nihs said, in a tone of finality.

For some bizarre reason, the very thought made Kyle shiver.

"Nihs is brilliant, in some ways. But this time I think he's missed the mark." Kyle turned. It was Meya. She was watching him with a steady, knowing gaze that was just shy of motherly. Kyle realized that he had no real idea how old she was.

"What do you mean?" he asked.

She drew up beside him, hugging herself across the stomach as she tended to do. "I don't think it's as simple as your phone influencing your thoughts," she said. "I don't think it *could* be."

Kyle could only nod. It hadn't *felt* as though Nihs was right. It was like being able to tell that a diagnosis was wrong even though one wasn't the doctor.

"What do *you* think?" he said.

"It's much simpler than that." She smiled, but it was distant and sad. "Have you ever been homesick?"

Kyle had to think for a moment. He realized with a pang that the answer was both no, and a resounding *yes.*

"I think I've been homesick most of my life," he said finally.

That smile again, like the last blossoming of a flower before winter. "You miss your world...or maybe your world misses you. Either way, you're drawn to each other. It's the same force that makes birds fly around the world searching for the Cross."

Sadness started to tug at Kyle's heart. Every word of it was true—Meya had seen what Nihs could not.

She tilted her head, her mouth drawn and her eyes fixed. "You couldn't stay here, even if you wanted to," she said. "You've known that all along, haven't you?"

Kyle couldn't meet her eyes, but he nodded again. "You're wrong about one thing, though. I *do* want to stay here."

He felt a hand on his back, then Meya leaned in and kissed him on the side of the forehead.

"You poor soul," she said.

As the *Markuss* picked its way southward along the coast of the Ar'ac, the land that passed by on the ship's port bow became progressively stark and dry. The lush greenery that surrounded Reno city became scrubland, which in turn gave way to wind-blasted badlands that stretched as far as the eye could see. Kyle's party soon resorted to staying below decks in order to avoid the boiling sun and hot wind—not to mention the sand which that wind often blew at one's face.

Near the end of the second day, when the heat had abated somewhat and the sun had turned the ocean's surface to molten bronze, the *Markuss* came to an enormous cleft in the Ar'ac's coastline. On the side of the cleft closest to them rose a soaring tower—a lighthouse, Kyle assumed—that for its graceful, organic shape looked as though it had grown out of the desert itself. A pennant decorated with what looked like a blue starburst was hung near its tip, and it snapped lazily in the oceanic breeze.

The cleft must have been several miles wide, for the far side wasn't visible from where Kyle stood. In fact, it was only intuition that told him this was not simply a peninsula jutting out into the sea.

"Is this a river?" Kyle asked Rogan, thinking of his own Earth's Amazon.

Rogan nodded in his ponderous manner. "One of its mouths, in any case. This is the grand canal."

The name wasn't familiar to Kyle. "What's that?" he asked.

"You'll see soon enough," Rogan said mysteriously.

The lighthouse passed by on the *Markuss*' port side, then the tub turned sharply and headed straight into the canal. There was a current pushing against them, but it was gentle, and the *Markuss*' Ephicer engines easily overwhelmed it.

Kyle's eyes were glued to the lighthouse as they passed. It looked like nothing he had seen in Loria so far; it seemed to be made of yellow sandstone, but stood as tall and graceful as any skyscraper he'd seen. There was a winding stone path that led down from the entrance, followed the bank of the canal for a while, then disappeared further inland. Kyle saw no people either in the lighthouse or on the path, but the place gave no feeling of abandonment.

"How far is it to Oasis from here?" Kyle asked, thinking they must be near the end of their trip.

"A day and a half still from here. But at least the scenery will be more interesting."

Rogan wasn't wrong about this. At first the grand canal was so wide that they might as well have been at sea, but soon the far shore came into view, and signs of civilization began to show themselves. There were more lighthouses and outposts on the banks, and soon they were passing by small settlements and even cities. Most everything was built of the same yellow stone, from the streets to the buildings. The occasional bridge that stretched across the narrowest parts of the canal was composed of wood, but otherwise that material was a rarity. The buildings were wide, flat and square, connected by curved archways and shaded by large squares of colorful canvas.

Kyle didn't recognize the architecture of these stone cities—it was different again from the steel and glass buildings of Reno, the black rock and iron of Buoria, and the ramshackle wooden construction of the Kol of Proks.

"Minotaur," was Nihs' explanation. "And redskin Orcs. Not to mention the nomadic human tribes of the south. Of all the races, only the Minotaur were born in the Ar'ac, and in the early years of the world they weren't ones for permanent cities. It wasn't until after the war with Wyvern that the south was truly settled, by a number of folk from different races."

"Redskin Orcs?" Kyle said.

"There are three main tribes of Orcs—grayskin, greenskin, and redskin. The grayskins are the oldest, the first Orcs who were born in Westia. After the meteor fell and Westia became an even harsher place than it already was, a number of Orcs piled themselves onto boats and set sail for the other continents. Those who landed in Ren'r or Eastia became the greenskins. Those who landed in Ar'ac became the redskins."

"So that's why there are so many Orcs in Eastia."

"Yes. It was the easiest trip by boat, but of course after that they had to scale the eastern mountains to reach their promised land in the valleys beyond them. It was there that they came into contact with the Kol. A strange pairing, but we found it mutually beneficial. Before then, practically no Orc could use magic, and practically no Kol knew how to build structures out of wood."

A huge chunk of Loria's history fell into place. "So all of the wooden houses in Proks—the Orcs taught you how to build those."

"Not only that, but a good number of them were constructed using pieces of the very same boats the Orcs had used to cross the ocean."

"Huh!"

True to Nihs' story, many of the folk they saw from the deck of the *Markuss* were either Minotaur, human, or Orcs with skin of a red so deep and muddy that it looked like they had been baked in a clay pit. There were also a number of Selks, the occasional Kol, and some of the catlike Chirpa, of which Kyle had only ever seen a few.

The grand canal itself stretched on interminably, widening and narrowing, bending and curving. Throughout their first day of travel, they encountered over a dozen other fingers of the enormous river's delta. There were also ships, most of them decidedly nicer than the *Markuss*, headed both toward Oasis and back out to the open ocean. The grand canal was mostly natural, but there were parts of it that had obviously been dug out by intelligent hands; the sandier sections of the river were shored up with yellow stone to keep them from eroding.

As they rounded the second day, the river straightened, its current hastened, and the density of ships in the water and buildings on the shore increased. The buildings became whiter and more polished, and the colorful bunting hung for shade and decoration appeared everywhere. Though the river was by no means narrow—it was still wide enough for twenty Markusses to sail abreast—more bridges stretched across it, stone pillars lifting them so high in the air that even the largest ships could pass comfortably beneath them.

By this time, the air was growing dark, and though Kyle wanted to stay awake and watch, his eyelids were becoming heavy. Rogan and Nihs, still easily tired after the fight with Radisson, turned in early, and for once Lugh recommended that the rest of them follow suit.

"We've got a big day tomorrow," he said, looking down the length of the river with his hands on his hips. "Looks like we'll reach the city around noon."

"How long will we stay?" Kyle asked.

"Dunno. All we really need to do is find passage to Westia. We could probably do that tomorrow, if we wanted. Seems a shame…Oasis is quite the city. But we shouldn't sit around longer than we have to."

Lugh didn't say it out loud, but Kyle understood what he had meant.

"I still don't get how Radisson found us," he said in a low voice.

Lugh looked at him sidelong. "You still wearing that necklace the Archmage gave you?"

Kyle nodded, touching at it just to make sure. The silver metal was cool against his neck. "Haven't taken it off once," he said. "Could Rosshku have been wrong?"

"Anything's possible, I suppose, but we could be overthinking things. We were pretty close to Reno city when they found us—maybe they did it the old-fashioned way. If that's the case, we need to be more careful. We barely got out of that last fight with our skins."

At this, Kyle's thoughts turned to Phundasa the Orc. *We were lucky*, he thought.

It could have easily been Lugh, Nihs or Rogan this time.

Yes—the sooner they left Oasis, the better. Yet Kyle wasn't convinced that they would be safe even in Westia. They had placed an ocean between themselves and James Livaldi once before, and it hadn't helped in the slightest.

There came a banging at Kyle's door that seemed, to him at least, loud enough to fill the entire world. In a sense, it did—the tiny, pod-shaped room he had been given aboard the *Markuss* was as soundproof as a metal bucket, and about as comfortable.

Kyle awoke with a cheek pressed against one of Deriahm's metal pauldrons; he must have rolled over while asleep. His arm was bent awkwardly behind him, and the air in the tiny room was stuffy. The banging at the door added to his growing headache.

With difficulty, he rolled over and then upright.

"Yeah?" He said to the door. He blinked, and the motion hurt his eyelids.

"We're nearly to Oasis," came the voice of Raghuz. "Your friends are waiting for you."

By this time, Deriahm was stirring beside him—though being a Buor, he didn't actually do anything as undisciplined as stir. What he did was sit straight up, bending at the waist like a marionette that had been jerked upright.

"All right," Kyle said. "Thanks."

There was no reply; Raghuz had already stomped off.

Kyle extricated himself from the tiny cabin, pulling his bag out with him and dressing in the passageway. Deriahm, for his part, had only removed a few outer pieces of his armor, which he screwed and belted into place as he stepped outside. Kyle wondered how many layers of the stuff Deriahm wore. Maybe Buors were nothing *but* armor, and if you kept peeling it off you'd eventually end up with nothing.

I'm in a funny mood, aren't I? Kyle thought as the two of them made their way to the deck.

They ran into Lugh before they had reached the top of the stairs. He waved good morning and pressed a loaf of spiced bread into Kyle's hands.

"You missed breakfast," he said by way of an explanation.

"Thanks." Kyle tore a strip off the loaf and tossed it in his mouth. It was just bad enough to want to keep eating. "Why didn't you wake us up earlier?"

Lugh shrugged. "Nothing to see then. Besides, you two need your beauty rest. Especially this one." And he clapped Deriahm on the shoulder.

"Indeed, sir," Deriahm said.

Lugh stared at him. Deriahm stared back—then suddenly Lugh burst out laughing.

"I'm sorry," Deriahm said, "have I said something amusing?"

"Yes," Lugh said, "but don't worry about it. Hey, you two, come get a look at this."

He led them to the *Markuss'* bow, where the rest of their party was already gathered. Kyle stopped short, a handful of bread halfway to his mouth.

"Saints," he heard Meya say. "It's *beautiful.*"

Oasis rose from the desert floor like a mirage of the most fanciful sort imaginable. Directly in front of them was the city's harbor, where boats and airships of every color and size were docked. Beyond that, at what must have been the center of the city, was one of the biggest buildings Kyle had ever seen, an ornate dome of glass, stone and golden metal. Around this in every direction rose building after building of white rock, each gleaming brilliantly under the boiling sun. A twin city, where the ships were glued to a watery ceiling and the buildings grew downwards like stalactites, could be seen reflected in the crystal-clear water of the harbor.

And that, Kyle realized, was what made Oasis such a shimmering, magical place, grander even than Reno city. The *water.*

It was everywhere—it gushed from fountains that lined the waterfront, shooting through air in graceful arcs over a hundred feet long. It spilled through doorways and down staircases. It ran in streams down pathways where denizens of the city walked in bare feet. It flowed down the sides of buildings, turning the already polished stone into a shifting, twinkling, cascade of beauty.

Soaring overhead were enormous stone aqueducts that ran as far as the eye could see, carrying Oasis' seemingly endless supply of water elsewhere—possibly, Kyle thought, to the outlying parts of the city.

"*Look* at that!" Meya said. "I've never seen anything like it!"

"You've never been here?" Lugh asked her.

She shook her head, red hair brushing the sides of her neck.

"Where does all the water come from?" Kyle asked.

"Everywhere," Rogan said. "Most of it comes from the main spring—the original Oasis—at the middle of the gardens there," and he pointed at what Kyle had come to think of as the palace in the middle distance. "But there's a thousand other wells all throughout the city, and all of them have run with water for as long as anyone can remember."

"Before you ask," Nihs added, "no one knows how or why. Some speculate that water which falls into Low Ocean somehow seeps through the ground and finds itself here, pushed to the surface by some unknown force. Whatever the explanation, it's thanks to this phenomenon that the Ar'ac has been tamed—to some degree, at least."

The *Markuss* picked its way into the harbor as Kyle continued to watch. Almost everyone in Oasis went barefoot; Kyle wasn't surprised, since it looked impossible to find a spot of dry land anywhere. Square-edged canals were interspersed with roads and bridges; boats and rafts sized perfectly to navigate the narrow streams were poled along lazily by their owners. As Kyle watched, a woman carrying a bundle of groceries used a slow-moving raft as a convenient bridge to cross a canal. The raft's owner took absolutely no notice.

"Remarkable," Deriahm mused. "I reflect that in this city the Buorish capital might find both its mate and its cardinal opposite."

"How so?" Nihs asked him.

"The fate of both cities is tied closely with that of a nearby natural phenomenon; the Heart of Buoria and the Grand Oasis, respectively. The denizens of each city admit aspects of this natural feature into their lives; the people of Buoria heat their houses with lava from the Heart of Buoria, and the people of Oasis walk barefoot in the waters of the spring. In other words, water is to Oasis what fire is to the Buorish capital."

"What an interesting observation," Nihs said. "How refreshing it is to hear some insight for once."

"Thank you, Nihs of the Ken folk."

"All right, you two, that's enough," Lugh said. "All this gushing is going to make me sick, and I don't think the people of Oasis will be too thrilled if I dirty up their nice water."

That, Kyle thought as the *Markuss* docked, was another thing. Not only was the water of Oasis plentiful, it was all sparkling clean.

Desert sand must be one heck of a natural filter, he thought.

Once the *Markuss* was tied up at the pier, they disembarked, and shared an emotional goodbye with Raghuz.

"We'll be heading out, then," Lugh called over his shoulder.

Raghuz, who was watching his men unload, waved a hand vaguely behind him. "Good luck with whatever you're doing," he said.

Lugh saluted, then turned about, and hoisted his bag further up his shoulder. "Right," he said, "what *are* we doing?"

Nihs got the first word in. "Arranging passage to Westia," he said flatly.

"Spending at least one night sleeping in a half decent bed," Meya countered.

"Eating some half-decent food," Rogan rumbled agreement.

"But we mustn't tarry," Deriahm said, "or we invite interception by our enemies."

"*Yes*," Nihs said fiercely. "At least one of us is speaking sense."

"If Livaldi knows we're here, we're already going to be fighting our way out of the city," Kyle said suddenly. "It took us four days to get here—plenty of time for him to send men ahead to wait for us."

Nihs looked surprised, as he always did when one of them brought up a point he hadn't considered.

"You know, I do believe you've got a point," he said. "Either it's far too late to run already, or we're safe provided we keep a low profile."

"Not really possible when your party is a Minotaur, a Selk, a Kol, two humans and a Buor," Rogan pointed out.

"You're not wrong," Nihs said. "In any case, our first step is to book passage to Skralingsgrad. Beyond that, we should either be killing time or holing ourselves up in preparation for our friend Livaldi's next assault—depending on how optimistic you're feeling."

"As long as we're holing ourselves up, can we do it someplace where there's food and dancing girls?" Lugh said.

"*Lugh!*"

"Just the food, then?"

Nihs' errand took them no longer than fifteen minutes; unlike Mjolsport, where any travel options outside of Reno or Oasis were extremely limited, in Oasis there were ships headed to every possible corner of the world. They booked passage on the biggest airship Kyle had seen yet—a gaily painted liner easily large enough for five hundred people—and that was that. It was scheduled to depart on late second sun of the same day, which gave them almost an entire period of light and dark to themselves.

Not to be dissuaded by any threat to his personal safety, or to his wallet, Lugh led them toward the center of the city, as he had so long ago in Reno. Try as he might, Kyle couldn't force himself to be concerned about Livaldi in the face of Oasis' splendor. They walked barefoot down winding streets that ran with cool water, over bridges hung with bunting of every color, and through hidden paths and archways disguised by creeping greenery. A group of children clad in nothing but their underclothes dashed past them, laughing and kicking up rivulets of water as they ran. Fountains shaped like beautiful women hoisted stone jugs over their heads, pouring endless streams of water into public baths the size of Olympic swimming pools—baths that were unerringly filled with women who were every bit as beautiful as the statues.

Kyle got a faceful of hot fur and realized that he had walked straight into Rogan.

"Sorry," he said.

Rogan raised his bushy eyebrows, but said nothing.

They happened across a public garden surrounded on all sides by water and filled to bursting with people of every race, shape and color. They seemed united in nothing but their desire to lounge about in the grass, talking, eating, and playing games. A number of boats had been tethered nearby, and some of them were even selling food off their decks. Kyle and the others, who had no place to go, decided to stay for a while. With difficulty they found an empty patch of land, then left two at a time to find something to eat. Kyle came back with a skewer of spiced meat wrapped in doughy bread, and a freezer—one of the astonishingly cold drinks that he hadn't had since his visit to Reno city over a month ago. He sat cross-legged, trying to eat without getting grease all over himself.

Across from him, Lugh sat back-to-back with Meya. He was scanning the crowd with his one good eye. He watched in detachment as a gang of Orcs picked up one of their fellows and threw him bodily into the canal, to shrieks of laughter from the onlookers.

"I ought to thank you for what you said about Livaldi before," he said to Kyle, his voice grim. "Now I'm watching for assassins everywhere I go."

"That's not a bad idea," Nihs said, but it was obvious that even he didn't believe it. Somehow, they knew that they were in no danger here—at least, not yet.

Still, Kyle found that he didn't want to stay here any longer than they had to. Oasis was stunningly beautiful, but something was already pushing him away from this place. It was the same drive that had haunted him ever since his fall into Loria.

He had to go home. The choice wasn't his to make, nor had it ever been. He might want to stay in Loria for another month or another year, but it didn't matter what he wanted; home was what he *needed*. And they were close, now. He could feel it, and the closer they grew, the stronger the pull became.

He looked up from his food, and was not at all surprised to find himself back on Earth. He was in college, sitting at the edge of the campus soccer field with his classmates. One of his computer science textbooks was open in front of him. He read an entire passage about the model-view-controller pattern before the vision melted and vanished. When he looked up again, he saw Lugh and Meya watching him intently.

"You all right?" Lugh asked him.

Kyle nodded. "Earth again."

That got Nihs' attention. "You had another vision?" he hissed across the circle.

"Yeah."

Nihs looked bitterly disappointed. "You didn't even make it a few days," he said, more to himself than anything. "I suppose it wasn't your phone after all."

"I didn't think it would be," Meya said, brushing her hands together to clear the crumbs of her lunch away. "There's only one cure for what Kyle has."

"And we'll be headed toward it in a few hours," Lugh pointed out. "In the meantime, let's enjoy this place, right? Now how about those dancing girls I've been hearing about?"

Suddenly Meya twisted sideways, leaping to her feet. Lugh wobbled, kicked his legs out for balance, then keeled over backwards, spilling his drink everywhere.

"Oh, I'm sorry," Meya said, not sounding it in the slightest.

Rogan rumbled laughter. "You'd better tread carefully, friend," he said. "The ice you're standing on is all the thinner for this heat."

Lugh, covered in drink and staring up at the sky, flashed a smile. "Just the way I like it," he said.

There were only a few hours left before sunset, but Kyle and the others made good use of them. They walked until they reached the massive glass dome at the center of the city, the mainspring of the oasis after which the city got its name.

The gardens were even more fantastic than Kyle could have imagined. Every surface was covered with lush vegetation, from delicate flowers shaped like fluted glasses to massive vines that reached greedily towards the dome's apex. There were blossoms wider across than Rogan was tall, and, in their own fenced-off area, creeping tendrils that were said to ensnare and mummify any animal that stepped too close.

The sun was setting by the time they left the gardens. Oasis at twilight was a sight to behold. The low-hanging sun reflected off of every jet of water and every smooth-faced building, turning the city into an orange blaze of firelight. The blinding orange turned to cool white as the sun gave way to the moon, and the canals, lit on both sides by Ephicer lights, looked like strings of blue pearls.

They wandered about in the dark for a while, looking for suitable lodgings. There were adventurers' hideouts here, but they had become suspicious of these places ever since the events in Reno and Rhian. They eventually found a small hotel tucked away inside a beautiful garden, and decided to rest there for the night.

Kyle couldn't remember when he had last been so tired. There had been nothing to do aboard the *Markuss* but wait and sleep, but somehow this had drained him of energy rather than replenishing it. He was also looking forward to going to sleep without one of the hard edges of Deriahm's armor pressed into the small of his back.

They gathered in Kyle's room before turning in, as had become their tradition over the past month. The sight of Rogan seating himself on the floor with Nihs perched on his shoulder sent Kyle all the way back to his very first days in Loria, which he had spent exclusively on the *Ayger*. Kyle felt a pang of regret when he thought of Lugh's beautiful golden airship, now long gone. Already that seemed like another life.

"Well," Lugh said, sitting back against the wall, "few hours from now and we'll be on our way to Westia."

"It's been a long journey," Nihs added, "but we're close to the end, now."

Meya shivered. "I'll tell you the truth," she said, "I'm not looking forward to finding out what the impact crater is like. We've got a hard road ahead of us."

You don't have to come. The words formed instantly in Kyle's mind, and he would have spoken them if he thought it would do any good. But he'd begged his companions time and time again not to put themselves in harm's way for his sake, and time and time again his pleas had fallen on deaf ears. He couldn't understand why his friends were so insistent on helping him, but he had at least come to accept it.

Rogan was nodding sagely at Meya's words. "We'll have to get ourselves some winter gear once we've landed in Skralingsgrad," he said. "And some camping supplies."

"What's our plan from there?" Lugh said.

"We'll be able to get transport further inland from Skralingsgrad," Nihs said. "At least as far as the boreal forest. Beyond that, we'll have to start travelling between Orcish settlements. We should be able to hop from camp to camp all the way to lip of the crater."

"And then?"

Nihs tugged his cloak tighter about him. "We'll have to make the final trek on our own. Point ourselves in the direction of Vohrusien's tower and make a break for it across the *adaragad.*"

The word *adaragad* tickled at Kyle's memory, and sent a frisson of fear up his spine. "What's the *adaragad?*" he asked.

Nihs sniffed. "A Kollic word that means 'wasteland', 'desert', or 'blight'. You may be familiar with the form of the word as it pertains to time—*adaragem.* It is our name for the age of the world after the meteor fell and the sun was blotted out. A time of great destruction and desperate survival."

Yes—Kyle remembered that word. Rogan had told him of the *Adaragem* back in Reno city. The age had ended with the defeat of the dread warlord Wyvern, and the re-emergence of the sun.

Meya leaned back. "Rosshku told us that the tower is at the very center of the crater. Even so, it's not going to be easy to find."

"The overhead will help us in this," Nihs said, "as will Deriahm's lodestone. He tapped his chin. "Could that possibly be why Azanhein chose to give it to us?"

"I am afraid that you have given even the Buorish king far too much credit, sir," Deriahm said. "No one could have anticipated that our travels would lead us to such a place."

"Yes, of course."

Lugh stood up and stretched. "Well, I'm tired. Talking about it isn't going to bring that tower any closer. So let's rest up tonight and get to it tomorrow. Right?"

"Bit of a slip-up there, Nihs," Lugh said later as they undressed. "You must be getting old."

Nihs harrumphed. "I can't imagine it makes any difference. Azanhein might as well have told us when we were leaving Buoria, and Deriahm nearly told us again just now."

Rogan, who was killing time before he moved into his own room, knitted his bushy brow and said, "Are you talking about the fact that that Deriahm lad is almost certainly a spy for the Buorish king?"

"Not *almost*. Azanhein gave him a lodestone right in front of us as we left the capital. It was his way of telling us without telling us."

Rogan rubbed his shoulders into the wall, scratching his back. "Is that going to be a problem?"

"It's already saved our lives once," Lugh said.

Rogan's face was grim. "And how better to save our lives again than by stopping us from flying to Westia?"

"If that's what you're worried about, it's far too late already," Nihs said. "The Buors know every move we intend to make from here on out."

Rogan snorted assent.

"You two worry too much," Lugh said, tossing his overshirt on a chair. "If the Buors wanted to keep us grounded, they wouldn't have let us leave the capital. They gave us weapons, a pat on the head, and Deriahm to keep an eye on us. That's all they'll do unless they think we're going to kill ourselves."

Nihs sniffed. "They must have a remarkable amount of faith in us. *I* think we're going to kill ourselves."

Lugh chuckled. "It wouldn't feel right if you didn't." He leaned back, bringing both the tiny Nihs and the massive Rogan into view. "It's been some time since it's been just the three of us, huh?"

"Not all that long," Rogan said. "Hardly been a month since Kyle fell into our lap."

Lugh shook his head. "What a time it's been." He counted on his fingers. "Ar'ac, Ren'r, Eastia, Ar'ac again, and soon Westia. Shame we didn't visit Nimelheim—that would've been all five continents in one."

"Don't speak too soon," Nihs said, "who knows to which corner of the world Vohrusien will send us."

"Hey, one step at a time. Got to the find the bastard first."

Rogan stood, his hooves clacking against the marble floor. "I thought that talking about the tower wasn't going to bring it any closer?"

"Yes!" Lugh said. "Thank you, Rogan, we'd been led astray." And with that, he jumped backwards, arms spread wide, flopping down on his ornate bed.

Rogan barked laughter. "Hah! Sleep well, you two." And putting a massive hand on the frame of their door, he shouldered his way out, his blushing fur collar trailing behind him.

The next day dawned brilliant, dazzling, and boiling hot; stepping out of the hotel was like stepping into a solid wall. Luckily, Oasis had no shortage of shade, and walking in the ankle-deep water that flowed through most of the city made a remarkable difference.

They picked their way through the city, stopping to eat a late breakfast at a cafe that was actually a large raft tethered to a pair of trees planted at the side of the road. As they ate, the proprietor, a lanky redskin Orc wearing a dazzling array of golden jewelry and a bizarre hairdo, jumped ship and began to unmoor his restaurant.

When Lugh gave him a quizzical look, the Orc said, "Heading to centerville, my friend. Feel free to ride along!"

Lugh shrugged, and so it was that they rode most of the way to the city's core, the restaurant owner poling them along with an ease that suggested he had made the trip many times before. He sang as he steered, with as much gusto as Sersi the Lizardman and only marginally more skill. He hailed his fellow raftsmen loudly, once lifting his pole out of the canal and trying to prod a fellow Orc into the water.

The owner's mood was catching, and they were all in good spirits by the time they reached their destination, a large square near Oasis' waterfront. The Orc crammed his raft into one of the few empty spaces, then leapt to dry land so he could fasten his restaurant in place and help them to shore.

They left in search of the liner they had booked the previous day. It wasn't exactly hard to find: brightly colored and the size of a small mansion, it stood out even against the festoon that was Oasis' waterfront. They boarded and found their rooms without incident, then gathered on the terrace—which was the size of a baseball diamond—to watch the ship take off. Ephicer engines fired with the distinct *whum* of magic, and ever so gently, the city of Oasis began to fall away. A cool breeze stirred, sending a sigh of relief though the group.

"Enjoy the heat while you can," Lugh said. "We're headed to the coldest place on earth in the dead of winter."

And enjoy the heat they did, at least for the first day of their flight to Skralingsgrad. They lounged on the terrace or in their rooms, playing siege, mareek-check or just talking, as the liner left the Ar'ac behind and glided out over the western ocean. It was peaceful, but Kyle was restless, even though he knew there was nothing they could do to speed their way.

A few days later, the coast of Westia came into view. It was a rocky, fractured expanse blasted clean by wind and surf. A hundred feet inland from the tideline, scrub began to grow, and several miles beyond that, the first skeletons of enormous needled trees rose into the sky. Far in the distance, they could already see the first of the white-capped peaks that covered most of the continent.

Though it was nearing midsummer in Reno, it was barely spring here on the eastern coast of Westia. The wind that blew down from the mountains was cool, and a few snowflakes brushed against Kyle's cheek as he stood on the liner's terrace. He started wearing his black coat again, and Nihs took to wrapping his red sagecloak tightly about his body.

It was in the afternoon of the fourth day that the party first caught sight of the city of Skralingsgrad. At first, Kyle wasn't sure what he was seeing. The city looked like a massive shipwreck, as if an entire fleet of boats had foundered on the edge of a plateau that overlooked the gray forest below. As they drew closer, rather than being proven wrong, Kyle found that his first impression had been absolutely right: the city was formed from the skeletons of hundreds, thousands, of land-locked wooden ships. Some sat upright; others were tilted back, with their bows jutting into the sky; still others were laying on their sides, entranceways carved into the decks.

Nihs, who was sitting on Kyle's shoulder, noted his look of disbelief.

"'Skralingsgrad' is an Orcish word," he said. "I don't suppose you can guess what it means?"

"'Ship?'"

"Close—'shipyard'. Not all of the ships that the Orcs built during *adaragem* made it across the ocean, and they built quite a few. Those who hadn't launched by the time the sun re-emerged were put towards a new purpose."

Kyle leaned out over the railing of the terrace. "Is there a single normal city in all of Loria?"

"Plenty, but who would be interested in those? Now we'd better get ourselves near the ramp if we want to get off this ship in the next hour."

They joined the crowd of people waiting to disembark as the ship came down smoothly in the city's airdocks, one of the few boroughs where golden tigoreh was in prominence.

The ramp lowered, and they were carried along by the sea of people out into the streets of Skralingsgrad. It was Kyle's first time touching the soil of Westia, though he supposed streets didn't count. He drew a breath of cold air into his lungs and looked about himself. Everywhere he looked, he saw ships; not every building was an entire boat in and of itself, but the city's origins revealed themselves in thousands of tiny ways. A stairway was actually a set of wooden ribs; a roadside stall was a repurposed hull.

Skralingsgrad was an Orcish city, grayskin Orcs making up fully half of the people out on the street. But there were a number of Minotaur here as well, not to mention humans and Selks, who had appeared in almost every city they had visited save for Proks and the Buorish capital.

Lugh put his hands on his hips and heaved a great sigh.

"Hah! Westia! Right, who wants some food?"

Food was found in the form of an Orcish restaurant that served meals only slightly less dense than the wooden tabletop upon which they were served: meat dumplings drenched in fatty gravy and an unknown vegetable of a violently orange color, mashed, pressed into cakes, and then fried. Lugh and Rogan ate ravenously, helping themselves to Nihs and Meya's portions when they failed to finish. Deriahm produced his fussy little *rouk* pipe, and sat smoking demurely as the rest of them tackled their improbable food.

Though lunch was enjoyable, it was clear that the danger and urgency of their mission was sinking in now that the party was in Westia. Lugh paid the restaurant owner and they stepped outside, on to their next task: finding gear that would take them all the way to the *adaragad*.

Though Skralingsgrad was an ancient city—nearly as old as Reno itself—it had been modernized in a number of ways, as had every city that performed regular trade with Centralia. It was the work of half an hour to find an outfitter that sold winter gear so modern, and so expensive, that it might have come from Reno's shopping district. There were coats, boots, gloves, Ephicer-powered furnaces, ice picks, collapsible tents—as well as, to Kyle's surprise, adventurers' weapons that doubled as travelling tools. Kyle had nearly forgotten that adventuring was what the others had done before he had come to Loria: getting contracts, slaying monsters, and then trading in the spoils for toys such as these. It had been some time since they had filled a regular adventurers' contract, and it all seemed so alien to him now.

In the end, they bought out nearly the entire store; Nihs, who normally scorned Lugh's lavish use of money, insisted that they spare no expense in outfitting themselves. No one argued; Kyle knew little about Loria, but from what he had heard, the mountains surrounding the impact crater were among the coldest on the planet, along with the continents of pure ice that sat at its poles.

They bought heavy, hooded coats for each member of their team, including Rogan and Deriahm, even though the former had a thick fur coat of his own and the latter had so far seemed immune to any and all changes in the weather. Pants, gloves, and boots followed, then a pair of sturdy canvas tents and an Ephicer-powered heater for each. Lugh hemmed and hawed over some more serious climbing gear, but in the end, they let it alone.

"Mountaineering isn't really part of the plan," he said. "If we end up climbing the side of a mountain to get to that bloody tower, I think we've already lost our way."

It wasn't quite so cold that they needed to don all of their gear now, so whatever they weren't using was divided between them and slung over their backs. Kyle huffed as he got used to the weight; secretly he wished their stocking up could have waited, but he knew they would need everything they had bought soon enough.

Lugh took a glance at his wallet before stuffing it back into his pocket. "I do believe I'm running out of money," he said.

A knife of guilt immediately wedged into Kyle's chest. "What?" he said.

Lugh winked. "Don't sweat it. Nihs and I have been more broke than this before. We wouldn't be adventurers if we couldn't make something out of nothing."

"I seem to remember a time you were so poor you couldn't afford to repair the *Ayger*," Rogan offered.

Lugh heaved a sigh. "That's dirty fighting, Rogan. I *wish* we still had the *Ayger*. We could fly ourselves right into Vohrusien's lap."

"You know that wouldn't work," Nihs said. "There's a reason ships don't fly over the *adaragad*, and it's not because of bad luck."

Kyle knew what Nihs was talking about; just like Low Ocean, the mysterious patches of empty air that dotted Loria's seas, airships could not fly too close to the meteor's impact site. The magic currents there were too strong, and they caused Ephicer engines to go wild. No, there was only one way to make it to Vohrusien's tower: on foot.

But that didn't mean they had to make the trek across Westia by themselves. They spent the rest of the day looking for transport that would take them further inland, as far northwest as they could go. They had a hard time of it; most people's business with Westia ended at the coast. Travel just a few hundred miles inland, and you'd encounter little more than loggers, miners, and hunters. A few hundred miles more, and you were entering the dominion of the grayskin Orcs, the hardiest and most stubborn tribe of a hardy and stubborn race. The grayskins were those Orcs who had refused to abandon their ancestral home even when the world was shrouded in darkness and plunged into an endless, freezing winter.

As it so happened, they did find a transport that was willing to cart six unknown adventurers halfway across the continent. A logging group that had just returned from the boreal forest to sell a load of lumber was preparing to head back out into the wilderness. Their destination was an outpost that the Orcs of the group called Torrvald, and the others called Timberfall.

The logging transport was an anvil-shaped machine the size of a large house that crawled along the ground with the help of two massive treads. They were walked to the machine by a town Selk who reminded Kyle more than a little of the grease-stained engineer who had organized the *Ayger's* repairs back in Reno. His crew was a motley assortment of tough-looking men: Orcs, Selks, and a couple of Minotaur. At first, Kyle was intimidated, until he realized that *his* party was about as motley as any party could get. Rogan and Lugh, with their fur collar and stone eyepatch, were fearsome. Nihs had his resplendent sagecloak and an aura of fiery power surrounded his tiny being. Deriahm was alien and inscrutable. Even Meya, who was the only woman on the entire transport, garnered respect; everyone could sense, as Kyle had when he had first met her, that she was possibly the most powerful of any of them.

Kyle recalled the time in the small church in a nameless village in Eastia, after he had woken up from Lacaster's arrow wound. Lugh had mentioned, almost in passing, that Meya was not a cleric but a bishop—she had been hiding from the others just how powerful she was. Though it had been gratifying to finally understand why she had intimidated him so when they had first met, he'd otherwise taken the news with indifference. *Normal people don't become adventurers.* It hadn't been long since Lugh had taught him that lesson, but Kyle had already taken it to heart.

Now, as Kyle and Lugh found themselves alone again, lounging in a corner of the huge transport, Lugh told him something else about the companions with which he was sharing his adventure.

"By the way," Lugh said, "I thought you should know—Deriahm is spying on us for the Buors."

"*What?*" Kyle said.

Lugh grinned at Kyle's reaction, his cheek scrunching his good eye nearly shut. "Don't look so surprised. It was bound to happen. No way the Buors were letting you wander around the world without keeping an eye on you."

Kyle tried to fit this into his mental image of Deriahm. He couldn't see it; Deriahm seemed about the least likely spy in the entire world. He said this, and Lugh laughed outright.

"For sure. He's not a spy by profession, he just makes regular reports on us back to the Buorish capital. That's why Azanhein gave him that lodestone."

"But he did that right in front of us."

"Exactly. He wanted us to know. That's how the Buors do business. Like I said, there's no way they'd let you run free knowing what they do. But they didn't want to spy on us without our permission, either, in case we found out and decided to be difficult about it. So, they let him join us and fight for us, in exchange for letting him in on everything we were doing."

Kyle was struck by the simple brilliance of this arrangement—as well as the fact that Lugh had picked up on it so easily. He felt more than a little bitter about how naive he was here in Loria; on Earth, he would have picked up on a scam like that right away.

I keep underestimating these people, he thought. *Somehow, because they're from Loria I haven't been taking them seriously. Well, I'd better start.*

"Anyway," Lugh was saying, "don't think too much about it. Buors might be good at keeping secrets from the rest of the world, but between themselves they're nearly as bad as the Kol. If you said that every Buor in existence was a spy for their king, you wouldn't be too far off. They think it's his right to know everything about everything."

Kyle shivered. The more he learned about the Buors, the more he came to both respect and fear them. Not for the first time, and not for the last, he thought, *I'm glad they're on our side.*

Over the next five days, the transport rolled doggedly across the vast landscape of Westia. The going was slow, and far different from what Kyle was used to from Loria's airships. The roads that led into the heart of the continent varied greatly in quality; some were paved, some beaten, some barely more than twin ruts carved into the countryside by vehicles much the same as theirs.

There was a sense of scale and majesty to this continent that Kyle had yet to see anywhere else in Loria; even the ancient forests and mountains of Eastia couldn't compare to the endless rock-strewn hills and valleys through which they travelled. As the roads wound further and further west, scrubland gave way to the forest proper, and the horizons closed in, shielded by enormous coniferous trees. The ground first twinkled with frost, then became dusted by snow. Finally, as they passed under the canopy of the winter forest, it became buried by a layer of white, the road turning into a muddy brown streak that scarred the otherwise pristine scenery.

Still the transport trundled on, weaving between trees, rolling over fallen logs, climbing zigzagging mountain paths with engines roaring, then gliding down the far sides almost, but not quite, out of control. Twice, progress was halted completely, the first time by an enormous fallen log that was too large even for the transport's spiked treads, and the second by a boggy stretch of road that had absorbed the water from a flooded river nearby. They dealt with the first roadblock easily enough, by chopping the log into segments and rolling it off the road, but the second was misery. Kyle and the others did what they could to help, but for the most part they could only sit and watch as the loggers swarmed about their vehicle, running it forwards, then backwards, shoveling snow and mud out from under it, then shoring it up with wooden planks. They tethered it to a nearby tree and winched it forwards, until the vehicle began to roll sideways, threatening to tip over. They attached grapples to its roof, and Rogan lent his enormous strength to righting the machine again.

By the time they were free of the mire, night had fallen, and they were forced to set up camp by the roadside on the far bank of the river. They lit a fire and sat outside for a while, shivering miserably, then gave up and retreated into the belly of the transport for the night.

That morning, they spent some time scraping the transport's golden hull free of the mud it had gathered during the previous day's adventures. They then set off once more, engine sputtering to life, treads squealing in protest as the vehicle slowly built up its momentum.

They broke free of the forest a few hours later, and found themselves back in the rocky, icy countryside. According to the Selkic logger, who was difficult to understand at the best of times, they were to cut northwest across the plains and re-enter the forest on the far side. Nestled in that stretch of forest was their destination, Timberfall.

Westia, however, was not about to be bested so easily, and had thrown one final roadblock in their path. This became known to them as soon as they passed out from underneath the forest canopy; the driver of the transport, an Orc with ashy skin and long braids of bristly, straw-like hair, uttered a word in Orcish that Kyle nonetheless had no problem understanding, and cut power to the engine. Had the transport been a more responsive vehicle, the jolt might have thrown them off their feet. As it was, they shuddered to a slow halt while the driver embellished his previous statement in a tone that was more surprised than it was angry.

The Selkic logger, swift on his feet, was the first to join the driver at the window. He grabbed hold of an overhead pipe and swung himself forward, his lanky frame silhouetted against the brilliant afternoon sun. Helpfully he provided a translation to what his companion had said.

"Piss in me eyes. It's a herd o' Phundar."

Kyle heard *herd of thunder*, and as he approached the front window along with the others, he realized he hadn't been completely wrong. The earth was trembling, and there was a low rumbling, much like thunder, that came to his ears and stomach.

He peered outside and at first saw nothing but the vast valley ahead of them. It was dotted with shiny black boulders, each the size of their transport, strewn across the ground like a forgotten game of marbles. But as he watched, he realized that the boulders were moving—trundling across the plain on short, stout legs, in a way that was bizarrely similar to the way their own vehicle moved.

"Phundar," Meya said. "I've heard that name. They're a kind of monster."

The Selk sniffled in disgust. "Yar, and they'll squish us flat soon's they catch sight of us. Damn! We'll 'ave to take the forest road. That's a whole day we lose."

Deriahm shouldered his way to the front. "Pardon me, sir," he said, "but are Phundar not meant to be rather passive beasts?"

"Not to us they won't be. Somethin' this size'll draw their attention in no time. They'll charge us fer sure."

Deriahm coughed politely. "Perhaps not," he said. "What if they were to perceive us as one of their own?"

The Selk's mouth hung open. The Orcish driver twisted in his seat.

"*Rodr?*" he said.

"What are you on about?" the Selk translated.

"I possess a moderate amount of skill in the school of mysticism," Deriahm said. "I believe I should be able to cast a glamour about this transport that will fool the Phundar into seeing one of their own kind when they behold it."

The mouth stayed open, and above it the brows knitted themselves into a knot. "You've got to be kidding," the Selk said.

By this time, most of the logging crew had gathered about. Their faces had tightened at Deriahm's proposal, and now they rumbled agreement with their Selkic companion.

"Get us killed, a stunt like that."

"I thought Buors couldn't use magic."

"Damn adventurers, have to do everything the hard way."

Deriahm dipped his head meekly. "It was only a suggestion, good sirs," he said. "This is your excursion, and I merely thought to divulge a manner in which we might save some time."

The word *time* made a noticeable effect on the loggers. Kyle could see each of them weighing the risk against the time and money they stood to save.

"I think we should do it," Meya said. "Deriahm wouldn't have suggested it if he didn't think he was capable."

There came a series of metallic *clangs* as Rogan strode forward, using Ravigan's double-bladed axe as a walking stick. "And if any Phundar charge at us," he said, thudding the butt of the axe into the ground, "I *personally* guarantee that I'll meet them head-on."

Few could be as persuasive as Rogan when the mood struck him; there was some grumbling, but eventually the crew agreed to try Deriahm's idea. He dipped his head and said, "Thank you, sirs. You will not regret it. Only one thing: I believe some of our time would be well spent by recoating the transport in mud."

"*What?*" The Selk said.

"It will render the illusion easier to complete, as the brown will be closer to the Phundar's black, and will disguise our scent."

There was some more grumbling from the crew, and a few dirty looks and uttered oaths, but loggers and adventurers alike stepped outside to follow Deriahm's instructions.

It was the work of fifteen minutes to get the transport even more covered than it had been that morning; though the ground had frozen in many places, there were a number of ponds and underground springs in the area to provide more mud than they knew what to do with. Kyle found the act of flinging shovelfuls of mud at the transport's sides and watching them strike home with wet *sploshes* oddly satisfying.

Once the transport was coated to Deriahm's satisfaction, he instructed them all on board and then took up a position in the middle of the cabin. He stood stock-still, fingers twisted before his chest. Gentle magic began to whisper forth from his frame, and the space between his hands glowed purple. Kyle watched— and felt—an immaterial bubble expand outwards, engulfing first Deriahm, then the crew, then the entire transport. When Kyle next looked out of the front window, the view was wavering slightly, as if the glass had become slightly warped.

"It should now be safe to proceed across the valley, good sirs," Deriahm said. "Miss Ilduetyr, sage Nihs of the Ken folk, I may require your assistance should my magic reserves prove insufficient."

"Of course," Meya said, stepping to his side with Nihs on her shoulder.

"Saints," the Selk said. "All right, Rundoll, let's go."

The Orcish driver blustered for a moment, then kicked the transport into gear. There was a slight jolt, and the vehicle started to move.

The atmosphere was tense as they broke free of the forest's cover and made their break across the valley. Kyle spent the first hour watching the distant Phundar, trying to figure out what manner of beasts they were. He couldn't decide if they were more like shaggy oxen, or massive black beetles; their legs were stout and covered in hair, but their round, glossy coats had an oily sheen that looked like no fur Kyle had ever seen. More than anything, they reminded him of horseshoe crabs, those prehistoric creatures from Terra who did nothing but scoot around the ocean floor looking for food. They certainly didn't seem threatening, and they took absolutely no interest in the imposter that had entered their herd.

They made it a third of the way across the valley in such a manner, passing the Phundar on the left and on the right, but drawing no attention. Still Deriahm stood in the middle of the room, weaving his magic, visored face inscrutable. If holding the illusion was causing him strain, he kept it well hidden. Meya stood at his right, arm linked in his, supporting him with her own vast reserves of magic.

Something changed as they were halfway to their destination. One of the Phundar, which had been grazing off to their right, caught sight of the transport and turned to face it. Or at least, Kyle thought it did; it was incredibly hard to tell which was the front end of a Phundar. The end that was facing them was round and ridged, like a wrinkled forehead. It was definitely some kind of shell, and had a black, leathery sheen. Though it was impossible to see the creature's eyes, or indeed its head, Kyle could tell that they were being watched. The monster's legs—were there four or six?—were kicking up clods of earth as they shuffled themselves around, keeping the frowning forehead pointed at them.

"I don't like the look o' that one," the Selk said quietly, eyes glued on the Phundar. Rundoll grunted his agreement, and sped the pace of the transport slightly. Deriahm tottered in surprise, kicking a leg out for balance. For a moment, Kyle saw the watery barrier around the transport flicker and waver.

The Phundar stepped back in surprise. A deep huffing noise began to come from under its shell, and Kyle saw blades of grass being flattened by its breath.

"Saints, man!" Rogan growled, as Meya helped to steady Deriahm. "Be careful!"

Rundoll glowered and said something under his breath, but didn't touch the controls any further. His Selkic friend was now gripping the back of his seat, lanky frame twisted so he could keep an eye on the monster. It was still huffing, stepping forward then back, caught in indecision.

It watched them for a while longer, well beyond the point that it had fallen out of view of the front window. It wasn't until ten minutes later that one of the crew, who had been watching it from the back room, came to tell them that it had finally ambled off. There was a collective sigh of relief. Now Kyle understood why the loggers had wanted to avoid the herd altogether; the creature had seemed a lot less silly up close.

Another twenty minutes or so passed without incident. Deriahm had started to dip his head as if falling asleep, but had assured them that he had energy enough to keep up the illusion for a while longer. They were just starting to relax again following the last encounter when suddenly the Selk pointed off to their left and said,

"Watch that one, he…shit! *Shit! Look out!*"

A massive crash shook the transport; Kyle fell to one side and landed heavily on a pipe that ran across the wall. Deriahm staggered and landed on one knee. Instantly the illusion that had shrouded the transport fell to pieces, falling in tatters of luminescent magic all around them. Rundoll swore sulfurously in Orcish and heaved on the wheel, trying to keep the transport from tipping over. The room was filled with the sounds of men shouting over one another.

Rogan roared in anger and leapt to the steel door that led outside.

"I'll handle this," he shouted into the cockpit. "Don't speed away! Deriahm needs to get his illusion back up and it won't work if we move too fast."

"I need to go with you," Meya said. "Nihs, help Deriahm."

Nihs leapt from one shoulder to the other, claws kicking up sparks as he scrambled for purchase against Deriahm's armor.

"Is there anything we can do?" Kyle said. A moment later, the Phundar rammed into the transport again, and he nearly lost his feet.

"Afraid not," Lugh said. "We'd just be in the way. Let Rogan do his thing."

It is now time for us to fulfill our promise to you. Lugh had a different way of saying it, but his words reminded Kyle of what Deriahm had told him back in Mjolsport, when the party had been gearing up to fight Radisson.

"At least let me help keep Deriahm upright," he said.

Nihs nodded. "Not a bad idea. Now be careful, you two," he added to Rogan and Meya. "It wouldn't do for you to get trampled this far into our adventure."

R ogan's hooves thudded against the ground as he leapt from the door of the transport, leaving twin impressions in the soft earth. Beside him, Meya had a much lighter landing. He was wielding the double-bladed axe of his father, and she the staff of Buorish obsidian given to her by King Azanhein. Though her magic would be of little help in warding off the Phundar, she did have one skill that was absolutely indispensable: the ability to pull Rogan's mind back from the dark place into which it wandered when he went berserk.

Although, to say true, it wasn't so much a wandering as it was a possession. Rogan could feel Gershel's soul inside him now, pacing back and forth, gnawing at the shackles that held him in place. His fur collar felt fiery hot about his neck.

I'll have need of you soon, he said in the recesses of his mind. He looked down at Meya, the tiny human with the thin frame and white dress. *And you as well.*

"Ready?" he said.

She nodded. "Are you really going to kill it?"

"I may not need to. But I'll need at least some shred of my wits about me if my plan's to work. Can you grant me that?"

Meya nodded again. "Count on it."

By this time, the transport had pulled ahead, and they had full view of the Phundar that was harassing it. It was a large bull with a heavily mottled brow, huffing and snorting its aggression. It was recovering from its latest charge, backing up and building distance from the transport. Rogan didn't give it the time. He rushed forward, coming between the creature and the vehicle. His collar was burning about his neck. He breathed heavily, letting the heat spread. He pounded one hoof against the ground and raised the axe above his head, willing his heart to beat faster and faster.

"Come!" he shouted at the huge beast in front of him. "Come, face me!"

The Phundar reared and pitched, surprised. But one target was much like another for such a stupid creature, and this one was already conveniently placed directly in front. It took a few more steps back, gauging the distance, then charged, all six legs treading furiously.

Rogan met the charge head-on. Though he was a fraction of the monster's weight, he had metamagic on his side, not to mention a dash of cunning. He shot one leg back and lowered his stance, vented his combat energy, and caught the lip of the Phundar's shell on his axe. The impact pushed him back in the mud and jarred him to the bone, but he held firm, and began to heave upwards mightily. It wasn't nearly enough; the creature bucked, and after a moment broke free. It thrust forward, knocking Rogan back with the weight of its body alone, then stepped backwards, preparing for another lunge.

Gershel had already taken control of Rogan's throat, and was using it to growl low under his breath. Rogan felt a bitter satisfaction. *If you would take charge of me, do it now. Now! Now!*

His head shook, and his eyeballs rolled in their sockets. The fur collar grew down his back and up his neck, until his entire body was wreathed in red. His vision swam, though while the earth became nothing but a dull smear, the body of the Phundar—the *ENEMY*—became a bright orange beacon in his mind's eye.

For a moment, Rogan was entirely gone; his world had been lost to darkness and boiling, raging heat. But then the faintest breeze teased his ear, a slash of blue in a sea of black and red.

Be careful, Rogan, the voice of Meya whispered. *Remember your plan.*

At first, Rogan didn't understand; his mind struggled to comprehend the words of sane folk. But then the voice came again, and his head cleared just enough to grasp hold of the idea like a drowning man to a riverbank.

The plan. Yes. He faced the Phundar, the blazing orange sun that consumed his world. *Let us finish this, then, and quickly.*

Meya stood firm, staff planted in the ground, the area between its two prongs glowing white. Eyes half-shut, she forced calmness upon herself as she watched Rogan face down the huge monster. If she let her anxiety show through, she and Rogan would feed off of each other's emotion, and her tenuous grip his mind would be lost. He was as close to fully berserk as could be, a state which Meya didn't care for in the least—but he would need every ounce of strength he could muster if his plan were to work.

The Phundar charged again, and for a moment Meya was afraid that Rogan had forgotten what he'd meant to do; but he crouched down, axe held low, and caught its shell with the blade as he had done before. Muscles bulging, skin foaming, he began to hoist upwards. The Phundar bellowed and bucked, but Rogan matched its movements, pulling upwards all the while. Soon Meya could see its furry underbelly, and the two front legs pinwheeling in the empty air.

Amazing, she thought. *Who knew that even Rogan was that strong?*

Huffing and bellowing himself, Rogan began to step to the right, axe skating against the lip of the Phundar's shell. It was too long to tip over along its length, but if he could push at one of its narrower sides, he could flip the entire thing over. His whole body was trembling, and the veins in his neck were threatening to pop, but he held firm. Soon it was the three legs on the Phundar's left side that were kicking at the air, and the creature was trumpeting in distress.

Rogan had risen to his full height, arms stretched above him, but even this wasn't enough to tip the animal over. In an incredible feat of strength, he threw the monster off his axe, stepped forward, and regained his purchase inside the shell. The Phundar held for a moment, then its right legs buckled, and the far edge of its shell came down in the mud. Rogan stepped forward again, then again, and finally, the creature toppled over with a ponderous crash.

Phundar were some of the mightiest creatures in the land, but they were not built for being thrown onto their backs. The beast thrashed to and fro, and its tail slammed against the ground, but try as it might it couldn't right itself. Meya felt pity for the creature, but knew that it would succeed in turning itself over eventually. By that time, their party would be long gone.

Now there was just one more thing that needed taking care of.

Rogan was bellowing his victory at the sky, but as Meya watched, he lowered his head again and pawed at the ground, framing the vulnerable Phundar between his curved horns. Meya ran forward and placed herself between Rogan and the Phundar. The tip of her staff glowed brilliantly, and when she held it out in front of her, Rogan's eyes followed it as if hypnotized.

"Come, Rogan," she said softly. "Come back to us. We don't need Gershel anymore...we need you."

She wove her staff in a slow cross (that Kyle would have called a *figure-eight*), and Rogan followed sleepily. His breathing slowed, and his muscles grew lax. His eyelids fluttered shut, and when they next opened, it was a different creature that looked out from underneath them.

Rogan heaved a breath that was equal parts sigh and groan; now that he was back to himself, his body was collecting on the debt of pain it was owed.

Meya herself sighed in relief and put a hand on his shoulder. "You did wonderfully, Rogan," she said, "but we need to get out of here before another one of those things comes after us."

Rogan, panting heavily, hefted his axe onto one shoulder and held out his free hand, palm upwards. Meya jumped lightly onto his forearm and wrapped one of her own arms about his neck. Rogan stood and turned. Off in the distance, a

Phundar that looked almost, but not quite like the others, was moving away from them at some speed.

"Not a bad illusion," Rogan said. "Little Deriahm is full of surprises."

"That he is," Meya agreed.

Rogan huffed. "Hold on."

She felt his muscles bunch beneath her, and grabbed an extra handful of fur as he galloped after the roving transport.

The reception back in the transport was as Rogan expected, equal parts hero's welcome and angry resentment. After all, though Rogan had been the one to save the crew from the Phundar's attack, Deriahm had been the one to put them in danger in the first place. Rogan didn't much care; soon, the two parties would be taking leave of one another, and he was exhausted besides. He collapsed gratefully against the wall as soon as he was inside. Meya jumped down from his arm, and put her hands against his chest.

"You're more tired than hurt," she said, "so there's not much I can do to help you. But I can at least keep your muscles from seizing up."

Rogan grunted understanding. Legs, arms, chest and neck—all ached horribly, and without Meya's help he'd be next best thing to paralyzed by tomorrow morning. He sighed in relief as her magic burrowed into him and detangled his knit muscles.

Lugh sat down next to Rogan and winked at Meya. Funny how the man could wink with only one eye.

"Wouldn't be an adventure if there weren't monsters to fight along the way, huh? Phundar…That's one thing we never had to deal with in Centralia."

Meya smiled, but it flickered out as quickly as it had appeared. In an instant, a familiar, aching sadness had stolen over her, climbing up her arms and legs from the fingers and toes as if she'd just dipped them into cold water. At first, even she wasn't sure why. Then a snatch of conversation came to her—one she'd held with Lugh only a halfmonth ago.

It's like a 'b', 'p', and an 's' all together. It's supposed to imitate the sound of a drum beat. Phun-dar.

Fun-*dar.*

Close. Bfun-dar.

Phun-*dasa.*

That's it.

Meya felt tears welling up in her eyes. She stared into the soothing light of her own healing magic, willing it to burn them away, but they came and came and before she knew it they had spilled out over her eyelids and onto her cheeks. Vision blurring, she pulled her hands back and hugged herself across the stomach. She felt Lugh put his hands on her shoulders, then pull her into his arms, as someone else had once done.

Timberfall was more of an outpost than a village, a cluster of buildings nestled at the foot of one of Westia's many mountains. There couldn't have been more than a hundred people living there when the logging transport rolled up and Kyle's party stepped out.

Their goodbyes with the logging crew were as brief if not briefer than those they had shared with Raghuz, the young captain of the *Markuss*. Though Deriahm's plan had saved them a day of travel, it had also given them a large dent in the side of their vehicle to contend with, and it was all too obvious that they considered themselves well rid of Kyle and his band of adventurers.

Deriahm did not take their dislike well. There was a visible sag to his shoulders as he watched them gather their belongings from the belly of the transport and step into the town's single watering hole.

Lugh drew up beside him and laid an arm around his shoulders with a metallic *whang*.

"Chin up, friend," he said. "We got to Timberfall, and that's what matters."

Rogan grunted. "This place barely exists. Will we be able to find all the supplies we need?"

"We'll have to make do," Nihs said. "I, for one, am more concerned about where we go from here. All we know is to head northwest."

"The entirety of Westia is dotted with Orcish settlements," Deriahm said. "If we are to locate one, we should be able to receive directions to the next, and so on. In this manner we should be able to travel all the way to the *adaragad*."

"That's a lot of 'shoulds'," Nihs said.

Lugh reached back and flicked him on the nose. "And that's enough from you. Let's not give up before we've started, all right? Now, first things first."

Meya smiled, with some effort it seemed. "Food?" she said.

Lugh winked at her.

Timberfall was graced with a single tavern that served as a poor watering hole and an even poorer restaurant. The cramped space was full to bursting, thanks mostly to the logging crew with which Kyle and the others had just parted ways. Kyle caught a glimpse of Rundoll the Orc and his Selkic friend before they turned their backs on the party and huddled closer to their food. He caught Lugh's eye, who rolled it before accosting the proprietor.

After one of the more bland and forgettable meals Kyle had ever eaten, they walked two doors down and stepped into Timberfall's general store, which, like the tavern, was the only one of its kind to be found. Here they would be stocking up on whatever supplies they hadn't purchased in Skralingsgrad, which mostly meant food. It was just as well that they had carried as much as they could with them: everything was exorbitantly expensive.

Now that it was loaded down with food, Kyle's pack was heavier than ever. Still, it was nothing to the massive pack that Rogan wore. Though it seemed now that they had enough food to hike across Westia five times over, Kyle knew that they would be needing every last scrap before their journey was over.

Lugh hefted his own pack, which in size was an appreciable fraction of Rogan's. "Great," he said. "Now what?"

"We need information," Nihs said. "Directions to the nearest Orcish settlement, or better yet, a ride there. I don't care much for the idea of wearing ourselves to the bone before absolutely necessary."

Deriahm cleared his throat politely. "I may be of some assistance in this," he said. "Good sage Nihs of the Ken folk—may it be possible for you to enter the overhead and determine if any of your kinsmen live in the settlements nearby? And, if so, whether they know of any sons or daughters of Buoria who also live close by?"

"What's this?" Lugh said. "You're going to call in some help?"

"I believe that one of King Azanhein's gifts may be put to good use, yes."

"I'll ask," Nihs said, "but I doubt there are many Buors to be found in this part of the world."

"You may be surprised, sir. Indeed, I hope that you are."

They found a secluded part of town (a rather easy feat) and kept watch over Nihs as he brushed a small plot of land free from the snow and settled down, legs crossed. Deriahm spoke to him in a low voice as his ears unraveled and his eyelids drooped; he nodded sleepily and then fell into the overhead. They watched him for a while, body swaying slightly, ears undulating as if caught in an ocean current. Then he resurfaced, and the expression on his face was triumphant.

"I'm astonished," he said. He stood and brushed the snow off his sleeves. "You'd better watch this one, Lugh," he added, nodding at Deriahm. "He has a way of getting things done. I'm considering making him my new partner in crime."

"Well!" Rogan said. "What is it?"

Nihs sniffed. "There's a Buorish researcher living in an outpost some miles from here. He owns a drifter—and within seconds of hearing about us he jumped into it and sped off. He should arrive here tomorrow, and he's willing to take us farther north."

Kyle felt like cheering, but he also remembered what Lugh had told him about Deriahm just a few days before. *I bet the Buors would move heaven and earth to make sure this quest was a success*, he thought. *And they probably could.*

As if reading his mind, Deriahm tapped at a metal cheek and said, "There was a slight factor of bribery to my kinsman's agreement to help. Being so far removed from Buoria, he knows not of you, Kyle, nor of our plight. But, I made an offer of the king's *rouk* to him, and this opened his eyes to our legitimacy and our need."

The king's *rouk* was one of the many gifts that had been given to them by King Azanhein of Buoria. It was a single small *rouk* cake stamped with King Azanhein's seal—nothing special in and of itself, but the very fact that it had been bequeathed to them by the Buorish king made it extremely valuable.

"That's great!" Lugh said. "Buors will do anything for a loaf of bread, eh?"

"Of course, sir."

Having little choice in the matter, they spent the night in Timberfall. They slept in the loft of the tavern, along with a dozen other people who had nowhere else to go. There were no private rooms, and the loft was freezing cold.

"Look on the bright side," Lugh said as he stretched out, "it'll be good practice for when we're up north."

Kyle slept fitfully. Every time he dozed off, a draft would inevitably find its way to an exposed ankle or wrist, and the snap of cold would jerk him awake. He took to looking around the loft, eyes half-closed and vision foggy. Occasionally, the dim shapes that were their fellow travelers shifted or rolled over in the gloom. A single tigoreh light left on downstairs was casting dramatic shadows onto the ceiling. The wind was blowing outside; Kyle had it to thank for the tendrils of cold that stroked at his cheek.

He curled up more tightly, bunching his knees to his chest, turning his bedroll into a pocket of warmth. His angle of vision shifted; now he was looking back at his companions. He saw the nest that Nihs had constructed out of blankets and pillows, and behind him the looming bulk of Rogan. The edges of Deriahm's armor gleamed in the gloom.

Kyle tilted his neck further. Two figures were sitting apart from the others—and they were sitting, side-by-side, backs propped up against the freezing wall, the head of one resting on the shoulder of the other.

Kyle allowed himself to smirk and rolled over. Then, mind turning to thoughts of someone he himself had left back in Terra, he fell asleep.

Meya was tired. She felt it in every component of her being—mind, body, soul. Her head throbbed. There was a pain in the small of her back. It hurt to turn her eyes in her sockets. She had become so tired, in fact, that her body had ceased to recognize her fatigue for what it was, and her eyes remained firmly open though she wanted to squeeze them shut.

She'd been sleeping poorly ever since the party arrived in Westia. At first, she'd thought it was the accommodations—the logging transport and the makeshift camps they'd put up along the way had been rude and often cold, much like this loft. But now she knew that the fatigue had come from her mind, or perhaps her soul, and found its way to her body, rather than the other way round.

Everything here reminds me of him, she thought. *The mountains, the cold weather, all of the Orcish names.*

For much of the last halfmonth, she had been too busy to grieve; from bishop Abel's church to Proks, then to their meeting with Archmage Rosshku, then to the plains of Ar'ac and the city of Oasis. But the last few days had been nothing but travel, and as they had drawn close to Westia, she had found her mood deteriorating along with the weather. And now she knew why.

Senseless, she thought. It was strange, but that was what bothered her the most about Phundasa's death: the cruel, pointless stupidity of it all. He had survived so much, *they* had survived so much, only for him to be killed by a stray bolt that had been intended for someone else. That such a radiant life would be snuffed out by such an idiotic event made her question the sanity of the world.

She didn't blame Kyle, not in the least. She could hardly bring herself to blame Lacaster, the assassin who had drawn the bow. He and his brother had been lost, tortured souls, hounds let loose by a careless master.

But she could blame the master, and indeed she did. She had promised to follow this quest through to the end. This was partly out of curiosity, largely out of love for Kyle and his companions. But it was also because of the chance, however slight, that their mission would eventually bring them face to face with James Livaldi. And when that happened…

It was no use; she wouldn't be sleeping tonight. She put her palms against the cold wooden floor and lifted herself up, the covers running off her slim frame. She sat there in the darkness for a moment, wondering what to do. Then she heard someone behind her speak in a low voice.

"Can't sleep either, huh?"

She twisted around, and saw Lugh sitting propped up against the back wall of the loft. His stone eyepatch was glinting in the dim light, and his grinning mouth was an arc of white below.

He's always smiling, Meya thought. *How does he do it?*

On an impulse, she stood and stepped carefully over to where Lugh was sitting. He looked surprised, but shifted to make room in the cramped space. She sat down next to him and leaned back. An instant later she gasped and pitched forward; the wall was like an icy palm pressed against her back.

Lugh chuckled silently. "You get used to it after a minute or two."

She sat back again, slowly, but the cold still stung. There was something satisfying about it, however. It felt alive, as if her entire soul was in that moment compressed into the icy plate between her shoulderblades. She sighed, and her own breath made her shiver as it ran over her knees. She looked over at Lugh, whose own knees were propping up his arms. He was still wearing a smile, but his teeth had disappeared. Now one cheek was bunched tighter than the other, giving him a lopsided grin that was equal parts weary and mischievous.

"Not the place I would've chosen to kick off the grand adventure," Lugh said. "But life would be boring if we always got what we wanted, huh?"

Meya smiled. "That's true."

Lugh tapped at his eyepatch with a dull *thud*. "Though come to think of it, I suppose the grand adventure started when Nihs and I found *that* one lying in a crater in the Ar'ac. Who would've known we'd wind up here at the end of it all?"

"It's a good thing you were the ones to find him," Meya said. "Who knows what would have happened if it had been someone like Livaldi?"

Lugh nodded, rocking back and forth on his tailbone. For a moment they sat in silence, then Lugh said, "You know, I think I'm going to miss the guy when he goes back home. He needs to learn to take it easy, but I think he could've made a good fourth member of our party."

"Fourth?" Meya repeated, injecting a note of mockery into her voice.

Lugh cocked an eyebrow. "You weren't thinking of joining our merry band after this was all over, were you?"

Meya was going to tease him some more, but found that she didn't have the energy. She sighed, giving herself another shiver.

"I have no idea what I'll do after this is all over," she said. She realized too late that she was hugging herself again. It was a childish habit that went all the way back to her earliest days at the church, but she'd never managed to rid herself of it.

Lugh had been watching her. Now, he pulled the blankets of his bed free, and wrapped them around his shoulders like a cloak. When Meya looked over to see what he was doing, he reached out one arm and met her eyes without saying anything. Meya realized with a jolt that Lugh's smile was as unreadable as Deriahm's visor; he wore it so often that you couldn't tell which emotions came along with it.

She realized a moment later that she couldn't care less. She shifted closer, and Lugh put his arm around her. Instantly she felt warmer, and the cold plate pressing into her back was gone. She sighed, and let some of the tension flow out of her body. She looked back up at Lugh. He was still smiling.

"You really believe it, don't you?" she said.

"Eh?" Lugh said.

She reached up to brush hair away from her face. "You said 'when he goes back home'. You really think that we're going to find a way."

"Of course! Don't you?"

His tone was so surprised—so *disbelieving*—that she looked at him again, searching his face for a sign of insincerity. She found none.

His question was hanging in the air, and she found she couldn't answer it. *Das is dead. You nearly died, and Kyle, too. We're going to the most dangerous place on earth. How can you not be afraid?*

But he wasn't. He really wasn't. She searched and searched, and there was nothing but confidence, and warmth, and that smile that never wavered.

Her silence must have been answer enough, because Lugh blew air out the side of his mouth and sat back. "Nihs must have given me that look a thousand times since we started travelling together," he said, in long-suffering tones.

"Sorry," Meya said. "It's just…"

Lugh smiled his lopsided smile and shook his head to show that he knew what was coming. "Listen," he said, "I know that not everyone thinks the way I do. People don't get how I can always see things turning out right. But the truth is, *I* don't get how other people can go through their lives thinking that everything's going to come out wrong. My brother always told me that if you want to get something done, you have to set your mind on it. So if your mind's set on everything going badly, how do you ever move forward?

"I've seen the kinds of things that people can do if they give it their all. Taken apart, we're strong—put us together, and we're even stronger. We fill each other's gaps—watch each other's backs. We all have the same goal, and we all have each other. Ninety-nine out of one hundred times, that's enough."

He glanced over and caught her expression. He added, "Now that's a look I don't often get. What's that one mean?"

Meya was smiling despite herself. "I was just thinking that you could teach most clerics I know something about faith."

Lugh winked. "I'll take that as a compliment."

Silence descended, and Meya's thoughts wandered. She remembered something that her old mentor, Meya the Kol (whose name she had later stolen) had once told her. The Kol believed that there was a word for everything. Their alphabet might have consisted of a finite forty runes, but their language was endlessly complex and endlessly evolving. They had a word for a sense of loneliness felt in the middle of a crowd; a word for the invigorating cold that accompanied early morning; a word for trying to read the thoughts of another by looking into their eyes.

To a Kol, naming and existence were one and the same. An *it* could not exist until it was named; and if it had a name, it had to exist.

Upon hearing of this theory, the other races had expanded upon it, and the concept of the true name had emerged. Everything and everyone had a true name, or so the theory went. A magical name, the aural equivalent of the unique soul. To learn the true name of a being was to gain complete control over it.

The theory, however popular, had never been proven, and the Kol, with their typical disdain for anything that originated outside of their caves, had dismissed it. Meya did not know whether or not she believed in it. Certainly, she'd never heard of anyone using a name to control someone else. But every so often she found herself thinking about names: if she were to distill *this* or *that* down to its very essence, which word would it become?

Now, she pictured Lugh, with his warm arms and confident smile, and thought, with a touch of sadness,

'Friend'. That's you. You're a friend to everyone, and you convert everyone into friends of yours. That's why you smile at everything the same—you like any one person just as much as any other.

"Hey," Lugh said.

Meya turned her face up. She felt Lugh's nose brush against her own, and then lips—soft and incredibly warm—pressed against hers. Her sadness disappeared in a moment of giddy realization, and was replaced by something else entirely. Her first thought as she returned the kiss was,

Well—perhaps not quite *as much.*

Astevyr of Buoria was a scientist who lived his life among the Orcs of Westia, hopping from settlement to settlement as his research demanded. He was also the most bizarre and eccentric member of his race that Kyle had ever met.

Prior to making his acquaintance, Kyle never would have imagined that the word 'lanky' could apply to one of Deriahm's countrymen. But Astevyr of Buoria was exactly that; nearly six and a half feet tall, thin as a rail, and possessed of an energetic, animated jerkiness that made him look like a life-sized marionette. His sash was five separate strips of yellow cloth tied around each of his knees, elbows, and waist. The shocks of color that bisected his limbs only added to their elongated appearance.

He arrived in Timberfall early in the day, two hours following sunrise. Kyle and the others had been trying to eke out a few last minutes of rest when they heard raised voices and the loud hum of an Ephicer engine coming from outside. Lugh twitched aside the curtain covering the loft's only window, just in time to see a tigoreh vehicle come shooting down the path toward the outpost at an incredible turn of speed. It was flat and golden, its shape reminding Kyle of a stingray with square wings and a triangular tail. It glided down the snowy path— although *glide* was far too soft a word—and at the last possible moment turned to one side, coming to a screeching halt before the wayhouse's front porch. As the whine of the Ephicer engine died down, and Timberfall's residents congregated around the apparition, Astevyr stood up behind the controls, his head poking into the air like that of a newly-hatched chicken. Kyle could tell even from this distance that he was sizing up the wayhouse, wondering if he had come to the right place.

"Well!" Nihs said. "I'm glad we're not trying to keep a low profile. But I can't fault his punctuality."

They hurried downstairs to meet their benefactor. He was still appraising the front of the wayhouse when they came outside; he jumped in surprise and bent backwards like a reed in the wind when he caught sight of them.

"Ah!" he said. "Success! My orienteering has proven satisfactory. I have not had the pleasure of visiting this lovely village before, but I remained confident that I would be able to locate it by following the young *irushai*'s directions. You must be the party of Kyle Campbell! My name is—"

At that moment, Astevyr, who had been stepping out of the drifter's pilot seat, caught his foot on the door and tumbled forwards. Arms pinwheeling, he failed to catch his balance and fell face-first in the snow. Kyle winced in sympathy.

"Are you alright?" Meya said. Her voice was all concern, but she was pressing a knuckle to her lips to keep herself from laughing.

Astevyr sprang to his feet, brushing down his chest. "Not to worry, not to worry!" he said. He took stock of their entire party in one movement of the head, left then right. It was Deriahm upon whom his gaze settled. "You must be *irushai* Deriahm. Greetings, kinsman. I am diligent Astevyr."

Deriahm came to the fore of their party, and the two sons of Buoria shared a rather formal handshake. Astevyr positively towered over the young *irushai*, but it was with an odd kind of submission that he continued talking.

"I hope that my arrival has been timely, good sir, and that I may prove of use to you and your kin. It is an honor to serve one who has earned the king's *rouk*."

"Thank you, brother," Deriahm said. "I am certain that this will be so. Would you accept the king's *rouk* now, as payment for your services?"

"Absolutely not!" Astevyr said at once. "I provide my services freely, and would hear no more talk of the king's *rouk* being given away for such paltry assistance."

"I thought that was the whole point," Kyle said to Nihs in a low voice.

The little Kol rolled his eyes. "Who can guess what goes on in the mind of a Buor? As long as he agrees to take us as far north as he can in that skiff of his, I won't complain."

Deriahm and Astevyr, meanwhile, had been discussing just that. "I am prepared to depart immediately, good sirs. Please, direct me to your effects and I will haul them aboard."

"Not so fast, friend," Lugh said. His hair was still rumpled, and his eyes half-shut with sleep. "I want a hot breakfast inside me before we go skimming through the snow in *that* thing."

Kyle noticed that he and Meya were standing very close, arms brushing together at their sides. He wondered if what he'd seen the previous night had been only his imagination. He thought not. He also found that he was happy for both of them. *At least you're getting one good thing out of all this.*

"Yes, of course!" Astevyr was saying. "Regular nourishment, the keystone of all non-Buorish life! Very well. Let us retire to yon watering hole and sate our appetites."

"Yeah," Lugh said absently. "Let's do that."

They ate a breakfast that, while indeed hot, was as bland as dinner had been the night before. Deriahm and Astevyr shared a *rouk* pipe between them, Deriahm once again offering and Astevyr once again refusing the special cake that had been awarded to them by King Azanhein. Kyle had a feeling that this was some kind of ritual.

After breakfast, they retrieved their bulging packs from the attic and tossed them rather unceremoniously into the back of Astevyr's drifter. Kyle wasn't sure what the scientist normally used his vehicle for; it certainly wasn't for transporting people.

At the front of the vehicle was a small pod containing the driver's seat. Behind this stretched a smooth golden cylinder like the abdomen of an insect, within which was housed the drifter's single Ephicer engine. To either side were the square compartments Kyle had thought of as wings. They were little more than buckets of metal, hastily cleaned but none too comfortable. Some attempt at creating seating had been made in the past—wooden planks were screwed into the inner wall of each bucket, forming rudimentary benches. One of them had recently been repaired, but the other was rotting apart.

Kyle glanced inside, shared a look with Lugh, and then shrugged. He'd seen worse. Besides, he was with Nihs: if this drifter would take them where they needed to go, he could handle a little discomfort.

There was a problem, however, that became obvious as soon as Rogan placed one massive hoof inside the drifter. The entire vehicle tilted to one side, and a groan of metal came from deep within.

"Are you sure this thing can carry all of us?" Lugh said. Really, he should have said 'carry Rogan', since he weighed nearly as much as the rest of them put together.

"Do not fear!" Astevyr said. "This transport is sturdier than it appears."

But the rightmost metal bucket was carving deeply into the ground by the time Rogan was entirely inside. The rest of the party squeezed itself into the leftmost bucket in an attempt to even the load; not only was it incredibly cramped, but Kyle got the horrible feeling that the vehicle was about to tip over backwards. Astevyr sat in the cockpit and opened the drifter's magical intake; the engine roared, but the machine failed to move. Kyle didn't know what the Ephicer equivalent of redlining was, but he imagined that this must have been it.

The drifter, hovering on a cushion of magic, skidded sideways for a short while before Astevyr shook his head and cut the engine. As the noise died and the machine came to a rest, he said, in a tone of almost comic dejection,

"I believe, sirs and madam, that we may have a slight problem."

Rogan growled in frustration. "We're wasting time!" he shouted, swinging one massive leg over the lip of the drifter. "So here's your solution. You take the drifter; I'll run alongside!"

Nihs scoffed. "You can't possibly."

Rogan knotted his bushy eyebrows. "Oh no? Don't insult me, little one. Not only will I run to wherever it is we're going; I'll beat you there!"

He stepped out, and the rest of them yelped in surprise; the drifter pitched too far the other way as soon as his weight was gone.

As ludicrous as Rogan's idea seemed, none of them argued. It was obvious that Astevyr's poor drifter couldn't hold them all, and none of them could think of a better solution. Kyle and Deriahm jumped into the right bucket, and this time the sound made by the drifter's engine was a joyous thrum.

"Splendid!" Astevyr said. "Our destination lies many miles to the north. Shall we begin?"

"Let's," said Lugh. "It's not getting any warmer in here."

They took off, skirting the edge of Timberfall and then joining up with a forested path that ran northwards from the village.

Riding inside the drifter was exhilarating, particularly after spending so much time in the slow, ponderous logging transport. Astevyr wasted no time in getting the drifter back up to the breakneck speed it had been going when he came upon Timberfall. Kyle clung to the edge of the bucket, watching the trees on either side of him blur past. It was hard to tell because the ride was so rough, but Kyle thought they might be going forty or fifty miles an hour.

Still, when he twisted around in his seat and glanced behind (partly to give his eyes and ears a rest), he saw Rogan pounding along in their wake, muscles bunching as his legs worked like pistons. Kyle couldn't believe that he could move so fast for so long. Every so often, he would fall behind, but he inevitably gained his ground back once the terrain was in his favor.

While the ride might have been much faster than the logging transport, it was also even less comfortable, which was no mean feat. The drifter had no roof, and the wind which blew in their faces was so cold it burned. Kyle had wrapped his scarf around his neck and pulled the hood of his new coat as far over his head as it would go, but it wasn't long before the exposed part of his face was completely numb. Eyes watering, he jammed his chin into his collar and focused his eyes on the metal floor between his boots.

They soared ever northwards, following a winding mountain path that carved a meandering route through the foothills of Westia. There was naught here but trees, rocks, and more trees; whenever they crested a hill, all they saw for miles around were gray-green trunks and snow-covered needles, growing so densely together that it was possible to see every bump and gash in Westia's landscape by the shape of the forest canopy.

The air grew colder, the trees taller and the mountains grander. By a few hours into their trip, the world had taken on a strange quality that Kyle couldn't quite define. Sometimes, it was hard to tell whether a given landscape belonged in Loria, or in his own world of Terra. He'd grown used to this world's bright colors, and to the strange plants and animals which he couldn't quite recognize. But there had been a few places in Loria—Buoria, the Kol city of Proks, and most recently Oasis and Skralingsgrad—where even these differences paled in comparison to the sheer *otherness* of the world as a whole. Some parts of Westia might have been the Rockies or even the forests of Ontario in winter, where he'd been a couple of times; but this familiarity had been fading as they travelled further north.

Now, Lugh called for a halt so they could all warm up and recover. Astevyr pulled off the path and parked the drifter on the lip of a hill overlooking a valley. Beyond the valley, cutting across the horizon from southwest to northeast, was a line of mountains. It was these mountains, and their jagged, distorted shape, to which Kyle's gaze was drawn. They looked like they were made of crumpled metal rather than stone, a jagged line of shrapnel laid across the horizon. Spiraled horns of rock jutted into the sky, and swoops of ice and snow that looked like cresting waves hung over the empty air.

As he looked, a fancy jumped into his head, and he fielded Astevyr as the Buor walked past.

"Are those part of the meteor crater?" he asked.

Astevyr spun on one foot and looked at the mountains as if it were his first time seeing them. He thought a moment, then said,

"It is difficult to tell in this part of the world, for indeed, even this far south one can see signs of the meteor's influence. But I believe that this particular range predates even the age of *adaragem*. Look, good sir," he added, pointing. "The sky is clear, and our path across these mountains is visible even from this distance."

Kyle followed the line of Astevyr's arm, and saw—just barely. Far ahead and above, a spear of rock jutted out from the side of the valley closest to them. Its tip tapered, tapered, then tapered some more, but didn't quite vanish. Instead—and now Kyle had to squint to make sure his eyes weren't fooling him—a thin bridge extended all the way across the intervening space, to join up with another formation on the far side.

"You can't be serious," he said.

Astevyr looked delighted. "You needn't fear, my friend! The *vleyrpast*, which is to say, 'sky bridge', is a common phenomenon in Westia. They are treasured by Orcs as a means of travel over otherwise impassable areas. While some are temporary and crumble over time, others—such as this one—can stand for hundreds of years."

There was much Kyle could have said about this, but he chose not to. Instead he made a promise to himself to brush up on his leaping before crossing the *vleyrpast*.

Rogan, who had been lagging behind, caught them up a moment later. His chest was heaving, and his chestnut fur was covered in foam.

"Hoo!" he bellowed. "What a run! Why have we stopped?"

"To warm up," Lugh said, rubbing his hands together for emphasis.

"Warmth? Hah! You can borrow some of mine!" and Rogan spread his enormous arms wide.

"Don't mind if I do," Lugh said. He ran forward and put his arms around his friend. Rogan returned the embrace, and Lugh let out a sigh of pleasure.

"Excellent. Better than any coat. But the smell could use some work."

In an instant, without so much as a grunt of effort, Rogan lifted Lugh clear over his head and threw him across the clearing. Lugh tumbled in the snow and rolled onto his back, laughing at the clear sky.

At first, Kyle thought he was hearing the echo of Lugh's laughter on the wind. Then he realized that there was a cry mixed in with the noise; a distant shrieking noise that cut through the air and struck needle-sharp at his eardrums. His teeth buzzed; he looked at his companions and saw discomfort on their faces. Nihs actually sucked a breath through his teeth and clapped his hands to his ears.

"What was that?" Meya said.

"I cannot rightly say," Astevyr replied. "There are many strange creatures in this land. That call was unfamiliar to me."

Rogan unslung his massive pack and set it upon the ground. "If it's a monster, we can worry about it in due time. Sound carries far in the cold; for all we know it's on the other side of those mountains."

Lugh sprang to his feet, dusting the snow off his jacket. "Spoken like a true Selk!" he said. "Now who's getting the fire started?"

"You."

Their break was a short one, as it was too early in the day to set up camp for good, and Astevyr wanted to get closer to the sky bridge so they would have ample time to cross it the following day. They skirted the edge of the valley, drawing closer to the base of the peninsula from which the *vleyrpast* jutted. The drifter climbed and climbed, and Kyle was grateful to be sitting in the bucket farthest from the lip of the valley. As it was, his stomach flip-flopped every time the machine began to swerve, which happened far too often. More than once the engine's hum climbed to a hysterical wail as Astevyr forced it up a steep slope; if the terrain got any rougher than this, the drifter would be no use.

Finally they came to a plateau of sorts and set up camp for good. The sun had started to set, and the temperature was plunging with it. The cold was a deep, biting chill, and Kyle couldn't rid himself of it no matter how close he sat to the fire. His fingers and toes had gone numb, and even his chest, wrapped within layer upon layer of fabric, was shivering.

Going to have to get used to it, he thought. From now until the end of his journey, he was likely to be cold every single night.

The air in Livaldi's study was warm and still. Saul stepped inside, gauging as he always did the young's master mood from a safe distance. What he saw heartened him; James looked better than he had in days. His clothes were still wrinkled, and his hair was growing long—*I shall have to schedule an appointment soon,* Saul thought—but the haunted look had departed from his eyes. Someone had been in to clean: the coffee mugs had been cleared off of James' desk and the stain in the carpet blotted out.

The desk was now instead covered with hundreds of tiny pieces of metal, and the tools with which to work them. Most shone brilliantly gold with tigoreh, and a few with blue Ephicer light. In the middle of all was a beautiful golden rifle, over four feet long, its innards exposed and scattered on the desk nearby.

The scene looked chaotic to the unlearned eye, but Saul knew that Livaldi would be keeping track of every last piece, and how it could be fit to every other.

Perhaps this is all the young master needed, Saul thought. *Some tactile work to occupy his hands and mind.* It was his own thought, but he didn't believe it one whit.

Still, Livaldi looked serene enough as he selected one metal tube and lifted it to his eyes, a needle-nosed pair of grippers in the other hand. He was wearing a set of delicate, gold-rimmed glasses which glinted in the light streaming in from the windows behind his desk. He peered over their rims as Saul approached, giving him a look which said, *you are interrupting some very important work.*

"My report, sir," Saul said.

The look didn't waver. Many men had withered beneath it, but Saul's resistance to it had been honed by his decades of service to the Livaldi family.

James sighed. He set the piece down and laced his fingers together on the desk in front of him.

"Let me guess," he said. "Nothing."

"Yes, sir."

"You've heard nothing. You've seen nothing."

"I'm afraid so, sir."

"No, you're not," James snapped. There was so much venom in his voice that Saul rocked backwards on his heels. "You're relieved. You think it's a good thing that Kyle's gotten away, don't you?"

Saul was dumbfounded. It had been so long since he'd seen Livaldi operating in his proper frame of mind. He'd forgotten the true extent of the young master's genius, and had made the mistake that most only made once—he'd underestimated James.

You know? How? And if you know this, what else? Had Livaldi even seen through what Saul planned to do when he did catch wind of Kyle?

"Of course not," he said. "Your goals are my own, as they have always been."

James sniffed. "How touching," he said. "Would that your commitment was of more use to me."

He didn't realize it, but that simple remark hurt Saul more than most anything else ever had. He felt tears welling up in the corners of his wrinkled eyes and blinked them back.

James, oblivious, had selected another piece of metal and was performing surgery on the weapon in front of him. "It hardly matters," he said. "For you see, I've been struck by a revelation."

Saul said nothing; his throat felt raw. Any words he tried to speak would surely come out as a croak.

"I've been expending far too much energy trying to chase Kyle down," Livaldi continued, "and frankly, I've grown tired of it. So I've decided to take a more strategic approach."

Despite himself, Saul was intrigued. This was so very different from the single-minded Livaldi he had known for the past halfmonth.

James discarded his grippers and pressed the piece into place with his thumb. Holding it still, he flipped the gun over and grabbed another. His eyes narrowed in concentration as he slid this one home. There was a moment of tension, then a *snap* of metal. Livaldi set the gun down and went searching through his tools.

"I know where he is," he said. "And what's he's doing. Furthermore, I know where he's going next."

"I thought that your second sight was no longer working?" Saul said.

Livaldi gave him another withering look. "I don't need some rock to tell me Kyle's movements," he said. "He's as predictable as the market. But I'd been so focused on the chase that I had failed to notice."

He mused for a moment, tapping his chin. He then bent to his work and continued.

"There's no need to go chasing after him; our paths will cross sooner or later regardless. All *we* need do, my friend, is prepare for his arrival."

And with that, the final piece of the rifle slid into place. All of a sudden, what had been a dead, dissected object came to life.

Livaldi opened the rifle's magic intake and there was a tangible *pulling* sensation as the fuel cell within it began to charge. A low whine was heard, climbing in pitch and volume as more and more magic was drawn inside.

At their core, Ephicer rifles were incredibly simple machines. A fuel core made from crushed, liquidized Ephicers—the constructor—formed a bullet of pure magic inside the rifle. Then, a secondary Ephicer, the accelerator, launched the pellet forward with a pulse of magic.

Saul was no engineer, but one could hardly spend much time in Livaldi's company without picking up the basics. As such, he immediately noticed that while this rifle was equipped with a constructor, it was missing an accelerator. Instead, there was a circular insert, about five inches across, sitting empty at the base of the barrel.

Any renewed sense of hope or serenity Saul had felt upon entering the office vanished as he watched Livaldi heft the rifle. His eyes strayed to the coffee machine sitting ten feet to Livaldi's right. James must have noticed, for he said,

"Indeed. Conventional weapons are of no use against a vagrant. To penetrate Kyle's defenses will take an extreme amount of energy. And if even that proves insufficient…I suppose I'll have to blow one or two of his adventurer friends to bits. Kyle may be invulnerable, but he still has vulnerabilities. Don't you agree?"

Saul was so shocked that, for a moment, the requested agreement caught in his throat. When he finally voiced it, James looked at him with mistrust, but said nothing.

"Good. Off you go, now. Schedule me some menial appointment. I have a need to clear my head."

"Yes, sir."

Kyle awoke early the next day. At first, he thought that he had shivered himself awake; it was certainly cold enough. Then, as the blotches of his memories ran together, he realized that it had been a loud *pop* of the fire that had shaken him from his sleep.

He rolled into a sitting position, making sure not to wake the others. His own tent was full; it must have been Lugh, Meya, Nihs, or more likely Astevyr who had gotten up early and rekindled the fire.

He stepped outside, and froze in the tent's threshold. Seated not ten feet from where he stood, hunkered over the blazing fire, was a huge Orc with skin of such a pale gray that it was bordering on white. He had a large crop of unruly brown hair and was dressed in clothes made of monster hide. He had a small axe belted to one hip, as well a larger one and an unstrung bow on his back. As Kyle watched, he bent over with a grunt, grabbed a large branch from a bundle of wood, and fed the fire.

Kyle's initial shock of fear gave way to disbelief.

The hell kind of prank is this? Break into someone's camp so you can use their fireplace?

He stepped forward, reaching for his sword. The Orc turned before he'd gotten two paces, twisting in his seat with his hands resting on his thighs.

"Ah!" he said. "The first to rise is the first to strike, as we say! Come, warm yourself by the fire." His accent was thick with a quality that Kyle might have called 'gravelly', or possibly even 'purring'. His face was flat and blocky, and his eyes were narrow. Save for being an Orc, he could not have been more different from Meya's dead companion, Phundasa.

"Who are you?" Kyle said.

The Orc laughed out loud, slapping his own leg. "The keeper of your fire!" he said. "To lay down and sleep while it fell to ashes—a tragedy! You must be easterlings, to let such a thing happen!"

Kyle found himself loosening his grip on his sword. He came around and seated himself next to the newcomer.

"That's right," he said. "I'm Kyle. You still haven't told me who you are."

The Orc grinned, revealing square, chomping teeth that were far too large for his mouth. "Grul is my name," he said. "And I make my home on the far side of yonder *vleyrpast*. Or, I should like to. But when the *gordja* flies, so I do not."

Kyle caught the shape of the sentence, but not the meaning. "*Gordja?* What's that?"

He'd been expecting Grul's look of stunned disbelief, but not for him to reach out, seize Kyle by the chin and forehead, and turn his face sideways.

"What's this?" Grul said. "I see you have ears. How is it you did not hear the *gordja's* cry? Are they stone ears, perhaps?"

Kyle pulled his head away. "*Oh,*" he said. "You mean the shrieking noise? We heard it yesterday."

Grul's face opened into another grin. "Ah, good! I was starting to worry for you, my friend."

"So what is it? Some kind of monster?"

Grul linked his thumbs and flapped his fingers in tandem. "Ar. A great bird demon. It would pluck the likes of you into the sky in a heartbeat. Wise men keep to the trees when such beasts are about."

The flap of Lugh's tent was pulled back and Lugh stepped out. His hair was rumpled and his good eye was foggy, but he blinked his drowsiness back as soon as he caught sight of Grul.

"Who're you?" he said.

Grul's story came in bits and pieces as the rest of them awoke. He was a hunter who lived in one of the settlements that lay beyond what Kyle was coming to think of as the shrapnel mountains. He had crossed the *vleyrpast* to do what he called long-hunting, which involved chasing a monster across the snowy miles until it died of exhaustion or he did. He'd come across a herd of *dhalor*, which to Kyle sounded like a smaller version of the Phundar they had encountered a few days ago. He'd selected a target—an old buck arthritic with age—and separated him from the herd. The two had chased each other all through the forest, into the valley, and finally underneath the *vleyrpast* itself.

Grul's quarry had only just collapsed when he'd heard the cry of the *gordja*. It had swooped down and stolen the *dhalor*—four hundred pounds of monster crushed between the great bird's talons and lifted into the sky. Grul could only watch as his prize was carried up over the lip of the shrapnel mountains, away to the *gordja*'s nest. Since then, he had seen it several times, circling the valley, and heard its distant cry pierce the air.

"So I am trapped," he said. "I cannot go home, for if I try to cross the sky bridge the beast will catch sight of me at once."

"So now you wander around and tend to the fires of foolish easterners?" Lugh said.

Grul barked laughter. "Firekeepers you are not, but I see you have weapons. Tell me, friends—are you warriors?"

"Adventurers, actually," Lugh said. "Do you know the word?"

Kyle found it odd that Lugh saw fit to ask, and even odder that Grul shook his blocky head, locks of unkempt hair striking his cheeks.

Lugh sat down and stuck his palms out to the fire. "It means we fight monsters for a living," he said. "Usually for money. But we want to cross that *vleyrpast* as badly as you do. So sure, we'll help you kill the *gordja*—that *is* what you were going to ask, isn't it?"

Grul's brow lifted, and his narrow eyes were pulled open. They were gold, as Phundasa's had been, but trimmed with white instead of black.

"We are brothers in mind!" he said. "Do you say it can be done?"

"I'll let you know once I can feel my fingers again. In the meantime, let's hear more about this demon-bird of yours."

Kyle had come to recognize the rhythm that was shared by all adventuring jobs. He'd first experienced it during the raid of the goblin mine in Donno, and was now experiencing it again, sitting around the blazing fire with Grul. The gathering of information always came first. What enemies were they to face? What were their numbers? What were their strengths and weaknesses?

Now, they learned of the monstrous bird demon that Grul called *gordja*.

Wings spread, it was over fifty feet across. Even if it weren't gigantic, Grul said, it could easily be recognized by the green trim of its pinions and tail, and by the golden mask it seemed to wear about the eyes. Like any bird, its greatest weapons were its beak and claws. Most prey it didn't even bother killing, but rather lifted them back to its nest live. If they weren't killed by the cold or crushed between its talons during the flight, the fall was sure to finish the work.

"One of us being carried off is our biggest risk," Nihs said. "Having soul shields, we could survive for a time in its grip. But we would be sure to perish eventually, and none of us could survive the fall to the valley floor should we be dropped."

Lugh was nodding, eyes closed, in a way that made it look like he was falling asleep. "If only we had something big that we didn't mind it snatching. We could've fed that to it and made a break for it while it was busy."

"We are brothers in mind," Grul said once more, "but the *vleyrpast* is long and the bird swift. We might still be in the shadow of its nest by the time it had finished with its last prize."

"Right, then. We fight it on the valley floor before it can pluck us off of the sky bridge. If one of us starts to get lifted, Nihs, Meya and Grul hit it with everything they have to make it drop whoever it is. Anything else?"

"The *gordja's* cry," Grul said. "You heard it from afar, yes? It made your head hurt, teeth hurt, yes?"

"What of it?" Rogan asked.

"From close, that cry can give you *rosshku*—er, shaking of the head…" words failing him, Grul raised his hands to either side of his head and vibrated them all together.

"Madness?" Rogan guessed.

"Or some kind of seizure," Nihs said.

Grul shrugged. "The word makes no difference," he said. "But when it strikes, you cannot fight, and some fall from their feet."

"I can help with that," Meya said. "My magic can keep your ears and mind safe. It will dull your sense of hearing, but it will be worth not being paralyzed every time the monster shrieks."

"Ah!" Grul said, delighted. "I feel our odds of living are growing with every moment!"

Kyle, however, was stuck on something that the Orc had said earlier. "Grul," he said, "what was that word you used just now? For shaking of the head?"

"*Rossh-ku*," Grul said. "Orcish word. Means many things. Why do we ask?"

"We know someone named Rosshku," Kyle said.

Grul's eyes opened wide, then he let out a gust of laughter. "As a name, 'Rosshku' means 'mad-in-the-head'. Who do you know who has such a name?"

Kyle was amazed; 'mad-in-the-head' couldn't have been a less fitting name for the Archmage, who was one of the sanest, wisest people he had ever met. Perhaps that name had been given to him as a kind of irony.

"Someone who doesn't suit it," Kyle said. Grul laughed even harder at that.

"Right," Lugh said, rising to his feet, "I think we've done enough talking. Time to get to some killing. If we're going to do it, we might as well do it now, when we're all still warm and have some daylight left. Right?"

"Right." Rogan stuck the point of his axe in the ground and heaved himself upright. "Astevyr, will you be joining us?"

The scientist shook his head in apology. "Though I was submitted to mandatory military training alongside the other sons and daughters of Buoria, I take no pleasure in fighting, and my skills have atrophied with long disuse. If it pleases you, I will remain here and tend to your belongings. And, of course, to the fire!"

Finding a way down to the valley floor would have miserable were it not for Grul's help. He led them down a zigzagging path of sorts that was half buried in snow. Finding decent footing involved a great deal of trial and error, but they were all agile adventurers, and even Grul had some skill in leaping. What likely would have taken Kyle an hour on Earth was thus cut down to little more than half.

As Kyle leapt thirty feet downwards, coming to a sliding stop in a snowbank, he thought, *This is me. I can do this. Will I really lose all of this when I go back to Earth?*

But that wasn't the truth, not entirely; it *wasn't* just him who could leap, who could fight gigantic monsters, who could draw a soul sword at will. The world of Loria was his crutch, the magic that made everything possible. He could feel it swirling around him; the atmosphere of this world was so *rich*. Nihs had once described the soul as a magical pair of lungs that pulled energy in from the world outside, as physical lungs did for air. When Kyle went back to Terra, his magical lungs would shrivel and starve, and surely eventually fall off. For Earth, his Earth, had no magic upon which they could feed.

All of a sudden, he felt such an aching sense of loss that he almost called the others to stop in their tracks. *I can't leave. I won't. I want to stay here. I can't give all of this up.*

And then another thought, following on the heels of this one: *I haven't even started to test the limits of how powerful I can become here. If I stay, I'll get stronger and stronger. Lugh, Nihs, Rogan and I—Meya and Deriahm, if they want to come, too—we can start doing more adventuring work, save up enough money to buy another airship. We'll get stronger and stronger, and soon there will be no job we can't do. I'll learn how to leap, and dash, and then soar. We'll be the most famous group of adventurers that ever lived.*

He saw the picture clearly in his mind's eye: he and his friends stood shoulder-to-shoulder, resplendent and mighty. He, Kyle, was the endless well of power that could make that vision a reality. What had Rosshku once told him as they stood on the bridge of the *Aresa Bign*? *One particle of your soul contains as much energy as the rest of the universe combined.*

But then another voice came to him, as it had several times since the words had first been spoken. *I can only implore you, as a friend, to follow a righteous path, and not to turn your immense strength against this frail earth.*

It was King Azanhein who had said this: King Azanhein, the mightiest member of the mightiest race in Loria. Who, like Rosshku, knew more about Kyle than Kyle did himself.

At first, he'd thought that Azanhein had been begging him not to use his power for evil—*beware the Dark Side, Luke*. But now he realized that it didn't matter whether he used his power for good or ill. If he wished to be righteous, there was only one path he could follow, and it was the one that led back to Terra.

He would return. He had to. But for now, he meant to do the job that was in front of him.

By the time they reached the valley floor, Grul's eyes were glued to the sky. He formed a visor with one hand and bent his neck backwards, watching the shrapnel mountains for any sign of their foe.

"The distance is long," he said, "but the *gordja* is swift. Once she catches sight of us, we'll have but seconds before she strikes."

Kyle wasn't sure he believed that—the mountains looked so distant from here. They gathered in the bowl of the valley. It was a nice, flat, open place, nothing but snow and scrub for a mile in each direction. They found a likely spot and began work on another fire. Having nothing but bush to work with, and wet bush at that, their fire would be short-lived; but if all went well, it would help them attract the demonic bird, and keep themselves warm in the process.

They piled sticks together until they had a mound as tall as Kyle. Nihs thrust an arm forward and a gout of flame belched forth. The fire caught at once.

There they stood shivering and watching the sky for over half an hour.

Soon there was a starburst of footprints surrounding the fire, as they took turns stepping away to fetch more fuel.

"Seems the bird is taking its sweet time," Rogan rumbled.

Grul snorted. "If we were to try crossing the *vleyrpast*, it would be upon us at once."

Another ten minutes trickled by. Kyle's feet had started off stinging, and were now completely numb. His hands, stuffed as close to the fire as they would go, were faring better—at least he would be able to hold on to his sword.

"The *gordja* comes," Grul said.

His voice was everyday, nonchalant, and for that reason it took a moment for the others to react. Then, suddenly, all was excitement. The others gathered around Grul, craning their necks, trying to catch sight of the enemy.

When Kyle first saw the *gordja*, the bird was barely a speck; he almost mistook it for a bit of ash blown from the fire. It grew in size, shockingly fast, and soon Kyle could distinguish the flapping of its wings. Before long, it was an inch wide in the sky, and its eerie, piercing shriek trickled into Kyle's skull and jabbed at his eardrums. By the time his teeth had stopped buzzing, Kyle could see the green trim on the monster's wings.

"It has caught our sight!" Grul shouted. "It will circle and make sure of us, but not for long. Brace yourselves!"

Kyle felt a warm softness wash over him, as if the air had suddenly turned to cotton. He turned round, and saw Meya give him a thumbs-up. Sound had become muffled, but it was soothing rather than irritating, like wearing a hat lined with thick fur. Still, they would have to be careful; their communication, and therefore their coordination, would suffer for this fight.

Kyle turned back to the *gordja* and was shocked to see how large it had grown. It passed across the sun, and he could see every pinion at the end of its squared-off wings. Its tail was long, and its claws enormous.

It dipped to one side and flew in a graceful arc, letting go its strange cry once more. This time Kyle heard it with his ears instead of his teeth. It began to circle as Grul had said, but must have liked the look of their party, for it hadn't made half a turn around them when it turned sharply and *dove*. Just like that, the battle was on.

The *gordja* wasn't just fast—it was nearly supersonic. It came out of the sky like a missile, wings pulled back, beak thrust forward like a lance. At first Kyle thought it was simply going to crash into them. Then, not a hundred feet from the ground, it spread its wings, flipped backwards, and extended its claws to grab. Rogan was its target; it must have seen him as the most substantial member of their party, his bestial appearance possibly even reminding it of the meal it had stolen from Grul.

Rogan leapt to one side, lashing out with his father's axe. The blade scraped against the *gordja's* scaled talons, but Rogan was missing the leverage he needed to drive the blow home. At the same time, Grul let loose an arrow and Nihs a fiery bolt. The arrow was batted aside by a beat of the bird's wings. The fireball struck home, but had little effect.

Kyle had started to move, but saw at once that it was a waste of effort. The *gordja's* swoop carried it past where Rogan had been, and its talons dug up great clumps of earth and snow. It beat its wings once, twice, three times, and in that short time gained so much height that it was nearly out of bowshot, let alone melee range. Kyle felt each wingbeat press against his body like the palm of a giant hand. Even if he had gotten closer, he would have been knocked off of his feet by the pressure.

The *gordja* circled tight around the group, and then swooped again, once more at Rogan. This time, he stepped more tightly, keeping his feet planted so he could swing. Swing he did, and caught the bird a great blow to one claw; it wasn't quite sheared off, but Kyle thought it was a close thing. But as the *gordja* passed him by, its hind toe struck at Rogan's ankle, pulling him straight off his feet. He dangled upside-down for a moment, then pulled free, falling fifteen feet to the ground.

"*Rogan!*" Lugh bellowed to make himself heard over Meya's protective magic.

Rogan sprang to his feet, and waved behind him vaguely to show that he was unhurt. By the time he'd done this, the *gordja* was coming back around. Kyle watched carefully—he had to be ready to dodge if it came for him.

Instead, the bird opened its beak and uttered its shrill cry. Kyle gasped in pain: even with Meya's spell, his head jangled like the clapper of a bell, and his balance nearly left him. It was just as well that the *gordja* did not come for him. It went for Lugh instead, who leapt straight up, past its claws and snapping beak, then twisted in mid-air, swords drawn to strike. But the monster was moving so quickly that by the time Lugh came down, it had passed underneath, and he struck at nothing but its lime-green tail.

Lugh cursed and waved a few tattered feathers from his blades. "This isn't going to work!" he shouted at the others. "We need to bring it down somehow! Grul, Nihs, Deriahm—and you, Meya—hit it with everything you have!"

They did that, and again the next two times it dove. Meya's aim was unerring, as was Deriahm's; Nihs struck home twice and Grul once, but it mattered little either way. Only Meya's magic seemed to hurt the bird at all, and this did more harm than good. The bird screeched every time it was struck, and each shriek cut deeper than the last. By the third, Kyle's vision was swimming, and he was sure his ears would be bleeding were it not for the magical cotton stuffed into them.

The next time the bird dove, one of its talons got caught in the brush. It squealed, twisting itself around, and employed its beak for the first time. It lunged at Rogan, lightning fast; he blocked with his axe, but the tip of the beak closed around its haft and yanked it free of Rogan's grip. A twitch of the neck, and the axe was sent flying through the air. The beak shot out again, but a black smudge had positioned itself between Rogan and the *gordja*. It was Deriahm— the one member of their party who carried a shield. Beak met shield with a loud *clang* of metal; Deriahm was nearly knocked from his feet. The next peck came, and this time the beak closed around the shield's rim. Deriahm, arm strapped to his shield, was pulled to and fro; Kyle could clearly see the blue flicker of his soul shield as it struggled to keep his arm from being broken.

Seeing their chance, Kyle and Lugh closed in on the monster from one side, and Grul from the other. Kyle focused, pouring his soul sword into the special weapon the Buors had given him. The metal blade collapsed in on itself and gave way to a blade of pure blue energy. He ducked under a wing and swung his sword overhead. It cut through the air with a keening *whummum*, and he was rewarded with a hail of green. He'd taken off the last foot of a few of the great bird's pinions, but he guessed that it would take a lot more than that to ground the *gordja* for good.

He ran under the wing in a crouch, then rose and sprinted at the bird's unprotected side. But the great wings beat again before he could close in, and he was nearly flattened against the ground by the wind and pressure. He broke his fall with his free hand and felt the bones of his wrist grind together. Had he been on Earth, he surely would have broken it.

The bird was away again, but at least now they had gotten a chance to strike at it. Rogan went running for his axe, and Meya put Deriahm's shield arm back into working order. They regrouped around the remains of their fire, which had been scattered to the winds with the *gordja's* descent.

"Hit everything you can," Lugh said. "Wings, tail—anything that will get it on the ground and *keep* it there. We'll be at this forever if all it does is keep diving at us."

"But leave *some* of the tail safe," Grul cut in. He was grinning with suicidal joy. "What's the use of killing such a mighty beast if one has no trophy to take at the end?"

"Your trophy will be getting back to your clan in one piece," Rogan growled. "Now here it comes again."

The *gordja* screamed out of the sky, faster than ever. Its wings bent low, and Kyle realized that for the first time he was in danger of being struck. He braced himself to dodge, but just before the creature struck, it screamed again, and Kyle's body betrayed him. His back arched, and his limbs went stiff. The bird exploded past him, and though its talons were not aimed at him, he was buffeted by the edge of its wing. It was a glancing blow, but still enough to knock him from his feet and send him flying into the snow. He would have braced his fall, but feeling was just coming back to his limbs. As it was, he struck hard against the rocky ground. His soul shield held, but barely, and for a moment he was completely stunned.

White light washed over him, and the pain receded almost at once. Kyle's eyes focused, and the number of fingers on Meya's outstretched hand shrank from ten to five. He took it, and she hauled him into a sitting position.

"*Look out!*"

There was a rush of wind overhead and Kyle thought the *gordja* had passed above them; then he realized that it had been Lugh. He was standing between them and the monster, who was less than fifty feet away. Both his swords were drawn and held aloft. He stood stock-still, facing the bird down as its claws extended.

"*Lugh, move!*" Meya screamed. Kyle heard the edge of hysteria in her voice and thought he knew why. She rose to her feet, but before she could act, Lugh cut down with both swords. The innermost toe on each of the *gordja's* feet was hewn clean off. Lugh was thrown backwards, but worse, the bird shrieked and twisted in mid-air just as Meya stood at full height. Its leg slammed into her, and she went flying just as Kyle had done. All at once the comforting cotton was ripped from Kyle's ears, and the next time the bird sang it was from directly overhead.

Blinding, incredible, all-encompassing pain exploded in Kyle's head. He felt like his skull had shattered into a million pieces. His eyes rolled back, and his teeth chattered; they came down on his tongue, and blood gushed into his mouth. He fell on his back and writhed, the sound worming into his muscles and stiffening his joints.

Rosshku. Mad-in-the-head.

Mad in the *body*—mad in the *soul.*

Kyle could do nothing but let the pain run its course. It could have been a minute or ten before his senses came back to him. He rose groggily to his feet, deathly afraid of what he would see when he did. But his companions were all still there. Rogan, Nihs, and Grul were battling the beast, while Deriahm was tending to Meya. Lugh was still sprawled at Kyle's feet. There was a thin trickle of blood coming from his ears.

Agony of indecision. Kyle wanted to help Lugh, but Meya was their healer. If she fell, their odds of winning were scant.

But when he came to Deriahm's side, he saw that the worst had already happened. He could sense rather than see that Meya's soul shield was broken, and she'd fallen into unconsciousness. Deriahm was doing his best to heal her, but his strength was nowhere near hers. He looked up at Kyle, and somehow there was fear visible in that inexpressive visor.

"I am afraid that miss Ilduetyr will likely not be in a condition to re-join this fight, even if I am able to revive her," he said. "Mister Campbell, tell me—what can I do to help ensure our victory?"

Kyle's first thought was *why are you asking me?* Then he realized that there was no one else to ask. Lugh had always been the strategist of their group; Kyle hadn't truly understood this until his friend was gone.

He stood, watching his friends battle the *gordja* in the near distance. Truly, it was a beautiful creature. Swift and agile, resplendent in its coat of green and gold. But deadly, so very deadly.

Think. What would Lugh do?

Apparently, what Lugh would do was stand face to face with the enormous monster, and chop off two of its toes in one blow. Kyle didn't believe he could do that, but...

It's got three weapons. Its claws, its beak, and its cry. There's nothing we can do about the one. But maybe we can still get three down to two.

"Come with me!" he shouted at Deriahm, forgetting for a moment that there was no need to shout, not with Meya out of commission.

The two of them ran to Rogan and Grul, ducking under the bird's great wings at its next pass.

"Listen!" Kyle said. "Lugh cut off two of its toes. We can get the rest—me with my soul sword and Grul with his axe. We just need to hold it still."

Rogan looked down at Kyle, chest heaving with exertion. No one else knew it, but it was taking every ounce of self-control he possessed not to let Gershel into his mind. With Meya gone, there would be nothing to pull him back from that darkness once it fell.

"What are you suggesting, little one?" he said.

"Block it," Kyle said. "The next time it swoops. Deriahm with his shield, you with your axe. Grul and I will wait on either side, and cut its legs."

Rogan and Grul shared a glance. Nihs made a keening noise from Rogan's shoulder.

"Madness, but then again, we need to finish this fight now if we're to finish it at all. Go, then. Go!"

They had seconds to spare before the *gordja* descended once more. It had fixated on Rogan, which right now suited them fine. He shifted at the last moment, focusing on the leftmost claw, while Deriahm stepped in and took the right on his shield. The *gordja*, a slave to its instinct, bit its claws into axe and shield and hovered, beating its wings to stay in the air while the two adventurers strained against it.

Kyle, ducking underneath one wing, saw his opportunity and took it. He vented all of his magic and launched a gaiden strike, the blow that was the adventurer's hallmark. Bolstered by his soul sword, the cut was devastating; a blue arc tore through the air and did not so much sever the *gordja's* leg as shatter it. The monster shrieked, and though it was piercing, it was a cry of pain rather than one of its ear-splitting hunting cries.

Grul hadn't managed to cut through the other leg with his first blow; it still clung to Deriahm's shield. When the bird next beat its wings, its back rolled away from Kyle, and its belly was exposed to him. He didn't hesitate for a moment—he stabbed, sword plunging through a foot of downy feather before finally meeting flesh. He ripped his sword upwards; he cut more feather than skin, but was still rewarded by a red stain that blossomed in the creature's stomach.

The *gordja* finally managed to untangle itself from Deriahm, and beat its wings furiously to escape from the blue fang that had bitten into its belly. Nihs sent a gout of fire chasing after it; close as he was, Kyle felt the tremendous heat of the spell. It struck the monster in the flank, and for the first time it reacted, shrieking in pain and veering sharply to one side. Suddenly, Kyle realized that they were not the only ones who had soul shields—the *gordja* had just lost its own, and Nihs' magic could finally harm it.

The bird gained height, more than it had before, and for a moment Kyle thought it was going to flee. It swooped at them, but veered away again, changing its mind at the last moment.

"Come, come!" Grul bellowed. "I will have your head before the day is out!"

The *gordja* plummeted towards them once more. This time it was aimed at Grul. He drew his bow and cast an arrow; it fell to one side. He drew again and this time held until the monster was shockingly close. Finally he let fly, and this time the arrow struck one of the eyes behind the bird's golden mask.

The gordja shrieked and threw its head back; its balance was thrown, and it lost control of its dive. One wing ended up crumbled underneath the body, pressed against it by the force of the wind. It fell into a mad spiral, hurtling towards the ground at tremendous speed. Grul sprinted to one side as the monster crashed into the earth, its wings splaying every which way. It rolled and slid for fully a hundred feet before coming to rest in the snowy ground. It was still thrashing, trying to get its feet below it, the stump of its severed right leg wiggling uselessly in the air.

Kyle ran towards it, but Rogan had beaten him there. From behind one flailing wing, Kyle saw him raise his axe and bring it down with incredible force. There was a deep, tearing, *whock* sound, and all at once the thrashing stopped completely. The body went limp, wings floating gently down to earth. The *gordja* had cried its last.

Grul held two of the *gordja's* tail feathers to the sides of his head, imitating the headdress that he had immediately promised to craft to celebrate his victory. The feathers, a foot across at their widest and bright green, were long enough to brush at the snowy ground beneath his feet. He was dancing a joyous but utterly undisciplined jig, kicking his feet together and throwing up clots of snow and mud.

"Warharharharr! No beast can stand against the mighty Grul and his brothers in arms! Men weep when he walks by, and women lay on their backs!"

"Glad to hear it," Lugh said breezily. "But you've made a little mistake—there's at least one woman among your brothers in arms."

Grul's eyes popped out of his head. "Of course! The red witch, the angel of battle! Men bellow and beat their chests that they cannot be with her!"

Meya smiled, though it was soon replaced by a grimace of pain. "Not that I wouldn't appreciate it," she said, "but for the moment I'd prefer it if bellowing was kept to a minimum."

As soon as they had been sure of the *gordja's* death, Deriahm had returned to Meya's side to revive her. Once his power was bolstered by magic borrowed from Kyle and Nihs, Meya's eyes had finally fluttered open. She'd immediately squealed in pain and clamped her palms to her ears; they were bleeding, just as Lugh's had been. But she was awake, and that meant that everything would be all right.

She'd tended to Lugh first, bringing him back from the edge of unconsciousness, then had taken some time to repair her own ears. Now she was back to Lugh, cupping his chin in one hand and shooting a delicate stream of magic into his ear with the other. Kyle, whose soul shield had saved him from the worst of the cry, would be last.

Still Grul jigged and jogged, quite literally dancing on the grave of his enemy. He plucked several feathers from the *gordja's* tail and shared them among his 'brothers in arms'. These, he said, were the trophies that marked their legendary victory against the demon bird.

Nihs ran a clawed finger down the length of his own feather. "I believe I could make real use of this," he said. "There is an incredible potential for magic in these feathers. That was no ordinary beast, for sure."

Once they were all fit to move once more, they climbed the side of the valley, looking for their campsite. Grul was loath to leave the carcass of the *gordja* behind, but as Lugh put it, "If there's anything around that can steal *that* thing from you, we're *not* helping you kill it."

They rejoined Astevyr, who, true to his word, had kept their fire burning in their absence. He stood and welcomed them with open arms.

"Splendid! I watched your battle from afar. Your performance was spectacular. Come, sit, and rest. I trust you are all unhurt?"

"More or less," Meya said.

Lugh was peering along the length of the *vleyrpast*. "How long do you reckon it will take to cross that? I think we should get it over with while we've got some daylight left."

"Don't be silly," Nihs said, "we need rest."

"I'm with Lugh," Rogan said. "We're racing against time here—the longer we stay out here, the less food we'll have, and the deeper we'll fall into winter. We can rest on the far side."

Nihs heaved a great sigh and muttered something in Kollic. "Fine, then. I only hope everyone's ears have recovered enough to keep us from tumbling off the side."

"Take heart, brother!" Grul said. "The *vleyrpast* is broader than she seems from here."

"I can only hope that you're right."

As they set to work striking their camp, Grul untied a decoration from his hair and handed it to Lugh. It was a small talisman made of bone, feather, and wooden beads.

"My clansmen await on the far side of the bridge," he said. "When you find their camp, give them this, and tell them that Grul waits in the valley below with a prize beyond their knowing! I will stay and tend to the *gordja* until they come!"

"Will do," Lugh said, tucking the talisman away. "Take care, friend, and happy hunting."

Grul bellowed laughter. "Very happy indeed!"

They could still hear him singing half an hour later as Astevyr's drifter climbed the last mile or so to the base of the sky bridge. The view from up here was dizzying, and the air thin. Kyle felt light-headed every time he caught a glimpse of the valley floor below, which became more and more often as the spire continued to narrow.

Trees and scrub gave way to snow, and then even snow was blasted free of the rocky bridge. The winds here were high and capricious; they tugged first in one direction and then in the other, as if willfully trying to pull the party to their doom. Kyle wasn't normally afraid of heights, but his stomach still tied itself into knots every time this happened.

Soon they decided to dismount from the drifter and follow along behind it. The engine hummed and whined, as if in reply to the gusting wind. They climbed and climbed, the outcropping wedge of rock becoming thinner and thinner. Soon it was no more than a hundred feet wide, with a sheer drop on either side. Still they climbed, and still the path shrank. Eighty feet, then sixty, then fifty.

Kyle couldn't tell at what point the rock spire disappeared completely and the true *vleyrpast* began, but half an hour into their walk he realized that this was now the case—there was nothing beneath them but a beam of rock some fifty feet across and thirty feet thick. His vertigo got worse and worse, and his legs started to betray him; they grew stiff and unwilling, and he found he could only make small, shuffling steps. A fear that had nothing to do with conscious thought and everything to do with primal instinct was screaming at him to turn back and leave this wretched bridge behind.

Of his companions, Astevyr and Deriahm seemed completely unaffected, and Nihs, with his climber's instinct and small frame, walked with confidence. But Meya was clutching at her staff with white-knuckled fingers, and even Lugh was starting to look sick. Kyle thought that his missing eye must make the walk that much harder.

But the real problem was Rogan. Rogan, who weighed several hundred pounds, and often heard the cracking of the earth below him; Rogan, who was used to the vast, open plains of Ar'ac; Rogan, whose hard hooves were terrible at finding purchase on the slippery, rocky ground. He crossed the *vleyrpast* first with hesitation, then with outright fear, and finally, when they reached the thinnest section of the bridge, he did not move at all.

A few minutes earlier, a cloud had come drifting across their path, borne by the high winds. It had swallowed the party shockingly fast, and each of them could only see the one in front, the one behind, and up ahead, the lights of Astevyr's drifter.

Kyle had been walking behind Rogan, and had heard his grumblings of discontent all throughout the trip. Now Rogan stopped, and stood stock-still, shivering in the cold fog. The wind was snagging at his blushing collar, and the moisture was turning his chestnut fur into sodden clumps. His shoulders were hunched, his broad back hiding his face from view. Kyle couldn't see what was up ahead, so for a moment he wasn't sure why Rogan had stopped.

"Rogan?" he said. "What's going on?"

Rogan mumbled a reply, but Kyle couldn't hear it. He stepped as close as he dared, trying to see what was beyond.

"Rogan?" he said again.

"Murdon's horns," Rogan said. Still Kyle barely heard; the words were being forced through gritted teeth and a jaw clamped shut. "This is madness. I can't do this."

Kyle was afraid himself, and the thought of being caught behind Rogan was almost too much to bear. "Of course you can," he said. "This is the thinnest part. Once we're past here it'll only get better."

"The bridge is going to come down if I take another step," Rogan said. Kyle could tell that he believed this wholesale. The problem was, he half-believed it himself. But they had no other options.

"The drifter's already gone across," he said, fighting to keep his voice calm. "It weighs more than you."

Rogan shook his head stubbornly, and wouldn't speak, as if he were afraid that even this would cause the bridge to collapse.

Kyle felt Meya's hand his shoulder. "What's wrong?" she said into his ear.

"Rogan won't move," he answered, keeping his voice low. "He's scared."

There was a pause, then Meya said, "All right. Don't move. I'm going to step around you."

Using his shoulder as an anchor, Meya shuffled past Kyle on his right. The bridge was still forty feet wide, but the last ten on either side sloped into nothingness, and instinct shrank the remaining space to something that felt little more than a foot wide. Kyle's own legs locked as Meya stepped past, and he narrowed his eyes to slits. When she was finally past, he had to step backwards to give her room to work. It was the hardest couple of steps that Kyle had ever taken.

"Rogan?" Meya said, laying a hand on his back. Kyle saw white light spill from her palm and into his body.

"Leave me be!" Rogan growled. But he couldn't move to get rid of her, and she stood behind him, wordlessly pouring magic into him. Kyle watched as Rogan's muscles slowly lost their tension, and his breathing calmed.

"Please walk, Rogan," Meya said finally, rubbing his back. "One step at a time. I'll stay here behind you."

Ever so slowly, Rogan lifted one leg and took a step. He took another, and another. True to her word, Meya followed closely behind, one hand still raised.

In that manner they finished their crossing of the *vleyrpast*. It seemed forever until their path started to widen again, but once it did, their pace quickened, and soon they were passing between the jagged spires of the shrapnel mountains. Finally it was over, and they found themselves gathered in a snowy pass on the far side of the valley. The rest of their companions were standing in a huddle around Astevyr's drifter.

"*There* you are!" Nihs said. "What happened to you?"

Silently, Rogan strode forward and sat cross-legged on the snowy ground, leaning on his axe for support. Meya patted him on the shoulder.

"We had some trouble," she said, "but we're all right now."

Nihs nodded, and said nothing else.

The pass in which they found themselves was snowy and winding, turning south and north as often as it cut west. Astevyr assured them that they would come out all right on the far side, but they had little choice but to follow the path regardless. It wound between the mountains for a time, then hugged the side of a slope on the left, a steep drop falling off to the right. Once again they dismounted from the drifter so Astevyr could maneuver it down the narrow road.

They came to a fork, a second path cutting off from the first and carving a way up the mountain to their left. The fork was marked by a crude wooden sign; Kyle couldn't read the wording, but recognized the runes as being Orcish.

"What do you want to bet that those are Grul's friends up ahead?" Lugh said.

"It seems likely, sir," Astevyr agreed. "That sign reads 'village'."

They left the drifter behind and made a detour up the side of the mountain. Soon the path was beaten clean by footfalls, and not ten minutes later they came upon Grul's village.

It was everything that Kyle had expected an Orcish settlement to be—which was to say, not much. Three crude huts made of wood and hide were clustered about a pair of roaring bonfires. An Orcish woman was sitting by the fire nearest to them, sewing a hide shirt together—though "sewing" was too delicate a word for her work. She was as tall as Lugh, thin but solidly built, with several long braids of hair spilling down her back and framing her face. Her head snapped up when she heard them approach, and she immediately reached for the spear that had been propped up beside her. She relaxed when she caught sight of the intruders.

"Hoo! You're lucky I didn't put one of your eyes out, friends. Wise men make themselves known when they enter another's camp."

"Funny you should say that," Lugh said, "because Grul didn't seem to have any trouble wandering into our camp and lighting our fire for us."

The she-Orc's narrow eyes opened in recognition. "You have met Grul?"

By now, they had drawn the attention of a few men who had been seated at the far fire, and another woman emerged from one of the nearby tents. Lugh pulled the talisman from his pocket and held it up for inspection. "Met and battled as brothers in arms. He left us with a message for you."

"Well?" one of the men asked. "What is it?"

In response, Lugh pulled from his pack the second treasure that Grul had given him—the *gordja's* bright green tailfeather. There were shouts of amazement and Kyle clearly heard "*gordja! gordja!*" spoken by a few in the back.

Lugh scratched the side of his head with the tailfeather as if struggling to recall the message—*laying it on a bit thick,* Kyle thought—then said, "'If you wish to lay eyes on a true legend, and the legend who slew it, come to the valley below the *vleyrpast!*'"

Kyle couldn't believe what an impact that small statement made. There was an instant eruption of cheers, and they were pulled into the Orcs' camp, given seats close to the fire and hot drinks. Questions flooded in in no particular order—what had happened, who was Lugh, where were Grul and the *gordja,* who was Rogan, from where in the east did they hail (their identity as easterners being a given).

More drinks were brought out, and food, as well—'food' being 'meat'. Kyle had never seen a reception go from chilly to boiling hot with such speed, and secretly he wondered how their meeting would have gone if they had not had Grul's talisman or the *gordja*'s feather.

Their story was dragged out of them in bits and pieces, no two of Grul's tribesmen getting the entire picture at once, or in any sort of order. Somehow, at the end of it all, the clan came to one mind.

"A prize like this has not been known in years," one burly male said. "We must celebrate in proper fashion. We should strike camp and join with our kinsman south of the *vleyrpast*."

This statement was met by a loud rumble of agreement. Lugh raised his arm like a student at school.

"Before you take off," he said, "we would ask a favor of you, if you don't mind."

Loud shouts of "anything!" and "out with it!" Lugh smiled graciously.

"We're looking to head further north, into the *adaragad*—the meteor crater. Would one of you be willing to travel with us and guide us there?"

The camp, which seconds ago had been full of loud conversation and laughter, fell deathly quiet. For a moment, all that could be heard was the crackling of the fires, and Kyle, sensing the tension in the air, thought, *he's said something wrong. Things are going to go bad.*

Then laughter erupted throughout the camp: roaring, booming laughter that thrummed against Kyle's sore ears. It struck every man, woman and child (there were a few, Kyle had noticed) equally. Amid the gales of laughter were shouts of "*rosshku! rosshku!*"

That word again. But Kyle was too busy being perplexed about the Orcs' reaction to be perplexed about their use of the Archmage's name.

The Orcs began to question them, asking why they wanted to travel to the crater—which they simply called 'the black lands'—and how they hoped to survive. They wasted no time in letting Kyle's party know just how foolish, how *rosshku*, their undertaking was. This, Kyle reasoned, was why the tribe had laughed so. They found the concept of such a suicidal journey to be hilarious.

That, of course, didn't mean that they would be bereft of a guide. Within seconds, a fistfight had broken out between two males who each wanted the honor of guiding Kyle's party to their doom. The rest of the clan roared and clapped as the men pummeled at each other, darting around the fires that formed the core of the Orcs' camp. Kyle and the others watched in utter confusion.

"I've never had men fight over me before," Meya said to Lugh.

He punched one hand into the palm of the other. "Should I get in there so I can win your honor?"

She gave him a kiss on the cheek. "You know you don't need to do that."

Lugh, grinning from ear to ear, stepped forward and stretched his arms wide. "Gentlemen!" he shouted. "Gentlemen, please!"

The fight ground to a halt, the two contenders looking to Lugh eagerly, wondering if he'd made his decision.

"There's no need to fight over us," he said, once relative silence had descended. "Trust me, we're not worth it. In any case, our guide won't need to do any punching—they just need to take us as far north as they're willing, and drop us off at another settlement, if they can. We need a tracker or a pathfinder, not a warrior!"

This generated some confusion. Kyle could practically see the brains of their two champions working as they tried to understand why fighting was not a metric of success in this endeavor. Then a she-Orc came forward; it was the same spear-carrying woman they had met when they first entered the camp.

"I ought go!" she said. "I am the best hunter and tracker in the clan. My eyes see true and my spear strikes truer. I offer them both!"

There was a chorus of cheers and hoots. "I'd offer you my spear, Dorma, if you'd but take it!" one man shouted, to great laughter.

"And I'd take your spear, Cros, if I could but find it!" Dorma shouted back, to even more hilarity as Cros groped at his own crotch in mock distress.

"Disgusting," Nihs muttered.

"I like her," Kyle said.

As before, the clan's mind was made up in an instant. Dorma's speech, coupled with her exchange with Cros, had been enough to convince them to the last that she was the best woman for the job. She presented herself to their group, thumping mightily at her chest just below the breasts.

"I will guide you true, as far north and farther than any of us dare go," she said.

"Glad to hear it," Lugh said. "When are we leaving?"

"We will strike our tents before dawn tomorrow. The clan will go south; we will go north."

Astevyr turned to the group and made a shallow bow. "I believe, good sirs, that I will accompany the clan when they depart southwards in the morning. You are entering the wilderling north of Westia; soon the geography will turn, and my drifter will be nothing more than a burden to you. Moreover, the north is a harsh place, more suited to hardy Orcs and brave adventurers than Buorish scientists."

Lugh took his hand and clapped him on the arm. "Say no more, friend. Thanks for everything. We wouldn't have made it this far without you."

"On the contrary, good sir. Having seen your battle with the *gordja*, I am convinced that this continent holds no dangers that you cannot face."

"Let's hope for our sakes that you are right," Nihs said.

Grul's clan consisted of no more than thirty Orcs, who shared three tents between them. The largest, in the back, was the women's tent, shared by Dorma, the clan's mothers and their children, and three elderly matriarchs who were past childbearing age. It was into this tent that Meya was ushered. She disappeared inside after wishing them all a hasty goodnight.

Immediately following this, another fight broke out over how the remainder of Kyle's party would be split between the other two tents. Like Meya, Kyle had never been fought over before, and it was an experience he hoped never to repeat. Lugh, with his sharp tongue, was in high demand, as was Rogan with his immense presence; the inscrutable Buors, meanwhile, were all but ignored. Lugh solved the problem as he'd done before, by making an executive decision.

"Rogan, Astevyr, Deriahm," he said, pointing at one tent. Then, at the other: "Kyle, Nihs and I."

A great groan escaped from Orcs on both sides, but they bowed to Lugh's authority and shuffled into their tents, leaving awake two sentries to tend to their still-blazing fires.

Kyle had fully expected to freeze that night, but the inside of the tent was astonishingly hot. It certainly didn't hurt that there were ten men stuffed into a space that couldn't have been much more than that many feet across; every square inch of the floor was taken up either by an Orc or his stash of personal belongings. Orcs kicked each other out of the way to make room for Kyle and Lugh, who settled down in their bedrolls, using wads of clothing as pillows.

Dusk had been falling by the time they had crossed the *vleyrpast*, and now it was pitch-dark outside. Kyle had lost all sense of time, but figured that it must have been near the dead of night. He was bone-weary; their battle with the bird demon had taken nearly all of his energy, and the fatigue from Meya's healing had taken the rest.

Mercifully, those of their sleeping companions who were not already semi-comatose with drink seemed to recognize this, and let them be after only a few minutes of conversation. The tent was soon filled with the sounds of Orcs industriously falling asleep, which they did with as much enthusiasm as anything else. Lugh shrugged, winked at Kyle, then stretched out, crossing one leg over the other and his hands behind his head. Kyle, sensing that sleep would be at a premium for the next halfmonth, followed suit.

On the other side of the camp, Meya was being introduced to the women of Grul's clan inside a tent that was considerably more spacious and organized than the one shared by Lugh and Kyle. The clan's three matriarchs, wrinkled with age and half-blinded by woodsmoke, had a corner of the tent to themselves. The clan's young children—two at a toddling age and two only slightly older than this—lived here as well, along with their mothers and some half-dozen other women who, like Dorma, were of a fighting and marrying age.

Unlike the men's tents, there was a fire pit dug out in the center of this one. The fire burning here was little more than smoldering, but its presence was felt throughout the room. Meya's eyes started to burn as she undressed and set up her own bedroll next to Dorma's, and they didn't stop until she was seated, safe below the pall of smoke that hung in the air.

Meya sat cross-legged on her bedroll and watched their new guide as she hung up her equipment, casually slapping at one of the older children who tried to paw at her spear. Meya envied her physique—she was tall and lithe, with not an inch of fat about her hips or stomach. No doubt she was considered very beautiful by Orcish standards, and Meya suspected that little exaggeration had been involved in her boasting about her hunting abilities. Though they'd come to the decision in a strange manner, Meya could tell that their choice of guide had been a good one.

Dorma sat across from her and exhaled a long, huffing breath that Meya recognized well. It was a breath that said *the work of the day is done. Now I can rest.*

"Thank you, Dorma, for agreeing to come with us," Meya said.

Dorma grunted. "You have slain a great beast and rescued one of our brothers. It is an honor to help you."

Meya nodded. She wanted to warn Dorma of the road ahead, and tell her not to put herself in danger for their sake, but knew that this would only insult her. The surest way to get an Orc to do something was to tell them it was a bad idea.

"Is it true that your road will lead you into the black lands?" Dorma said.

"Yes. We have business with a man who lives there."

Dorma sniffed through her squashed, slitted nostrils. "I have been to the edge of the black lands," she said. "It is a cursed place. All that grows and feeds there is poison. I have never heard of any man who calls those lands home."

"There's at least one," Meya said. *Or so we hope,* she thought. She chased the thought from her mind.

Dorma sniffed again and shrugged. "*Rosshku.* But no business of mine. I will take you to the edge of the lands, where I have been before; you will meet no Orc who will take you further."

"Thank you, Dorma," Meya said again. Dorma nodded, and then jabbed her chin at Meya's bedroll.

"Sleep is scarce in the wilderlands. You ought to gather as much as you are able now."

Kyle awoke, sweating and cramped, to the sensation of a million icy spiders crawling over his flesh. Orcs were coming in and out of their sleeping tent, and each time the flap was pulled back, a blast of cold air washed over him.

The cold jolted him awake better than any alarm clock ever had. He sat up and began to pull on his warm clothes.

Today's the day, he thought. The next leg of their journey was soon to begin. The icy expanse of the wilderlands loomed ahead; beyond that, the black lands, the *adaragad.* Beyond those, the tower of Archsage Vohrusien himself.

They had come so far already—more than halfway up the continent of Westia. But this had been by airship and logging transport and Astevyr's drifter; the final stretch would make for a more difficult journey than everything they had done so far taken at once. From here, it was only to get colder and darker, colder and darker. He'd likely sweated his last inside the cramped Orcish tent.

They stepped outside to a flurry of activity. Grul's clan were striking camp, preparing to head further south. The women's tent was being picked apart, and already there was no sign of the other men's tent. As soon as Kyle's own tent was empty, it was swarmed and disassembled with practiced efficiency. Posts were pulled out of the ground, canvas sheets were bundled together with rope, and the resulting load was shared between the members of the tribe. Before long there was no camp to speak of, and Grul's clanmates were bidding them farewell. They shook Lugh's hand and thudded their chests as they saluted Dorma.

"Bring us honor! Do us proud!" were the words that came back time and again. Dorma bowed at each farewell, standing tall with her spear by her side.

Astevyr made his own farewells, bowing gracefully at the waist in the Buorish manner.

"Best of luck, my friends. I eagerly await the news of your safe return!"

"Hold for the moment, brother," Deriahm said. "I believe there is something you have forgotten."

"Oh?"

Deriahm nodded. "The king's *rouk.* You have yet to accept it."

Astevyr swatted the statement aside. "Say no more on the subject, comrade, lest I leave you in bad humor! You requested my aid and I provided it freely, with no expectation of payment. Save your breath, for I cannot—*will* not—accept your gift!"

Deriahm sighed. "You are truly immovable?"

"I am."

Deriahm extended one gloved hand. "Very well, then. I will not try to persuade you. Take my hand, instead, as well as our deepest thanks."

Astevyr did, with great enthusiasm. "I wish you well, young *irushai*. As Dorma's brothers and sisters said to her, so do I say to you: make our countrymen proud!"

"I will," Deriahm said. "You have my solemn oath."

Astevyr clambered into his drifter and opened the magic intake. He brought the machine around, gave the party one final nod, and then sped off after Grul's clan, which had already vanished into the snow.

"I'm surprised you let him get the better of you," Rogan said. "I was expecting that argument to go on for hours."

"I would expect the same, sir," Deriahm said cheerfully. "That is why I decided to spare us the trouble, and packed the king's *rouk* among his effects early this morning."

Rogan blinked in surprise, then gave a hearty laugh.

"You're craftier than you look, little one."

Dorma strode forward, stabbing the butt of her spear into the ground. "Talk, talk, talk!" she said. "Do all easterners talk so much? We must use every second of daylight we have, unless you want to be old and gray when you finally reach this wizard's tower of yours."

"Yes!" Nihs said from the crook of Rogan's shoulder. "Well spoken. I couldn't agree more."

Dorma wasn't paying attention; she was cutting a path north, her footfalls light upon the snowy ground.

"Then walk, don't talk," she said over her shoulder. "And mayhaps you will live to see the east again."

Looking back, Kyle wouldn't have been able to say whether their first day in the wilderlands was the easiest or hardest of the lot. Many things went well—the sun shone well into the evening, the air was still, and their trail, which wound up, down and around one featureless snowy hill after the other, was easy enough. But Kyle had never walked so far in so long on any other day of his life, and was woefully unprepared for how excruciatingly difficult it was.

The cold was not so terrible—not yet. The clothes they had bought in Skralingsgrad were some of the thickest and warmest that Loria had to offer and, if anything, Kyle's chest was burning with heat by the end of the day. But his fingers and toes were numb within the first hour, and the exposed part of his face stung with cold.

Far worse than the cold was the walking itself. Kyle had done his fair share of walking since coming to Loria, but never across such rough terrain, and never with such a heavy pack on his back. The sheer effort it took to lift one foot, drag it through the thick snow, and then press it down beyond the other became insurmountable as the day wore on. His thighs burned, and a wedge was driven into the small of his back. He didn't know if they were high up enough for the air to thin, but it certainly felt that way—or perhaps it was just the chill in the air he sucked into his lungs that led him to believe each breath was doing more harm than good. Water ran from his nose and froze into the hairs of his beard above his lip.

In that manner he carried on doggedly, determined not to be the weak link of the group. His companions walked alongside him, some faring better than others. Rogan, carrying his enormous pack, was walking with mulish determination, his energy seemingly endless. But Nihs, who rode on his shoulder, looked much the worse for wear even though he wasn't doing any of the work himself. His tiny green face was puckered with discomfort, and he had dug himself deeply into the fur of Rogan's collar for warmth.

Only Dorma, their guide, walked with any kind of energy. Her straight-backed poise remained unchanged even after five hours of walking, and she often kept thirty paces ahead of the rest of the party. When they came to a hill, she would crest it in one swift dash, and then stand atop it, squinting at the land beyond for signs of danger. She would wait for the others to catch up, then take off once more, leaving them no time to gather their energy.

"Move, swiftly, while the sun is still with us," she would say. "There will be time enough to rest when darkness falls."

Enchanted by the promise of rest, it was darkness for which Kyle began to pray as they walked.

Please. He projected his prayers at the bronze disc hanging in the sky, not caring that he had it to thank for whatever warmth he felt. *Please, set. Let Dorma tell us it's time to rest.*

A Kyle who had not spent the last six hours trudging through the snows of Westia might have found this foolish, even juvenile, but he was tired and sore, and his fingers were stiff and throbbing with pain. When their walk had first begun, he'd felt at least some semblance of energy, and had even taken time to appreciate the raw beauty of the landscape that surrounded them. But now he dug his chin into his scarf, squinted his eyes as close to shut as could be, and had no mind for anything but putting one foot in front of the other.

Left, then right. Left, then right. Each step is bringing you closer to the tower. Each step gets you one step closer to Archsage Vohrusien.

How many miles until they reached Vohrusien's tower? They couldn't be sure, as no one knew where the exact center of the *adaragad* was. At least one hundred. Possibly as much as two.

How many miles could a human walk in a day? A human who was tired, and sore, and homesick, and bent double under the weight of his travel pack—the thing that was, ironically, supposed to keep him alive? Kyle couldn't remember, and he was too tired to do the math.

Don't think about that. Think about left, then right.

Finally, finally, the sun dipped below the horizon—or more accurately, behind a ridge of mountains in the far distance—and Dorma called for a halt. Kyle wanted nothing more than to let his legs give way and sink to the ground, but there was still more work to do. They found a sheltered plot of land and set up camp, pitching their tents, unrolling their beds, and gathering wood for a fire. What they managed to find was scant, but burned merrily enough, and that was enough for Kyle. He took off his gloves and laid them flat by the fire, and thrust his hands out until they sang with pain. But it was a good pain, and though his fingers started the night off swollen stiff, he found he could soon move them again.

They ate a small meal of packaged food, and Kyle ate with all the more enthusiasm knowing that his pack was getting lighter with each bite. The fear that they might not have enough food to finish their journey was distant, for the time being.

They talked a little, though having spent the day doing nothing but walking, there was little to talk about. Lugh bent his head back and forth and then knuckled roughly at his own neck. "I think those straps need a few more layers of padding. I feel like I've been whipped." He leaned his neck toward Meya. "I don't suppose you could help a poor cripple out?"

Meya smiled indulgently—and yes, there was something behind that smile that hadn't been there before. She reached out and there was a flash of white light. Lugh sighed with relief.

"We oughtn't do that as the days wear on," Nihs warned. He was sitting no more than a foot from the fire, with his sagecloak wrapped about him. He looked like a small red bean. "We users of magic need to conserve every ounce of our power, so we can use it when it's needed most."

"Oh, go on," Lugh said, but without much enthusiasm. It was obvious he knew that Nihs was right.

They spoke little after that, and when the fire started to die down Dorma ordered them into their sleeping tents. Kyle's party had brought two, and Dorma, working off the Orcish wisdom that there was always room for one more, hadn't brought one of her own. Kyle, Deriahm, Meya and Lugh shared one, while Rogan, Nihs and Dorma took the other. The arrangements reminded Kyle most of the *Markuss*, the tub they had ridden from Mjolsport to Oasis—there was absolutely no personal space to go around. It mattered little, because they all slept fully clothed, shivering together in the darkness. Deriahm wrapped himself in his cloak to spare the others the agony of touching his bare armor; though

Kyle could feel heat emanating from Lugh behind him, nothing came from Deriahm's form to indicate that he was anything but an empty shell of metal. Try though he might, Kyle couldn't force himself to be curious about this. His whole body ached, and his eyes couldn't keep themselves open. The wind picked up and battered at the sides of their tent. The sound was deafeningly loud, but somehow soothing. Kyle curled up, holding in heat as best he could, and allowed it to rock him to sleep.

They awoke to a steady wind blowing from the east, and a foot of fresh snow piled against the flaps of their tents. Light and fluffy, it skipped along in the wind in wisps of white, carving delicate, undulating dunes into the landscape. It was pretty, even beautiful, but Dorma sniffed in displeasure when she stepped outside.

"A storm blows in from the east. We must move all the more quickly today if we are to outrun it."

This caused general groans of protest, but Dorma was unfeeling.

"You easterners came to this land and asked I be your guide. Heed me or perish; the choice is yours."

They ate a hasty breakfast and struck their tents—or, more accurately, watched Dorma strike their tents for them. She moved incredibly fast for someone completely unfamiliar with modern equipment, and before long they were stepping through the fluffy snow, cutting north while the wind tried to blow them off-track.

Kyle's back and shoulders were afire with pain, and the thought of spending another day laboring underneath his pack was almost too much to bear. But he grit his teeth and stepped left, then right, never missing a beat despite the breakneck pace Dorma had set.

During the second day, Kyle discovered two new foes that inhabited the snowy foothills of the wilderlands. The first was wind. It seemed mild at first, but as the day wore on, its playful touch became a sting, and then grew to a sharp pain. He pulled his scarf up over his ears and pulled his hood down, and that worked, for a time. But the wind would inevitably find a way underneath the lip of his hood and go shooting around inside, freezing his forehead and the back of his skull in equal measure. Or, worse yet, it would yank his hood straight off, and the bubble of warmth he had spent the last half hour building up would be gone in seconds. He began to walk at a ridiculous forty-five-degree angle, trying to put his back to the wind while moving straight ahead.

The next was boredom. Boredom and pain went hand in hand, Kyle discovered. The more he felt of the former, the more time his mind had to dwell on the latter. To make matters worse, defending against boredom was if anything much harder than defending against the wind. No one was in the mood to talk, so Kyle retreated into his own mind in an attempt to distract himself. He thought of the mild, blue-skied, pre-summer heat of Reno city, and the thick, oppressive atmosphere of Buoria. He thought about Proks, and the comfortable cave home of Jire and Rehs. Finally, he thought of Oasis, the boiling heat cut by the cool water underfoot; the sparkling, gleaming houses and the beautiful women that bathed in outdoor pools.

It helped, for a time. But Westia asserted itself in each gust of wind that lanced down his ears, and each flake of snow that found its way into his boots. His teeth chattered, and more and more he found himself being tugged back to reality.

Resigning himself to being stuck in Westia—at least for the time being—he took some time to look around. They had been moving steadily downhill through the foothills of the shrapnel mountains, and had emerged in the remains of a boreal forest. Few of the trees here were still upright, and fewer still were alive. Most had fallen years ago, and were buried under layers of snow and ice. They walked single file among the petrified stumps. Seen from above, their party would have looked like a gaily-colored caterpillar, gray Dorma in her brown furs taking the lead, chestnut Rogan and his red collar in the rear.

There was little sound here but the howling of the wind and the creaking of ancient trees. It seemed the storm that Dorma had promised was indeed blowing in; the wind was picking up, and angry clouds rolled overhead. Snowflakes the size of thumbnails were nipping at their cheeks and burying themselves in the crooks of their clothing.

Beyond the forest was a dark, icy plain—a frozen lake that stretched from horizon to horizon, its far coast dimly visible in the gray air.

Dorma called for a halt as they were coming to the lake's shore. She turned to glance behind them, her narrow eyes held almost shut, lids forming a V-shape on her face.

"The worst is behind us," she said, "but if we stop here, the storm's tail will lash us in the night."

"So we carry on, over the lake?" Rogan said.

Dorma grunted. "The winds will be higher—if we go out, we must walk enough to escape the storm, or suffer a worse fate than being caught on the shore. Do you easterners have the strength for this?"

"Let's do it," Nihs said. "The sooner we finish this cursed journey, the better."

Kyle was surprised by the anger in his voice, and when he looked at the tiny Kol he saw that Nihs was not faring well in the cold at all. His skin had been leached of some of its green color, and he was shivering intensely. His ears, usually ready to break from the sides of his head and undulate in the air, looked like they were frozen in place.

Dorma grunted again. "If we walk, we must walk," she warned. "Two...no, three hours more."

That statement made Kyle want to cry, but he nodded, and saw that the others were nodding, as well.

"Very well. We walk."

The wind out on the lake felt at least three times more intense than it had among the trees. Keeping a straight path was like swimming against a strong current of water. At least here the ground was perfectly flat, and Kyle no longer felt in danger of stumbling every time he put a foot down.

They struck out straight across the narrow part of the lake, headed for the mountains on the far side. At first, Kyle fixed his gaze forward, willing the mountains to draw closer. But after an hour walking, the horizon seemed as far away as ever, and he gave up.

Left, then right. His shoulders and hips were burning. His arms were about ready to fall out of their sockets. But Dorma had not ordered them to stop, and so Kyle would not.

It was a full three hours more before Dorma was satisfied with the lead they had built against the storm. The wind was still high, but no snow was carried upon it. Looking back, Kyle was secretly glad that they had pushed on for so long; the coast behind them and a good deal of the lake's surface had been swallowed by boiling gray clouds.

They pitched their tents in the middle of the lake, driving the spikes directly into the icy surface. Lugh squatted down and brushed a square of ice clean with a gloved hand as if trying to peer through.

"There's water somewhere down there," he said. "Wonder if there's anything swimming in it."

Dorma laughed shortly. "For certain. But we will never know of them and they will never know of us."

They ate, then squeezed into their tents. Kyle was now grateful for the tiny size of their sleeping arrangements; even without a fire, he managed to feel something at least approaching warmth as the tent gradually heated up. The wind teased at the walls of their tent, but it lacked cutting power. Exhausted, he fell asleep within minutes of laying down.

He awoke to more aches and pains—a throbbing between his shoulder blades, a stiffness of his back, and a twinge on the right side of his neck. He also awoke to Dorma's shouting, which was even more painful. It heralded another day of endless walking.

"Come, you lazes! Get up, unless you want to spend another night sleeping on the lake!"

"She's going to make an excellent mother someday," Lugh said. Kyle heard Meya giggle from his far side.

It was a dismal-looking day. Dark, brooding clouds formed a gray ceiling overhead, which was mirrored by the icy lake below. A white band of clear sky was sandwiched between them, featureless but for the far coast in the distance, and the near coast behind them. Kyle estimated that they were almost halfway across the lake, which meant he had four hours of even ground to look forward to before they began to climb anew.

They ate and then struck their tents. This time, Dorma took one while the rest of the party took the other. They very nearly beat her to the finish.

More walking. How far had they come in the past two days? There were no familiar sights behind—no sign of the shrapnel mountains. But there was, Kyle knew, an incredible amount of Westia out there. Could they really hope to traverse even a small fraction of it by foot?

He forced himself not to think of this. Of course, that meant that he had to distract himself with something else. Today, he chose music: he fetched up songs from the back of his mind, songs that he had known back on Terra, and played them to himself in his head as if it were an mp3 player. He chose long ballads and entertained himself by trying to piece together the lyrics: he spent half an hour on *American Pie* and then another on *Won't Get Fooled Again*. Then he visited *Hey Jude*, which was a mistake—he spent fifteen minutes on *na, na, nanana na* before he could thrust it out of his mind and replace it with something else.

He found that he was having an amazing amount of fun. Nostalgia and homesickness (was there really any difference between the two?) swept over him in waves as each song came back to him, carrying its own set of memories with it. An amusing thought occurred to him: *If I had any musical talent at all, I could release these songs in Loria and make a fortune.*

Then again, perhaps not. Kyle strongly believed that success was ten percent talent, ninety percent marketing, and this was the ninety percent he was missing. Not to mention that the musical tastes of Loria's denizens probably differed from those of the average American. He doubted the electric guitar had made its debut in Loria, as well.

Oh well. He didn't think he would have done it even if he could have. What kind of absurdity would it be if he stayed in Loria just so he could plagiarize The

Beatles and Don McLean?

Thinking thoughts such as these, and resolutely putting one foot in front of the other, Kyle whiled away the time while the lake's far shore grew ever so slightly larger in the distance.

By the end of the day they had reached the lake's opposite shore, though it was a close thing. Twilight was falling as the *clup-clup* of their footsteps again became a snowy *crunch*. This shore looked much like the one they had left behind, but here there were no trees, and the slope of the land was greater. At first, Dorma wanted them to scale the vast hill ahead of them before resting, but she relented when she saw the condition of her charges. Instead, they stepped a short distance back over the lake so they could rest on flat ground.

Kyle lay flat on his back, hoping against hope that the fiery kink in his spine would be gone by morning, having taken the endlessly repeating coda of *Hey Jude* with it.

The next day they awoke to high wind, icy flurries of snow, and the most biting cold Kyle had experienced yet. The day was otherwise sunny, which somehow made matters worse; Kyle had dared to feel optimistic when he first poked his head out of the tent.

As usual, Dorma had been the first to awaken, and was waiting for them when they stepped out of their tents. Kyle wasn't sure if he should be comforted or concerned by the slight look of pain she wore on her face.

"This will be a bad day," she said flatly. "Cover your fingers, toes, ears. Do not stop moving, and do not step out of each other's sight. The snow will swallow you if you let it."

They set off, Dorma's warning ringing in their ears. Kyle forced himself to keep his eyes on Lugh's back as he walked. He was not the world's greatest survivalist, but he understood what would happen if one of them got lost in the snow.

As the storm got worse, his field of vision shrank and shrank, until all he could see was Lugh in front of him and Deriahm behind. His heart was already pounding with exertion, but now it began to pound with claustrophobia as well. It was fine as long as he focused on Lugh, but whenever his eyes wandered, he would see nothing but a sea of white in all directions, and his chest would tighten in fear.

The snow will swallow you if you let it. Yes, that's certainly what it felt like. They were headed down a white gullet, pressed in on all sides by the storm.

With the disappearance of sight came the disappearance of time. It stretched out in both directions, until Kyle couldn't tell whether they had just started the day's walking or were nearly finished. There were no landmarks to go by, and if the ground in front of them hadn't been sloping steadily upwards, Kyle would have been certain that they were going in circles.

Eventually, all thought wore away, and Kyle shambled forward in a half-doze. His eyes had drooped next to shut, and he was no longer looking at Lugh, only the footprints he was leaving behind. In such a manner he actually ran into his friend's back when they finally stopped at Dorma's signal.

"Stay here," she snapped at Kyle and Lugh. "Wait for the others. Do not move from this spot."

And without another word, she bounded into the endless whiteness that surrounded them, long legs skipping through the snow.

Kyle, Lugh, and Meya all shared a glance. Eventually Lugh shrugged.

"I'm sure she has her reasons. Let's wait—I certainly don't want to wander off into *that*."

They were soon caught up by Deriahm, then Rogan and Nihs. Nihs was bundled in Rogan's arms like a baby, and had never looked so miserable. All but his eyes and part of his nose were wrapped in his red sagecloak, and his gaze was sleepy and unfocused.

"This one isn't doing so well," Rogan said quietly to Meya. "We'll have need of you before the day is out."

Meya nodded. "I'm not surprised. I can give him enough energy to keep him going for a while more."

"Mm," Rogan said. "Where's our guide?"

"Out playing with the snow sprites," Lugh said. He'd set his pack down and was lounging against it, half-sunk into the snow. "She got sick of us and left us here to die."

"Very funny," Rogan said, then added, "you're going to freeze your rear end off."

"That's what you're here for, isn't it, you big rug?"

Rogan huffed. "You've got something else coming if you think I'm going anywhere near your rear end."

They had all reached a point of exhaustion where they found this to be the height of humor. Their laughter rang out in the cold air and was snatched away by the wind. A moment later, a dark shape emerged out of the storm, and Kyle had reached for his sword by the time he realized it was Dorma. She was wearing an inch of snow on her head and shoulders and a deep scowl.

"Noise, noise!" she said. "You easterners are all noise!"

"It's part of our charm," Lugh said, vaulting to his feet.

Meya turned away from him, trying not to smile. "What's going on, Dorma?"

Dorma sniffed and spat into the storm. "We can go no farther tonight. But we walk in another tribe's shadow. They will not take kindly to our trespass if they find us."

"What does that mean?" Lugh said.

Dorma treated him to a dark look. "If we go to their camp and offer gifts, they may let us pass. If our gifts are splendid enough, they may even help us. But it might amuse them to drive us off and let us freeze. They would think the fate fitting of a bunch of easterners."

A chill ran down Kyle's spine. He thought of the warm welcome they had enjoyed at Grul's camp, and how even at the time he'd wondered if all Orcs were so kindly.

Lugh was hissing breath through his teeth. "What kind of gifts would they want?"

"Hide whatever you do not want demanded of you. Food, furs…weapons make a fine gift."

Weapons? Yeah, right, Kyle thought. "If we give them our weapons, we'll get ourselves killed as soon as we reach the *adaragad* anyway."

"My thought exactly," Lugh said. "All right, you heard the lady. Hide everything you can't give up and let's talk to these Orcs."

Meya drew up beside Dorma as they walked.

"We won the favor of your clan by killing the *gordja*," she said.

Dorma barked laughter. "These folk will not be satisfied with a few feathers."

Meya's red hair brushed her cheek as she shook her head. "Not feathers," she said. "But there are ways that we could turn them to our side without giving them gifts, aren't there?"

Dorma gave her a sidelong look. "Say whatever you mean to say, and stop wasting your breath."

Meya told her of the plan that had been cooking in her mind ever since the party had visited Grul's camp. Dorma's thin nostrils flared.

"I would not do something so cowardly!" she snapped.

"But it wouldn't be," Meya insisted. "Because we would tell them afterwards. And the story of how we got them would win them over even more. I'm right, aren't I?"

"I don't care if you're right," Dorma growled. "I will have no part in this… *trickery*."

"*Yes, you will!*" Meya shouted, so loudly that she had to turn back and wave Lugh away to convince him she was all right. She turned back to Dorma. "We can't afford to give away anything—no food, no weapons, no clothes. All we brought with us is *all we have*. And it still might not be enough. Our lives are in your hands. And if you won't help us get where we're going, you might as well turn around and let us make our own way."

Dorma stopped short, and looked down at Meya with eyes hard as flint. Meya forced herself to meet them, though they floated nearly a foot above her own. For a moment she thought Dorma might hit her. Then she unfroze, and all at once continued to walk.

"There is some she-wolf in you, girl," she said to the snow before her. "Perhaps *you* should be the one to earn the clan's favor."

That was the closest thing to a compliment Dorma had paid any of them, so Meya thought she was in. "I can't," she said. "I don't know the first thing about fistfighting, and even if I did, the clan would never accept my victory. They'd say I was—" *what did Grul call me?* "—a witch."

Dorma grunted. "You are right." Her tone was surprised, even wondering. "Very well, red one. We do things your way. Tell the men."

Meya allowed herself a smile. "They'll find out soon enough."

Kyle had no idea how Dorma had found the Orcs' camp, or even how she had known it existed in the first place. They travelled along the side of the mountain for a while, then came to a black outcrop of stone. Nestled on the windward side of the rock was an Orcish camp about twice the size of Dorma and Grul's. Its dark silhouette had only just emerged from the white when Dorma called for a halt.

"We must make noise and announce ourselves, or they are liable to think we are monsters stalking through the snow." She addressed Rogan. "You. Hold out your axe for me."

Rogan did so, and Dorma banged against it with her spear.

"*Ho! Ho!*" she shouted, and then bellowed a few words in Orcish. She began to step forward, still shouting, and the rest followed behind her.

The camp grew out of the storm as they approached, and soon they could see that a half-dozen Orcs were standing, facing them, weapons in hand. Most had spears similar to Dorma's, and some had axes similar to the one she banged against (though none near as grand). They were quite indistinguishable from Grul's band, at least to Kyle's untrained eye; he had no head for the significance of the various furs and bangles that each Orc wore.

Unlike Grul's band, Kyle could sense hostility emanating from these Orcs before the first one spoke. They were large, hulking men—no women had come to greet them—and the one who first came forward to speak was badly scarred about the face and arms.

He bellowed a challenge in Orcish; even through the storm, Kyle could clearly see flecks of spittle flying between his tusks. Dorma replied in kind, and the harshness of her voice, made harsher by the language she spoke, made it clear that any welcome they could earn among these people would be hard-won indeed.

A few sentences were traded. The male Orc laughed, and his companions laughed with him, but it was not a kindly sound.

Finally Dorma said, in words Kyle could understand, "Then be sure of us, and let us by the fire. If we are but feeble easterners, you have nothing to fear from us."

"Sure, sure!" the male Orc replied. His accent was so heavy—*sshoor, sshoor!*— that at first Kyle didn't realize he could understand what was said. "Come in by the warm!"

The Orc stood to one side and waved them in. His tone was mocking, and his companions were still laughing; there was some kind of joke here that Kyle wasn't privy to. He felt color rising in his cheeks. He didn't take kindly to being teased. If these Orcs gave them trouble, they would soon find out just what a feeble easterner could do.

They stepped into the camp, each of them keenly aware of the tension in the air. Kyle stiffened as he stepped past the lead Orc. He was taller even than Dorma, and more than twice as broad. He smelled strongly of sweat and animal fur.

"I don't like this," Kyle said in a low voice to Lugh. His friend nodded sagely.

"Don't need to speak Orcish to see what's going on here. But let's not get ahead of ourselves. I trust Dorma's judgement."

Of course you do, Kyle found himself thinking, but he kept his doubts to himself.

They were led into the circle of light generated by one of the camp's three firepits; safe beneath a canvas shield, it was burning, though barely. More Orcs turned out to see what was going on. Men, women and children alike watched them with flinty, narrowed eyes.

The Orc who had waved them into camp now strode forward and spoke to his clanmates. His voice was loud and carrying, and halfway through his speech he gestured to Kyle's group in a grandiose fashion. There was more laughter. Finally he turned, hands on hips, and said, "So! The easterners seek passage through our land. What do they offer in return?"

Dorma stepped forward. "I offer the gift of truth!" she said in a ringing voice.

The Orc's white brows met, his balance thrown. "What?" he said.

Dorma thrust her arms forward and waved them rather dramatically. "I am a gifted seer, and can tell you truths about yourself yet unknown to you. Give me your palm, Aggar, and I will tell your fortune." And she held out one slender hand, palm up, fingers spread.

The other Orcs of Aggar's clan were stepping forward, interested. Aggar himself had now folded his arms, and his expression was thunderous.

"What is this?" It was a deep-chested growl.

"Do you fear the truth?" Dorma pressed.

"I fear nothing!" Aggar boomed, more spit flying from his mouth. He slapped his palm down on Dorma's, hard enough to make her whole body shake. "Here, witch! Tell me of all the women I will bed before the long night comes!"

A laugh rippled through Aggar's clan, but it was hushed. Most were fixated on Dorma, who had closed her eyes and who was keening softly under her breath. A moment passed, then another.

"Yes..." she said finally. Then, in a loud wail: "Yes, I see! Oh, fates!"

"What is it?" Aggar said, trying and failing to hide the tension in his voice. "Out with it!"

Dorma looked at him with shining eyes. "You...are a lover of mules! But your manhood is so small, even the mules don't know it!"

Kyle almost swallowed his tongue, but the Orcs of Aggar's clan burst into a roar of laughter. They slapped each other on the back and stamped their feet. Children rolled around on the snowy ground, and Aggar was tackled and pounded at by his friends.

Kyle couldn't help it; he started to laugh, too. And as he did, he watched the Orcs around him and thought, *is it really so simple?*

But Aggar was throwing his friends off and clambering to his feet. His face was flushed. He drew a dagger made of bone from his belt and pointed at Dorma with his free hand.

"Your tongue is smart enough, woman," he said, "but that makes for a poor gift. Still, if you have nothing else to offer, I will gladly take it from you."

The laughter died out as quickly as it had started, and Kyle knew that if Aggar were now to make for Dorma's tongue, his fellow clanmates would hold her down as he cut it off.

But Dorma raised her fists, and for the first time Kyle realized that she had acquired two new pieces of jewelry—a heavy silver band worn around each wrist. They were a little large on her, hanging from her forearms like bangles, and looked bizarrely familiar.

I've seen those before. Where?

"A knife is a woman's weapon," Dorma said—a little ironically, Kyle thought. "If it is my tongue you want, come tear it out with your bare hands."

Now interest was building again. A hot lust was simmering among the folk of Aggar's clan. They fanned out, creating a ring around the firepit, enclosing the two would-be fighters.

Aggar paced back and forth, trying to get a measure of what was going on. "There's no honor in hitting a woman," he said.

"Then you have nothing to fear," Dorma said. "For you won't hit me, not once."

Finally goaded beyond self-control, Aggar bellowed and lunged at Dorma. His fist shot out, fast and incredibly strong. Dorma blocked, and the sound of the two arms meeting each other was a deep *whock* of flesh. He lashed out again, left then right, his fists blurring, but Dorma knocked both aside before following up with a punch of her own. As she did, there was an angry *buzz* of magic, and the bracelet on her right arm glowed Ephicer blue. Her curving fist burned an arc of blue light into the air that hung in place even after her punch connected. And connect it did, with a burst of magic like a small explosion. Kyle felt the impact of the blow in his gut.

Aggar was knocked back, almost off his feet. His eyes bulged in confusion, then narrowed in anger. He charged forward, and he and Dorma exchanged more blows, lightning-fast. Every time Dorma blocked or threw a punch, her wrists flashed blue, and Aggar was blown away as if struck by an invisible wall of energy.

Kyle watched the two Orcs tussling, and suddenly comprehension dawned. He *had* seen the bracelets before—worn, but never used. Phundasa had never gotten that chance.

Dorma was wearing the enchanted bracelets that had once been given to Phundasa the Orc by King Azanhein. Kyle had completely forgotten that they existed. He sidled up to Meya and said in a low voice: "I didn't know you'd held on to them."

Meya's eyes were shining with a light that was half triumph, half sadness. "I was going to bury them with his body. But I kept hearing his voice in my mind, laughing at me, telling me what a stupid waste that would be, that we needed all the help we could get. So I kept them. Now I'm glad I did."

Kyle watched Dorma chasing Aggar around the ring, untouchable behind the powerful bracelets. "What will the clan say when they find out Dorma was cheating?"

"We'll take care of that," Meya said, and Kyle didn't dare dispute her.

The fight, for all its ferocity, did not last long. Aggar was formidable, but he was no match for Dorma and her enchanted armor. Still, Dorma did lose her bet; Aggar succeeded in touching her a half-dozen times before she finally laid him out with an uppercut to the jaw. He flew backwards and slammed into the ground on his back, groaning and semi-conscious. A great cheer erupted from the clan, and Dorma was instantly swarmed by admirers. Aggar had snow pressed to his bruises and his face slapped, and he soon woke, but it was a while before he could walk without help.

Dorma threw her arms up in the air and shouted something in Orcish. Another cheer arose, then was chased away by a wave of silence. Dorma spoke for a while, pulling the bangles from her wrists and holding them out before her, as if asking forgiveness for cheating. Kyle had no idea what she was saying. Instead, he watched the faces of Aggar's clanmates. He saw surprise, disbelief, a few flares of anger—but mostly, awe and acceptance.

"These, then, are our gifts!" Dorma said finally, lapsing out of Orcish. She held the bracelets aloft. "These magical bangles, given once as a gift by the Buorish king!"

Kyle sucked in his breath. "*Meya!*" he said.

She was nodding. "It's all right. If there's anything we can afford to give up, it's them. Besides—" and tears were standing in her eyes when she next looked at Kyle "—you could say that Das is now back in his homeland. He might have been a greenskin, but Westia is the Orcs' home. I'd rather they end up here than anywhere else."

The Orc who had helpfully slapped Aggar awake now stepped forward.

"The bangles are not enough!" he boomed, holding up one thick finger. There was a clamor of agreement, and Kyle's heart sank like a stone.

The Orc continued: "We also demand the tale of how they were won!"

Cheers, even louder than before, and suddenly Kyle and the others were being pulled forward, given seats by the fire, given food and strong drink, surrounded by a horde of new friends. Kyle was completely overwhelmed. He'd never seen such a volatile people in all his life. Ten minutes ago, he'd been fully prepared to cut his way out of Aggar's camp. Now, it looked like they would be still fighting their way out, but for a completely different reason.

Rogan had Orcish children climbing all over him. Dorma and Meya were surrounded by groups of admirers, as was Lugh as soon as he downed his first drink in a single gulp. Deriahm, quiet and reserved, was left alone for a time, until the men of Aggar's clan discovered the joy to be had in pummeling at his rock-solid breastplate while he stood politely still, never once showing that the blows did him any harm.

All in all, the only person less popular among Aggar's clan than Kyle was Nihs. The little Kol had recovered somewhat but still looked very ill, and his face was sour as a lemon. Kyle, for his part, didn't mind the lack of attention. He was bone-weary and was enjoying both the fire warming him from the outside, and the drink warming him from the inside. A stew was made, and a bowl of bubbling meat and fat was pressed into Kyle's hands. He ate ravenously, then sat back, half dozing, as Lugh kept their promise to the clan, and recounted the tale of how they had won Phundasa's bracelets. His audience was equal parts rapt and raucous; Orcs listened intently, then interrupted, then started shouting over one another. Blows were exchanged, and they fell silent once again.

It wasn't until later that Kyle realized he had actually fallen asleep where he sat, and missed the conclusion of Lugh's story. Night had fallen, and the storm had stilled; now it was only the errant flake of snow that hung suspended in the warm air over the fire. Rogan and Nihs had gone to bed; Deriahm was sitting alert at Kyle's right, reminding him oddly of a watchdog who was standing guard over his fallen master. *He probably* has *been ordered to protect me*, Kyle thought sleepily.

Seated on the far side of the fire were Lugh and Meya. Meya was curled up under Lugh's arm, her eyes pressed tightly closed. Lugh's head was bowed, his cheek resting in Meya's hair, but he was awake: Kyle could see a golden sliver of light reflecting off his good eye. It caught Kyle's own, and flickered briefly as Lugh winked.

Orcs were still scattered about, some seated near the fires, some talking, some simply laying spread-eagled in the snow.

"I think, good sir, that we had best rest," Deriahm said at Kyle's elbow. "We have many more harsh days ahead of us."

Kyle nodded. Deriahm's was the voice of reality, of the miles and miles of snow and mountain they had yet to cross.

"You're right," he said. He caught Lugh's eye again, who was watching them curiously.

"What's this?" Lugh said.

"Bed," Kyle mouthed across the fire.

Lugh nodded, then looked down at Meya with the expression of a man contemplating his mortality. He shook her ever so slightly, and she responded by pulling her arms tighter around his neck. Kyle started to laugh.

"Good luck," he said.

Lugh winked and said, "I've learned this trick. Watch." He shook her again and said, "Hey, Alexis."

Meya's eyes snapped open. They were glowing red, and at that moment Kyle thought she looked incredibly beautiful and incredibly dangerous. She looked up at Lugh.

"Yes, *Lughenor?*" she said.

Lugh was smiling. Kyle thought that Lugh would have smiled at a hooded cobra.

"Time for bed," he said.

While she treated Lugh to a look with which Kyle was all too familiar, he decided rather unwisely to ask, "Your real name is Alexis?"

The look darted from Lugh to Kyle, and he found himself pinned to his seat by it.

"I'm not in the habit of telling people," she said. "As *some* of us don't know how to keep our mouths shut."

"Did I mention it's bedtime?" Lugh said.

The night at Aggar's camp passed much in the same way as it had at Dorma and Grul's. They awoke to a day that could not have been more different from the one before; the air was perfectly still, the sky a clear, beautiful blue, and the sun was blazing. It was still cold, but Kyle could almost forget this as he warmed himself by the fire, drinking leftover stew from the night before.

Though food was scarce, they were given a gift of salted meat to help fill out their packs. Kyle's spirits were soaring. It was impossible to be gloomy in the face of the sunlight glinting off the fresh-fallen snow, listening to the laughter of Aggar's Orcs, who were now their loyal friends. Aggar himself had forgiven Dorma completely once his senses had come back to him, and had several times proclaimed his intention to make her his wife. Dorma, to Kyle's surprise, did not seem entirely at odds with the idea.

All too soon, it was time to head out again. Aggar's Orcs, for all of their friendliness, didn't prolong the goodbyes. Aggar head-butted Dorma and bade her take care of the easterners. Women and children lined up at the edges of the camp to see them off. Kyle shouldered his pack, now heavier than ever, and found that despite this the pain in his shoulder and back had faded away.

With Dorma once more in the lead, they fell into single file and headed north.

Days later, they had finally crested the mountain ridge and picked their way carefully down the far side. Beyond was another forest, sheltered on all sides by mountains. The trees here grew thickly together, and immensely tall. As Kyle and the others passed under the forest canopy, the day immediately grew dimmer and colder.

The entire forest was trapped under a thick layer of ice, from the ground to the boughs of the trees beneath which they walked. It was beautiful, but chilling all the same; Kyle had spent too much time in Westia to ignore the menace implied by this display.

The forest was completely and utterly silent. The ice covering the ground made movement incredibly slow; it was not quite thick enough to take the weight of a footfall, so every step inevitably broke through to the soft snow underneath. The ice would catch their boots on the way back up, making it all too easy to stumble.

Each cracking, shuffling step sounded like a gunshot in this empty world. Even Dorma, who usually moved like a cat, made noise—the most of any of them, in fact, as she was the one blazing the trail.

The forest was more interesting to look at than the mountains had been, but Kyle began to feel uneasy as their route took them deeper and deeper into the trees. The trees were grand, for certain, but they did not look healthy. They had shed everything but the very highest of their needles, and the branches below were dry and dead. They were sharp and crooked, like bony fingers, and sagged under the weight of the ice. Several trees had exploded into splinters or collapsed entirely.

But the silence was worst of all. After days of wind and snow and animal calls heard in the far distance, the stillness of this place was disturbing. It was almost as if time itself had been frozen in the storm. Kyle imagined animals entombed in the ice below, birds frozen to the branches of the trees. Whenever he came to a mound of ice in his path, he half-expected his clumsy footfall to reveal the furry back of an animal unfortunate enough to have been caught outside in the storm. He started to step around these mounds instead of on them, though he knew it was a colossal waste of energy.

It was both comforting and disconcerting to see that his friends were picking up on the strange atmosphere of the forest, as well. Rogan, who normally used his axe as a walking pole, was gripping it in both hands, his red eyes alert behind his shaggy brow. Deriahm, walking alongside him at the back of the party, was resting one hand on the sword belted at his hip. Oddly enough, he was looking upwards, sweeping his eyes (or at least his visor) over the dead, icy branches that hung overhead.

Kyle realized that Dorma was watching him. He caught her eye and she said, in a low voice,

"I see that your animal-mind is not completely dumb after all."

"What is it?" Kyle asked.

"What else? Monsters," Dorma said, "but of what kind? I am not sure. So we walk, and keep our eyes and ears open."

Kyle nodded. He felt for the sword he'd been given by King Azanhein. He wasn't afraid of a few monsters, not after everything they'd been through—but he wasn't looking forward to the waiting.

Within minutes, the tension in their party had become palpable. Their animal-minds were clamoring, and feeding off of each other's alarm. Kyle's eyes were coated with adrenalin, and he was seeing danger behind every tree, within every hump and mound on the forest floor. But there was nothing, not anything to see or hear, and so they walked on.

Not too long after, it began to snow again. It was a delicate, dainty snow—there was not a mite of wind, and thin, threadlike flakes drifted softly down from the canopy above, alighting gently on their heads and clothes. It was so slight that Kyle didn't even notice it at first, at least not consciously. But something in the back of his mind was screaming at him, crying foul even before Dorma whipped around and Deriahm raised his voice from behind.

"Have a care, dear friends!" Deriahm cried. His visor was still turned up at the sky. "Our foes lurk above!"

Dorma's warning was more straightforward. "*Monsters! Run!*"

She bolted off into the woods, and Kyle sprinted after her as quickly as he could manage. It was like running in a bad dream; between his pack and the icy ground, he could barely manage a jogging pace. Still, he ran as best he could, ran until his thighs and calves burned, followed Dorma's retreating back through the woods.

"What are we running from!?" Lugh's voice, clear and carrying, rang out from behind.

Dorma, twisting herself around, shouted backwards. "Ice-spiders! They mean to trap us!"

That sounded like so much nonsense to Kyle until a few moments later. His flight carried him into the path of one of the snowflakes—no, one of the snow-*threads*—that hung suspended in the air. It struck his cheek, and he immediately felt it tighten and freeze, sticking to the exposed flesh of his face. He scratched at it and it broke off, a thin line of ice, as if he had cried a tear which had snap-frozen in the cold air.

It was then he realized that his slow pace was not just due to his backpack or to the icy ground, but to the hundreds of threads that had already landed on him. They were clinging to his clothes, stiffening his limbs and weighing him down. The fingers of his gloves had fused together; with difficulty, he cracked them open and drew his sword, not knowing how much help it would be against enemies they couldn't see.

Have a care, dear friends! Our foes lurk above!

Kyle looked up and gasped in fright. Perched in a tree above him was an enormous spider, six feet long from its head to its bulbous abdomen, slender legs splayed wide enough to stretch across a four-lane highway. Its body was a gleaming, milky white. Its eyes, six, were bright blue globs of color that stood out like dots on an impressionist's painting. If it weren't for those eyes, Kyle might not have seen it among the dead branches of the trees. As he looked, he picked out another, then another, then another still. They were all completely immobile, their inky blue eyes fixed on Kyle's party.

Threads were cascading down from the spiders; threads of that strange substance that turned to ice as soon as it struck something solid. Kyle forced himself to look away and focused on running. He didn't know how many of the spiders there were, but did know that stopping to fight them here would be suicide. How long would it take before Kyle collapsed, helpless, under the weight of the ice if he stopped moving? Not long. Not long at all.

He ran and ran, and then Rogan came up beside him, bearing Nihs on his shoulders.

"To the front, to the front!" Nihs was shouting. Rogan, threads of ice burrowing into his fur, grunted and redoubled his pace. As soon as he was past Dorma, Nihs reared up onto two legs and let loose a gout of fire into the air ahead of them. It was a wide spray of flame that plumed into the sky; Kyle could feel the heat from thirty feet back. Nihs was not aiming at the spiders—they were well out of range of the fire, and scurried higher into the trees when it licked at the limbs below them—but rather at the air itself.

They ran and ran, Nihs burning a safe passage through the thread. Kyle stole glances upward as often as he dared, hoping to see an end to the horrific spiders. But his eyes picked out more every time he looked, and for a time it almost seemed as if there were more than ever.

"Don't stop!" Dorma shouted. "We'll break free of the trees soon enough."

The spiders, as if knowing this, finally began to move. Snow—regular snow—fluttered down from the canopy as they climbed about, trees groaning under their weight. All of a sudden, one of them dropped, and thudded to the ground behind Nihs and Rogan, cutting Kyle and Dorma off from the safety of the fire. Kyle reacted without thinking. He ducked under a leg, slipping close to the bulbous abdomen, and swung outward with his sword. The spider's leg, tough but brittle, snapped off at the second joint. Ichor sprayed from the wound, and the monster recoiled without making a sound. The other legs seized inwards and Kyle found himself momentarily pinned; he called his soul sword to hand and swung again. This time two legs snapped and the spider darted away, body listing heavily to one side.

"Good!" Dorma said. "Keep moving!"

More spiders dropped from the trees, their bodies thudding against the ground. Kyle and the others were beset on all sides. Meya fired a blast of red magic at one creeping up from the side. Dorma, long legs working in great strides, vaulted off an exposed tree root and drove her spear into the eyes of another. The spiders were huge, but they scurried away as soon as they were struck. Kyle imagined that they didn't often have to fight with prey that fought back.

Still, it was an awkward, desperate fight. They couldn't afford to drop their packs as they might never be able to retrieve them, and they were slow and clumsy in the cold and snow. The spiders were cowardly but fast, and those wounded tended to loop around to strike again from another angle. They were easy to wound but hard to kill; Kyle had yet to see a single one of them stop moving.

And still the threads fell, threatening to suffocate them with their gentle touch. Kyle stole a glance upwards and a thread fell across one of his eyes, sealing it shut. He cursed and clawed at it, but in that time was borne to the ground from behind.

It was a lucky thing for him that his pack was between the spider and himself. It stepped on him and picked at him furiously with its mandibles, but couldn't find a way through to his flesh. Kyle did as he had been trained to do when pinned down: he rose to his knees, grabbed his sword in both hands and threw it at the ground. It vented its pent-up magic, and a dome of energy expanded outwards from the point of impact, throwing the spider off. The sword snapped back into his hands and he stood. He turned just in time to see the spider lunging at him again. Before he could react, a sword black as midnight thrust past him and into the spider's eyes. The spider lurched backwards off of Deriahm's sword and scrabbled away, jelly flowing from the wound on its head.

"Thanks," Kyle said.

"It is of no moment," Deriahm replied. "I suggest we—"

Another spider thudded down behind them and latched on to Deriahm's pack. Six rear legs pedaling, it began to back up to a nearby tree, trying to yank Deriahm off his feet. Kyle lunged forward, reversing his grip on his sword, and plunged it into the creature's head. It ignored the wound and continued to yank, mandibles furiously feeding folds of Deriahm's cloak and backpack into its mouth.

Kyle stabbed again as Deriahm threw his pack off and fell to the ground. The spider pitched upwards, and Kyle was knocked away. It was still forcing the pack into its mouth, not realizing that there was no food underneath the tough hide of the animal it had captured—at least, none that it could enjoy. As Kyle watched, the spider's mouth and throat distended, and the backpack disappeared inside it.

"Come, sir!" Deriahm shouted. "Do not worry about the pack!"

Kyle obeyed, and the two of them sprinted after the others, Deriahm now significantly lighter on his feet. He danced left of some questing legs and struck out with his black sword—whose hilts, Kyle noticed for the first time, were themselves styled after the crooked legs of a spider. The spider dropped as if bending the knee, and Deriahm followed up with a stab that felled it for good.

The trees were thinning up ahead. They could see the gouts of Nihs' fiery shield, and flashes of Meya's hurting magic. A spider jumped at them from the left and Kyle struck with his soul sword. The swing raked across the spider's face and it fell twitching to the ground.

Finally, they broke free of the trees, and of the terrible threadlike ice that the spiders wove. They were instantly beset by a frigid, blasting wind, but Kyle accepted it gratefully. Their party was gathered at the forest's edge, battling with the spiders that had been bold enough to leave the cover of the forest. Kyle came up beside one and split its abdomen open with his sword. Hot guts spilled out; the spiders weren't *all* ice.

Lugh came forward and shredded the spider's face with his razor-sharp swords. Behind him, Dorma was plunging her spear into the face of another. Rogan came up beside it and chopped the head clear off the abdomen with a single blow of his mighty axe. The head continued to move for a time, mandibles grasping at the shaft of the spear. Then it, too, was still.

A few stragglers remained, but they soon retreated, being cut and stabbed from all angles. They scurried back into the forest, as silently as they had appeared. And just like that, the danger was over.

Kyle's legs felt made out of jelly. He dropped his pack where he stood and sat in the deep snow, not caring when some of it found its way to the skin of his lower back. Lugh sat on his haunches; Meya made the rounds of the party, but astonishingly, none of them had so much as broken their soul shield.

All of them had patches of ice crisscrossing their packs and clothing; Rogan had large mats of his fur clumped together. Dorma, to their surprise, suggested they head back under the cover of the forest to gather wood and make a fire.

"They only followed us so because they already had our scent," she said. "Normally they stay only in the deepest parts of the forest. And the fire will scare them off."

As far as Kyle was concerned, both of their options seemed just about as undesirable as the last—they could stay outside and be frozen by wind, or go back into the forest and be frozen by spiders.

They walked a short way back into the woods, just enough to dull the screaming wind, and started to build a fire. The wood was icy, but bone-dry beneath, and once the fire was burning hot they had no trouble keeping it going. The blaze made Kyle feel better; he recalled how frightened the spiders had been of Nihs' magic.

As he ate, he caught sight of Deriahm, who was sitting staring into the fire, head bowed, elbows resting on his legs. The pose, which on others would have appeared relaxed, looked forlorn on Deriahm.

It prompted Kyle to say, "I'm sorry about your pack."

"Think nothing of it, mister Campbell," Deriahm said, sitting up straighter. "Chattels are replaceable; lives are not. I am thankful that my pack was the only thing lost in today's excitement."

"What was in it?" Kyle asked, then added: "Not your lodestone?"

Deriahm shook his head, patting a small square pouch on his hip to indicate that the lodestone was safe and sound.

"A few pieces of armor, a couple of books, and some study materials that I thought worthwhile to bring with me. And, of course, my supply of *rouk*."

"*What?*" Kyle said. "*All* of it?"

Deriahm looked uncomfortable, as he always did when others showed concern for him. "Have no fear, mister Campbell. *Rouk* is carried more as a precaution than a necessity; in Buoria, it is not needed at all, and only occasionally in other parts of the world. I am confident that I will be able to survive to the end of our journey without it."

Kyle wasn't sure he believed that, but he wasn't about to call Deriahm a liar. "Is there anything we can use to replace it?" he asked instead.

"I am afraid not. Regular smoke contains very little that is useful to us; it is not worth the effort it takes to harvest. I appreciate your concern, mister Campbell, but I assure you—I will be fine."

Kyle looked into the dark visor, trying to imagine the face behind those words. As usual, he failed utterly.

"All right," he said. "I trust you. And I'm sorry—you wouldn't have lost it if it weren't for me."

"It is of no moment, mister Campbell," Deriahm said. "It is an honor to serve you." And there was an odd hitch in his voice that Kyle couldn't quite identify, and wouldn't be able to until years later, when he was back in Terra and his adventures in Loria were nothing but a fond memory.

They awoke warm and rested, having taken it in shifts to keep the fire burning throughout the night. The forest was still frozen and eerily quiet, but its magic had been broken, in a way, by the appearance of the spiders the day before. There was evil to be found there, for certain, but now it was a known evil.

They struck camp (they now worked fast enough to be helping Dorma with her tent rather than the other way round) and left the protective cover of the trees once more. It was a dark, dismal day, and the wind blowed constantly. The temperature had dropped even further compared to the days before, and fire or no fire, it wasn't long before Kyle was chilled to the soul.

One good thing had come out of Deriahm losing his pack: he was now able to take some weight from the others. This, coupled with the fact that they now had less food, meant that Kyle's felt positively featherlike on his shoulders. He supposed he was becoming stronger, as well; no training could quite match the exertion of carrying a pack across the wilderlands of Westia.

A day passed, and then another. On the third day, they came to an enormous slope that reared, featureless and grand, into the sky. It was not a mountain, but a plateau of sorts, with a distinct ridge that ran from horizon to horizon. Kyle felt dizzy just looking at it.

Dorma paused, setting the butt of her spear against the ground. Her braided hair blew in the wind.

"The black lands lie beyond this ridge," she said, her voice uncharacteristically quiet.

"You don't say?" Lugh said. He peered up at the slope ahead. His breath was haggard, his face lean, and his hair, normally his pride, had fallen untidy. "That hardly took any time at all."

That earned him a slap on the arm from Meya. "Idiot," she said, not unkindly. She turned to Dorma. "Will you be leaving us, then?"

"I told you I would take you as far as I had ever come," Dorma said, "and so

I will. When last I journeyed this far north, I crested the top of the ridge—and so I will again."

Meya nodded wearily. She, like the rest of them, was thinking about the hard climb ahead of them.

It took another two days to reach the lip of the crater. They were the hardest of the entire journey. They were exposed to the worst of the snow and the wind, and the constant upward slope meant that they could make barely a third of their usual speed. Kyle's ears popped as they climbed, and his breath started to catch in his lungs. He was reduced, once more, to playing games with himself to take his mind off the terrible pain and boredom. The others slogged with little more energy than he; Nihs, cradled again in Rogan's arms, seemed completely asleep more than half of the time. They finally had to pause so Meya could cup his tiny head in her hands and gift him some of her magic. That gave him energy—for a time—but it wasn't long before he fell asleep again.

For as slow as they were moving, it caught Kyle by surprise when they finally came to the lip of the meteor crater. Dorma, as always, was the first to crest it, vaulting ahead like a gazelle. She stood stock-still, silhouetted against the dark sky, and Kyle thought that there was a fierce beauty to her—this woman who had led them quite literally to the edge of the world.

Slowly, now not sure that he wanted to know what awaited them beyond the ridge, Kyle drew up beside her and saw what she saw: the black lands. The *adaragad.*

They were not black, at least not at first. Snow blown free from the other side of the ridge had settled here, and coated the ground in a thin powder until several miles in. Then, indeed, the world turned black; raw stone stood exposed beneath a tumbling, cloudy ceiling. The sky reminded Kyle of two things: first, Deriahm's home of Buoria. Second, the way the sky had looked above the *SS Caribia* on the night Kyle had fallen into this world.

The ground fell smoothly downward for a time, but in the far distance Kyle could see disturbing shapes: columns of stone like knuckled fingers, mountains that looked like shards of jagged glass. Though night was just barely falling, the air was dark, and alive with a subtle, sickly glow that seemed a different color every time Kyle noticed it.

Kyle looked at Dorma. As always, she was peering into the distance. He wondered what she could see that he didn't.

She said something, quietly enough that at first he didn't even notice she'd spoken. Then his brain pieced together what his ears had heard: "Foolish easterners."

She looked at him, and he realized that the foolish easterners had grown somewhat in her esteem in the days since they had left Grul's clan. She was worried for them.

"I do not pretend to understand your business," she said in her frank manner. "But in that place awaits death."

"I know," Kyle said, "but we don't have a choice."

Dorma shrugged, and said nothing else.

They camped on the inner lip of the crater, where they were braced from the wind and the worst of the snow. The *adaragad* loomed in the distance, silently threatening, as they tried to focus on eating and sleeping.

That night, Kyle dreamed a familiar dream for the first time in months. It had been a staple of his life before Loria, but he hadn't experienced it once since coming here. Now it came back in full force, and with a Lorian twist to boot.

He was running through the streets of Cleveland at night, panting, nearly suffocating in the humid summer air. Someone was chasing him; he didn't yet know who. He turned a corner drunkenly, shooting off the sidewalk and out into the middle of the road. The streets were devoid of cars and people alike. He tried to keep running, but his legs had gone suddenly numb, and he found he could barely limp. He turned around, expecting to see, as he always did, the face of a friend or co-worker (or *her* face, and that was worst of all)—but it was no one he recognized from Earth. Instead, one of the massive ice-spiders was skittering along the ground, speeding towards him at a breakneck pace. He fell over backwards, and the spider had just begun to clamp its jaws down on one of his legs when he awoke.

Panting, he propped himself up on his elbows and looked around. It did little good; the night was pitch-black, and he couldn't even make out the walls of his tent. At the very least, there were no ice-spiders. He settled back down and slept fitfully until dawn.

"The influence of wild magical particles on the unconscious mind," Nihs said later.

He was seated at the center of their fireless camp, once again wrapped in his sagecloak, looking foul and sounding fouler. His diagnosis followed stories from all members of their party—Dorma included—of nightmares experienced the night before.

"The *adaragad* is a cursed land saturated with wild magical particles," he went on. "Their corrupting influence affects everything they come in contact with—plants, animals, even the landscape itself. It's no wonder we all suffered nightmares. I would expect many more vivid dreams in the nights to come— some fair, some foul, all intense. I trust none of you are prone to sleepwalking."

"Great," Lugh said. "One *more* thing we have to worry about."

Dorma unfolded her muscular legs and stood. "This is where I leave you," she said simply. "I have taken you as far and farther than any other would go, as I promised."

"And we couldn't thank you enough," Meya said, also standing. "Be safe, Dorma. I hope the road back is safer than the road out has been."

"It always is."

Lugh stepped forward, hands in his pockets. "Can we give you anything for the road?" he asked. "Food? Water?"

Dorma laughed. "Keep your food for yourself," she said. "You will need every scrap before your journey is done." For a moment she looked as if she was going to say something else, then she shook her head. She vaulted off the ridge, landing on the snowy outer slope of the crater, and began to walk.

"Strike first, strike last, strike true!" she called over her shoulder, plowing through the deep snow.

"And you!" Meya called back.

They watched her for a time. Before long, she was a small gray speck disappearing into the distance.

Rogan was the first to turn away. He struck the butt of his axe into the ground and said,

"We're killing daylight."

"You're right," Nihs said, and he flung himself at Rogan, claws digging into fur as he climbed to the Minotaur's shoulder. Perched there like a vulture, he looked down at the rest of the party.

"I will say this once," he said. "Be on your guard. Always, *always*, be on your guard. The *adaragad* cannot be mapped. It cannot be understood or predicted. It is a land of wild magic, and it does *not* follow the rules. Question everything. Do not fall into complacency because of how something looks or feels. We would rather run than fight, whenever possible. Understood?"

Perhaps it was because Nihs still looked the worse for wear, or because there was a tangible note of fear in his voice, but none of them said anything following this speech. They just nodded, somberly, to show they had taken the warning to heart.

"Good," he said. He turned back around. "Now, let's go. As Rogan said, we're wasting daylight."

It was warmer here than it had been in some time. Kyle should have felt relieved, but all he could feel was fear. Fear, and another, more terrifying emotion that could only have been the beginnings of insanity.

Wrong. This land was *wrong.* It was the only word that could give due justice to the complicated blend of feedback that Kyle's senses were throwing at him, a pervasive sour note that saturated every aspect of this place.

Chernobyl, Kyle thought. *Fukushima. This must be what it feels like to walk through one of those places.*

The land was indeed black, the stone blasted clean of snow. The texture of the ground changed constantly; here it was perfectly flat, here it was folded into delicate curves and waves, here it was bubbled like volcanic rock. There was no sane or predictable path through the formations; all they could do was aim themselves north and work around the landscape as best they could. They would climb a small mountain only to find that it was bisected by a fissure that ran along its ridge; they would follow a path only to find that it was consumed by jagged reefs of rock a short while later.

Worse yet was the air. When they first entered the *adaragad,* there had been a steady wind blowing from the east; a few minutes later, it had reversed direction, and not long after that was blowing directly into their faces. Occasionally a smell would be carried on this wind; first it had been a pleasant smell of peppermint. Then it became bloody iron, and then something more unpleasant still, a rotten, burning smell that none of Kyle's experience could place.

Every so often, red lights began to dance at their feet, as if stirred up from the ground. At first Kyle thought they must be some kind of lightning bug, but when he finally got fast enough to catch one of the lights in his hand, he found that it had disappeared completely.

"They're illusions," Nihs said from his perch. "Caused by tiny magical reactions. Ignore them."

That was easy enough, but soon they became plagued by illusions of sound, as well, and ignoring these was much more difficult. Kyle's steps started to echo a good two seconds after his foot came down. Rogan heard his own breath puffing into his ears. Meya, for the longest time, swore that she could hear the call of a small animal nearby, and began peering into every nook and cranny of the landscape searching for it.

Nihs had perked up somewhat now that the air was warmer, but he still looked sickly. His skin had taken on a yellowish, waxy hue, and there were bruised patches under his eyes. In Dorma's absence, he had become their guide. He led them toward certain areas and away from others, warning them of the dangers he could sense lurking in the *adaragad's* volatile atmosphere.

They came to an empty plain, at the center of which stood a large formation of stone. Nihs actually flinched when his eyes beheld it.

"In there," he said, pointing. "Buried beneath the stone is a shard of the meteor. I would stake my life on it. It's no wonder the air has been so foul; we've been walking in the shadow of that mountain."

"Does that mean it will get better once we pass it?" Lugh said. His voice had lost its essential sparkle. He now sounded nothing but tired.

"For a time," Nihs said. "But as we draw closer to the center we're bound to run into more shards. Come—let's have this place far behind us when we rest for the night."

They chose to skirt the great plain rather than cross it; none of them wanted to get any closer to the shard than absolutely necessary. Kyle could hear his heart beating in his ears, and it seemed the very air was buzzing—but so far they'd not seen a single living thing since passing into the crater.

The shard well behind them, they walked for a few hours more, while the temperature plunged and the ground again became dusted by snow. Kyle found that he felt better as soon as the black rock beneath their feet was hidden from view, as if this were enough to dull its power. The rest of the party felt it, as well, and by unspoken agreement, they made camp in the direct center of a snow-covered field. It was freezing, but Kyle would have happily taken the cold over the thick, living warmth of the *adaragad*.

Kyle lay down in his bed, and as soon as silence fell, he realized that he could hear voices whispering in his ears. They spoke no language he could understand, and were so quiet that he couldn't be sure they existed at all.

Nightmares, Kyle thought. *Just waiting to get in.*

He sighed, rolled onto his back, and closed his eyes.

Their time in the snow was blissful but short. Less than an hour after they started walking the next day, the snow fell away, and the ugly black stone of the *adaragad* emerged once more. Rogan suggested they skirt the edge and try to find a way around, but this idea was quickly shot down. Vohrusien's tower was said to be in the exact center of the crater; they were on track to find it if they continued to head straight north. Even then, their chances were not good. If they started to deviate from their path, it was likely that they would wander these wastelands forever.

Meya, of course, had the ability to escape them—perform the magic she had performed when Lian and Lacaster had shot down the *Ayger*, and warp the party away from this place. But escaping was a last resort; if their luck was poor, they could end up in a part of the world just as deadly as the one they had left.

And so they walked north, directly into the *adaragad*'s dark embrace.

So it went for three days: a sprint across a patch of corrupted ground, followed by a reprieve found in an area free of the worst of the *adaragad*'s influence. These areas became rarer and rarer as the days went on; on the first day, they passed right over one and found another a few hours later. By the third day, they had to walk well into the night to find a place relatively free of the frightening illusions that plagued them while awake.

On the fourth day they found no reprieve at all, and for the first time resigned themselves to making camp in the middle of the corrupted ground. It was as bad as Kyle had feared it would be. He woke no less than five times throughout the night, heart thrumming, voices whispering in his ears and lights dancing before his eyes like the aftereffects of a camera flash. Shapes appeared in the shadowy corners of the tent: faces, bodies, nonsensical fractals of darkness. Kyle, exhausted as he was frightened, clamped his eyes shut and tried to fall asleep, knowing that dreams would worm their way into his head as soon as he did.

It was pitch-dark when they awoke, as it had been when they first made camp. Had they slept for one hour? Five? A hundred? There was no way to tell, but it felt like no time at all. Kyle was still bone-weary, and he hefted his pack with something approaching dread.

Though it was not until the fourth day that they entered the worst of the crater's realm, it was on the second that they met the first of its denizens. Meya had been walking a slight ways off from the group—she was searching for the mystery animal again, and it was impossible to stop her from doing so—when she suddenly shrieked and jumped in the air as if she'd seen a mouse.

Lugh's sword was instantly in his hands, and he put himself between Meya and the creature. It was no mouse, but a lizard whose body was almost completely flat. It was three feet in length, and its hide was mottled to blend in almost perfectly with the diseased-looking ground. Meya had nearly stepped on it.

It burst to its feet and skittered away, incredibly fast. Its nails scratched against the exposed rock with a frantic *scrfscrfscrfscrf*. Within two seconds it had scrabbled up a small boulder and disappeared down the far side.

Meya was panting with fright; Lugh put his arms around her to calm her down. Nihs sniffed.

"We should be lucky if all of the *adaragad's* denizens are so passive," he said. "Would that I could believe that will be the case."

It wasn't long before they saw another monster, then another; it was as if the first sighting had opened their eyes to everything around them. Kyle spotted what looked at first like the grasping root of a tree, which turned out to be a centipede-like monster over eight feet long. As soon as they drew close, it flowed away from them like a snake, legs striking the ground with a sound like a rain-stick being turned. Not long after, a beetle the size of a football trundled across their path, chittering constantly. "Gwip," it seemed to say, as if greeting them hello. "Gwip, gwip."

"They're ugly enough," Lugh said, watching the beetle disappear behind a rock, "but *duoneys ezeran lydlde sool.*"

Kyle blinked. It sounded to him as though Lugh had lapsed effortlessly into another language—Selkic, perhaps. He supposed that Lugh must be able to talk some language other than what he'd heard, but Lugh had never used it before.

"What's that mean?" he asked.

Lugh's head snapped around so quickly that Kyle backed away, afraid. Lugh's own face looked concerned.

"*Nlyd hyde eh yo?*" he said.

Kyle could only stare, dumbfounded. *Am I having a stroke?* For a moment he thought Lugh was playing a trick on him, but his friend's expression was enough to convince him otherwise.

"I can't understand you!" he said, trying to keep the edge of panic out of his voice.

"*Sheed ze han eh?*" Lugh said, still in that strange, garbled language. It sounded like his words were being delivered from under a foot of water.

The others came forward. Meya put a hand on his cheek, her eyes glowing red. Kyle felt a pulse of magic, then Meya spoke. Her voice sounded just as Lugh's had, and Kyle couldn't understand a word of it.

Nihs was next. He spoke rapidly to Lugh and Meya, then held up a finger and went rummaging around in his satchel. He produced a notebook and a glass pen. He wrote something and then held it up to Kyle to inspect, eyebrows raised. His question was obvious: *Can you read this?*

Kyle looked at the runes written in Nihs' hasty scrawl and found that he could not. It was a word, he could tell; but the letters meant nothing to him. They shifted and wavered, promising to make sense until his eyes had pinned them down—then devolved into nonsense the second they did.

Kyle shook his head. Nihs made a face and spoke a word: "*Dasha!*" This one was Kollic, and Kyle knew well what it meant.

Deriahm spoke, his voice measured and considering. Nihs snapped a response. Rogan rumbled something. Lugh shook his head, arms folded. Kyle watched all with rapidly growing fear and sadness. What was going on? Was this another effect of the *adaragad?*

We barely stood a chance while everything was going well, Kyle thought. *How are we supposed to get to the tower if I can't even understand what my friends are saying?*

But his fear of never reaching the tower was not the real reason for his distress. *My friends.* These people *were* his friends; the first real friends he had ever had. They were the only people who had ever understood him—and now he couldn't understand them. With every word they spoke, he felt he was falling further away from them. From them, and from the world from which they came.

Kyle thought of the dreams that had been encroaching upon his reality for the past halfmonth—the waking dreams of Earth that had intruded upon this world. *Loria is falling apart. I'm losing it. How long do I have before it disappears completely?*

As if to confirm his suspicions, the earth and sky around him began to tear apart and fall away, like a sheet of parchment being burned at by a candle. A tear separated Lugh's head from his shoulders and slashed Meya diagonally across her body. Nihs dissolved into nothingness and fell away. Bright summer sunshine shone through the holes in reality. Kyle saw the silvery gleam of a skyscraper and heard the honking of cars. There was the sound of the wind rushing through leaves.

Kyle could enjoy none of this. He was watching his companions being torn to shreds before his very eyes, and in that instant, all he could think was,

Not yet. Not in this horrible place. Not before I've said goodbye.

And, ignoring Terra, ignoring the bright sun and the buildings and the cars, ignoring the wind through the trees, he pushed the illusion aside and fell back into the *adaragad*, the black, blighted plain that was an affront to all natural life. Back to where he belonged.

"*Stop! Wait!*" he shouted, not sure who he was shouting at.

Heads snapped to look at him. Lugh's face split into a massive grin, and he spread his arms wide.

"*Hey!* You can speak again!" Then: "Can you understand what I'm saying?"

Kyle almost cried with relief. He staggered and almost fell, but Meya and Deriahm caught his arms.

"*Yes*," he said. "Yes, I can. Can you understand me?"

Lugh nodded. "Clear as anything."

"Saints be praised," Meya said, and kissed the side of his forehead.

"What happened?" Kyle asked.

It was Nihs who answered. He had jumped from Rogan's shoulder to Lugh's, and his face showed no happiness or relief.

"The gift of the ten races," he said. "The ability to understand and be understood. To speak without language. You lost it, for a brief time."

That brought Kyle all the way back to his first days in Loria. *Wait a minute*, he had asked, when he realized how odd it was that Lugh and Nihs could understand him. *What language are you two speaking?*

Language? Lugh had said, confused. *We're not speaking any language. We're just speaking.*

Kyle could only ask, "How? Why? Is it because of the meteor?"

Nihs' face was dour. "That certainly isn't helping," he said. "But I suspect Terra's influence here as well. Your world is exerting its power over you, and the *adaragad* is amplifying the effect."

"So what do we do?" Rogan said.

"We move. Quickly. Before it's too late."

A nd so they did, their mission taking on a note of urgency that it hadn't had before. Kyle's brief experience in losing the ability to speak like a Lorian had shaken him to the core. He began to worry every time one of his companions opened their mouth to talk, fearing that their words would come out as the garbled non-language he had heard earlier.

They descended deeper and deeper into the *adaragad*. The air grew darker, and the land grew twisted, until it looked more like the bottom of an ocean trench than high up in the mountains of Westia. Soon they were encountering not just monsters but strange plants as well: bulbous cacti, their skin as hard as turtle shells; nettles with acid-red needles that crouched defensively in crooks of rock. These grew thick around pools of a mysterious, bubbling liquid that looked like molten mud. It was a dark, bruised purple and smelled like bile.

Illusory light danced around their feet and voices whispered in their ears. And Kyle's weary party moved on.

A monster that looked like a fat, bloated frog that had been run over by a truck watched them balefully from a pool of liquid. Its eyes were a dull gold, and it seemed completely gormless right up until it opened its mouth and shot a long tongue, yellow and barbed, directly at Lugh's head. Meya shrieked, and Lugh swore and ducked away as the tongue, fifteen feet long, wriggled and grasped at him of its own volition. It landed on his shoulder and began to wind around his upper arm, while the frog made a *gak-ak-ak* noise and tried to pull Lugh close.

Kyle drew his sword and cut down as hard as he could, but the tongue was gummy and elastic; his blade sank in and bounced off.

"Gak-ak-ak!" The frog said, pulling itself onto the bank. Purple ooze sloughed off its body, and they saw that it was much larger than it had appeared—at least the size of a fully-grown hippopotamus.

"Shit!" Lugh had drawn his dagger and was hacking at the tongue, but it was nearly impossible to cut. The yellow barbs were soft, but incredibly sticky, and already it looked as though the tongue had fused to his arm.

Rogan came forward with Nihs on his shoulder. Nihs blasted fire into the creature's eyes; it cawed in pain and shrank back. Muscles heaving, Rogan hefted his great axe and brought it down on the tongue. It bent all the way to the ground, where it was finally severed with a great *whap*. It still hung on by about two inches of flesh; Rogan put a hoof down on it and drew his axe across it like a knife. One end snapped against Lugh's arm; the other was returned to its owner, and slapped against its face between the eyes.

They ran, Lugh still trying to detach the severed half of the tongue from his arm. The 'frog' watched them disappear into the distance, the same expression of harmless vapidity on its face.

Lugh was still picking bits of tongue off of his sleeve when they made camp that evening; they had cut most of it away, but it was incredibly sticky, and nothing seemed able to shift the parts of it that had already bonded with Lugh's coat. He scratched and picked all the while they set up their tents, muttering about the defilement of his expensive new jacket.

It had gotten warm throughout the past day; so warm, in fact, that it was now hot, and tents were quite unnecessary. Kyle couldn't believe how quickly the temperature had shifted, or how quickly he had gotten used to the heat. Already he was wishing for a cool breeze as he sweated through his coat.

Still, not one of them suggested that they sleep under the open air.

Kyle's dreams that night were particularly horrific. He sweated and shivered in equal measure, drifting in and out of a feverish sleep. He saw toads and centipedes, lakes of fire and mountains of ash; he dreamt of his blood boiling in his veins, of their tent catching fire and cooking them alive. Hideous heat raked across his cheeks and singed the hairs of his beard. His companions screamed, and hands grabbed at him, trying to pull him to his feet.

Leave me alone, he thought desperately. *I'm trying to sleep.*

His next breath drew in a lungful of smoke, and he fell into a coughing fit. His eyes snapped open, and he realized that part of his dream had been no dream at all.

Their tent was on fire.

Pain instantly struck in several places at once; his eyes watered until he was nearly blind, and his chest burned. A hand was indeed grabbing at him; it was Deriahm. Kyle let him pull him upright, and the two of them forced their way out of the burning tent. More hands, belonging to Lugh and Rogan, pulled them free and away from what was quickly becoming so much charred and crumpled canvas.

"My pack," Kyle croaked, thinking of the precious food he had been carrying.

Deriahm patted him on the shoulder and hefted it. "Have no fear, sir," he said. "I have retrieved it."

Meya was soon there, pressing her palms to his chest. "Breathe out," she said.

He did, and smoke bellowed from his mouth and nose in incredible amounts, feeling foul, but much better than it had on the way in. "Thank you," he said.

She nodded, her face weary and grim.

Kyle turned back to watch the burning tent. He saw that the other one had caught fire, as well; it had already burned completely to the ground.

"What the hell happened?" he said.

"We're fools, that's what happened," Nihs snarled from his perch. "This entire area is saturated with fire magic. We're lucky our own skin didn't burst into flame. I can't believe I didn't notice."

"It's hot," Kyle said. "But it's not *that* hot, is it?"

"The actual heat doesn't matter," Nihs said. "What matters is *potential*." And he thrust an arm back and then out, fingers splayed. An enormous pillar of fire exploded from his hand and seared through the air. There was a thunderclap of pressure and Kyle had to slam his eyes shut to keep himself from being blinded.

"*Hey!*" Lugh said. "Watch it!"

Nihs ignored him. "I couldn't have worked a spell like that anywhere else on earth. As I said, the very air here is fire. It was only a matter of time before our tents went up."

Lugh rubbed at his neck. "Let's look on the bright side," he said. "At least we don't have to carry them around anymore."

Nihs shot him a murderous look. Kyle wanted to laugh but found that he could not. In fact, none of them were laughing. Lugh sighed and let his hand drop from his neck.

"All right, let's go," he said. "I wasn't tired anyway."

We're fighting the adaragad, Kyle was thinking later. *And the* adaragad *is winning.* It was all he could think of as he looked between the faces of his companions. Lugh, for once, was not smiling, and Meya was downcast. Rogan was surly, and Nihs looked like an angry, bitter gremlin. Deriahm, of course, seemed to have no capacity for anger whatsoever, but he was completely silent, and worse, the discipline with which he had always carried himself was slipping. He had not had any *rouk* in several days, and the effect of hunger on him was starting to show. Whenever they stopped to eat for the night, he would sit with them, motionless, hands clasped in front of him, saying and eating nothing. He politely waved away their concern about his lack of food, but it didn't fool any of them in the least. He was hungry, and it was unknown how much longer he could carry on.

Kyle, for one, had no idea how much farther they still had to go. Between Lugh, who could sense the distant ocean, and Nihs, who could position himself using the overhead, they could at least be sure that they were still travelling north. But where, exactly, was the center of the meteor crater? And—Kyle could hardly bear to think of this—would they even know it once they found it?

He forced these thoughts from his mind and focused on walking. Being in this place was exhausting, in every possible way. The nature of the world around them changed constantly; first it was hot, then cold, then bright, then dark. They traversed lakes of glass and forests of stone, wind-blasted valleys that smelled of burning sand and silent bogs that smelled of death. Sometimes they would go hours without seeing any living creature; then, over the next rise, they would come across a fetid plain crawling with insect-like monsters. Nihs would lead the way, shooting gouts of fire into the writhing mass, chasing them away with a look of fierce ecstasy on his face.

Occasionally, they would hear the call of a much larger monster carried on the non-existent wind. These were strange, unnatural sounds that sent shivers up and down Kyle's body. He would whip his head around searching for the origin of the noise, and once, he saw it: an enormous, shambling, six-legged shape that loomed far in the distance.

That night, they slept in the open air next to a single, petrified tree, which rose slender and graceful into the sky. It was black as night, as everything was here, but at least the ground was flat, and it smelled nice enough. Two of their bedrolls had been lost in the fire, so Deriahm volunteered to go without while Nihs slept between Lugh and Rogan. Kyle was quite convinced he would never fall asleep, not while exposed to the horrible atmosphere of this place, but eventually his fatigue won out, and he slipped into dreams.

In the middle of the night, when the party was sound asleep, one of the upper branches of the tree detached itself and began a slow and stealthy march downwards. It was a monster, a bug demon about a foot in length, its sleek, cylindrical body lined with legs on the bottom and rudimentary scales on top. It had been sitting, frozen, at the top of the tree, two long feelers extended above its body, looking exactly like a black branch with two smaller branches sprouting from it. Now, the long feelers twizzled prissily back and forth, tasting the air. There was life below, and the monster marched towards it with a blind addiction.

A circular mouth opened, revealing a set of small teeth. The monster's bite was not very strong, but it didn't need to be. It only needed to bite once.

Hanging upside down, legs trundling, the creature drew closer to the sleeping forms. Its feelers brushed against the trunk of the tree, then began to tease at errant wisps of Kyle's hair.

A black streak shot through the air and pinned the creature to the trunk. It was an obsidian dagger, wielded by a hand also clad in black.

"I think not, sir," Deriahm whispered, as the creature squirmed and writhed, feelers working frantically, wrapping themselves around the blade that had skewered it. "We have come too far to be undone by one such as yourself."

He picked the creature off the trunk, and instantly its legs hugged his hand. It bit desperately at his black glove, but its feeble teeth were no match for Buorish leather.

Deriahm rose, stepped a ways off from the others, and carefully set the creature against the ground. He put his metal boot on its back and crushed the life out of it. Green-purple guts sprayed from both ends of the creature as its exoskeleton collapsed.

Not a one to leave anything to chance, Deriahm stepped on it twice more, spreading its body across the rocky ground. Only when its feelers had finally stopped their endless dance did he rejoin the others. Hands on hips, he examined the tree in detail, but saw no sign of any other creatures.

Work done, he lay down on his back, folded his hands across his chest, and continued his watch.

Two more days passed. With their tents gone and their food supplies running low, their packs had become very light indeed. For the first time since their journey in Westia had begun, Kyle started to seriously fear that they might run out of food before arriving at the tower. They held a vote and decided to cut rations. Lugh clapped Deriahm on the shoulder.

"We'll be joining you in your fast soon. How does that old saying go?"

Misery loves company, Kyle thought, but didn't say it. It wasn't likely to go down well given the current climate.

The joke, they found out later, was on them. That night, Rogan was rummaging through his enormous pack, digging into all of the pockets to make sure there was no food he had missed. His brow creased and he pulled out a circular package.

"What's this?" he said to no one in particular.

Deriahm let out a gasp of surprise. "Why—that is the cake of king's *rouk!*"

And so it was. The crest of King Azanhein stamped on the front was unmistakable. The cake of *rouk*, perfectly circular and exquisitely packaged, looked like a cookie when held in Rogan's enormous hand.

Deriahm stepped over, and Rogan proffered it. Deriahm took it in both of his hands, staring down at it in wonder.

"But...I hid this inside Astevyr's drifter before we parted ways," he said. "How has it come to be here?"

Lugh started to laugh. It was the golden, sunny sound that Kyle remembered from happier days, and he started to smile. Meya was smiling, too; she was flushed with happiness and love, and her face was radiant. Even Nihs momentarily shook himself free of the ghost that had been clinging to his shoulders ever since they entered the wilderlands.

"Looks like Astevyr was one step ahead of you!" Lugh said. "He must've noticed you'd given it to him and gave it right back. Hah!"

The hands that held the *rouk* cake were trembling.

"I...I..." Deriahm said, and Kyle realized that he was trying to say *I cannot accept this*. Lugh must have realized this, too, because he put a hand on each of Deriahm's shoulders and said,

"Listen. Tonight you're going to smoke that stupid cake, all right? We need all the strength we can get. You can get revenge on Astevyr later."

"I...I shall," Deriahm said to the cake.

"Right." Lugh looked up, and he was smiling again, cheeks creasing under his stone eyepatch. "Right," he said again. "Let's get going, shall we?"

It had been such a simple thing, but the effect that the king's *rouk* had on the entire party was remarkable. Deriahm had indeed smoked it that night, improvising in the absence of his *rouk* pipe. He'd crumbled the cake into a bowl (with noticeable regret) and set it alight, draping a blanket over it so he could catch as much of the smoke as possible. It had looked rather silly, but he emerged noticeably more energetic, and in great spirits. His joy and relief were almost childlike, and Kyle reflected that Deriahm had an awkward charm about him that, in some ways, even Lugh couldn't match. His energy had given them energy, even though they were eating less and less each day, and still had seen no sign of the tower.

The following day, they came across a deserted field at the center of which stood a bulbous outcrop of stone. Or, so they thought at first. No sooner had they entered its shadow than it split open, revealing a gigantic, glowing eye, bright red and over a hundred feet across. Kyle let slip a horrible word and Meya screamed outright. They dashed backwards, hiding behind another mound of rock at the edge of the plain.

Slowly, the eye swiveled around, its gaze scanning the field that they now instinctively understood to be its territory. It had not one but several hundred pupils, scattered across its front like bubbles clinging to the side of a soda glass. Veins, red and orange and black, spidered from these pupils in all directions, reminding Kyle of the pictures of nebulae taken by the Hubble telescope.

The eye was so vast that they could *hear* it shifting around in its bearing—the gentle *shrrr* of lubricating mucus, and the *whoosh* of air being displaced by its movement.

"What happens if it sees us?" Kyle asked, grinning in manic fear.

"Let's not find out," was all Rogan said.

They skirted the edge of the field, sticking to the shadows, staying well out of the eye's field of vision. Kyle couldn't stop looking at it. There was something so disturbing, yet so enrapturing, about its gaze. Despite himself, he was burning with curiosity, wondering what *would* happen if it were to see them. Surely this was not an ordinary monster—no, this was something more, some greater being whose true nature was unknown to them. Was there more to the creature, hidden beneath the ground? Or was this the eye of the *adaragad* itself, on the hunt for interlopers?

Their detour took over an hour, but eventually the horrible eye and its patrolling grounds were behind them. Kyle stole one last glance behind as the eye passed out of sight. It was still open, still rotating lazily in its socket. Kyle wondered how long it would remain so before the great lid closed, and the creature that controlled it fell once more into slumber.

K yle was feeling ill, and a persistent headache was throbbing over his right temple. This was, he knew, partially due to hunger; they had cut rations again following Nihs' announcement that the magic interference had become so strong he could no longer orient himself using the overhead. Lugh, whose water sense was less dependent on magic, was still confident that they were moving at least mostly north, but it was becoming obvious to all of them that their chances of becoming completely lost were extremely high.

They were making progress; that much was certain. The nature of the *adaragad* changed with every mile, and they were in no danger of retracing their own steps by accident. But was it in the right direction, and was this a direction that would lead them to the tower?

Kyle began to do something that he hadn't done in over a decade. He prayed. He prayed to his God, he prayed to Loria's many Saints, he prayed to whoever would listen. In his feverish state, he even prayed to the monstrous eye they had seen days ago, thinking of its immortal, silent gaze as he did.

I don't know who or what you are, but if you can point us in the right direction…just give us a sign, anything…

The faces of his companions were drawn, weary. Rogan clopped along, looking less like a proud Minotaur and more like an old mule arthritic with years of work on the farm. Nihs' lips were drawn wide like a frog's, and his eyes were bloodshot. Lugh and Meya clung to each other for support. Kyle realized that, of all of them, those who were faring best were Deriahm and himself. Deriahm, because the effect of the king's *rouk* had still not worn off. Kyle, because…

Because why?

He shook his head. It didn't matter. What mattered was the truth of their situation. They were dying, all of them, and if they didn't find the tower soon, their quest would end in this forsaken place.

Kyle's nails scraped against the bottom of his pack that night as he searched for food. It was the first time this had happened, and the sensation of the woven fabric rasping against the tips of his fingers rekindled the fear in his chest.

Across from him, Lugh ripped a strip of salted meat down the middle and handed half to Rogan, who accepted it gratefully. Rogan's strength was immense, but this strength was paid for in food; he ate three times as much as any of the others at the best of times, and was not taking to their new diet well. After he ate, he collapsed backward onto the ground, not even bothering to roll out his bed. The air here was stale, neither hot nor cold, and Kyle was struck by the sudden fear that they would all asphyxiate in their sleep.

He laid down, praying again, this time for the simple miracle that he would live to see another morning.

He dreamt of the eye.

In his dream, he did not hide from it, but stood naked before it, staring directly into its multitude of pupils. Its gaze was a spotlight of orange light focused on him; he could feel heat radiating from it like a sunbeam.

The eye did not speak, nor did it waver or blink. It merely pinned him to the spot with its light and heat, bore down on him until he felt he could do nothing but curl up and wait to be blasted away, dried to a husk and disintegrated by the persistent beat of the eye's light. He fell to his knees, then to all fours. His head bowed, and his eyelids fluttered. His forehead was just about to touch the ground when he felt the heat lift from him, to be replaced by a cool wind. It was chilling, but somehow energizing.

He looked up. The eye had changed; it was no longer orange and black, but white, like a human eye, and had only one pupil. The iris surrounding this pupil was bright purple.

I know that eye, Kyle thought.

Now the eye did speak.

Poor child. If only you knew the truth of your mission. Your travels are nearly done; your final peace lies closer than you know. Come; I will show you.

Kyle was afraid but he did go, and when he reached the eye he instinctively embraced it, pressing his body against the massive iris. The eye slurred upward, and he clung to it, until it was facing directly into the sky and he was laying on top of it. Shaking, trying not to slip and fall on the jellied surface (somehow he knew that he could not fall from eye, or this dream—this *vision*—would end), he stood up. He looked all about himself and could see nothing but darkness in all directions.

But then the cool wind came again, and he was borne upwards into the sky. He was no longer naked; his black coat flapped around his ankles, and he understood that somehow this was helping him ascend. He flew a hundred, two hundred, five hundred feet up, until the air finally started to taste sweeter and his vision cleared.

Floating in space, he turned gently, not quite able to control himself. At first he saw nothing but black mountains; then, far in the distance, he caught sight of something else. It was a spire of obsidian rising into the air like a sword, a black nail jutting thousands of feet into the sky. He realized that he had seen it before, in another dream—in that dream, there had been a brilliant orange light glowing near the top. This tower was completely dark, but he still recognized it for what it was: the dwelling of Archsage Vohrusien.

Kyle's heart soared. *I can see it. We're close! We're actually going to reach it!* Then, another thought, hot on the heels of the first: *Please let this not just be a dream. Please let this not just be a cruel joke...*

As if in response to this thought, Kyle felt his eyes snap open, his *real* eyes, and knew that he had awoken. The dream world wavered and broke apart, but the tower still stood on the horizon.

And Kyle still floated in the air.

It took him a moment to realize that it was happening. But his coat was still flapping around him, his sleeves still billowing out with wind. He could still see the endless darkness of the *adaragad* laid out before him. And he could still see Vohruisen's tower in the distance.

He looked down, feeling an odd detachment. *I'm really flying. How? Why?*

He felt himself becoming ever so slightly heavier, and he began to sink towards the ground. He was still half asleep, and it wasn't until he started to accelerate that panic set in. Soon he was falling—not as fast as he should be by rights, but fast enough to break his legs and perhaps worse. He had no idea how to react, how to stop it. The ground rushed closer, and his ears whistled and stung. He pinwheeled his arms, trying desperately to stay upright, feet pointed at the ground. Still the ground came closer—two hundred, then one hundred, then fifty feet away. Kyle would have screamed, but his jaw was clamped shut, muscles in his neck stiffening to protect his delicate windpipe.

He closed his eyes at the last moment, and his feet slammed against the ground—hard, but not as hard as he had expected. He fell to his knees and pain exploded from them; his hands came down and he scraped both palms on the rocky ground. Momentum still unspent, he went sliding a couple feet across the ground, rolling over and over, then onto his back. He lay there for a moment, staring up into the sky, while his body throbbed with pain.

It's just like when I fell from the Ayger, he thought. *I should be dead—*would *have been dead if I'd been on Earth.*

Footsteps behind him. Lugh's face appeared in his peripherals.

"Hey!" he said. "Are you alright?"

"I think so."

Lugh helped him up, and Meya appeared to heal the cuts on his knees and palms. He hadn't been wearing gloves or shoes; he was in the pants and shirt that he'd been wearing to sleep, as well as the black jacket he had bought in Reno, the one with the silver bird stitched into the back. Too light to be of any use in Westia, he'd been keeping it rolled up in the bottom of his pack ever since they'd arrived here. As it had been the first time he'd tried it on, he was amazed at how comfortable it felt around his shoulders.

Rogan, Nihs, and Deriahm arrived, Nihs clinging to the front of Rogan's chest like a monkey.

"What happened?" he snapped. "Where did—*how did you do that?*"

"I don't know what I did," Kyle said, wordlessly nodding at Meya once she drew her hands back.

"You *flew!*" Lugh said, his voice full of wonder.

Nihs shook his head. "Not flew. *Soared.* You used metamagic to fly."

"If I did, I did it in my sleep," Kyle said, put off a little by Nihs' tone. "I was dreaming."

"About what?" Nihs asked at once.

Memory flooded back. "The tower!" Kyle blurted. "It's close! I could see it from where I was floating!"

"This was in your dream?" Nihs said.

"No! I mean—yes, it was, at first. But then I woke up and I could still see it."

He looked around, caught sight of a familiar mountain ridge, and pointed. "It's just past that! We'll be able to see it once we get over there!"

Lugh actually laughed with relief. "That couldn't be more than two days' walk from here!"

"You're *sure* about this?" Nihs said. "Remember where we are. This could be just another fever dream brought on by the *adaragad.*"

Kyle shook his head vigorously. "I'm positive. This wasn't like the other visions. I know it."

Nihs opened his mouth to speak, but Lugh reached out and pressed his finger against his nose. Nihs hissed and swatted at the finger; Lugh said, "We don't know where we're headed for anyway, so we might as well go for it and trust that Kyle is right. We're going to need *some* kind of miracle to get out of this place."

Their trip up the mountain was the longest two days of their journey thus far. Its face was stark and bare, stripped clean of plants, monsters, and even loose rocks. It was like climbing a single chunk of smooth iron ore: rippled, slippery, and sharp in equal measure.

In the evening of the first day, they reached the foot of the mountain, and set up camp in its shadow. They ate their meagre rations, then spent the night shivering in their bedrolls, exposed to a strong wind that blew icy air in their faces. Nihs took the time to question Kyle further about his vision. It didn't take him long to come to the same conclusion that Kyle had as to the identity of his benefactor.

"It was Archmage Rosshku," he said. "That was his eye and voice that guided you to the tower. I wonder where he is—and how he managed to find you to plant that vision into your mind."

"I think he was the one who helped me soar, too," Kyle said, thinking of the cool wind that had borne him into the sky.

"If so, his power is even greater than I had known," Nihs said. "To hypnotize you from such a distance and bid you to use an ability you didn't even know you had—that is incredible magic indeed."

"I don't think I could soar again if I tried," Kyle admitted.

"That may be true now, but I wonder for how long. Rosshku said before that your power was limited by the edges of your mind rather than those of your soul. I suggest you reflect on that in the days to come."

Morning came; they struck camp and set to climbing the mountain. Kyle was so exhausted he could barely walk, let alone climb. But climb he did, feet struggling to find purchase, knees scraping against the ground, breath coming in shallow puffs. He focused on keeping up with Nihs, who was several feet ahead of him and probably could have scaled the mountain in minutes had he been at full strength.

Kyle paused to rest, digging his elbows into the rippled ground so that he didn't slip and slide halfway down the mountain. Meya drew up next to him, and she collapsed, as well. She lifted her eyes to the ridge above them. The distance defied being measured; it looked close enough to reach out and touch, but they had been climbing for hours, and Kyle guessed they were little more than halfway up.

"We're so close," Meya said, though Kyle wasn't sure just who she was trying to encourage.

Suddenly, Kyle heard a bellow coming from behind them. There was the sound of heavy footfalls, and then Lugh went dashing past them, closing the space to the mountain's peak. He was leaping, devouring the mountain fifty feet at a time. Kyle couldn't believe he had the energy.

"Stop that, you fool!" Nihs shouted after him—but Lugh was already at the edge of hearing, and wouldn't have listened even if he had heard.

By the end of his climb, he was so far away that Kyle lost sight of him for a moment. Then he re-emerged at the top of the ridge, silhouetted against the sky. He stood still for a moment, a tiny black shape. Then they very clearly saw him raise both fists into the air in a sign of victory.

Meya gasped. "He's seen it."

"So it would seem," Nihs said, allowing optimism to creep into his voice for what seemed like the first time in years.

They climbed to the sounds of Lugh whooping and hollering above them, shouting at them to hurry up. When they finally crested the top, he went to Meya first, sweeping her into his arms and twirling her around.

"Look! Look!" he said, and carried her to the far side of the platform like a groom carrying his bride over the threshold.

There it stood, just as Kyle had seen in his dream: a black sword rising into the sky, a shard of obsidian, a stone obelisk thousands of feet high. It stood at the center of a blasted plain directly below them.

Rogan laughed heartily. "We'll be knocking at Vohrusien's door before the day is out!"

Lugh kissed Meya right on the mouth. "And here I thought we were all going to starve and die," he said to her.

She slapped at his chest, cheeks flushed and eyes shining. "Put me down, you idiot."

"Something tells me food will be the least of our worries once we're inside *that*," Nihs said, but even he couldn't put a damper on their mood.

The tower was a skyscraper in the truest sense of the word; where it reached the cloud layer, the clouds split apart around it, as if they could not bear to touch it. Shining down through the crack in the clouds was something they hadn't seen in nearly ten days: a ray of sunlight. It was faint, but it was there. It fell upon the obsidian sides of the tower, reflecting off them, proving their solidity.

They had done it. They had really done it. They had reached the tower. All that was left was to climb it. Climb it, and hold audience with the Archsage.

They descended the far side of the mountain and struck out across the great plain. The tower drew closer, albeit slightly—it was farther away than they had thought. But none of them cared. Kyle's eyes were glued to it, warily at first: he half expected it to shimmer and vanish. But it did not, and by late that afternoon it was close enough that he could see the subtle marbling of its texture, the faint white-gray veins that ran up and down its facade. He wondered what it was made out of. His first thought was stone, but its reflective surface also reminded him both of glass, and of the pitch-black metal of Deriahm's armor, known as Buorish obsidian.

Looking up at the silent tower, Kyle felt a complicated blend of emotions. Chief among them were happiness and relief, but apprehension lurked close behind. It occurred to him that there was no guarantee that their trials were over; none of them had any idea of what awaited them inside Vohrusien's stronghold. Archmage Rosshku had taught them a great many things aboard the *Aresa Bign*, but the subject of his master was one he was loath to breach.

"It has been many centuries since I have seen him," he had said. "And I do not pretend to know his current mood. I suppose you could say that he is insane—but not in the traditional sense. All I can tell you is that while many things about him and his tower change constantly, some things always remain the same. He will seek to test you, and he may seek to manipulate you as well; trick or persuade you into giving up your quest. But I think that he will help you, if you stand true to your purpose."

The fact that not even Rosshku was certain if Vohrusien would aid them wasn't a very comforting thought—but in the end, it didn't matter. It was too late to worry about whether or not they had made the right decision. They walked in the shadow of the tower, and Kyle intended to climb it, for better or worse.

Night was falling by the time they reached the tower's base. The ray of sun that fell upon it had turned a deep, fiery red, and the structure's walls reflected it so brilliantly that Kyle was reminded of the water-drenched buildings of Oasis.

Like the mountain before it, the ground leading up to the tower was completely flat and featureless, a circle of sheer stone over a mile in diameter. Kyle got the impression that they were walking along the surface of a stone sundial, headed toward the gnomon in the center.

The spire itself was stark and featureless; it had no windows or balconies, nothing to indicate floors, and if it had a door, Kyle had yet to catch sight of one. No path led up to it, and Kyle couldn't tell if they were approaching it from the front or from behind.

Suddenly, they were there. The tower stood less than a hundred feet away, blotting out the sky, oily walls bearing down on them. They stood, six abreast—Rogan, Nihs, Deriahm, Kyle, Lugh, Meya—and regarded it.

Nihs was the first to speak. "I don't believe it," he said softly. "We actually made it."

"Didn't think we could pull it off, eh, Nihs?" Lugh said, his voice also quiet.

Meya slipped her arm into Lugh's. "What a horrible place," she said, her voice mournful and sad. "It's so lonely. What kind of a person could live here?"

"We'll be meeting him soon enough, if all goes well," Rogan said.

"Speaking of which," Lugh cut in, "I can't help but notice that there's no door."

It was true; not only was there no door, there was not a single flaw in the tower's makeup, nothing to even suggest that the structure was hollow. Were it not so perfectly shaped, Kyle might have thought that it was a natural spire of rock.

"Maybe it's on the other side?" Meya said, not sounding very convinced.

Lugh shrugged. "Might as well check."

For its height, the tower was incredibly thin—perhaps five hundred feet wide at the base. They circled it easily, finding nothing but smooth black walls on all sides. Soon they were back where they had started.

"The door could be hidden with an illusion," Nihs said, "or some other trick of magic."

"If that's the case, we're not likely to be getting in any time soon," Lugh said.

Kyle looked up at the blank, unfeeling walls. "Do you think Vohrusien knows we're here?"

"I'm certain of it," Nihs said.

"Then this could be one of the tests Rosshku told us about. He hasn't locked us out; but he's not about to show us the door, either."

"Maybe you could soar around and scout the place out," Lugh said. Kyle couldn't tell if he was being serious or not.

"I wonder if it could be something so simple as the fact that we have failed to announce ourselves," Deriahm said. "We are, after all, interlopers in Vohrusien's domain. It is only polite, not to mention prudent, that we make ourselves known to him."

"Not a bad idea," Lugh agreed. He turned to Kyle. "I think that one's on you. This is your mission, after all."

Kyle nodded. He stepped forward and looked up, imagining Vohrusien watching them from inside the tower, somewhere above them. A problem presented itself to him. How, exactly, were you supposed to introduce yourself to an immortal Archsage?

"Hello?" he said. Not a great start. He cleared his throat and tried again.

"My name is Kyle Campbell," he said in a clear voice. "I'm a vagrant—a traveler from another world. We met with your apprentice, Rosshku. He said that if there was anyone in the world who could help me, anyone who could get me back home to where I belonged, it was you.

"This is Rogan Harhoof, and Nihs Ken Dal Proks, Lughenor MacAlden, Meya Ilduetyr, and *irushai* Deriahm. They're my friends and travelling companions. We've come a long way to meet you. I know you have no reason to help us, but… we hope that you will. Loria is an amazing world, but I don't belong here, and I think that bad things will start to happen if I stay. So, will you please help us?"

The last echoes of his voice were swallowed by the still air. Kyle's companions were nodding in approval, but none of them spoke.

They watched and waited, hoping for something to change. A minute passed, and it became clear that nothing would. Deriahm bowed his head and Lugh sighed.

"All right. That wasn't it. What's next?"

But something had caught Kyle's eye. He had been watching the shimmering patterns of marble beneath the tower's surface. They were subtle, almost impossible to see even in the right light, but they were there, and Kyle would have sworn that they were moving. This small difference completely changed the way he saw the tower; where before he had thought it was solid rock or metal, now he wondered if it was in fact something else entirely. Water? Oil? Some kind of dark matter?

Silently, his companions fell into step behind him as he closed the distance to the tower. At thirty feet away, he was so close that the northern sky was completely blotted out. Ten, and he could feel a gentle coolness radiating from its walls.

He held out an arm, palm first. He didn't know why, but he wanted—*needed*—to touch the tower, to feel the texture of its surface, to try and solve the riddle it posed. *What's it made out of?* It was all Kyle could think.

His outstretched hand was a foot from the tower's base. He was shivering in its shadow, and could see his fingers trembling.

"Kyle," Nihs said behind him, but Kyle ignored him. He swallowed and grit his teeth, and took another step. His open palm connected with the tower's wall.

Water? Oil? More like molasses. No, more like a fog so thick that it felt solid. It was cool to the touch, and Kyle's palm met resistance, but even as he watched, his hand sank through the tower wall and disappeared. He pushed further, and his arm was swallowed up to the elbow. Frightened, he pulled back, and his arm reemerged, undamaged.

He looked behind himself. His companions were watching him, enraptured.

"It's not solid," he said. "I think…the entire tower's a door."

"A door to where?" Nihs asked.

Kyle didn't say anything. Of course he didn't know. He wasn't meant to know. This was one of Vohrusien's tests, and the only way to pass it was to move forward.

"I'm going through," he said.

"We'll be right behind you," Meya assured him.

Kyle nodded and turned back to the tower. Should he close his eyes? He thought not. He considered drawing his sword, then rejected that idea as well. He thrust both hands out in front of him, took a deep breath, and stepped forward, before he could think to hesitate.

There was a moment of stifling, all-encompassing blackness, as if Kyle had been sealed within the tower wall. His lungs restricted and his pupils dilated, desperately trying to pull in whatever light they could. Just as he was starting to panic, he emerged on the far side. He looked around in disbelief. Whatever he had been expecting, it wasn't this.

He was standing in the middle of a forest, lush with greenery and blanketed in fallen leaves. The air was dim and the sun—wherever it was—had nearly set. The air was cool, not cold, and smelled of sweet rot. A gentle breeze teased his cheek and rustled through the leaves above. Other than that, the forest was dead silent.

Kyle looked around in confusion. Where could he possibly be? Was he— his heart skipped a beat—even still in Loria? There was nothing extraordinary about the world around him, but then, the tamer parts of Loria tended to be indistinguishable from Earth.

He looked behind himself, expecting to see the tower wall behind him. He caught his breath—there was nothing but trees and brush in all directions. He was stuck here, wherever *here* was.

He turned back around and realized he was in danger of becoming lost— rather, he was already lost, and was in danger of disorienting himself even further. He scratched a rudimentary arrow into the soft earth with his boot, pointing the direction he'd been facing when he first came through the portal. If this was indeed the inside of Vohrusien's tower, then that arrow would point toward the center.

For a moment he stood, not sure what to do next. He didn't doubt that his companions had followed close behind him, as they had promised—the question was, would they emerge in the same place as he? He decided to wait, for the time being. If no one appeared, he would leave a message for them as best he could and take off in the direction of the arrow.

Mercifully, he didn't need to wait long. There was a shimmering disturbance in the air behind him, and a pair of gloved hands emerged from thin air. Kyle recognized the gloves as Lugh's, and he took one hand and pulled him gently forward.

Lugh stepped into the tower, blinking in the darkness and looking around. He flashed Kyle a relieved smile.

"Almost died when you grabbed my hand. Didn't feel like it was being eaten, though. Where the hell are we?"

"No idea," Kyle said, and was about to add more when Lugh suddenly doubled over, clutching at his chest with both hands. He made a low, groaning sound, grimacing in exquisite pain.

"What? What is it?" Kyle said, reaching a hand out to steady him.

For one heart-pounding moment, Lugh didn't answer. Kyle was starting to panic—he had no idea what was wrong and doubted he would be able to help even if he did. But a moment later Lugh moved his hands away and straightened up. His face was hurt and confused.

"I just felt..." He shook his head. "It really hurt for a second there. Like someone was trying to yank my heart out of my chest."

He was trying to sound nonchalant as always, but Kyle could tell that he was still in pain. He'd just opened his mouth to ask what Lugh supposed had happened when there was another shimmering disturbance in the air. Kyle and Lugh each took a hand to guide Meya as she stepped through the portal.

"Thank you," she said, looking around. "Where—*ah!*"

She shrieked and hugged herself across the chest with both hands, doubling over as Lugh had done. Her hair fell across her face, and Lugh put a hand on her back to comfort her.

"You alright?" he said.

She steadied herself against him. Her expression was the same worrying combination of pain and loss. "What just happened?" She sounded near tears.

"Haven't gotten that far yet," Lugh said.

The others came through moments later; Rogan and Nihs, then Deriahm. Rogan whooped as if punched in the stomach, and even Deriahm showed discomfort. But worst of all was Nihs. As soon as he was through the portal, his eyes rolled back into his head, and he fell into a swoon. He teetered on Rogan's shoulders, then tumbled off, and the big Minotaur just managed to catch him in his arms.

"Meya! Quick!" he said, setting Nihs down.

Meya rushed over, Kyle and Lugh following. She knelt down before him and reached out both hands, cupping his face. She held him that way for a moment, then suddenly recoiled, as if he'd turned into a snake.

"What's wrong?" Kyle said.

Meya was looking at her open palms. "I can't use magic," she said softly.

"*What?*" Lugh said.

Deriahm squatted next to Meya and touched her arm. A spark of understanding passed between them. He rose. "It is as miss Ilduetyr said. I am unable to perform magic as well—furthermore, we are unable to sense one another's souls."

Lugh rubbed the side of his head. "Shit. We have to help Nihs somehow."

"Who has water left?" Meya asked.

Rogan produced some from his pack. Meya took her coat off and wetted the edge of her sleeve. She dabbed it against Nihs' forehead and cheeks. Not long after, he started to stir, and eventually his eyes opened.

"Sick," he said in a whisper. "I feel sick."

Meya rolled him onto his side, where he retched, but didn't throw up. After a minute or two he got his hands underneath him and rose. His skin was incredibly pale, to the point that it looked almost like human skin, and his lips and eyes were red.

"What's wrong with him?" Lugh said.

"*Reursis*," Meya said, and Kyle recognized a condition that he himself had suffered when he first fell into Loria. "Magic deprivation. I think we all have it—but Nihs has it worst."

"Where are we?" Nihs asked. He wobbled, and Rogan caught him in his arms and lifted him off the ground.

A suspicion that had been forming in Kyle's mind now coalesced into a certainty. "We're on Earth," he said.

Meya's head whipped around; Lugh's turned slowly.

"Could that be true?" Rogan said. "I thought magical folk couldn't survive in your world."

Kyle looked around. Somehow, he had an answer to that, as well, but he didn't know how to word it. Just as he was sure that they were back on Earth, he was equally sure that they weren't. Not exactly. Not *completely*.

The forest around him looked real enough. The ground underfoot *felt* real enough. But there was a darkness to this world, an immateriality, something about the texture of the air that suggested it could all fall away at any moment. No, this wasn't the real Earth; he would have been able to tell if that were the case. This was some kind of...

Shadow world. The term appeared inside his mind of its own accord, and he shivered.

"Not the real Earth," he said. "I think it's some kind of copy."

Nihs was nodding groggily. "We could never...enter your world," he said, with great effort. "And if we could...we would die, instantly. This is...a pocket world, that obeys most of the rules of your own. But not all."

"Perhaps Vohrusien has cobbled it together using mister's Campbell's memories," Deriahm said. "With some provisions made so that we could accompany him."

"But we still can't use magic," Meya said, in that same tone of heavy grief. "Which means we won't be of much use anyway."

"Let's not worry about that," Lugh said. "Do the job that's in front of you, all right? Now, Kyle—if Deriahm's right, you should have some idea of where we are."

Kyle looked around for the second time, hoping against hope that something in the scenery would tell him where they were. There wasn't much to go off of; they were in a forest at night, during what might have been spring, summer, or early fall. The trees were broad-leaved and the bedrock was showing from underneath a blanket of ferns and grass. A botanist might have been able to identify the trees and plants, but Kyle's relationship with nature had never been very close.

"I can rule some places out," he said slowly. "But we could still be almost anywhere. These forests are all over the U.S. and Canada. We could be in Europe, even."

Despite herself, Meya smiled. "Such interesting names," she said.

"We *could* be," Lugh said, "but I don't think we are. Vohrusien wouldn't have thrown us somewhere that didn't mean anything to you. Any forests where you live?"

"There are a few," Kyle said, "but…" and he shrugged. Lugh nodded.

"Right. I get it. Well, what do you think? Pick a direction we like and walk?"

"Seems as good an idea as any," Rogan agreed.

But just then, Kyle's nerves twinged, and he instinctively reached for his sword. He had heard a sound in the near distance, so soft as to be nearly silent, but borne to his ears by the cool, quiet night. It was the sound of feet coming down on beds of leaves.

"Did you hear that?" Kyle whispered.

Lugh nodded, reaching for his own weapons. "We're not alone," he said.

"Protect Nihs and Meya," Rogan said, his voice deep and low. He hefted his axe and held it across his body, blade out.

Meya looked none too happy about needing to be protected, but she didn't argue. It was all too obvious that she and Nihs, who had once been two of the most powerful members of their party, had been all but completely crippled in this world where their magic was neutralized. Meya, at least, had the staff that King Azanhein had given her; but Nihs didn't even carry a weapon, as he had never needed one.

They formed a ring and stood facing into the darkness, eyes and ears pricked for any sign of movement. Kyle heard more footfalls, but they were so faint that he might have imagined them. He couldn't tell what manner of person or creature the sounds belonged to.

Then a sound erupted off to Kyle's left and all doubt was washed from his mind. It was a wolf's howl—pure, sustained, and eerily beautiful, but also terrifyingly close.

Kyle drew his sword, as did Lugh and Deriahm. The three of them and Rogan closed tighter around Meya, who had lifted Nihs also her shoulder and was holding her staff out in front of her.

Another howl came from the opposite side of their party, and more joined it. The echoes reverberated between the trees, scrambling Kyle's senses. How many were there? Five? Ten?

"You've got to be kidding me," Lugh said between gritted teeth. "Can't we catch a break?"

Now Kyle could see gray-white shapes moving through the underbrush; a shoulder here, a tail there. Kyle caught a glint of yellow eyes and turned his sword toward them, but they were already gone.

More howls, and the patter of feet all around them. Kyle strained his eyes, trying to see. He would have given anything for some of Nihs' fire magic, or even an ordinary flashlight.

He heard Lugh shout from behind him and turned just in time to see a huge wolf bearing down on him, emerging out of the darkness like a ghost. This was no regular wild dog; no coyote or even coyote-wolf mongrel. This was a purebred grey wolf, three feet high at the shoulder, fierce as it was stately and graceful. It locked its eyes on Lugh and paced back and forth, just out of range of his sword.

Kyle turned back as another wolf loped out of the forest near his side of the circle. It was perfectly silent, its face calm, but its eyes glittered, and its muzzle was pointed at Kyle. It moved low to the ground, while Kyle pivoted in place, tracking it with his sword.

Suddenly Rogan bellowed and swung his axe at a third wolf that had ventured too close to him; it danced backwards while his blade whistled past, burying itself in the soft earth. Kyle's wolf bounced back as well, its head weaving in the dark air.

"Come on," Kyle growled at it.

Two more wolves appeared; now there were five, and Kyle's eyes flickered back and forth as he tried to keep them in view. They circled his party, dipping in, jumping back, testing their defenses. Kyle had seen documentaries of wolves hunting before, but nothing could do justice to the feeling of being marked as their prey. They circled, always out of reach, but close enough to strike at any moment. Kyle's heart was pounding and he was shivering with icy adrenalin. He could feel his nerves starting to fray under the tension. If only they would attack! Then the fight they all knew was coming could begin.

"Come on!" Lugh shouted. "Poke at them! We need to chase them off!"

Rogan was huffing loudly, and Kyle felt a fresh pang of fear. If he went berserk here, none of them would be able to pull his mind out of the black depths to which it descended when Gershel's soul took over.

We need to end this, and fast.

The next time a wolf stepped close, Kyle lashed out with his sword. His swing was slow and clumsy; he'd gotten used to Loria's magical atmosphere, and the combat energies he could leverage there. The wolf he'd attacked slipped underneath his swing and galloped away in a wide circle. Before he could pull his arm back, another shot forward from his left like a bullet. Its head snaked out, and its jaws clamped around his wrist.

He gasped in pain as his bones ground together and blood streamed from his wrist. He drew his sword back and struck down at the wolf's back. His blade bit into its skin, and it whined and growled around his wrist, but it kept its hold on him. It braced its legs against the ground and yanked at him, trying to pull him off balance; this time, he cried out and fell to one knee.

Deriahm appeared on his left. His black sword shot out and skewered the wolf through its stomach. It yelped in pain and let go of Kyle, thrashing away from the sword. Its companion came charging back, paws drumming against the ground. This time, Kyle saw it coming and swung to the right. His cut was wild—his body was shaking with pain—but he clouted the wolf on the side of its muzzle and it retreated again, growling.

A new wolf—*six*, Kyle thought, *six of them, six of us*—came up from behind Deriahm and started to savage his back; but Deriahm, in his heavy armor, was the most protected of any of them, and was next to invincible in this fight where none of their enemies carried weapons. The wolf's teeth grated against his armor, searching for purchase, and its tongue spread slobber across his backplate, but Deriahm did not so much as lose his poise. He turned smartly about and bashed at the wolf with his shield. It yelped and retreated once more.

Kyle was staring at his ruined wrist, trying to keep himself from fainting. He'd suffered so many wounds since coming into Loria, some of which had threatened his very life. But somehow, none had been worse than this bite on the wrist. It was so much more painful, so much more *real*, than anything he had felt before.

This is it, he thought, light-headed. *This is our last battle. Not the twins, not Radisson, not the* gordja *or the ice-spiders. Just a pack of regular timber wolves, attacking us in some forest in God-knows-where.*

Lugh, who was the fastest of any of them, had severely wounded one wolf, fetching it two deep gashes that ran down its sides. Rogan was bellowing and swinging his axe, but so far none of the wolves had been bold enough to attack him. Meya was standing in the middle of them, clutching her staff, Nihs clinging uncomfortably to her neck.

Another wolf drew close to Kyle, and this time he didn't wait for it to attack. He lashed out, and when it splayed its front paws and ducked under him, he followed up, sword whistling through the air. He might only have one hand left, but he was starting to regain the balance he had lost when moving between worlds. Already he was getting used to the feel of the atmosphere, as someone would get used to the land after spending months at sea. He struck three more times in rapid succession. The third clipped the wolf on the side of its muzzle, and a spray of blood shot into the air. It yelped and tumbled over. Kyle was about to strike down when another wolf attacked from his right, and he was forced to focus his attention on it.

On and on it went, for what felt like hours. Feint, attack, dive in, dive out; the wolves were nearly impossible to hit, and perfectly filled the gaps in each other's defenses. They were panting heavily, and several of them were bleeding, but so was Kyle, and Rogan had been bitten on one arm, as well.

A wolf slipped under Rogan's guard and made directly for Meya. She shrieked and swung her pronged staff at it. It connected at the shoulder, but the wolf charged through it, jaws snapping at her stomach. It bit into her side and yanked; she yelped and fell to her knees. Nihs, still groggy, lost his hold on her neck and tumbled onto the ground.

The wolves, sensing a kill, abandoned their teasing of Kyle and the others and streaked past them on the way to Nihs. One of them closed its mouth around his middle and lifted him straight off the ground. He shouted in pain and slapped at it, but here he was little stronger than a child.

Rogan bellowed in fury and swung his axe lightning-fast. The wolf dodged, but not well enough. There was a sickening crunch as its ribs gave way and one hind leg was crushed underneath its body. But its grip on Nihs remained.

Lugh came forward and plunged his sword into the wolf's neck from the side; now the animal went limp and Nihs came rolling out of its jaws. A second later, another wolf clamped its jaw around Lugh's outstretched hand. Meya rushed in and grabbed Nihs. A wolf caught the back of her flowing suit and tried to pull her to the ground again. She ducked down, covering Nihs' limp body with her arms, blood streaming from the wound in her side. Deriahm came forward and chopped at the wolf that was savaging her; his sword bit deeply into its back and it fell to the ground.

All sense of tactics became lost. Kyle charged in and swung at gray fur whenever it presented itself to him. He sliced at a front leg, and was rewarded with a yelp of pain. He stabbed at an exposed flank as it streaked by him, and his sword became stuck. Desperately, he punched at another wolf that was approaching to his right until Lugh chased it away.

Rogan let loose a mighty bellow and charged directly into the fray, scattering wolves and his companions alike. He picked up a wolf that was nipping at Nihs from between Meya's arms, lifted the writhing creature right over his head, and threw it thirty feet away into a nearby tree. There was a loud *crack*, and the wolf fell to the ground, its back broken.

Finally, the pack's nerve broke. Half of them were dead, and the other half was wounded and limping. Without so much as a single bark, the wolves turned tail and ran, beating a silent and organized retreat. Silence reigned once more, and Kyle's party was left alone in the darkness.

Only Deriahm had escaped from the battle unscathed. Kyle, Lugh and Rogan had each been bitten on the arm at least once. Lugh was sweating profusely and uttered a stream of curses under his breath. Meya was sobbing, clutching at her wounded side. Nihs…

"Is he dead?" Lugh asked huskily. Then, louder: *"Meya, is he dead?"*

Meya shook her head silently. "I think…" she gasped in pain, squinching her eyes shut. She held for a moment, then her face relaxed, and she resumed. "I think it looks worse than it is. And he's still suffering from *reursis*. That's why he won't wake up. The bite isn't as bad as that."

He certainly looked bad enough; in fact he looked half-eaten, covered with slobber and a multitude of bite marks. A few small holes had been introduced to his beautiful red sagecloak.

Not important, Kyle thought. *I'm sure the Buors will be happy to repair it for him once we get back. If we ever get back.*

"What now?" Rogan said. "Do we try to patch him up here or get out of the woods first?"

Meya stood on shaking legs, tears still silently streaming down her cheeks. Her hand was clamped over her wounded side. "We need to get out of here," she said. "We need light, and shelter. And we're finished if more wolves show up."

Rogan nodded, bent, and scooped Nihs up into his arms. The little Kol was so small against him that he could lay flat along one of Rogan's forearms. His body was limp, and his eyes were closed, but his breathing was regular.

"All right, then," Lugh said. "Let's walk."

Kyle and Lugh took point, with Meya, Rogan and Nihs behind; Deriahm, who was in the best shape, came last, covering their rear. Kyle cradled his wounded arm, and Lugh limped.

"Just our luck," he said to Kyle. "We landed right on top of a wolf pack when we came in." His voice made it clear that he thought luck had nothing to do with it.

"If you think that's lucky, you'll love this," Kyle said.

"Yeah?"

"Those were grey wolves. They almost never attack people. And if we are where I think we are, they shouldn't have been here in the first place. There hasn't been a wild grey wolf population here in years."

"You don't say," Lugh said thoughtfully. His next step came down hard and he winced. Then he looked at Kyle again and said, "Did I hear you right? You think you know where we are?"

"I've got an idea," Kyle said. *I'll believe it when I see it,* he added to himself.

Wounded and weary, they limped through the forest, Meya trailing blood, Nihs shivering in Rogan's arms. They wound steadily downhill, then, to their immense relief, came upon a narrow, two-lane paved road. The sight of the crumbling blue asphalt, a streak of reflective yellow paint running down the center, brought to Kyle an immense and indescribable joy.

What's the opposite of homesickness? he thought, giddy with relief and leftover fear. He supposed the closest word was 'comfort'. And that was what this winding, poorly maintained road represented: comfort. It was a promise, a thread that, if followed, was guaranteed to lead to civilization.

Lugh scuffed at the yellow paint with his boot. "Human?" he said, and his tone of curiosity made Kyle laugh out loud.

"You better believe it," he said. "That's all there is in my world, remember?"

"Yeah, yeah. So which way do we go?"

Kyle shook his head, his happiness evaporating. "I don't know," he said.

"Wherever we go, let's go there fast," Meya said, a hand resting on Nihs' chest.

"Right." Lugh looked in one direction, pivoted and looked in the other. He turned back to the first direction. "*That* way," he said. It was as good a decision as any.

As they walked, the reality of their situation had time to sink in. *Earth!* The word bounced around inside Kyle's head. But of course it wasn't; it was a pocket world, a—

Shadow world.

Just as Loria's atmosphere felt different from Earth's in a way that couldn't really be described, so did the atmosphere of this copy that Vohrusien had thrown together. There was something essentially *dark* about this world, and not just because it was nighttime. A black fog groped at the edges of Kyle's vision, as if his sight were an island whose beaches were surrounded by inky water. The sky was dark and threatening, and the silence was oppressive. Kyle was struck with the sudden certainty that nothing lived in this world; nothing but them, and the wolves, and whatever else Vohrusien decided to call into being. There were no birds, no insects, and Kyle would have bet good money that you could take a microscope to the forest floor and find not a single bacterium. This was a world of death—no, this was a world that had never lived in the first place. A stunted, fake world. A—

Shadow world.

Kyle shivered, though the air was only cool.

Still, even this place was an Earth of sorts, and each familiar sight rekindled the swooping joy he had felt when they first came to the road. Here was a discarded pop can; there was a solitary orange traffic cone, forlornly announcing a roadside danger that no longer existed. Each was a reminder of the world that Kyle had left behind, a promise that the real Earth was within reach.

He could tell that his companions were burning with curiosity about his world, for all of their wounds and worries. They pointed out the most mundane sights and talked in low voices to one another. Lugh jabbed a finger at a white sign that leaned jauntily back from the roadside.

"What's that say?" he asked. Kyle looked up.

"It's a speed limit sign. Says you can't go more than 35 miles per hour on this road."

"Huh!" Lugh said, his tone wondering. Kyle laughed despite himself.

"You're too easily impressed," he said.

Lugh laughed as well, tapping at his stone eyepatch. "I guess some part of me never really believed everything you said about your world," he admitted. "But now it's right there in front of me."

Kyle couldn't take offence at this; he had a hard time believing it all himself.

They walked for fifteen minutes, and Meya had just suggested that they stop and administer themselves as best they could when the scenery changed. The trees broke on one side of the road, to be replaced by green fields (black in the current light). They had obviously been shaped by human hands, and Kyle could see an intersection up ahead. His companions cooed and pointed at the power lines running overhead, and the shape of a large house emerging in the distance.

Kyle's suspicion grew into a certainty as the house grew more defined. It was white, two stories tall, with a covered porch and columns running across the front and down one side. Next to it was a small, vintage gas station, also white, with two tiny pumps, one red and blue. A dark blue sign along the top read M.D. GARAGE. The gas station was dark and empty, but the lights in the house were on.

Kyle stopped in his tracks and stared, mouth agape. His companions turned to look at him.

"Cuyahoga!" he said in wonder. "That's where we are!"

"What's this?" Rogan said.

Kyle didn't know whether to start laughing, or crying, or both. "Cuyahoga. It's a national park just south of Cleveland. This is the Boston Store Visitor Center. I used to come here all the time."

"Cleveland…That's where you used to live, isn't it?" Lugh said. Kyle nodded.

Meya's tone was businesslike. "That building—will there be supplies inside?"

"There should be."

"Then let's go. We don't have any time to waste."

Yes, it was all here: the white columns, gray porch, and black rocking chairs on the outside; inside, the lavishly painted stern of the *Sterling*, the model village and the wall covered in logging tools.

They fanned out, wooden floor creaking beneath Rogan's weight. It was bright here, every light switched on, as if the center was open for business. But there was not a single sound as they stood in the threshold, listening.

"What kind of place did you say this was, again?" Lugh asked.

"It's a visitor center. It's where people come to get more information about the park. I think it used to be a general store or something."

"Food? Medicine?" Meya said.

"There's probably a kitchen in the back. And there's got to be a first aid kit somewhere. It'll look like a red box with a white cross on it."

They split up, knowing instinctively that there was no danger to this place. Kyle went right for one of the desks that once would have been manned by park staff, while his companions couldn't help but get distracted. Lugh went rummaging through the center's collection of cheesy historic clothes that had probably been worn by thousands of children over the years.

"*You* weren't dressed in anything like this when you came over," he said.

Kyle glanced up from what he was doing and chuckled. "That's not surprising. Those clothes haven't been in fashion for a hundred years."

He sprung open two cupboards, saw nothing of use, and closed them. He slid open a series of drawers, one after the other, and in the bottom one found exactly what he was looking for: a travel-sized first aid kit, the kind made out of canvas that zippered shut.

Just our luck, he thought.

"Hey, Meya! I found it."

She bustled over, pushing her hair back behind her ears so she could see. Rogan clopped over, holding Nihs in his arms. Kyle unzipped the kit and let it fall across his forearm like a book.

It wasn't the most well-stocked kit in the world, but there were bandages, aspirin, a bottle of rubbing alcohol, a roll of gauze, and even some Steri-Strips. Meya ran her eyes over the contents, moving things aside to see what she had to work with. She pulled out the bottle of aspirin and held it up to her face.

"What is this?" she asked Kyle. "I can't read the label."

"Aspirin," Kyle said. "It's a painkiller, and a blood thinner."

Meya nodded silently and held up the rubbing alcohol.

"Alcohol," Kyle said. "Antiseptic."

Meya heaved a sigh of relief, clutching the alcohol like a talisman. "It's not magic," she said ruefully, "but it'll have to do. Let's find a table."

They cleared a space and set Nihs down. He was awake, but his lids were drooping, and his mouth was clamped shut, as if he knew it would be painful to speak. Carefully, Meya unwrapped him from his sagecloak and set it aside, then worked open the front of the cloth suit he was wearing. His stout green chest was peppered with bite marks, running from his neck down to his stomach.

Meya tried to unscrew the alcohol, failed, and sat there staring at it as if it had called her a dirty name. Wordlessly, Kyle took it from her, unscrewed it, and handed it back.

"Child safety lock," he said, apologetically. "You have to press the cap down or it won't unscrew. It's so kids can't get it open by accident."

Meya gave him a look, but all she said was, "Thank you." She turned back to Nihs. "This will sting a bit," she said.

Nihs nodded slowly, then squeezed his eyes shut.

Once Nihs was sterilized and bandaged, they gave him more water, two of the aspirin, and a piece of dried biscuit to nibble on. He sat in one of the rustic wooden chairs behind the Sterling's stern, looking none too happy, but better for all that.

Meya's own wounds were the most serious next to Nihs', but being on her side, there wasn't much they could do to wrap them. They settled for sterilizing them and applying a half-dozen adhesive bandages. Kyle and Lugh got gauze wrapped around their wrists, but there wasn't enough left to wrap a single one of Rogan's massive forearms. He waved the bandages away, saying, "I survived Gershel's venom. It would take more than a few wolf bites to do me in."

Ministrations complete, they explored the visitor center, looking for anything else that might be of use. They had food—enough to stretch a couple more days, if necessary—but none of them wanted to waste it, not knowing what they would be able to find in this stunted copy of Earth.

Wonder if we could find a grocery store to raid, Kyle thought. He didn't doubt that any such place would be empty of people. Whether it would be empty of food was another question; he still wasn't quite sure of the rules of this place.

A shadow appeared on the wall in front of Kyle; it was one of the building's columns, a thick beam of darkness projected through the building's front window. It was joined by a half-dozen others, and they began to slide to the right, making Kyle feel as though he were inside a film reel. His subconscious understood what was happening before his ears heard the hum of the engine and the crunch of gravel coming from outside.

Someone had just pulled up to the visitor center in a car. Their headlights were shining through the front windows.

"Get down!" Kyle hissed, and they did just that, hiding themselves as best they could among the furniture. Kyle and Lugh fell behind the Sterling, Meya and Deriahm squeezed into corners, and Rogan left the room, knowing there was nothing here that could hide his bulk. They were still far too exposed, Kyle knew whoever was in the car had almost surely seen them when they pulled up.

"What is that thing?" Lugh whispered to Kyle.

"It's a car," Kyle said. "A vehicle, like a runner."

"How many people inside?"

"Could be one, could be as many as seven." Kyle sneaked a peek around the side of the Sterling. The car was in fact a truck—a black pickup. It could have been a Ford F-Series or pretty much anything else; Kyle could only catch a glimpse of its profile from where he crouched, and much of the detail was washed away by the truck's headlights. He could hear the engine idling, feel it through the creaky wooden floor.

"They make enough noise, don't they?" Lugh said. He'd drawn his two swords and had them gathered in his lap, leaning against the Sterling's back end as if he were lounging on the beach.

Kyle didn't answer. He had leaned over further so he could see the front half of the truck. He thought he saw a dark shape moving around in the driver's seat. The truck switched off, but its lights stayed on. The driver-side door opened, and Kyle heard the *clop* of shoes hitting pavement.

"I think it's only one," he whispered to the room. *But who?* In the real world, his money would have been on a ranger or security guard doing their nightly rounds. But regular people didn't live in this world—he was almost sure of it.

The wolves had not been natural; they had been a security measure, a trial, laid across their path by Vohrusien. Would this be the same?

Kyle watched as a figure stepped around the truck. It was human, tall and slim, hands resting on its hips. At first, it was nothing but a black shape outlined by the truck's lights, but as it stepped closer to the building, its features came into view. It was a man, skin so pale as to be milky, hair white, but with the body of a healthy adult. The face came into view, and Kyle gasped in surprise. It was Rosshku the Archmage.

The Archmage looked different in this *shadow world* than he had in Loria. His eyes, which were a glowing violet in his homeworld, were now a glassy blue—the same blue they had been when he had appeared in Kyle's dreams. He was dressed not in his flowing magician's suit of pastel colors, but as a young professional might have been for an afternoon walk through the city: navy slacks, a white shirt, and a loose-fitting gray jacket. Now he was sliding his hands into the pockets of that jacket, watching the front of the visitor center as if expecting something to happen. He still had his light touch of a white beard, and his many-lined face was crinkled and peaceful. Even in this world, Kyle could feel a sort of benevolent wisdom radiating from the Archmage. His face was every loving father, every patient schoolteacher, every understanding boss who had unfailingly taken problems that seemed to have no solution and dissolved them into nothingness. All at once Kyle felt an enormous relief wash over him.

"It's Todd!" Meya said in wonder. "It's the Archmage!"

"What's *he* doing here?" Lugh said, but he sheathed his swords and stood, scooping a grumbling Nihs into his arms.

They stepped outside, and Rosshku's pale mouth pulled into a warm smile. "Ah," he said. "I thought you would be inside. I was just starting to doubt myself."

Kyle shook his hand, still marveling at Rosshku's presence. He repeated Lugh's question as Todd was shaking hands with the rest of their group.

"What are you doing here?" he said.

Todd laughed. "A simple question with a complicated answer. Suffice to say that I became aware of you as soon as you entered this place; my history with Vohrusien gives me that ability. He wouldn't have suffered me to help you reach the tower, but now that you're inside, I thought I would come to welcome you."

"We are honored by your presence, Archmage *Solrusien*," Deriahm said, bowing deeply.

Todd smiled, but didn't bother correcting Deriahm's use of his title—it would have been a wasted effort.

"Think nothing of it. It's my pleasure to give you whatever assistance I can. Speaking of which, I don't suppose you have any idea of where we are?"

He asked this of Kyle, who said, "This is Cuyahoga park. It's just south of Cleveland, where I used to live."

Todd nodded, looking around himself. "The tower always looks the same from the outside, but its interior changes constantly. It wouldn't be inaccurate to say that the inside Vohrusien's tower and the inside of his mind are one and the same. No doubt he exists somewhere in this pocket world, waiting for you to reach him. You know where *we* are—can you divine where Vohrusien might be, as well?"

Kyle thought that Rosshku knew where the Archsage was; this was another test, another trial. He racked his brains, trying to think of where in Ohio an immortal sage might choose to reside.

"I'm not sure," he said slowly. "But I don't think it's a coincidence that we're this close to Cleveland. I think we should head for the city."

"Not a bad idea," Todd said, nodding. "In which case, you'll be needing this." And he reached into the pocket of his jacket and pulled out a keyring with a single key on it—the fob for his truck.

"Really?" Kyle asked. "Are you sure?"

Todd dropped the key into his hand and closed his fingers shut over it, shaking Kyle's hand with both of his. "I drove it here for this express purpose," he said. "I imagine you've had enough of walking for the time being. Please, take it—and make haste. It won't do to dally in this world."

"Right." Kyle tossed the key up and caught it again. This was going to be an interesting road trip.

"Thank you, Rosshku, for everything," Meya said.

"Really. We wouldn't have made it this far without you," Lugh added.

"I'm only sorry I can't help you more. But you'll do fine—I have no doubt you'll reach the Archsage. Remember what I told you when you meet him. He may be unwilling to help at first, but I believe that he will, as long as your resolve is unflinching."

"Don't worry," Kyle said. "We're not leaving this place empty-handed."

Todd smiled again at that, then waved, once, telling them in that simple gesture that the time for talking was over. "Good luck, all of you—and stay safe, though my intuition tells me that *that* part of your proving has passed."

They bade him farewell and turned to leave. Kyle glanced behind himself not five seconds after Todd had spoken his last words, but the Archmage was already gone. Kyle wondered where the real Todd Rosshku was at this moment. It must have been a tremendous effort to send himself here to meet them.

With the Archmage gone, they turned their attention to the truck. It *was* a Ford—an F-150, like the one that Kyle's father had once driven. But this was a newer model, and was brand new to boot, its black sheen flawless but for a few dings behind the wheel wells where gravel had struck. Lugh made a circle of it, examining it with his hands on his hips.

"So this is a car, huh?" he said, peering into the box.

"A truck, actually," Kyle said. He pressed the fob and the truck honked at him, lights flashing. Lugh jumped away with such a comical expression on his face that Kyle burst into laughter. He laughed until his stomach ached and his bad arm twinged, tears squeezing out of the corners of his eyes. The others laughed, too, and Meya rubbed Lugh's back, consoling him.

"Yeah, very funny," Lugh said, in a bad humor that wasn't entirely convincing. "I'm not sure we can trust this thing. What makes it go?"

"If it's good enough for the Archmage, I'm sure it's good enough for us," Rogan said. "Only one problem. Are we all going to fit?"

"Oh," Kyle said. It was obvious what Rogan's question had really been: was *he* going to fit?

"You could sit in the back," he said, rapping the edge of the box with his palm. "I won't be able to go too fast, but it'll work."

Rogan grunted. "I'll run alongside."

To their surprise, it was Nihs who spoke up. "You oughtn't," he said. "We should all ride—stay together, and safe."

"Why?" Rogan said, his tone a little surly.

Nihs coughed, then swallowed drily. "When traversing unknown waters, you take a boat. You don't swim."

They waited for him to keep talking, but that seemed to be all that was forthcoming. Eventually Rogan heaved a great sigh.

"Fine. Are you sure this thing can take my weight?"

"I wouldn't worry about it," Kyle said, though the axles did whine in protest when Rogan hauled himself aboard.

Kyle's other companions were having trouble with the doors, so he made a round of the truck, showing them how to pull the handles back and swing the doors open. Meya was first, and she laughed when Kyle offered his hand to help her up.

"Such a gentleman," she said, then made a delighted little noise as she climbed into the back. "There's *food* in here!" she said.

"Really?" Kyle and the others gathered round to look. And indeed there was a fair-sized pile in the middle of the back seat: a box of granola bars, a bag of red apples, another of beef jerky and two more of chips, a 24-pack of bottled water and even a few bars of chocolate. It looked as though someone had stocked up for a road trip—which was, of course, what had happened.

"Another gift from the Archmage," Deriahm said in wonder.

"Where would we be without him?" Lugh said, his voice muffled. He was halfway through an apple and was working the top off the box of granola. "Now how long are you all going to stand there looking at it? Let's go!"

If it felt strange to be behind the wheel of the F-150, it was only because of how *un*-strange it felt. Kyle turned the lights on and spent some time adjusting his seat and mirrors; the Archmage was several inches taller than he was. Of course, there was nothing to be seen out the back but Rogan's shaggy bulk, but old habits died hard. Deriahm, who had won the passenger seat, watched politely, while Lugh, who was sitting behind him, grabbed the back of his headrest and poked his head into the front of the car.

"What are you doing now? What're all these buttons for? What's this?" and he held a granola bar up for Kyle to inspect.

"It's a travel bar," Kyle said. "Tear at the frilly edges to open it."

"What's in it?"

"Just eat it," Kyle said, because Lugh was bothering him, and because he was trying to remember how to drive a truck, and because he was smiling like an idiot because this was all so strange but so *funny* at the same time.

He started the truck just as Lugh was figuring out how to open the back window and hand some food to Rogan. Nihs was sitting in the middle of their stash, drinking from a bottle of water more than a third his height. Meya was eating an apple, watching Lugh with a long-suffering look on her face. A granola bar was sticking out of his mouth like a cigar, and he was pawing at a bag of chips, trying to get it open. She snatched it from his hands.

"Save some for the rest of us, would you?" she said.

"This stuff is *delicious*," he replied, biting off his mouthful. "What the heck's it made out of, Kyle?"

"Sugar," he said, and nodding at the chips, added: "salt. We've got our junk food down to a science here. Now I'm going to take off. Everyone got their seatbelts on?"

He realized his mistake just before Lugh said, "our *what?*"

Kyle sighed.

"Forget it." He supposed it didn't matter, anyway. They would be driving down the freeway, but there wasn't likely to be much traffic, and having a Minotaur sitting in the back of the truck was probably about as unsafe as could be.

He put the truck into gear and pulled out onto the road. He was trying to remember where they needed to go to reach Cleveland. They needed to get on the I-77; that would be fastest. Instinctively, he touched at his hip pocket, wishing his phone were there so it could guide them home. That would have been fitting, he felt, but they had no such luck.

They pulled onto Boston Mills road and then turned right onto Riverview. *North through the park,* Kyle thought, *and then west on…whatever it's called.*

He accelerated, glancing through the rear-view window constantly to check on Rogan. His furry bulk shifted with each bump they hit, but his hooves were planted against the far side of the box, and his hands were gripping the sides. It would probably take rolling the truck to dislodge him.

Now Lugh and the others were looking out of the truck's windows, watching the world go by. At first he thought it was strange, then he remembered that he himself had been in their position only a few months ago. He'd probably looked just as silly to them then as they did to him now.

I wish I could show you the real Earth, he thought. *Not just this shadow world. Take you to a real American diner to get burgers, then go on a road trip across the Interstate. New York, Vegas, the Rockies, LA…*

Then, with a pang: *all the places I've never been.*

He whistled breath through his teeth and tightened his grip on the wheel until it creaked beneath his fingers. *I'll make it home. And then I'll see home. You can count on it.*

Snowville. That was the name of the road. Kyle turned west, and accelerated some more. They were on their way.

In a matter of minutes they had turned on to the I-77, and Kyle accelerated up to 50 miles per hour. He would have gone faster but for Rogan's presence; he still glanced fitfully behind him every couple of seconds to make sure the Minotaur was still there. The going was at least smooth, and as Kyle had suspected, there was not a single other car on the road. The world was still shrouded in darkness, that insistent and oppressive dimness that had nothing to do with the time of day and everything to do with the nature of the world they were in. The road ahead was clear, but when Kyle glanced to the side, he saw that the darkness intensified in the near distance. About a mile out, it grew so deep and all-encompassing that the world was swallowed by it. Kyle knew without being told that he was seeing the edge of this universe, the outer walls of the tower. This trip wasn't going to include any detours—Vohrusien had made sure of that.

"How long did you say this trip was going to take?" Lugh asked from the back seat.

"Half an hour, usually," Kyle said. "But I'm going a little slower than I usually do."

"How fast *can* this thing go?"

Kyle laughed out loud. "Faster than this. But most cars these days have speed limiters built in. This one's is probably around one hundred miles an hour."

"How fast are we going now?"

"Fifty."

Lugh whistled as if he'd just seen the perfect pair of legs. Meya sighed.

Kyle knew this route like the back of his hand, but things were different in Vohrusien's pocket universe. The darkness made everything seem alien and unfamiliar, and Kyle started to watch the roadside signs obsessively, worrying that he would get them lost. This was, of course, a completely irrational fear: the I-77 ran directly into Cleveland's downtown, until it finally merged with the I-90.

"So, where do we go once we reach Cleveland?" Meya asked.

Kyle had been thinking about this, as well. "I'm not sure," he said. "Todd told us to figure out where Vohrusien might be staying, but I can't think of anywhere in my world that would suit him."

"Perhaps that is the wrong question to ask," Deriahm said. "Perhaps we should be thinking instead of which location would suit *you*. After all, this is your world, and we emerged within driving distance of your hometown."

"You got a house in Cleveland?" Lugh asked, halfway through the second bag of chips. Meya reached over and stole one from him.

"An apartment," Kyle said, "but that doesn't seem right, somehow." *I don't want all of you to see it. It's not where I belong.*

"What about significant buildings or locations?" Nihs asked, his voice already getting stronger. "Any parks, government buildings, monuments—"

"Towers?" Lugh added, saying the word that had jumped into all of their minds at once.

Realization struck, to the point that Kyle had to fight to keep the truck steady on the road. "There is a tower," he said. "Key Tower. It's the tallest in the state."

"*Inter*esting," Lugh said. "What's it used for? Don't tell me it's a weapons manufacturer."

"I think it's just an office building," Kyle said. "It's owned by KeyCorp. They're an investment company or something. Not very interesting," he added, wondering if his intuition had been wrong after all.

"In *your* world it is," Nihs pointed out. "I think it's worth investigating."

"All right!" Lugh said. "You know the way, Kyle?"

Kyle nodded. "Not exactly, but I just have to get us downtown," he said. "You can't miss it after that."

The forty-minute drive to downtown Cleveland seemed both very short and very long. Kyle's companions let him drive in peace, for the most part, contenting themselves with eating and looking out of the windows at the limited scenery offered by the shadow world. This, of course, posed its own set of questions.

"What are all those ropes following the road?" Lugh asked.

"They're wires—power lines. They carry electricity between cities."

"Electricity? What for?"

"That's what we use for energy," Kyle said. "For heating and cooking and using all of our machines."

"Wow," Lugh said as another tower passed by. "So what, is the whole country covered in these things?"

"The whole of most countries," Kyle said.

Lugh whistled. He sounded both incredulous and impressed.

Kyle fiddled with the radio, but he couldn't get a sound to come through.

It was a shame; it would have been hilarious to expose his friends to some of Earth's music. But nothing but static came through the speakers, and they drove on in silence.

Eventually, Kyle saw signs for Cleveland, and his heart sped up. He wasn't sure he wanted to see his hometown again like this after so long, but he was sure that he wanted to find the Archsage and put an end to their searching once and for all.

Buildings—houses and high-rises—began to pass them by. On a better day, Kyle might have been able to name a good number of them. But he always drove this route half-asleep with familiarity, and in this shadow world, he couldn't tell exactly where they were. He only knew that they were still heading north, getting closer with every moment to Cleveland's downtown core.

The highway was lit, and such streetlights as they could see off the sides of the road were on, as well. But for the most part, the world was dark and dead. The road was still completely empty, and every building they passed looked deserted.

Their exit, when it finally came, caught Kyle by surprise. He signaled out of habit (he'd gone the entire drive staying within the lanes) and passed under the sign that read:

EXIT 163
E 9th St
Ontario St

"We're almost there," he said. "If the sky were bright you could see Key Tower right ahead of us."

"No kidding," Lugh said, leaning forward again. There was, however, nothing to see; the sky was as dark as ever.

They turned on to E 9th St and drove under the I-90 overpass. A shape, huge and metallic, loomed out of the darkness ahead of them. Even Deriahm gasped in surprise.

"What's *that?*" Lugh said.

The structure, all sheet metal and white scaffolding, drew closer. "That's Progressive Field," Kyle said. "Home of the Cleveland Indians."

"What's that supposed to mean?"

"It's a baseball diamond," Kyle said. Then, having learned his lesson, he added, "Baseball's a sport. Huge in America. The Cleveland Indians are our city's team."

Now the downtown core was coming into view. The buildings were mostly dark, but still retained a sort of essential glow, as if all their lights had been left on at twenty percent brightness. Now Kyle knew where he was going; here was the AT&T building on his left, The 9 on his right. Kyle's heart was beating faster. *We're almost there. Almost…*

"What are we looking for, here?" Lugh asked. He had picked up on Kyle's excitement; his face was pressed against the window, and his eyes were scanning the city. Even Nihs had gotten up from his roost. He was perched on Lugh's thigh, using it as a boost so he could see out the window as well.

"A square tower with a pointed roof," Kyle said. "There's a big red key high up on the side, but you might not be able to see it from here. Anyway, it shouldn't matter. You'll know it when you see it."

They came to the tower just a handful of seconds later. Kyle pulled over and parked—he wasn't too worried about getting a ticket—and there came an impressive groan from the back as Rogan hoisted himself out. Kyle himself jumped out, then helped the others work the doors. They crossed the lawn before the tower and the fountain at its center (it had some stupid name like 'the fountain of eternal youth', Kyle remembered) and gathered at its base, as they had done not very long ago at the base of Vohrusien's tower in the *adaragad.*

And they did know the tower when they saw it, every one of them, though Kyle was the only person who had seen it before. They knew it even though Kyle had been wrong about one detail: there was no red key on the side of the tower. Instead, a blazing neon 'O' shone down on them, so bright that it was clearly visible from dozens of stories above.

Not an 'O', Kyle thought absently. *A circle.*

Not a circle, another voice said, a voice that came from so deep within that Kyle wasn't sure it belonged to him. *A band.*

It was solid red, as Key Tower's famous key had been, but there was an unsettling, hellish quality to the light it gave off. Suddenly Kyle was reminded of the monstrous eye they had encountered in the *adaragad.*

"Thought you said it was a key," Lugh said, matter-of-factly.

"It was," Kyle said absently. "It should be."

"Does that symbol mean anything to you?" Meya asked him.

Kyle shook his head. "It's just a circle."

But it wasn't just a circle; it was a *band,* and Kyle knew that it was as deliberate as their landing in Cuyahoga had been, as the wolves had been, as Todd Rosshku's intervention had been. They were following a trail that Vohrusien had laid out before them, and this was another stop. The final stop.

"Well?" Lugh said. "Shall we?"

Kyle had seen Key Tower almost every day of his life back on Earth, but until today he'd never set a foot inside. Even still, he knew something was off from the moment they crossed the stone courtyard and stepped through the glass entranceway. Their feet fell on lush red carpeting, and all sound was muffled.

The first thing Kyle noticed was that the lobby was not deserted, as the rest of this world had been. There was a woman—a secretary—seated behind a massive faux-wood desk directly ahead of them. Her head was bowed and she was taking notes, though what there could possibly be to take notes on in this world was a mystery. Her hair was blonde, shoulder-length, and she was, outwardly at least, rather pretty. But there was something about the sight of her slim figure seated behind the enormous desk that twanged a chord of unease within Kyle's chest. She seemed somehow frail and insubstantial, as if she might shatter into glass if approached. Her note-taking was intense to the point of being feverish; Kyle could clearly hear the scritching, squeaking noises of her pen from across the lobby.

A sense of imbalance, of wrongness, of *dread* that had been building unnoticed in Kyle's stomach finally began to boil to the surface. His legs stiffened, and his heart thumped. He was scared of the woman behind the desk. At first, he wasn't sure why. But then understanding flowed, not from within, but from without, as if someone were whispering the answer to him from an unseen corner of the lobby. The dark, twisted, incomplete nature of this *shadow world*—it was given form in the shape of the woman before them. The dark sky, the abandoned streets…it was her doing; it was her fault.

Or was it? Kyle thought of the circle—the *band*—that had adorned the top of Key Tower. Where did it begin, and where did it end? Was this woman the creator of the shadow world, or one of its prisoners? Was she the queen, or merely…

…the secretary?

Kyle felt a hand on his shoulder. He turned and looked into Lugh's good eye.

"Remember what Todd told us," Lugh said quietly. "Anyway, we're right here behind you, no matter what happens."

Meya laid her hand, small and warm, on Kyle's other shoulder. Deriahm's cold leather gauntlet joined Lugh's on his right. Rogan eclipsed Meya's hand with his own massive palm.

Kyle drew a few quick breaths, then one long one. "All right," he said. "Let's see what there is to see."

The woman looked up just as they were drawing close to her oversized counter. Kyle recoiled instinctively, half expecting her face to twist into a monstrous grimace. But she merely glanced at them with pale gray eyes, eyes that flitted nervously back and forth.

"Yes?" she said. "Do you have business here?"

She was wearing a plain white blouse and had a thin silver bracelet (*band*) around one wrist. It clinked against the dark red finish of her desk as she set her pen down. Her face was narrow and her nose pointed. She looked small and sad. Kyle no longer feared her—but he thought he might come to pity her if they lingered for much longer.

He cleared his throat. "Yes," he said, as calmly as he could muster. "We have business with Archsage Vohrusien."

From the way the woman reacted, Kyle might have spoken an extremely bad word. She gasped, clutched her hands in front of her, and leaned back, as if afraid she might catch something off of him.

"I'm afraid there's no one of that name here," she said in a quavering voice.

Kyle had been half expecting this. *He will try to deceive you.*

"I think there is," he said slowly. "I saw his symbol on the building outside."

Now why would he say that? But he could tell from the secretary's reaction that he had been right. She looked at him in alarm, reaching impulsively for her pen. She started to pick it up, but it slipped from her fingers and clattered against the desk.

"Well," she said, breathless. "Well. That may be. But the Archsage does not hold audience with outsiders."

Kyle laid his hands on the smooth, polished surface of the desk. It was cold to the touch. "Please," he said. "We need his help. He's the only person in the world who can send me back where I belong."

The woman was eyeing Kyle with an accusatory look on her face. It was obvious that she wanted nothing more than for him to leave, but was powerless to turn him away. "Even *if* he were to see you," she said, her voice clipped, "he wouldn't help you. He would just turn you away."

"I'd like to hear that from him, please," Kyle said softly.

Now the secretary looked ready to cry. "Why won't you listen?" she said in a desperate whisper. "Why won't you just leave?"

"Because I have no choice," Kyle said.

She watched him for a moment longer, frozen in place, and Kyle felt the flutterings of fear once more. There was something very wrong with this woman. Her fragility was upsetting; Kyle felt like he was balancing a delicate china plate on his arm. The thought of letting that plate fall to the floor and shatter was almost too much to bear.

Let her fall, and our lives are forfeit, Kyle thought, and though he used the word 'our', the thought was not at all his own. It came to him in the same voice that the name of this world (*shadow world*) and the nature of Vohrusien's symbol (*the band*) had done.

"All right," the woman said finally. "All right." She grabbed at her pen, dropped it, and then reached for a sleek black phone sitting on her desk. She dialed a three-number combination—Kyle thought it looked like 223—and held the receiver up to her face. Her pale blonde hair fell in wisps at the sides of her head, much like Meya's often did—but this hair had none of Meya's fire and vitality.

Kyle heard the phone ring on the other end of the line, then heard someone pick up. The secretary didn't say a single word, only sat frozen in concentration. After a moment, she heaved a heavy sigh and hung up.

"He's waiting for you," she said. She pointed to her right, where stood an alcove lined with sleek metal elevators.

"Thank you," Kyle said, but the woman had already gone back to her writing. Her pen skated across the paper with a sound like a nail scraping across rough metal. Kyle glanced back at his companions, nodded, and left without saying another word.

The elevators were six, stark and imposing, two rows of three facing each other across the intervening space. Kyle thumbed the 'up' arrow and the center-left elevator slid open instantly. They stepped inside; there was more than enough room for all of them, and even Rogan didn't need to so much as duck his head to get in.

There was a huge array of floors to choose from, expressed as a grid of buttons four across that lined the elevator's front wall. Kyle ignored them, immediately looking for the very top of the grid. There, centered on its own row, presiding over the rest of the buttons, was a single red button marked with Vohrusien's symbol:

O

I hope the rest of the riddles are that easy to solve, Kyle thought, pressing the button. The doors sighed shut, and there was a barely perceptible lurch as the elevator started to move. They watched the floors light up on the panel as they ascended—3, then 5, then 10.

Kyle's apprehension—his *dread*—mounted along with the elevator. They were getting close now, incredibly close to that mysterious figure known as the dread Archsage. Already Kyle could feel his aura impressing itself upon his mind. If Rosshku's aura was one of benevolent sagacity, and Azanhein's was one of exquisite might, then Vohrusien's was one of a dull, familiar sadness that was somehow worse than outright terror. It was the knowledge that tomorrow would not be better than today; that the rain-swelled clouds would not give way to warming sunlight; that there was not, and never would be, a way for a lonesome vagrant to return to the world he had once called home. The oppressive blackness of the atmosphere grew in intensity, encroaching upon Kyle's vision, threatening to blot it out. The world was slowly leached of its color and Kyle's muscles of their vitality. His heart began to struggle, and his extremities felt numb.

20…25…30…the elevator continued its smooth ascent, stupidly unaware that it was killing its charges a little more with each floor.

Meya took Kyle's hand. Her other hand was taken by Lugh's.

"We are close indeed," Nihs whispered, his voice pained. "The dread Archsage looms above us."

40…45…50…Kyle wanted nothing more than to rip his hand free of Meya's and dash for the control panel. He would mash the emergency bell, the button for the ground floor or even floor 55, anything that would stop this elevator ride into hell. He was sweating and shaking like a convict approaching the electric chair.

The elevator slowed. The penultimate floor—floor 57—lit up, then this light, too, faded. The top floor, the band, began to glow.

The doors slid open. A rush of soundless, sightless despair boiled inside like an icy mist. Meya whimpered, and Kyle all but fell into a swoon.

"Stand true, my friend," Deriahm whispered. "Do not be shaken from your purpose."

Kyle stepped inside. His companions followed.

They emerged into a small anteroom, notable only for how mundane it was. It was carpeted in dark blue, and the walls were the same manila beige as a thousand other office buildings throughout the United States.

There were a few chairs, a potted plant (plastic), and some dreary black-and-white photography hung on the walls. There was a reception desk, but no one sat behind it. A handmade paper sign stuck inside a plastic frame set on its surface read:

Be Right Back!!

in cheery red letters. Kyle thought that this was a solid contender for the biggest falsehood ever written; it was obvious that the desk had never had an occupant, and never would.

Behind the desk was an entranceway into an office corridor. Through the doorway Kyle could see offices separated by panes of frosted glass, stretching off to the left and right.

The despair that had been felt on the elevator had abated somewhat, but it was still buzzing in the back of Kyle's mind like an angry insect. It was like a migraine headache that had been dulled by a heavy dose of aspirin; asleep for the time being, but threatening constantly to return.

This office felt *thin*, thinner even than the rest of the shadow world. Whatever this reality was, it was being held together by the most tenuous of threads.

Slowly, carefully, they spread out into the anteroom and looked around. Their footfalls made next to no noise on the plush carpet.

"Where is he?" Lugh whispered.

"Not here," Nihs whispered back. "He must be down that corridor."

Kyle didn't give himself time to hesitate. He stepped past the abandoned desk and into the hallway. He looked left and right. Offices lined both sides of the hallway. The one directly in front was numbered 212, even though they were on the fifty-eighth floor of Key Tower. Its door was locked shut and the frosted glass hid its insides from view.

Kyle turned right, the others following close behind. The next office down, 213, was also shut and locked. So were 214 and 215.

Kyle's apprehension mounted and he quickened his pace. It was too easy for the imagination to run wild with the locked doors and frosted glass. He imagined that they were not offices but unspeakable magical prisons; horrific creatures from Loria's equivalent of hell were trapped inside. He imagined many-fingered hands thudding against the glass, the door handles rattling from the inside. But the office remained deathly silent, and the doors remained closed.

They were just nearing the end of the corridor when Kyle came across an open door. It was office 223, on his left. He could see sunlight streaming into the hallway from through the door as they approached. Sunlight—here?

He drew closer, but his legs locked shut as he was about ten feet from the door. The fear was back, bubbling up from inside just as it had on the elevator.

This is him, Kyle thought. *It's really him.* And now that he was here, he found that he couldn't do it. He couldn't face the Archsage; he feared the man, but worse, he feared what the man would say. Feared that within this small office, his last flame of hope would be extinguished.

He started to back up into Lugh, who put his hand onto his shoulder and whispered, *"Go on!"* It did his nerves no good. He couldn't—he simply couldn't.

He had just opened his mouth to say so, to apologize to his friends for taking them all the way out here for nothing, when they heard the creak of a chair from inside the office. There were a few whisper-quiet footfalls, the door swung further open, and a man leaned out into the hallway.

"Well?" said the Archsage. "Are you coming in or aren't you?"

Vohrusien's office was large enough to fit all of them, if barely. Rogan had to hunker through the doorway, and the party had to spill into the corners of the room so they could all fit inside. They lined up against the far wall facing Vohrusien's desk, none of them wanting to draw too close.

Vohrusien himself had crossed the small room, stepped around his desk, and seated himself in the cold, metal-boned chair behind it. He now sat facing them, hands clasped on the desk in front of him. He looked like an angry school principal about to chide a bunch of unruly students. He lifted one hand and jerked the fingers toward himself.

"Come in, come in," he snapped. "Sit. And someone shut the door."

Deriahm, who was farthest back, did that. There were only two chairs in front of Vohrusien's desk, each with metal, pipe-like arms and legs and rough-woven cushions affixed to the seat and back. Kyle took one; none of his companions seemed about to take the other.

Vohrusien was a man—a very ordinary one, or so he seemed at first. He was tall, dark-haired and dark-eyed, with a sallow face showing deep and troubling lines of stress. His age, just as Rosshku's, was impossible to tell. Some moments he seemed to be thirty or forty; others he seemed seventy or eighty. He was dressed in a brown suit with a white shirt beneath; the brown matched the frames of his square glasses, as well as the leather strap (*band*) of the wristwatch he wore. He was clean-shaven, and his lips were pale and severe.

The Archsage expelled air out of his nose and regarded them. Kyle saw his temples bulge as his teeth ground together. Silence, hostile and stifling, permeated the room.

"Well?" Vohrusien said at last. No one answered; none of them dared. So he went on: "On what business do you come here? You must have some. My tower is little known and less easily found. Speak."

"My name is Kyle Campbell—" Kyle began. Vohrusien waved him away.

"I know that much. Kyle Campbell, from Cleveland, Ohio. You claim to be a vagrant from a sister world called Terra."

"Yes," Kyle said, his heart pounding. "I am."

"You came to Loria by a magical accident. You want to return to your world."

"Yes," Kyle said again. He sat up in his chair; the metal squeaked. "That's right. We were told you can help me."

"I cannot," the Archsage said.

The bottom fell out of Kyle's world. He was falling, falling, being devoured by sadness and panic. *No*, he thought. *This can't be real. I don't believe you.*

He might have lost his mind right there and then if Rosshku's warning hadn't come back to him: *he will try to deceive you*. Even this was cold comfort; Kyle couldn't shake the feeling that the Archsage was telling the truth. He struggled to calm himself and speak.

"What…what do you mean?" he said.

Vohrusien flashed him an angry glare. "It is impossible to send a vagrant such as yourself back to their home world. It defies the fundamentals of magic. If you had bothered to pay attention to this detail before seeking me out, you might have saved yourself a long and tiresome journey."

"But…" Kyle said.

His voice was washed away by a heavy sigh.

"*Zan*," Vohrusien said, and the word shot from his mouth like a dart, stinging Kyle between the eyes and vibrating down his spine. "That is to say, a *not-it*, a zone of utter nothingness, a hole in the magical fabric of the universe. Such is the phenomenon that gives rise to folk such as yourself. Vagrants, particles of energy pulled through gaps in space. In theory, one of sufficient power could invoke *zan*—open a hole in space large enough to fling the vagrant back to their home universe.

"However. At best, *zan* can only devour again which magic was consumed to create the phenomenon in the first place. Your soul, Kyle, has grown and swollen ever since your arrival in our world. By virtue of coming here, you have become trapped here; your soul is larger than the rest of the universe combined. There is not enough magic in this universe to create a *zan* large enough to devour you. That is all."

Kyle was at an utter loss for words. It wasn't that his mind was blank; rather, there were so many thoughts clamoring inside it that he had become paralyzed.

You'll never see Earth again.

You'll live and die in Loria.

That's not so bad; I can live with that.

No, you can't. Think of everything that's happened because you're here.

What about the illusions? Will I go insane? Will I go rosshku?

Maybe Todd can help with that, at least…

No. There has to be a way home. Vohrusien's lying.

Bigger than the universe…

What do I do?

WHAT DO I DO!?

Kyle jumped to his feet, as if his chair had suddenly grown red-hot. Vohrusien's eyes followed him. He was aware that his friends were watching him, concerned.

"There must be something we can do," he said.

Vohrusien's face was closed, hostile. "There *must* be no such thing. You cannot bend the fundamentals of magic."

"There *are* no fundamentals of magic," Kyle said, his voice getting louder. "Nihs told me that the very first day I came here."

Nihs cringed back at the mention of his name; obviously he didn't care too much for being used to defy the Archsage's words. Kyle didn't care. His fear and sadness had coalesced into a wild and desperate kind of anger.

"That," Vohrusien said, his voice clipped, "is a convenient falsehood used to explain the nature of magic. It is not to be taken literally."

"That's not true," Kyle said. "You *know* it's not true. Why aren't you telling the truth? What did I ever do to you?"

Vohrusien rose to his feet. For a moment Kyle balked; the Archsage's aura was billowing out from his tall frame, withering his resolve.

"The last visitor to my tower was a trespasser and a thief," Vohrusien said. "And now I have you, who presumes to know more about the nature of magic than the man who brought enlightenment to the Kol. I have nothing more to say to you. Begone!"

Kyle forced himself to meet Vohrusien's gaze. It was the hardest thing he had ever done.

"A thief?" he said softly. "Someone stole something from you?"

A momentary flicker of doubt; the Archsage hadn't meant to say that. His jaw clenched again and his temples bulged.

"That's no concern of yours. Leave now, and enjoy the remainder of your life in Loria; or stay here and die. It makes no difference to me."

Kyle was about to say something else, but a hand clamped around his arm. To his surprise, he found out that it was Lugh.

"Come on," his friend said softly. "Let's leave for now." He saw the look on Kyle's face—shock, hurt, betrayal—and added, "We're not giving up. You can bet your life on that."

Meya nodded vigorously, eyes shining; Rogan grunted in affirmation. Slowly, Kyle nodded back.

"All right," he said to Vohrusien. "We'll leave."

He allowed his friends to lead him out of the office and back down the hallway. Kyle glanced back just once; Vohrusien was still standing behind his desk, frozen as if in fury. His eyes were staring into nothing and his jaw was clenching and unclenching. Kyle heard the Archmage's voice in his mind, clear as daylight: *I suppose you could say he is insane.*

It doesn't matter, Kyle thought. *We're not finished with you. You're going to help us—I don't care what it takes.*

They left the office and rode down the elevator in silence. It opened on the ground floor of Key Tower, and they walked past the fragile secretary on their way out. She didn't even glance up as they passed by.

They exited into the cool night air—it was still nighttime here, even though the sun had been streaming into Vohrusien's office. It was only then that Lugh spoke.

"Where do we spend the night?" He asked no one in particular.

Kyle looked up from his thoughts. "We can pick a hotel and break in," he said. "Doubt anyone's going to come after us."

"Sounds like a plan. What's the ritziest place you know of?"

Kyle shrugged. There was a Marriott attached to Key Tower—he could see it from where they stood—but right now he wanted to keep his distance from that place. "There's always Metropolitan at The 9," he said. "We passed it on the way here."

"Shall we drive?"

Kyle shook his head. "Let's walk."

They did so, Kyle in the lead, and silence descended once more. Kyle thought it was because none of them knew quite what to say, how to react. Nothing had been as they expected—not the tower, nor the Archsage, nor his reaction to Kyle's plight. Kyle didn't know whether to be hopeful, desperate, angry, or sad. It was all too much. He just needed some time to get his thoughts together.

As they turned off of Superior and onto 9th Street, Lugh felt compelled to break the silence again.

"So. What do we think? Is Vohrusien telling us the truth or is he taking us for a ride?"

"We shouldn't have disrespected him so," Nihs said, his voice low and bitter. "Even if there was a chance of him helping us, we've all but thrown it away."

Lugh opened his mouth to answer, but Kyle stopped the argument before it had begun.

"I don't think so," he said. "I don't think we could have gotten him to help just by being polite to him. He's testing us—that's what he's been doing ever since we got to the tower."

"So what are we supposed to do?" Rogan said. "He didn't exactly give us much to work with."

"Let's talk once we get to our lodgings, yeah?" Lugh said. "I don't know about the rest of you, but I've had enough excitement for one day."

His words brought Kyle's attention to the needs of his own body, and he realized that he felt the same way. They'd been through so much over the past few hours; they'd escaped the bitter cold of Westia only to be attacked by wolves in Cuyahoga. They'd been rescued from starvation and given a truck by Rosshku only to be rejected by Vohrusien.

Kyle's fatigue, physical and mental alike, came back to him in waves as the day's events caught up with him. His bitten hand started to throb with pain, and a dull headache settled behind his temple. Lugh was right; he couldn't think about the Archsage any more tonight. Vohrusien would have to wait.

L ike the rest of the city, the Metropolitan was completely deserted, and its windows were cold and dark. The front door, however, was unlocked, and once they stepped inside the sumptuous lobby they saw that at least some lights had been left on.

Kyle had never stayed at the Metropolitan before, but he had no eyes for the place now. He led his companions to the reception desk and stepped behind it. He rooted around until he found what he was looking for: the hotel's stash of key cards. He grabbed a half-dozen of them and a ring of keys left on the desk for good measure. He stepped back around and handed the cards out to the others.

"What's this?" Lugh said.

"A key for getting into your room." Kyle looked at his own and froze; the number on it was 223.

"Yeah?" said Lugh.

Kyle shook himself. "Come on."

They found the elevators and Kyle jabbed the 'up' button. As with Key Tower, one of the doors opened instantly. They filed in and rode the elevator up a single floor. They found their rooms, and Kyle showed the others how to open them with their key cards. He swung the first room open and they stepped inside.

Lugh whistled. "Not bad. Shame about this world just being a copy—seems like it could actually be nice here."

Kyle nodded in agreement. He was by now so tired that he could barely stay standing.

They each took a room to themselves—why not?—which meant that Kyle entered room 223 on his own. The number concerned him, and he swung the door open slowly, half expecting to find himself back in Vohrusien's office. But the room was an almost identical copy of Lugh's: lavish, spotless, and completely dark.

Kyle threw his pack on the floor and turned on his bedside lamp. He never slept with a light on, but he thought that tonight he would make an exception. He danced out of his jacket and threw it over a chair, then turned down the bed's covers before pulling off his shirt and pants and climbing in. The sheets were cool and incredibly soft. He sighed in relief and allowed his tired eyes to close. He was asleep in seconds.

He woke not long after; he wouldn't have been able to say why, but he thought he had slept for little more than an hour. He sat up and glanced around, ready to reach for the sword propped up next to his bed, but his room was completely silent. He had no idea what had woken him.

He kept still for a moment, straining his eyes and ears, but heard and saw nothing. The tension flowed out of his body, and he fell back down against his pillow, hoping to fall asleep again. It was no use; he was as awake now as he had been sleepy not very long ago.

He found himself thinking about the tower, about Cleveland and the shadow world, and about their brief meeting with Vohrusien. The Archsage was nothing like Kyle had expected; then again, Kyle had a suspicion that the man they had met was not really Vohrusien. He was the lure of the anglerfish, the false eye of the killer whale, the *shadow* of the true Archsage. The form he had taken was a mystery to Kyle. If this shadow world was cobbled together from Kyle's memories, why had he not recognized the severe man in the dark brown suit?

I'd never been inside Key Tower or the Metropolitan, either, Kyle thought. *And yet here I am.*

Part of Kyle wanted to push the thoughts from his mind and try to fall asleep, but another part of him knew that this was important. *It's all a test. This entire tower is a test. Vohrusien can help us—I'm sure of it.* What did they have to do to earn his trust?

The last visitor to my tower was a trespasser and a thief. Who could that have been? The only person Kyle knew to have met the Archsage was Todd Rosshku, and he didn't believe the Archmage capable of stealing anything.

Suddenly Kyle kicked off his sheets and swung his feet down to the floor. There was no hope of falling asleep again; he might as well get some use out of his energy.

He dressed himself quietly, pulling his arms through the sleeves of his coat and buckling on his sword. He crossed the big empty room, grabbed his key card, and stepped outside. He glanced around as he put a hand on the door to keep it from closing. His eyes caught a dark shape standing a few doors down and he nearly jumped out of his skin. He drew his sword just as the figure stepped forward, and was lit by one of the smoked glass sconces that lined the hallway.

"Fear not, mister Campbell," the figure said. "It is only I, Deriahm."

Kyle relaxed. He sheathed his sword and stepped close.

"What are you doing out here?" he asked, keenly aware that Deriahm could ask him the same question.

"I found myself unable to sleep, and thought that I might make use of my insomnia by standing guard. I needn't have worried—it seems that many of us are having difficulty falling asleep in this strange pseudo-world."

"Oh, yeah?" Kyle said.

"Yes. Not too long ago I saw miss Ilduetyr…" Deriahm trailed off, looking at the floor as if the end of his sentence might be found there. Then he looked up again and said, "But what of yourself, mister Campbell?"

Kyle sighed. He'd barely gone two steps before being found out.

"I was going to go for a walk," he said. "Try to clear my head a little."

Deriahm nodded. "I see. I will not attempt to stop you, if only because I sense that whatever danger this world once posed us has passed. Still, there is no need to tempt fate by going alone; please, take me with you."

"Thanks," Kyle said. "But I think I need to be by myself." He tapped the sword at his hip. "Don't worry, I'll be fine."

Deriahm still contrived to look worried, so Kyle added, "I won't be gone long, promise. You can wake the others if I'm not back in an hour, all right?"

The young *irushai* bowed in acquiescence. "I shall do as you say, mister Campbell. Enjoy your walk, and please be careful!"

Kyle thought about Deriahm's behavior as he walked down 9th Street. When he had first joined their party, he had been meek to the point of being timid, almost never speaking without being spoken to first. Now his attitude was assertive, even motherly. Kyle wondered if this was a result of him being more comfortable with the others, or had anything to do with the commands he was no doubt receiving from his lodestone.

Kyle hadn't meant to walk back to Key Tower—in fact, he had meant to walk almost anywhere else—but he found himself strolling down 9th Street, turning left again at Superior.

What are you going to do, meet with the Archsage on your own? All of Kyle's instincts told him that this was a terrible idea, but still he walked.

I'll see what there is to see, he promised himself noncommittally.

There it was: the huge fifty-seven (fifty-*eight*) floored tower, marked by Vohrusien's red band. Kyle stopped for a minute and examined it, trying and failing to catch a glimpse of anything odd. There was no sign of the strange out-of-place top floor, or of the sunlight that had shone into Vohrusien's office. Not surprising, really.

Maybe the place will be closed, and I won't be able to get in, he thought as he approached the front door. But it was open as before, and the thin, worried secretary was still seated at her post, right where they had left her.

This time she did look up, and Kyle very clearly saw tears shining in her eyes.

"You *again!*" she hissed. "What do you want?"

That woman is the key. She is Vohrusien's gatekeeper.

Kyle stepped up to the desk and looked into the woman's face. *Who are you? Why did Vohrusien put you here, in our way? What do you know about him?*

"Hi," Kyle said, rather lamely. "I was just...going for a walk."

She blinked, disarmed. "Yes, and...?" she said.

Kyle sighed. "I couldn't sleep. This world...well, it's kind of like my own, but it's just different enough that I can't relax."

The woman had gone back to her mysterious writing. "Well then," she said, "why did you come here?"

"I didn't have a choice," Kyle said, for what felt like the umpteenth time. "I needed to see the Archsage. To ask for his help."

The woman made a fussy little noise in the back of her throat. "You always have a choice," she said. "You could have stayed in Loria where you belonged."

"But I *don't* belong there," Kyle said.

"You belong anywhere where you're happy." She pinned him down with her eyes. "You *are* happy there, aren't you?"

"Of course," Kyle said. "But..."

"But what?"

It was Kyle's turn to be disarmed. He cast about for an answer. "It's dangerous," he said. "If I stay too long I'll keep getting more and more powerful."

"You *know* there are ways of preventing that," the secretary said. "There are no fundamental laws of magic—you told Vohrusien that less than two hours ago. Or did you forget?"

"That's not the same!" Kyle said, shocked.

She gave him another piercing glare. "Of course it is. Didn't Rosshku give you that necklace so you could hide from your enemies? What else do you suppose he could make for you if you asked nicely? Of course, he would rather send you on a fool's errand to get you out of his sight."

The woman's voice had changed. It had lost its fragile quality and become stern and commanding. It was like talking to a completely different person.

"I'd still have to go my whole life lying about who I was," Kyle said.

"Don't be silly. You lost all of your memories in the accident, remember?"

"What do you—"

The woman leaned forward. "Don't waste your life trying for the impossible," she said. "Everything you need is here; you just need to see it. Forget about your world. Enjoy your life here—it will be rich and full. Rosshku and Azanhein will worry about your power; let them. *You* know that you are trustworthy. *You* know that you won't let it get out of hand. And you have friends here who love and support you. What do you have back home that's so worth going back to?"

"I—"

"I can see into your mind," the woman said, and she came forward more as if to get a better view. "Your mother is dead, taken by an illness that you couldn't pay to cure. Your father was never there from the start. You've never had a single real friend in your entire life. You pushed everyone away, even the woman who would have married you if you'd had the courage to ask her. You threw it all away until there was nothing left. And now you want to go *back?* Why are you so determined to hurt yourself? Was ruining one life not enough—now you need to abandon another?"

Kyle's heart was pounding, and his legs were shaking, but his mind, for the first time in days, was clear. He looked the woman in the eye and laid his palms on her desk.

"You're right," he said. "I've made a lot of mistakes. And there are plenty that I can never take back. But it's not all bad. That was my biggest mistake of all—only ever seeing the bad in things. I built my world around that. But even still, there were good parts to it. Only, I'll never be able to get them back if I don't go home. That's why I have to go—to rescue the parts of my life that are worth rescuing. So please, Vohrusien, can you help me?"

The woman held his gaze for a full five seconds, not speaking, not so much as blinking. Then, slowly, she settled back down in her seat.

"You're wrong about one thing," she said. "I am not Vohrusien. If you're to see the Archsage—the *real* Archsage—you'd best make sure your soul is strong. Can you claim that, *mister* Campbell?"

"Yes," Kyle said. "I can."

She eyed him as if she still didn't believe him. But finally she said, "Very well. Go on; I won't stop you."

She didn't give him directions, or so much as wave him on his way, but he felt that was the way things were meant to be. He nodded and left for the elevators as before, while she watched him from behind her desk, a pensive look on her face.

Kyle stepped inside the elevator and watched the smooth metal doors slide closed. He looked at the control panel and its fifty-eight buttons, wondering what he was supposed to do. The red band at the top of the panel beckoned, but somehow Kyle thought that was wrong. That was what Vohrusien *wanted* him to think was the answer.

He stared at the panel for some time. He considered just pressing the button for the second floor and seeing where it would lead him—perhaps he could look at the *real* room 223 and see what there was to see—but that didn't feel right either.

Then another idea struck him, and he knew it was the right one even before he tried it. He stuck out two fingers and pressed the buttons for floors thirty-nine and forty at the same time. He held them for a moment, then a deep chime sounded from somewhere inside the chute, and the elevator began to rise.

As the elevator ascended, Kyle felt an alien pressure assert itself over his mind. It wasn't exactly like the fear and despair they had felt when going up to Vohrusien's office on the top floor; rather, it was a directionless *force*, a weight of incredible density that was not evil, only incredibly vast, and dangerous for that. Kyle flexed his hands and touched at the sword he wore; but of course he wouldn't be needing it. He was scared, but also incredibly excited. He was close now, so close.

The elevator slowed, then stopped. The doors slid open silently. Kyle braced himself against the overwhelming force of Vohrusien's aura, and stepped out.

There was a small antechamber directly ahead of him, after which rose a staircase of naked gray-black stone. It looked nothing like the rest of Key Tower's interior or exterior; the stonework was rough and ancient, the lines swooping and oddly organic.

This isn't Key Tower anymore, Kyle thought. *I'm back in the real tower. Back in Loria.*

Kyle.

The voice came to him from the staircase, from the empty air, from the walls and the floor. It was as soft and discreet as a *sotto voce* comment made at a boardroom meeting, but it vibrated every atom of Kyle's being. It was low, calm. Angry, despairing…and tired.

If you would hold audience with me, then do so. Do not keep me waiting.

My God, Kyle thought. *Vohrusien.*

He was deathly afraid, but he could no more disobey that voice than stop the beating of his own heart. He clenched his jaw and began to climb.

The first fifty steps were gloomy and dark, but eventually Kyle saw a purple glow emanating from above him. It shone through what looked like an arched doorway—the top of the staircase.

His heart thumped in his eardrums, and he was sick to his stomach. Vohrusien's aura struck him in waves, threatening to undermine his balance and send him bowling back down the stairs to the elevator. He wished there was a handrail to hold on to and settled for the pommel of his sword, instead.

Closer, and Kyle could see a twirling, twisting shape at the center of the light. He couldn't divine its nature; it certainly didn't look human.

Suddenly he was there, standing in the threshold of the room at the top of the stairs. It was circular, irregular in shape, as if it had formed spontaneously from natural rock. Its ceiling was vaulted, coming to a point high above, and the floor and walls were completely stark. Eight stone pillars, each two feet across and as tall as Kyle's chest, sat in a ring around the room's center. At the middle of the circle formed by the pillars was the source of the purple light: the true form of Vohrusien the Archsage.

The true Archsage was not a human or even a physical creature. It was a ball of swirling, pulsing, thundering light, a violent purple corona like the birth of a galaxy. It floated high above the ground, out of Kyle's reach, and shone so brightly that he had to squint his eyes next to shut to keep them from watering.

Circling the light was the band.

It was about three feet wide and swung lazily about the light like an enormous gimbal. It was at once red, purple, green, yellow, blue, and purest black. Though it was only about a dozen feet in diameter, the sound it made as it spun was the low, deep booming of vast amounts of air being displaced at once.

The light was frightening, but the band was terrifying. It seemed not to be a physical object, but rather a window into some vast unseen space that could— and would—consume anything that drew too close.

Kyle watched in horrified fascination as the nature of the Archsage was revealed to him in this strange display. The light and the band; the prisoner and his prison. The light flashed and strained with a lunatic power; the band dampened and constricted with an implacable solidity.

Come, the Archsage said. It was now clear that the voice was emanating from the light behind the band. *Speak.*

Kyle stepped forward, his face taking on a ghostly purple hue. Every time the band's slow rotation eclipsed the Archsage from view, it was plunged into darkness. His mind was reeling. What did you say in the face of such a creature?

"Archsage," he said. "It's an honor to meet you."

Waste not your time on honey; your awe and honor mean nothing to me. Pose your questions…ask your favors. That is why you are here.

Kyle stepped closer as bid. The light shone so brightly it seemed to be pouring into his skin and irradiating his body. "The person we met before…the man in the office. Was he you?"

He was an aspect of me. As this world is a reflection of your mind, its inhabitants are a reflection of mine.

Kyle licked his lips. "So you know what he told us."

I do.

"Was it true? Is there really nothing you can do to help me?"

I did not lie. The energy needed to send you back to your world is beyond even my reach.

"But…could that change? There must be something we can do. If not, then…why did you bother to bring me here?"

The Archsage didn't answer. Kyle looked into the light as often as he dared, but it stabbed pain into his eyes whenever he did. He watched the band instead, marked its slow patrol around the Archsage's light.

"You're a prisoner here," he said, half to himself.

Yes.

"Why?"

Knowing this would bring you no closer to your goal.

"But what if we could help you break free? Would you be able to help us then?"

That wish is beyond your power to grant.

The light had become too much; Kyle lowered his gaze, biting his lip. The Archsage claimed he was beyond help. Was this another lie? No, not lie—the Archsage didn't lie. He merely obscured the truth.

"The thief," he said suddenly. He looked up again, squinting his eyes. "Your shadow said that the last person who visited you stole something from you. What was it?"

For a moment it seemed like the Archsage would not answer again. Then he said three words.

Look. Think. Remember.

What? Kyle looked around the chamber, wondering what Vohrusien possibly could have meant. There was nothing here but him, the light, the band, and the eight stone pillars that formed a circle around the Archsage.

He drew closer to one of the pillars. It was slightly shorter than him, a rough cylinder with an indentation in the top. Set into the top of the cylinder was a large glowing stone—it looked like an Ephicer, only it was deep red instead of blue. If it was an Ephicer, it was the largest Kyle had ever seen; the size of both his fists put together. It was cut into an organic, sanguine shape that looked both deliberate and naturally occurring.

He looked across to the next pillar over. There was an Ephicer here, too, but it was yellow instead of red, and its edges were sharp and jagged.

He stepped around the Archsage, going from stone to stone. Each was a different color and shape. Green, white, purple; round, square, cylindrical. Except…

"There's one missing," he breathed. "Seven instead of eight. That's what he stole from you? One of these Ephicers?"

These stones form the heart of my power. If but a single one is removed, the circle becomes incomplete, and my energy is sapped.

Kyle caught the Archsage's implication immediately. "You can't help us because the Ephicer is missing. If we found it, would you be able to send me home?"

He stared into the shining, purple light, and for the first time since coming into the Archsage's presence felt an emotion other than hostility directed at him. It was not enough to be called kindness, but perhaps it could be called satisfaction.

The subway will take you and your companions away from this place. Go. When you have brought the thief to justice and retrieved my stone, bring it to the place where you first entered this world. Do that, and the road to Terra will be revealed to you.

Kyle sprinted up the road toward the Metropolitan. The air, which had first had seemed cool, now felt icy going down Kyle's throat into his lungs. He barely felt it, just as he barely took note of his surroundings. He was filled with a blind elation that had only grown more powerful since leaving Vohrusien's chamber. It was an emotion brought on by the simple fact that, for the first time since coming to Loria, he *knew*.

He *knew* what he had to do to get back home; it wasn't a suspicion, a hope, or a clue. It was a certainty. It was a goal, a simple equation with only one right answer: *bring back the stone, and I will help you.*

Unburdened by his pack and brimming with energy, Kyle flew down the streets of Cleveland, redoubling his pace when he saw the sign for the Metropolitan up ahead. He burst through the front doors and jabbed the button for the elevator. He rode up to the second floor only to run into Deriahm, who hadn't budged from his post.

"Sir!" he said in surprise.

Kyle took him by the shoulders. "Help me wake everyone up," he said. "I need to tell you all something."

"Nothing is the matter, I hope?" said Deriahm.

"I spoke with the Archsage again," Kyle said, already knocking on doors. "He's going to help us after all."

"Ah!" Deriahm gasped, and seemed unable to say anything else.

By this time, Rogan had already opened his door, and was watching Kyle blearily from the threshold of his room.

"I suppose there's a reason for all the noise?" he said.

"I'll explain once everyone's up. Could you grab Nihs?"

Lugh and Meya emerged as Rogan was pounding on the door to Nihs' room, trying to wake him up. Neither looked as though they had slept a wink; Kyle must have barely slept himself, and his meeting with the Archsage, for as revealing as it had been, had only taken a couple of minutes.

Finally Nihs opened his door, and they all piled into his room. Nihs sat inside the nest he had made on his bed; Rogan sat on the floor next to him. Lugh pulled up a chair, and Meya sat on his knee. Deriahm, as always, found an unobtrusive corner to stand in. Kyle also remained standing—he was too excited to sit. He faced his friends, still panting from his sprint down the road, and thrust his hands into the pockets of his coat.

"Vohrusien's got a job for us," he said.

He told them of his walk to Key Tower and his second meeting with the secretary. He told them of the hidden floor that housed the true form of Vohrusien the Archsage, and about the seven Ephicers that surrounded it. He told them of the thief and of the missing eighth stone that Vohrusien had tasked them with finding. His companions were suitably awestruck when he described the light and the band—and for once, the most excited of his friends was Nihs.

"You've witnessed a magical phenomenon of the like that no other man has," he said. "Some kind of incredibly powerful magical seal that is holding the power of the Archsage at bay. The Ephicers must form some part of it; there is some relationship of power here that we are not privy to."

"I get the impression that he didn't want me to know too much about him," Kyle said. "He just told me to find the missing stone."

Rogan huffed. "Quite the errand he's sent us on. That stone could be anywhere in the world. How are we supposed to know where to look for it?"

Nihs shook his head vigorously. "If those stones are indeed Ephicers, then the eighth stone's presence in the outside world can't be kept secret for long. The power of an Ephicer increases exponentially with its size. An Ephicer half an inch on the side can power a firearm. An Ephicer an inch across can power a small vehicle. An Ephicer of the size that Kyle is describing could power an entire city. That amount of magical potential is bound to have left its mark somewhere. Furthermore," and now he looked at Kyle, "based on what Kyle has told us, I believe we can derive the stone's shape and color."

"How do you figure that?" Lugh said.

Nihs dove for his satchel, went rummaging through it, and pulled out his notebook and pen. As he flipped through the pages, Kyle recognized the last thing he had written in it: the message he had tried to get Kyle to read when he'd lost the Lorian language. Kyle could read it now as it flashed past: *Nod if you can read this.*

Nihs found a blank page in his notebook and drew an octagon of shapes. He connected the shapes on the opposite sides of the octagon, creating a starburst pattern, then began to label each shape.

"It is no coincidence that Vohrusien has eight Ephicers feeding his power," he said as he wrote. "Eight is a magically significant number. Specifically, it is the number of primary colors that exist on the color wheel."

"But there are only three primary colors," Kyle said.

Nihs stopped writing and glanced upward. In a single look he managed to convey his utter disdain for the foolishness of humans.

"Right," Kyle said. "Sorry."

Nihs finished his work and held up his notebook for them to inspect. There were eight shapes, all different, each labelled with a color.

"The eight primary colors, divided into four sets of opposites," Nihs said. "Red and blue, yellow and green, purple and orange, and white and black. I can guarantee you that the Ephicers surrounding Vohrusien followed this pattern. So, Kyle—which was the missing stone?"

Kyle squeezed his eyes shut, wanting to be sure. Vohrusien had told him *look, think, remember*, and that he had done.

"Orange," he said. "It was the orange one that was missing."

Nihs nodded and tapped the shape next to the orange label—it was perfectly round, an orb. Then he said something strange.

"Do you know why most Ephicers are light blue?"

Kyle shook his head, and to his surprise, Lugh and Rogan did as well.

"It is because that is the natural color of our world's atmospheric magic. The dominant wavelength, as it were. Though Loria's ether is purple in color, and purple is generally considered to be the true color of perfect magic, blue is the dominant color here on Loria—hence why our sky is blue."

Kyle wondered briefly what Nihs would say about Rayleigh scattering, and decided not to broach that particular topic now.

"For an Ephicer to appear as a color other than blue suggests that its power is heavily skewed toward that other color. In other words, each of the eight Ephicers surrounding Vohrusien grant very specific powers as determined by their color."

Nihs took a moment to bask in their confusion. He clearly took this as a sign that his lecture was going well.

"What's that all mean to us?" Lugh asked.

Nihs preened. "It means that not only do we know what the missing stone looks like, we know what kind of powers it's granting to the thief who stole it. Just as Kyle's phone warped the world around it when it landed in Loria, so the orange stone has been reshaping the world around it to suit its image." He tapped his drawing again, this time to the shape opposite the orange one. "Purple is the color of magic; of imagination, immateriality and transience. Its polar opposite, orange, is firmly rooted in the material. It is the color of wealth, science, and knowledge. Whoever has the stone now has these powers at their command."

"Livaldi!" Kyle shouted suddenly.

Nihs smiled broadly and closed his notebook with a *snap*.

"My conclusion exactly," he said.

L *ivaldi has the stone.*

They debated it at length, and other theories were put forward, but somehow they all knew that Kyle and Nihs' original guess was the correct one. It all fit too well to be mere chance. After all, Livaldi was the richest man in Loria, and he had made his fortune selling Ephicer engines. His company was producing such advanced weapons that even the Buors and their famed military might couldn't compete.

"I'd be willing to bet it's no coincidence he knows about you, either," Lugh said. He counted on his fingers. "Livaldi steals the orange stone from the Archsage. Then you show up. Livaldi starts chasing you. Then you meet the Archsage, and he tells you to take back the stone that Livaldi stole. It's all connected."

"I was thinking about that," Kyle said. "How *did* Livaldi steal the stone in the first place? How did he even know it was here to steal?"

"We can ask him that when we meet him," Meya said. There was a barb in her voice that made Kyle look over and search her face.

"That brings up another problem," Nihs said. "Vohrusien told us how to get back to Loria, but where do we go once we're there? We know who has the stone, but we're not sure where he's keeping it."

"'Course we do," Lugh said.

Nihs treated him to a raised eyebrow. "How do you figure that?"

"This might come as a shock, but I *do* listen to what you say—every once in a while. You said the stone was reshaping the world to its liking, right?"

"Yes."

Lugh tapped his eyepatch pensively. "I seem to remember a certain someone commissioning a giant tower to be built not too long ago. Kind of similar to the one we're in now, wouldn't you say?"

Nihs clapped his hands to his cheeks. "Of course! Livaldi didn't build Sky Tower for himself—he built it to house the stone! Possibly he didn't even realize why he was doing it. Lugh, you're a genius!"

"Oh, well," Lugh said, pretending to blush. "Let's not go too far."

"So he's keeping it somewhere inside Sky Tower," Meya said. "Probably close by, just like Vohrusien keeps his own Ephicers close to himself."

"On one of the maintenance floors, perhaps," Deriahm said. "For remember that it was this code Kyle used to gain access to Vohrusien's chamber. Or, perhaps he keeps it even closer, in his personal office on the top floor of the tower."

Rogan shifted on the floor. "Either way, it sounds like we're breaking into Livaldi's tower and searching the place. That's not going to be easy."

"Yup," Lugh said. "You can bet he's got the best security money can buy. He probably designed a lot of it himself with the stone's help."

"So? What do we do? Do we stay here where Livaldi can't reach us and make a plan?"

It was Kyle who answered. "No. We should leave this place as soon as we can—tomorrow, I think. Vohrusien's let us stay here so far, but I don't think he wants us here."

"I'm with Kyle," Lugh said. "This place gives me the creeps."

Nihs sighed and rapped his clawed fingers against his notebook. "So we'll stay here for the night, and leave for Loria in the morning. As for how we'll steal the stone back from Livaldi—we'll worry about that when the time comes."

"Right," said Lugh.

Meya reached out and rubbed Kyle's back. "We're going to get you home," she said.

"Yeah," Kyle said. He didn't trust himself to speak further.

He slept better that night than he had in weeks.

Lugh and Meya lingered in the hallway after Nihs kicked everyone out, and Deriahm had finally been persuaded to give up his watch and get some rest. Lugh leaned against the wall, his hands in his pockets; Meya stood in the middle of the hallway, hugging herself, rocking her weight from one leg to the other.

"You all right?" Lugh asked her.

She nodded, then sighed. "I'm worried," she said. "About going up against Livaldi."

"Worried one of us will get hurt?"

"More than that," Meya said. "I'm worried that he'll win. What if we drop Kyle right into his lap? Everything we've done, all we've given up, would be for nothing if that happened."

"It won't happen," Lugh said at once.

"Lugh," she said, exasperation creeping into her voice, "you would say that about anything."

"No, I'm serious." And Lugh kicked himself off of the wall and grabbed her shoulders, turning her so she could see his face. "You don't need to worry about that. Personally, I feel a little bad for Livaldi."

Meya's expression turned to one of mild horror. "What are you talking about?"

Lugh winked. "Remember what Rosshku said? Kyle is infinitely powerful in Loria. He just doesn't know it yet. But he's been getting stronger all the time. Even if the worst happened, and Livaldi took him prisoner, how long do you think it would last? Livaldi might have the stone, but Kyle's got the *universe*. Livaldi doesn't stand a chance against him."

Meya wanted to tell Lugh he was wrong, but she found herself starting to believe him already. *How does he* do *that?* She thought.

"Even if that's true," she said softly, "we still need to worry about ourselves. Livaldi's willing to hurt us to get to Kyle. We know that."

Lugh pulled her into his arms. Again Meya was struck by the all-encompassing warmth of his body.

"Right," he said again. "And that's why we'll be watching each others' backs when the time comes to storm his tower. I'll watch yours, you watch mine. Nihs, Rogan, Deriahm, and Kyle—we'll do it together. But listen." And now he pulled away and looked into her eyes again. "We'll need *you* to keep us safe, and you won't be able to do that if you're just thinking about getting revenge. So no going after Livaldi on your own, all right?"

She glared at him, shocked. She wanted to be angry but could only manage to be surprised. "How did you know that?"

He flashed a vicious grin. "I'm smarter than I look sometimes. So do you promise?"

She looked into his open, earnest face, and felt tears welling in her eyes. Lugh pulled her in close again.

"All right," she said to his chest. "I promise."

"The best revenge we can get is snatching that stone from him and getting Kyle out of his reach, anyway. Right?"

"Right," Meya said, though part of her still didn't believe it, and never would.

"Arriving at…Skralingsgrad…station. Doors will open on the left."
"Weird," said Lugh.

They were on the Cleveland Rapid, travelling east out of the city. The station had been completely deserted, full of that warm, stale wind that seemed endemic to subway stations throughout the world. As they stood on the platform waiting for the train, a discarded scrap of newspaper had blown by, borne by the wind coming from the tunnel. Kyle had snatched it up, curious to see what the contents of this *shadow world's* paper would be. What he'd seen had sent a thrill of fear down his spine.

The page was dominated by a black-and-white photograph of Vohrusien and his secretary. The Archsage was dressed in a sharp, well-fitting suit and his secretary was in a pencil skirt and white blouse. They were standing in front of an office building, and though the Archsage had his arm around his secretary's shoulders, both of their faces were grim and unhappy. The Archsage looked like a stern father, glaring out of the photograph from behind his rectangular glasses.

Every headline and every sentence in every story was the same:
Don't fail me.

Kyle let the paper slip between his hands and watched as it blew away. A moment later, the train arrived. Lugh whooped in excitement and Nihs gripped his cloak as it threatened to blow off his shoulders. The arrival bell tolled and the doors opened of their own volition. Kyle tried not to think of what was running these trains, where they came from and where they went, as he stepped inside.

The train looked and ran exactly as Kyle remembered, with a few slight changes. Firstly, he'd never before seen one of The Rapid's trains completely deserted, and in normal circumstances it would have been almost miraculous for them all to get seats (except for Rogan, who barely fit on the train and probably would have broken any seat he tried to use). Secondly, the stations at which this train stopped were about as different as could be from the ones Kyle knew.

"Arriving at…Okogan…station. Doors will open on the right."

"Where's that?" Kyle asked.

It was Lugh who answered. "There's a bunch of islands off the west coast of Ren'r, around where Elfland and the Selks' territory touch. Okogan's sort of the unofficial capital of the islands. Hey, how do we know what the next stop is? We should figure out where we want to get off."

Kyle stood and walked over to the route map. It showed a map of the entirety of Loria in miniature, with a string of glowing dots looping across the various continents. There were over three dozen stops, some of which Kyle recognized and many of which he didn't.

"Looks like it's going to take us down the coast of Centralia," he said. "Through Reno, to Ar'ac, then across the ocean to Proks."

"We need to be in Reno eventually," Lugh said, "so there's not much point in letting it take us too far from there. What stops are there around Reno?"

Kyle peered closer; the tiny stops were hard to make out. "There's one in a place called Coromb, across the bay."

"That'll do. Only about an hour's ride to the city center from there. That'll get us in without having Livaldi breathing down our necks."

Kyle nodded. "Three stations to go."

The mysterious train stopped at Okogan station, opened and closed its doors, then rolled on, moving at the apparent speed of several hundred miles an hour. Kyle thought that it wasn't actually speeding under Loria's earth and oceans; nothing in this realm was as it seemed. He imagined that they were still in the tower, merely selecting from a series of doors that Vohrusien was presenting to them. The train was here for their benefit, to help them cope with whatever magic the Archsage was working on them.

It was less than fifteen minutes later that the cool female voice (was it the voice of Vohrusien's secretary? Kyle thought it might be) announced that they were arriving at Coromb station. Kyle stood out of habit, though there wasn't exactly going to be a rush on the doors when the train arrived at the platform.

The train slowed then stopped, and its doors slid open.

They stepped out onto a gray concrete platform that was both completely alien to Kyle, and utterly nondescript. There was no signage, no advertisements on the walls, nothing to indicate where they were. In fact, the platform as a whole seemed unfinished, as if Vohrusien had just constructed it and hadn't had time to put on the finishing touches.

Best not think about it too much, Kyle thought.

They climbed the stairs from the platform, then followed the only available hallway out. There was another stairwell at the end of this hallway, which ended in a single door painted a noncommittal baby blue. Kyle pushed it open and then threw an arm over his forehead as sunlight burst into the tunnel.

They stepped out into a hot summer afternoon, vibrant and bright. Kyle knew at once that they were back in Loria; the colors, the smells, and the magic-rich thickness of the atmosphere were unmistakable.

They were standing in the middle of a green field, surrounded by hills and dotted with trees. A gleaming city rose up in the near distance; it looked very much like Reno, so Kyle assumed it must be Coromb.

Lugh breathed a huge sigh of relief and spread his arms. "Hoome!" he shouted into the air. "We did it!"

"We did indeed," Rogan said, blinking away the light. "Doesn't that sun feel good?"

It did feel good; Kyle might not have been a Lorian, but he could appreciate the bright sun above and the green earth below after spending so long away from both. He took off his coat and stuffed it in his pack, letting the breeze cool his arms and chest.

"Shall we head into town to plan our next move?" Deriahm said.

"Let's," Lugh said. "But first we're going to a restaurant and ordering one of everything they serve."

"Meals or drinks?" Kyle asked.

"Both."

Coromb, as one of the many towns that surrounded the greater city of Reno, was essentially a smaller, slightly less intense version of its larger cousin to the southeast. The buildings were sleek and modern and the streets gleaming clean. It wasn't quite as nice as Oasis, but it was a welcome departure from most anywhere they had been since then.

They stumbled into the first restaurant they found, and Lugh nearly held to his promise of ordering the entire menu. Nihs, however, vetoed drinking outright, to which the rest reluctantly agreed. They were close enough to Reno to feel under Livaldi's shadow, and they feared him more than ever now that they knew the source of his power.

After eating, they found a hotel to check into and spent the better part of two hours washing their clothes, washing themselves, sorting out their belongings, eating more food, and generally enjoying the kind of mundane comfort that only civilization could provide. Though the Metropolitan hotel in shadow-Cleveland had technically been theirs for the using, none of them had felt completely at ease there.

They emerged clean, satiated, and in high spirits—the fact that Westia, the *adaragad*, and Vohrusien's tower were all far behind them was finally starting to sink in. They left the hotel to go walking through the streets of Coromb, looking for a safe place to figure out their next move. They found a park filled with stout, full-bodied trees dressed in their summer finest. Their leaves were colored anywhere from a pale lime to a deep forest green, and many of them were flowering, covered in buds and petals of bright pink and butter yellow. Meya looped her arm in Lugh's as they strolled down the white stone pathways. They were all trying and failing to be concerned about Livaldi, as they had done back in Oasis.

Eventually they found a shaded seating area in a semi-secluded spot; it was quiet enough that they could speak without being overheard, but public enough that they didn't need to worry about being taken unawares.

Lugh clasped his hands together behind his head and leaned back into the latticework created by his fingers. "All right," he said. "What's our plan for taking down you-know-who?"

"We're not here to take him down," Nihs said at once. "We're here to get the stone back. If we can avoid a confrontation, all the better. Besides, I think that things will end up going poorly for him before long once he no longer has the stone to rely on."

"Right," Lugh said. "So how do we pull it off?"

That was a problem. None of them knew the first thing about thievery, nor about what they could expect inside Sky Tower, nor about where Livaldi might be keeping the stone. They mulled it over, trying to focus as the sun did its best to put them to sleep.

"Let's start with the stone," Nihs said. "We work on the assumption that it's somewhere in Sky Tower. Livaldi will have protections around it—I guarantee you it's stored somewhere that you need a special key or code to access."

"Livaldi doesn't seem the type to leave keys lying around," Rogan said.

"I agree with your assertion," Deriahm said. "It is likely a code, or perhaps something that is attuned to Livaldi's own magical signature."

"So all we need to do is knock him out, kidnap him, and cart him around the tower looking for a door that will only open to his touch," Nihs said sourly.

To their surprise, Lugh laughed out loud. He then laughed even harder when he saw the dirty looks he was earning.

"You're all forgetting something!" he said. "We don't need to worry about any of that—we have the best locksmith in the world with us!"

"What are you talking about?" Nihs snapped.

Lugh pointed at Kyle. "Kyle's got a sword that can cut through anything! It doesn't matter what kind of security Livaldi has around the stone—we can just carve it out of the way!"

"I don't know if that's still true," Kyle said. "My sword's not as strong as it used to be ever since I got hit by that arrow."

But Nihs was nodding pensively. "No…Loath as I am to admit it, I think Lugh is right. Your sword doesn't have the raw power it used to, but the nature of its being hasn't changed. It can still lyse anything in this world, just perhaps not as quickly as it used to."

"It sounds like you're saying we throw caution to the winds and storm the place without a plan," Rogan rumbled.

Nihs sniffed. "I wouldn't go *that* far."

Lugh leaned forward and crossed his hands before him. "All right," he said, "what about Livaldi's men? He's sent the twins and Radisson after us before, but the twins are dead and Radisson's in jail."

"There are sure to be security guards in Sky Tower," Nihs said.

"And don't forget Saul," Meya added.

"That's the old man we saw when we got captured?" Kyle asked Lugh. Lugh nodded.

"Livaldi's personal magician. He's supposed to be a very powerful wizard. And I guess we need to worry about Livaldi himself, too, right? He's supposed to be quite the swordsman."

Rogan snorted. "It's one thing to play with swords, and another thing entirely to use them. I doubt that little pup has ever bloodied his blade."

"True, but he also has guns, and you don't need to be a warrior to use one of those," Lugh pointed out.

"We're getting ahead of ourselves," Nihs said. "I would prefer to get through this without carving our way up the tower."

Lugh shrugged. "Better to be ready for the worst."

They talked throughout the afternoon, tossing plans back and forth. Their task seemed about as simple as could be. Break into Sky Tower, hopefully on a night when both Livaldi and his magician were out of the city. Find the stone, get past whatever security Livaldi had in place to protect it, steal it and make their getaway. Easy. Only there were several steps missing from their plan, and for each of the steps they did know there were several things that could go wrong. Plan as they might, they could not find the answers to the questions that remained.

How would they know when both Livaldi and Saul were out of the tower? What if that opportunity never came? More pressing: what if they couldn't find a way past James' security to reach the stone, or worse, what if they couldn't find the stone in the first place?

They left the park to find food, then returned that evening to plan some more. But it was clear to all of them that they had reached a dead end. Kyle's spirits, which had soared upon leaving the shadow world, began to sink once more. The stone was infuriatingly close, which made their lack of a plan all the more frustrating.

It was Lugh who finally gave voice to what everyone was thinking.

"We can talk all we want," he said, "but it's not going to do us any good. We need more information. I don't know where we're going to get it, but until we do, we might as well stop wasting our breath."

"So what do you propose we do?" Nihs said, his voice more than a little testy.

"Right at this moment?" Lugh glanced upwards at the sky, which was a deep, vibrant purple. "Nothing. I don't know about you, but my wrist is killing me and my back feels like I just carried a pack halfway across Westia. Let's sleep on it and see what comes to us tomorrow. Maybe we try talking to someone who's been inside Sky Tower, or someone who's met Livaldi. Maybe we check the tower out ourselves. But we're not doing any of that tonight. Right?"

Nihs complained, and Kyle wanted to protest, but he knew that Lugh was right. He *was* tired—exhausted, in fact—and his brain had all but checked out for the day.

They packed up and headed back to the hotel, the question of how they were going to pull off their heist still nagging at each of them. Kyle was frustrated; it felt like answers to their questions were hanging just out of reach, and whatever Lugh said, he wasn't confident that a night's rest was going to bring them any closer.

But in the end, it didn't matter. The Archsage had given them a task, and they were going to complete it. Complete it, or die trying.

That night, Deriahm sat alone in a private corner of the hotel's lobby. He pulled his lodestone from his satchel—a pale, oblong disc of stone fitted with a metal antenna—and set it down on the table in front of him. Detaching the tiny communication crystal from the collarbone of his armor, he set it down on top. The crystal glowed, and the metal antenna of the lodestone began to vibrate ever so slightly. Deriahm, statuesque, watched and waited, gloved hands clasped before him.

A voice, faint, sounded from the crystal.

"*Irushai* Deriahm?" it asked.

"Yes, it is I," Deriahm responded.

"What is your report?"

Deriahm shifted in his seat, metal slats of his armor clinking together. "We have arrived once more in Centralia," he said. "Coromb, to be precise."

"Did you meet the Archsage Vohrusien?"

"Yes. I apologize that I did not contact you sooner; the lodestone was unresponsive inside Vohrusien's tower."

"It is of no moment. What have you learned?"

It was much, but it was still only the work of a few minutes to relay their fantastical experience to the Buor on the other end of the crystal. His story caused some consternation; as soon as his tale was done, he was asked to reiterate several aspects of it, then elaborate on pieces he had missed. The questioning went on for some time, at the end of which his contact said, "Understood. Please standby."

Deriahm did, sitting in perfect silence like a robot waiting for further instructions. Several minutes later, he received them.

"We have established contact with one who will help you achieve your objective. We are able to put him in your way tomorrow afternoon. Do not move from your position until then."

Deriahm was shocked. "One who will help us storm Livaldi's tower?"

"Indeed. Listen now closely. Managing the expectations of your companions is of the utmost importance."

"Of course."

Deriahm listened with growing amazement as the voice relayed his instructions. Once it was done, he nodded out of habit, though there was no one there to see him.

"Very well," he said. "I will proceed as instructed, and inform you when the key moment comes."

"Good. I wish you luck, *irushai*, on behalf of all of Buoria. You are doing your country and the world a great service."

"Thank you, sir."

The crystal's glow faded. Deriahm plucked it from the lodestone and fitted it back into his collar, then closed the lodestone into its box and pushed it into the pouch on his hip. He sat for a moment, his visor betraying nothing about the thoughts passing by behind it. He then rose from his seat and walked quietly back to his room.

They took a different route through the city the next day at Deriahm's suggestion. He argued that it was best they didn't make their movements too predictable in case there was someone following them, and so they turned into the city and walked the busy streets at its downtown core.

It was Deriahm who stopped them again when they passed by a grand stone building with a heavy ironwork sign out front. Or rather, he stopped dead in his own tracks and stood staring up at the sign; they had left him about five yards behind before Lugh thought to turn around on check on him.

"Hey, Deriahm," he said. "You coming?"

Deriahm didn't answer. Kyle, following the arrow of Deriahm's visor, looked up and saw the sign. It was picked out in plain black letters and read:

Baccalade's
Rouk and Apparati

"Ah…My apologies, good sirs and madam," Deriahm said, sounding flustered. "It occurs to me upon seeing this sign that I have not eaten since the king's *rouk* in the *adaragad*; and also that I do not have any stock, nor a pipe with which to smoke. Might we make a brief stop so I may resupply?"

"Of course," Lugh said. "Why didn't you say so before?"

Deriahm contrived to look embarrassed. "I'm afraid I have only just remembered. It is easy to forget one's hunger in the face of excitement."

Stepping into the *rouk* store was like stepping inside a cask within which an expensive spirit had once been aged. The interior was plain but scrupulously clean, with walls made of weathered stone and furnishings of polished wood. Most of the floor space was taken up by small wooden tables with ornate *rouk* pipes set in the center, though the far wall was covered in shelves of 'apparati' for sale. The wall to their right was dominated by a bar behind which rose a tremendously tall display of *rouk* cakes. They were all wrapped in different colors of canvas or paper and stamped with different seals. A smattering of Buors were inside the store; one couple sat near the window, sharing a pipe, while a few others were shopping at the counter or sitting in the back of the room. A stout Buorish man stood behind the counter, hands behind his back, and nodded to them respectfully when they came inside.

"Good afternoon, sirs and madam. How may I help you?"

Deriahm went to the counter to speak to the owner while the others fanned out to explore. Kyle found himself reading the labels and prices of the various cakes, wondering how they all differed. He was still curious to try *rouk*, no matter what Deriahm said about humans not being able to smoke it.

A Buor approached from Kyle's left, armor clanking softly. "Excuse me," he said in a low voice. "Are…are you Kyle Campbell?"

Kyle froze, instantly alert. He turned his head to the side to bring the Buor into view. He was tall and stiff-backed, but he did not seem like the other Buors Kyle had met. He realized it was because this man did not stand like a Buor; he moved slightly even when standing still, while most Buors could pass for statues when they were not moving. He didn't speak like a Buor, either—Kyle had never known one of their kind to stutter.

"Who are you?" he asked, also keeping his voice low. He flexed his palm, feeling the blue-white sparks dance beneath his skin. He was ready to drive his soul sword into this man's chest if he saw something he didn't like.

"I hope to be an ally. I have information for you about ma—James Livaldi."

Kyle looked into the dark visor. "You're not a Buor," he said.

"No. This is a magical glamour—a disguise."

A strange question occurred to Kyle. "Do the Buors know you're here?"

"Yes. They are the ones who sent me. Please, can we talk privately?"

"*Who are you?*" Kyle repeated in a low hiss.

It was a moment before the man replied; Kyle got the impression that he was struggling to get the words out.

"We have met," he said finally. "My name is Saul. I am master Livaldi's manservant."

They sat in a secluded corner of the *rouk* store, Deriahm smoking one of his recent purchases using the ornate silver pipe that sat at the center of the table. Saul was seated in the corner, with Lugh to one side and Rogan on his other. To an onlooker, they would have appeared as a group of people keeping their Buorish friends company as they ate; only those seated around their table knew that Lugh and Rogan were positioned so to cut off Saul's means of escape.

"How did you find us?" Lugh hissed at him. "And how'd you get your hands on a set of Buorish armor?"

"I didn't, on both counts," Saul said. His voice was trembling ever so slightly. "This is a magical glamour, a disguise of light. The Buors told me to come to you this way. Everyone inside the store now is an agent of the Buorish king."

Kyle looked around. The man behind the counter was watching them, but it seemed to be only because he had nowhere else to look. No one else was paying them any attention.

"Is that so?" Nihs said. "Deriahm, are you aware of this?"

Deriahm lowered his pipe. His manner was somewhat sheepish. "I am, sage Nihs of the Ken Folk. I was informed of Saul's cooperation with the police via my lodestone."

"And you led us here so we could meet him," Lugh said, leaning back and folding his arms. "Well, well. So what's the deal? Why are you working with the police?"

Saul's head was bowed, and his shoulders were hunched. He looked like a man consumed by doubt. It took him a long time to answer.

"I have served the young master for all his life," he said finally. "When he was in his cradle, I was his nursemaid; when he was a young boy, I was his guardian. Now, I am his obedient servant. I served his father, the late James Livaldi senior, before him, and his father, Johann Livaldi, before that. Everything I am, I owe to the Livaldi family. I would rather die than betray the young master."

"And yet here you are," said Nihs, with his usual lack of tact. "So obviously something has changed."

Saul's head dipped even further. "The young master is in a…troubling state of mind. I am worried for his well-being. That is why I've decided to turn to you for help. It's…not easy for me to do. But I know it to be for James' own good."

"A troubling state of mind, you say," Nihs said nonchalantly. "Let me guess. Some time ago, he went somewhere he oughtn't have, and took something he shouldn't have. And now, it's come to possess him, rather than the other way round. Does that sound about right?"

Saul gasped audibly. "How do you know that?"

"Never mind that," Nihs said. "What do *you* know?"

Saul sighed. "I will start from the beginning."

"It all began last Off-Cross—half a year ago now. Maida had just finished rolling out its latest line of products, and the young master was intent on launching a new project for his engineers to undertake.

"James, as you may know, is never content with making small improvements to his products. He demands the best of himself and of the machines that his company produces. I suppose that is why he began to research alternative materials and methods of powering the next generation of firearms.

"You see, our research had shown that the products we had most recently released were approaching the limits of what could be accomplished using traditional materials—tigoreh wiring and fuel cells. And so, his focus turned toward other potential sources of power."

Saul paused. "You might not believe the next part of my story," he said.

"You'd be surprised," Rogan said companionably. "We're very open-minded people." He was sitting next to Saul on the bench, and one of his arms was laying across the headrest behind them; he could have drawn Saul into a bear hug with one flex of his muscles.

Saul sighed once more, then went on. "On the continent of Westia, at the very center of the crater left by the world's end meteor, there lies the tower of an incredibly powerful sage. To this day, I don't know how the young master learned of this tower's existence; but learn he did, and it became his goal to reach the tower and discover the secrets of the Archsage's magical power."

"You succeeded," Nihs said. He didn't bother trying to make it sound like a guess. "But how did you reach the tower?"

Saul swallowed audibly and shivered. Kyle got the impression that it was costing him everything he had to reveal Livaldi's secrets to them.

"The *Aether*," he said finally. "An airship that can travel over the mountains of Westia. The young master designed it, and his engineers built it in secret, all with the aim of reaching the Archsage's tower."

"That's impossible!" Nihs snapped. "No ship could fly that high."

Saul regarded him solemnly. "The *Aether* can," he said simply. "Its frame is light, and its engine draws so little magic that it can fly several miles above the earth, if necessary. It is Livaldi's masterpiece. If only he could have put his focus into more creations like it." He trailed off, then continued: "Disbelieve me if you will, but the *Aether* is docked at one of Maida's secret hangars now, and I rode in it myself when we travelled to the Archsage's tower."

Nihs waved a hand as if to say the existence of the *Aether* was not important. "So you found the tower. Then what?"

"It's...hard to explain what happened inside the tower. My memories of the place are foggy...If it weren't for what we brought back, I would say that I imagined the entire ordeal. We met the Archsage...or some reflection of him. Either way, he rejected us. He wouldn't listen to anything the young master said, and demanded we leave not long after we arrived. James, however, wouldn't be deterred, and refused to leave the tower empty-handed. It was then he decided to steal one of the Archsage's possessions."

"And what did you steal?" Nihs asked, as if he didn't already know.

"An Ephicer...an orange Ephicer. It's the largest I've ever seen, five inches on the side, and its *power*...well, it's nothing short of incredible. To look at it makes one sick, and neither James nor I have ever touched it, for fear of what might happen."

"I see," Nihs said. "But Livaldi's obviously been using it somehow."

Saul nodded. "He found a method to acclimatize himself to the stone's power in a controlled way. He has been increasing his exposure to it slowly over the past months."

"How?" Nihs said. He sounded enraptured—there were few things that could hold Nihs' attention better than talk about magic.

Saul's answer was as bizarre as it was slow in coming. "He...built a coffee machine that houses the stone inside. When the machine is run, the coffee is poured over the stone's surface, infusing it with some of its power."

Lugh's mouth hung open. "He put the stone in a *coffee machine?*"

"Incredible," Nihs sounded impressed despite himself. "That's the last place anyone would look if they wanted to steal the stone from him. Where does he keep this machine?"

"In his office on the top floor of Sky Tower. In recent days, he almost never leaves his office, and the machine is hardly ever out of his sight."

"So he's drinking coffee touched by the stone, and it's been influencing his mind," Nihs said. "How so? What does the stone actually do?"

"At first, it seemed only to grant James clarity—a source of inspiration, you might say. He claimed that it brought the world into greater focus, allowed him to see what he normally could not. He used it as…a cheat of sorts, I suppose. If there was a problem of business or engineering that he could not solve, he would use the machine, and the answer would inevitably come to him."

"No wonder Maida's been doing so well recently," Lugh said.

Saul glared at him sharply. "The young master did not need the stone to get his company where it is. His mind is incredible—he is a visionary, a genius, in the purest sense of the word."

"How can you say that?" Meya snapped suddenly. Her red eyes were shining, and Kyle could feel the gentle pull of magic as her soul swelled with emotion. "After everything he's done?"

"The man who has been pursuing you is not Livaldi," Saul said, his voice and body trembling. "It is a mockery of the man he was, and will be again, once the stone is taken from him."

Meya stood, fingernails digging into the table in front of her.

"Meya," Lugh said, but she ignored him.

"The stone didn't order him to send killers after us," she said.

Saul met her gaze. "He never ordered any such thing. The twins Lian and Lacaster were meant to capture Kyle. They were never instructed to harm anyone."

"*My friend is dead!*" Meya screamed. "*You're going to look me in the eye and tell me that Phundasa's death wasn't James' fault?*"

Saul recoiled, and as he did, the Buor in front of them flickered. For a moment the shape of the armor thinned, and Kyle saw the image within the image; the glamour had grown semi-transparent, and Kyle could see Saul's silhouette trapped inside the armor. Then the illusion shattered completely, and Saul sat exposed before them.

He looked as Kyle remembered, though now Kyle had the opportunity to see him closer than before. He was an old man, at least seventy or eighty, and his cheeks were sunken and his narrow face heavily lined. His eyes were milky blue, and what was left of his hair was iron-gray and combed back from his face. His mouth was a thin line, and a brown liver spot was growing on one cheek.

There were tears running down his face.

Meya froze, her eyes locked with Saul's. He reached out with trembling, arthritic hands—one gloved in white and the other in black—to grasp both of hers.

"Sir!" one of the Buors at the front of the room snapped. "Restore your glamour!"

Saul made no indication that he had heard. He was staring into Meya's face.

"Yes," he said softly. "Yes, it was James' fault. At first I told myself otherwise… because I could not bear to think of the young master as a murderer. But whether it was the stone or just ill luck that brought the twins to us, it was Livaldi who gave them the black arrow, Livaldi who was so blinded by his desire to capture Kyle that he failed to see how dangerous they were. I tried to warn him against them, but he didn't listen—and now your friend's blood is on his hands. His, and mine. And so it will be until the day that both of us are dead. I am sorry. I am so sorry."

"*Sir!*" Now the Buor—the one who had looked to be on a date with his partner—had stood. "Restore your glamour at once!"

Saul, still looking at Meya, closed his eyes, and a moment later a shifting, spinning cloak of light and shadow engulfed him. It formed into a helmet and breastplate, pauldrons and greaves. Soon, the Buor was seated in front of them once again. Saul sat back, head hanging in shame. His voice was barely audible when next he spoke.

"Over the past months, I have watched a most brilliant and promising young man degenerate into a heartless, single-minded predator. The stone has taken him over completely. He has forsaken everything else in his pursuit of Kyle… his business, his reputation, even his own humanity. I ignored it for too long, and everything has gotten far out of hand. I know that nothing can undo what's already been done, but if we can return the stone to its rightful owner, we can at least put an end to this madness."

There was a moment's silence. Meya looked as though she might speak, but in the end no words came out. She sat back down, and didn't move when Lugh put a hand on her arm.

"We're missing a few pieces of this story," Nihs said at last. "Livaldi found the stone, and started to use it to make business decisions. Where does Kyle fit in all of this?"

Saul nodded, raised his head, and continued his story. "Some two months ago, the visions that the stone granted changed abruptly—or so the young master told me. Instead of getting a vague sense of inspiration about what was on his mind at the time, he began to receive consistent visions of a single man. It wasn't long before Kyle was all that the stone would show to him."

"But *why?*" Kyle said. "Why would it focus on me?"

"At first, the young master was as confused as you. He began to increase his exposure to the stone, and as he did, he saw more and more. It revealed much about you, and James deduced the rest. He figured out that you were not of this world, and reasoned that the stone was showing you to him for the same reason it showed him everything else—that you were a potential source of wealth, scientific advancement, or both."

Nihs made a soft 'ohh' sound. "Of course," he said. "What Livaldi could accomplish if he got his hands on a vagrant would be far beyond anything else in Loria—so the stone fixated on Kyle as soon as he arrived here."

"Yes. The young master became obsessed with Kyle—or rather, the stone did, and it passed its obsession to James. He began using it more and more, and the visions it provided became clearer and clearer. Before long, he knew exactly what Kyle looked like, and even had a fair idea of where he was in the world."

Saul looked at Kyle. "The first time he captured you—when you and Lugh were in Reno city—he had just dispatched a group of salesmen to the area around the city. The stone had told him that you were close, and sure enough, one of the salesmen soon reported back with the information that you were travelling with a group of adventurers."

Lugh gasped in surprise. "The salesman in Donno!" he said. "Livaldi sent him out there just to look for Kyle?"

"Yes. As I said, the young master was obsessed. He didn't think twice about using the company's resources to search for him. In any case, Livaldi hired Radisson to help hunt you down, and we later captured you in Reno with the help of his men. You know the result of this encounter."

"We met you," was all Kyle said.

Saul nodded. "And the young master as well."

"What?" Kyle said, confused. "But he was out of the city that day."

"No…His double was. We hired an actor to play the part of James that day. I used a pair of glamours similar to the one I'm using now, to turn James into the actor and the actor into James. He left the city to make a presentation on James' behalf, and James remained in Sky Tower to question you."

Kyle's mouth hung open. "The man in the gray suit," he said. "That was Livaldi."

Lugh smacked his forehead. "I can't believe I didn't see it!" he said. "He was even using Livaldi's sword—that golden rapier."

Saul nodded in acknowledgement. "A foolish oversight, but James was convinced that it would make no difference. We never thought you could escape. Then again, at the time we didn't know of Kyle's soul sword.

"The young master was furious after you escaped—it was then that he chose to send the twins after you. They first attacked while you were flying over the eastern ocean, in the form of an eyrioda swarm."

"That was *them?*" Nihs said. Saul nodded.

"Lian was an incredibly powerful sage. He could control the weather, and all manner of sky-attuned beasts. His brother was a danger, but Lian was a terror. I could hardly believe it when you defeated him.

"In any case, when their first attack failed, James gave Lacaster the black arrow and sent them after you again." He bowed his head once more. "That, of course…" he couldn't bring himself to finish.

A silence descended, until Nihs said, softly, "The black arrow. What *was* it? Did Livaldi make it?"

Saul nodded. "I was not privy to the details of its making, but I suspect that the orange stone told James how it could be done. As for what it is…" he looked at Kyle in sudden realization. "Does it bind you still?"

"Partially," Kyle said. "We found a way to weaken it."

Saul sighed in relief. "I am glad. I was worried that it would have unforeseen effects. As for what it was," and now he spoke to Nihs, "it was a bolt that carried an enchantment the young master refers to as a black soul container. It's a magical seal that can bind any soul, no matter how powerful."

"Can its effect be nullified?" Nihs asked. Saul shook his head.

"It's possible that the young master knows a way. But I do not."

Kyle nodded slowly. It was as much as he'd expected.

"Something changed not long after you defeated the twins in Eastia," Saul went on. "The young master stopped receiving visions of you. He increased his dosage of the stone more and more, but he could no longer see where you were."

"That was us," Kyle said simply.

Saul nodded. "I thought you must have found a way to defend against the stone. In any case, the young master was furious, and ordered me to send out more of the company's agents to find you. We did find you one more time, in Mjolsport, and James sent Radisson himself to capture you. Once again, he failed, and now…" he paused, then said, "It would not be enough to call the young master 'desperate'. He is livid, obsessed, insane with desire. I am afraid of him now, and I'm afraid of what will happen to him if he keeps using the stone."

Lugh kicked back onto two legs of his stool and said, "So you went to the police and told them everything, hoping they'd help you."

Saul, to their surprise, now looked at Deriahm. "My original plan was to speak to Kyle's party without the police's knowledge. I thought that we all might benefit from not involving the Buors in these affairs. I see now that this was a pointless endeavor—we are all your countrymen's pawns in this, are we not, *irushai?*"

"I would not say that," Deriahm said quickly. "But it is true that we know of mister Campbell's existence, and are heavily invested in leading these events to a positive outcome."

"Then let's talk outcomes," Rogan cut in gruffly. He seemed, as usual, to be annoyed by the fact that details had gotten in the way of the big picture. "Livaldi's got the rock. All of us want to see it taken from him and given back to the Archsage. How do we do that?" He looked at Saul. "You said the stone's in his office. Why don't you just steal it and give it to us?"

"It's not so simple. The stone hardly ever leaves James' sight. He spends almost every hour of every day in his office—lately it has been hard to persuade him to leave the tower for any reason. On the odd occasion that he does, he locks the top floor of the tower so no one can enter until he gets back. Not even I can get into his office then."

"How does he do it?" Nihs asked. "Could we break in?"

"The elevators are locked by Livaldi's magical signature, and won't run to the top floor for anyone but him. There is an emergency passage out of the office, but opening it sounds every alarm in the building. Knowing how paranoid the young master has become, I wouldn't be surprised if there were other defenses as well—most likely alarms that sound if you enter the office."

"Guards?" Rogan asked.

"Maida security, armed with the latest of the company's weaponry. Normally they would answer to me, but they would alert James if they caught me in his office while he was away."

They questioned Saul for a while longer, forming a mental picture of Sky Tower and the defenses that Livaldi had in place to protect the stone. Soon, fronted by Nihs, the beginnings of a plan emerged. Finally Nihs pressed his thumbs into his eyes and asked one last question.

"When is the next time that Livaldi will be out of the city?"

"He has no appointments now that will take him out of Reno," Saul said, "but I can arrange one. He has some business with a wealthy client in Oasis. I will suggest that they meet in person to discuss it."

Nihs nodded. "Do. And contact us again once you know the date. We'll have to be ready when the time comes."

The next day, they received a letter to their hotel from a diffident Buorish messenger. The letter was plain and unmarked, containing a total of twelve words and two sentences.

Second sun tomorrow, three hours after sunrise. Meet me at the entrance.

"Well," Nihs said, crumpling up the paper and incinerating it in his hand, "that's that. I suggest we take the day to rest."

They did just that, filling up the hours with pointless excursions and meaningless chatter. Try as he might, Kyle couldn't enjoy anything they did—he was too tense and nervous to focus on anything. Tomorrow, everything would be decided, for better or worse.

They retired early that night, shuffling into their rooms and promising each other that they would sleep.

Rogan slept, cradled to sleep by a procession of thoughts, calm and slow. He thought of the plains and of his wife, Graysa, and of the interesting turn his life had taken since he had met Lugh and Nihs. The coming day's events didn't trouble him overmuch. He was, as the Minotaur would put it, a man with his hooves planted firmly in the earth. He knew who he was and what he needed to do, and was confident that the man was great enough for the deed.

Nihs slept, light and fitful like a bird, then woke, and lay in bed shivering despite the heat. He thought of his sisters, his father, of the Archmage and of Livaldi. He turned his plan over in his mind, prodding at it, trying to see if there was something he had missed. He was all too aware that their success, and possibly their lives, depended on it being as foolproof as possible. A small, secret part of him was convinced that he would lead them all to their doom, and it was this part of him that kept him awake for the rest of the night, no matter how tightly shut he squeezed his eyes.

Deriahm slept, though not as well as one might have thought upon seeing his still form. He lay on his back like a mummified king, arms crossed above his chest. His thoughts were of his home in Buoria, of his father, his tutors—of King Azanhein and his agent, Sardassan, whose voice had guided Deriahm through the past month. He felt an enormous pressure resting on his shoulders; a multitude of faceless bodies whom he would never meet, but who nevertheless depended on him to see Kyle safely home. As a Buor, he had no Saints to pray to, but he invoked the name of the first Buorish king, Ozdohtr, as he wished for strength of body and clarity of mind to grace him during tomorrow's events.

Meya slept, but only after a hard-won battle that lasted for most of the night. Two faces dominated her thoughts: that of Phundasa, and that of the man responsible for his death. It felt as though those two faces had been haunting her thoughts for as long as she could remember; only Lugh's presence could keep them at bay. But Lugh was not here, so she hugged herself across the stomach and hissed between her teeth *go away, go away, go away,* until her mind became so tired that everything melted into blackness and sleep overtook her.

Lugh slept as he always did, after hours of lying awake on his back with his arms crossed behind his head. He thought of his brother, his friends, of Meya and of Kyle; he'd started to miss this last one already, since he knew that Kyle would be leaving them in a little over a day's time. His mind didn't allow him to doubt that for a second, and so it was that his breathing slowed and his good eye drooped shut as it always did.

Kyle didn't sleep a single minute that night.

It was a classic Reno summer afternoon; the sun was blindingly bright, its light glinting off of the forest of multicolored metal and glass that was the city's downtown core. The air was hot, but the heat radiating down from the sky and up from the paved streets was cut by a cooling wind that blew in from Centralia Bay.

Reno's youth, many of them still basking in the afterglow of the city's On-Cross celebration, took to the streets in droves, their eclectic choices in fashion filling the city with undulating waves of clashing colors; bright primaries, rich darks, and the occasional stark black or white all vied for the eye's attention.

Amidst the colorful chaos that was Reno's downtown, two groups of men and women walked all but unnoticed toward the sprawling glass complex that sat at the base of Sky Tower. Construction was now complete; the outer shell of the tower was finished, and now it was the inside of the tower and the complex below that were to be wired, ornamented, and finally occupied. Though Maida would be taking the tower for itself, the complex was to be rented out to several hundred businesses, creating a shopping center that would rival Reno's current sprawling market district. For the time being, the only people who ever set foot inside the complex were Maida staff on their way to Sky Tower proper, construction and renovation crews, and the occasional security guard hired to keep Reno's more curious residents from wandering where they didn't belong.

The two groups of people who now entered the tower drew little attention from the guards. They were dressed in sharp business attire of black, grey and navy blue, and wore badges of purple and gold on their chests. There were seven of them in all, six men and one woman, all of them human but for a single Kol who sat at the shoulder of the man at the front of the group. Their ages ranged from thirty to forty, and most were wearing dark-tinted glasses to shield from the summer sun.

Kyle felt cool relief wash over him as they passed between the first set of guards, who were keeping a lazy watch at one of the complex's many entrances. The relief was mostly physical—the air in the complex was cool and air-conditioned, a welcome change from Reno's stifling heat. If there was a reason his mind didn't share in the relief his body was feeling, it was because he knew that they had passed only the first and easiest obstacle they were to overcome.

Their group of seven was divided into halves: in front, Saul, Nihs, Lugh and Rogan; in the rear, Kyle, Meya, and Deriahm. Saul's glamours had transformed Rogan, Lugh, and Deriahm into humans, and Kyle and Meya into completely different people. Their party of adventurers was now a group of Maida businessmen, at least to the eye—Saul's illusions were of light but not of sound or touch, so he'd instructed them to keep quiet and let him talk to anyone who accosted them.

The complex was huge, airy, sleek and modern. Empty glass storefronts shone down on them from all directions. Highlights of gold metal accented columns and floors of blinding white marble. It was at once sterile and sumptuous, a testament to Livaldi's obsession with cleanliness and simplicity.

Their shoes clicked against the marble floor as they made their way deeper into the building. They passed by a handful of workers who were starting to add the human touches that would defeat the vast emptiness of this place. The workers paid them no mind and they walked past in silence.

At the far end of the complex was the entrance to Sky Tower itself. The second pair of guards let them pass with nothing but a cursory nod from Saul.

Kyle, of course, had been in Sky Tower before—he had faced Saul and the gray-suited man he now knew to be Livaldi in this very lobby. But he'd had no time to take in the details then, nor did he now. Saul had warned them all to look purposeful so they didn't get stopped, so Kyle kept his head pointed forwards, allowing his eyes to flit around behind his darkened glasses. The glamour that Saul had cast over him looked solid enough, but it didn't feel like anything—Kyle felt nervous and exposed.

Sky Tower had more than two dozen elevators; row upon row stood gleaming and silent at the far end of the lobby. The vast empty space reminded Kyle more than a little of Key Tower back in shadow Cleveland, as did the way in which one of the elevators instantly slid open as soon as Saul pushed the button.

They stepped inside, and the doors slid shut. The array of buttons on the elevator's panel was massive, though some of the buttons—most near the top—were unlit. Saul reached into his pocket and pulled out a small orange Ephicer on a length of chain; keeping the chain woven through his fingers, he pressed the Ephicer to a small panel on the elevator's console. A soft tone sounded from somewhere inside the machinery, and most of the missing floors lit up. The very top floor was conspicuously not among them. Saul tapped the button with his finger.

"This is good," he said. "I can access this floor when the young master is in the tower. This tells us that he is gone for certain."

With that, he pressed the button for the penultimate floor, and the elevator accelerated upwards at a breakneck pace. Once they passed the first thirty floors, they burst free of the lower complex, and brilliant daylight streamed in. The elevator was now climbing the outer edge of the building, and the view was fantastic, but nauseating.

The elevator slowed, and the doors glided open. The floor onto which they emerged was plush and refined. There was a reception lobby directly ahead of them, and beyond that, rooms which branched off to the left and right. Kyle half expected to see a sign reading "Be Right Back!!" in cheery red letters on the desk.

"Eventually this floor will house a restaurant, a private reception hall, and some office space," Saul said quietly.

"Lovely," Lugh replied.

Saul said nothing, but his lips tightened, and he stepped forward as if to acknowledge that this was no time to admire Sky Tower's offerings. They followed him as he led them down the dark hallways toward the back of the floor.

Finally they reached a dark wooden door with a golden handle. Saul put his glove on it and turned, then shook his head and stepped back.

"Locked," he said.

They had prepared for this. Deriahm stepped forward, looking utterly bizarre wearing a youthful human face with blond hair. He put his hand on the lock, and there was a gentle whisper of magic. Before long the lock had sprung, and Deriahm swung the door open.

The room beyond was clearly intended to be one of the posh reception halls that Saul had mentioned, but at the moment the only testament to this was the rich red carpet and the gold filigree that crowned the walls; the room was otherwise dark and empty. Saul stepped to the center and craned his neck upwards.

"We should be directly beneath the young master's office now," he said. He turned to the others and waved a hand; their glamours melted away, as did Saul's own. His exposed face was haggard and stressed. "Kyle, now is the time for you to use your sword."

"You're absolutely sure that this won't set off the alarms?" Nihs said.

Saul shook his head. "I'm sure of nothing," he said.

Rogan shrugged, cricking his neck. "We're wasting time. We know what to do if this sets something off." And they did; between them, Nihs and Saul had covered what felt like every possible contingency.

Rogan stepped to where Saul hand been standing and crouched down, exposing his furry back. Kyle clambered on top, stood, and drew his soul sword. Rogan straightened his knees, bringing Kyle closer to the ceiling overhead. Once it was within reach, Kyle drove his sword upwards into it.

The ceiling split open with a loud *crack*, and stone and plaster rained down; Kyle ducked instinctively, shielding his face. Rogan grunted as a fist-sized chunk of ceiling struck his lower back and rolled off.

"Here," said Saul. "Let me help you."

He raised his white-gloved hand and a shield of light appeared above Kyle's head. When Kyle next struck, his sword passed through, but the bits of ceiling that came raining down rolled off it and fell to the side.

Working carefully, Kyle carved a hole three feet wide in the ceiling, exposing tigoreh wiring, beams of steel and concrete, and giant foam squares of insulation. Rogan stood taller and taller, allowing Kyle to reach further and further upwards. Soon his sword was biting through a final layer of concrete and plush carpet, and light was breaking through the hole. Kyle, tense, was expecting something to happen with every moment, but everything was still and silent.

He completed the hole, widening it another half a foot. He then jumped off of Rogan's back, taking care to avoid the circle of debris that surrounded them. Lugh took his place, looking up with his hands on his hips.

"So far so good," he said. "Nihs? Saul? Meya?"

Kyle and the other magically-disinclined members of their group stood back while Meya, Saul, Nihs and Deriahm gathered about the hole, trying to determine if there were any magical wards in place in Livaldi's office. This was the part of the plan about which Nihs was most concerned; while they had between them a talented sage, bishop and wizard, they did not have a mystic, and this was the school of magic that any traps were most likely to fall under. Deriahm's skill wouldn't be enough to detect the more subtle traps that might be protecting the orange stone, but they had little choice.

Kyle, Lugh and Rogan waited several minutes for the others to finish their work. Kyle wrung his hands together and Rogan picked bits of plaster out of his fur. Finally Nihs shook his head and turned to them.

"Nothing—at least, nothing we can detect. Perhaps James isn't as paranoid as Saul thought. Or perhaps we're underestimating him."

"One way to find out," Lugh said. Meya nodded.

"We shouldn't spend any more time here than we absolutely have to. We'll just have to risk it."

"All right," Lugh said. "Who first?"

Saul volunteered. Rogan bent over once more, and Saul climbed on top. They made for a rather ridiculous picture, but Kyle found little humor in it at the moment. He watched as Rogan straightened up, tall enough for Saul's head and shoulders to peek up into Livaldi's office. Saul grabbed at the carpeted floor and lifted a leg; Rogan made a platform with his palm and boosted him up by the foot. Soon Saul's other leg disappeared into the hole, then his face reappeared as he leaned over it.

"I will look around for a moment," he said. "Stay there."

They heard his first two footfalls, and none after that—the building was brand new and there was a not a single creak of the floor to betray his presence.

They waited for a half minute that felt like a half hour. Kyle watched the hole he had carved in the ceiling, waiting for Saul's face to reappear, not understanding what could be taking him so long. He gripped the sword at his waist, growing more tense with every second.

Finally Saul's face did pop back out over the lip of the hole, but instead of triumph, it displayed confusion and naked fear. He swung his legs out over the hole and Rogan raised his arms to help him down. Saul landed heavily, white dust smeared all over his suit.

"What's going on?" Nihs hissed. "Where's the stone?"

Saul was gasping, clutching at his chest. "It's gone!" he wheezed.

"*What?*"

"The stone! It's gone! The coffee machine is empty, and I couldn't find it anywhere else in the office! James has moved it!"

Nihs lapsed into his native tongue and unleashed a stream of curses. "Livaldi must know we're after it! That's the only reason he would have moved it! We need to—"

His voice was drowned out by a shriek of magic so sharp and so loud that it struck the ears like a *gordja*'s cry. It was accompanied by a great thunderclap, the awesome ripping sound of lightning incinerating the air around it. There was a flash of orange light, and something struck Kyle with so much speed and power that he went from being alive to being dead without feeling the slightest twinge of pain.

Many things happened at once. Kyle's body was thrown from the ground and went rocketing across the room, smashing into the opposite wall with such force that it formed a crater, a cloud of plaster blooming into the air around it. Kyle's companions, owing to a lifetime of instinct, had their weapons drawn and had formed a defensive circle inside of two seconds; all but Meya, who at once ran for Kyle's corpse. But before she could reach it, all of them were stopped in their tracks by an awful, groaning, booming noise that suddenly erupted from the ground beneath their feet. All at once a thick black fog boiled up from the floor, a living, writhing fog gilt with edges of silvery white.

Meya watched as the fog latched onto her ankles and climbed up her legs. She didn't have time to take even a single step; as soon as the fog connected, it brought with it a chill numbness so profound that Meya felt as if her legs had been detached from her body. They gave way instantly, and her kneecaps bounced against the carpeted floor. Her hands shot forward to catch her fall, and she lost control of them the second they plunged into the fog. She locked her shoulders and somehow managed to keep to all fours, head dangling dangerously close to the fog's surface.

She could hear the others crying out in pain and shock. She wanted to call out to them, but her chest had constricted in fear, and any air she managed to get into her lungs was immediately forced back out.

What...what is this? How is this happening?

She heard the *click* of hard leather shoes crossing the reception room floor, and with a tremendous effort managed to loosen her neck enough to raise her head. She saw him step out of the shadows, as calmly as if strolling down a park path. His purple suit was vibrant and exquisite, and he held a rifle of resplendent gold. Nestled at the base of the rifle's barrel was a massive Ephicer that glowed a merry orange.

It was their enemy, James Livaldi. And somehow, *somehow*, he'd gotten behind them.

James popped the spent fuel cell from the Wyvern's breach and slotted in a new one. The weapon made a low whine that grew slowly in pitch as it cycled up to full strength. He stepped forward from his hiding place, hoisting the gun up and resting it indifferently against his shoulder. The orange stone was inches from his ear—close enough that its whispering drowned out virtually all thought. He heard it all the time, now, whether he was drinking coffee or not. But when it was close by, the whispering grew in intensity to the point that James couldn't tell which were the stone's thoughts and which were his own.

He saw Kyle's party through a wavering orange filter, as if looking through a pane of colored glass. He saw the shock and horror on their faces and felt a vicious energy coursing through his body. It was thrilling and triumphant. The fools had actually done it! They'd delivered Kyle right into his hands!

"Well, well," he said, watching them struggle against the soul-containing fog. "What a sublime irony this is. I went to such lengths to chase Kyle to the ends of the earth, and after all that, here we find ourselves right back where we started."

"You bastard!" shouted the Selk. What was his name again? Something common—*Leffe? Lugh?* Yes, Lugh. He was fighting valiantly against the fog, trying to get his head and shoulders free of it. He reared up, but his arm betrayed him, and he went falling again to all fours. The fog sucked greedily at his exposed cheek.

James picked a bit of lint off his sleeve. "There's hardly any call for that. I've made it clear from the first that all I've ever wanted is Kyle. I would have been happy to take him peacefully, but you all expended so much effort in ensuring that wouldn't happen. The twins, Radisson—frankly, it's been an absolute mess. But I'm certain the results will be worth it."

Meya had been desperately crawling over to where Kyle lay. Now she reached his supine form, and her trained eyes picked out the details of his injuries. At least one arm and the opposite leg had been broken, and his entire chest where the slug had impacted was a mass of burnt flesh and clothing. The smell was so strong that it cut through even the numbness of the fog and struck deep into Meya's forehead.

She felt tears welling in her eyes as she reached out to peel back an eyelid. What she saw confirmed her worst fears. Kyle's eyes, normally so bright and blue, were now gray, drained completely of color. His soul was extinguished.

He was dead.

James was not often surprised, but it shook him to the core when the bishop rose to her feet in the middle of the fog and faced him down from across the room. She, like James himself, was a monochrome, through red instead of purple. She was clearly immensely strong; to stand against the fog would take incredible willpower, and James could see her eyes shining red even from where he stood. She was looking at him with pure hatred on her face. Suddenly she screamed like a tortured spirit and sprinted forward, one hand raised and alight with magic.

Livaldi had been surprised by her resistance, but he never remained surprised for long. He trained the Wyvern on her and had just begun to press the pad of his finger against the trigger when the fog did its work. The light died from her eyes and from her hand, and she collapsed to her knees again, the strength of her soul undermined by the suffocating containment field.

"*Meya!*" Lugh shouted.

For a moment Meya didn't answer; her chest was heaving with the effort of keeping herself conscious. Then she looked up at James.

"He's dead," she said. "You killed him!"

"*What?*" Lugh bellowed. The Minotaur—James had never bothered to learn his name—roared in animal anger and tried to rise to his feet as Meya had done, and the Buor let out an almost childish cry of despair.

But James was laughing. These adventurers were not just foolish; they were nothing short of clueless. Were these really the warriors that had beaten Radisson and the twins?

"Don't be ridiculous," he said. "Do you really think I would go to all this effort of capturing him only to kill him? Of course he's not dead!"

Their expressions became awed, confused. James grinned openly at their distress. The moment of his victory had finally come—and the satisfaction was far greater than he ever could have imagined.

"Kyle is immortal in our world," he explained, in the tones of one talking to a small child. "Didn't you know even *that?* How did you think he survived everything that's happened to him so far?

"Kyle's soul is more powerful than the sum of all other energy in this universe. To undo it would take at least that much power. His body can be traumatized to the point that it could be considered dead…but his soul will preserve it, and eventually repair it to the point that Kyle will revive. Remarkable, really. Just one of the many things about your friend that I greatly look forward to studying in the years to come."

He smiled down at them, while the black smoke spread further to the edges of the room. Though it curled around his feet as it had the others', he didn't seem to even notice its touch. "Speaking of which—time is wasting. Kyle and I have a date to keep. Don't worry, the fog won't kill you; it will merely hold you here until the trap switches off. Goodbye!"

And he stepped around the party, walking through the fog as if it were nothing. He stopped when he reached Saul, who had collapsed and was clutching at his heart. Saul looked up, and James looked into his eyes. They were haunted and ashamed. James smirked, and Saul looked away, his lower lip quivering.

"My own manservant, conspiring to steal from me with a group of adventurers." Livaldi shook his head. "I'm so very disappointed in you, Saul. I didn't think it possible for you to sink to this level."

"Young master—" Saul began. His voice was wheezing and broken.

"Shut up." And Livaldi stepped past not a foot away from him, his eyes fixated on Kyle.

He reached the corpse and slung the Wyvern to his back before stooping down to lift it. He had considered bringing some help along with him for this— but no. If Saul had had the capacity to betray him, then whom in the world could he trust? The answer, as it had always been, was no-one—no one but himself.

Kyle was quite light, and Livaldi hoisted him up with little effort. He turned on the heel of his polished leather shoe and left the adventurers to their suffering. They shouted after him, they tried to reach out to him, they promised they would find him—but of course hurling abuse had ever been the last resort of the losing party.

After so much time and so much trouble, Kyle was finally his. He cradled the vagrant's body as he stepped into the elevator, ready to take Kyle where no one would ever find him.

The elevator doors closed, and Livaldi reached forward, pressing the button for floor thirty-one. There was an exit on this floor to the roof of the market complex, on which could be found a small airship hangar. Livaldi's ride was already waiting for him there. It was not the *Aether*, the miraculous ship that had taken him directly to Vohrusien's tower; that ship was too precious to leave out in the open where someone might find it. Of course, as soon as Livaldi began to unravel the secrets of Kyle and his world, he would be able to create ships that would put the *Aether* to shame.

Excitement gripped James' heart, and it fluttered against his ribcage. *All in due time.*

The doors opened, and Livaldi stepped out, then turned a left on his way to the open-air hangar. He already knew the entire tower's layout by heart—after all, he had helped design it.

A large glass door led to the outside; arms full, James pressed it open with his hip and stepped into the blinding sun. It was a beautiful day…yes, an absolutely marvelous day.

The hangar consisted of a large circular landing pad, and beyond that, a covered area where ships could be permanently docked. His own ship—a nondescript five-passenger colored the default tigoreh gold—was crouched in the corner of the parking area. It was, for the time being, the only one here.

Livaldi carefully laid Kyle down in the back and then climbed into the front of the ship himself. This ship was a fraction of the size of the *Ayger* and did not have a standing wheel; instead, James strapped himself into the driver's seat, slotted the key into place, and took hold of a steering yoke on the control panel in front of him. The ship hummed into life, and its wings unfolded. James brought it into a low hover and emerged from the covered portion of the airdock; then he opened the magic intake, pulled back on the wheel, and took off into the sky. He grinned viciously as he accelerated past the first layer of cloud cover and broke into the vast blue above.

He was not afraid of Kyle's companions, nor of Saul, nor of the Buors, whom he knew must be on his trail by now. Once he was away from Reno city, not even they would be able to find him. By the time that they did, it would be far too late.

Lugh had been in pain many times in his life. The way of the adventurer was one fraught with any number of dangers, and even the best of them picked up nicks and scratches from time to time. Not a month and a half ago, he had picked up his biggest 'nick' yet—a piece of the *Ayger's* debris had struck him in the head, taking out his left eye and partially crumpling his skull for good measure.

But the black fog that now held him crippled against the ground was something he had never experienced before. It didn't exactly *hurt*, in the same way that it didn't exactly hurt when you sat on your leg until it fell asleep. No, the effect it had was something far subtler, far more terrifying. If Nihs had been in any condition to talk, he might have been able to put it into the following words: the fog was like a cold black wall that was separating their souls from their bodies.

As soon as a limb was consumed by the fog, you lost the ability to feel it. If your head dipped in—as Lugh's had done—your thoughts became scattered and distant.

Now, Lugh was fighting to remember where he was, and what he was trying to do. He realized, after some time, that it was the silver-lined fog that was keeping him from thinking clearly.

If I could lean back on my knees, I could get my head out of the fog. That's good. That's a start.

The only problem was, he couldn't feel his arms. They seemed to end at the shoulders. Something was obviously propping him up, but he had no more control over his own arms than he did over someone else's.

He was dimly aware of the others around him. They were struggling as well, crawling through the fog, trying to speak to one another. Though they couldn't have been more than a few feet away from Lugh, they felt like they were on the far side of a vast black plain.

Come on, think! Remember what you were trying to do!

Slowly, laboriously, Lugh managed to push his head out of the fog and rock back to his knees. Understanding flooded back into his head as it broke free of the miasma. *Kyle!* Livaldi had taken Kyle!

He looked around. The fog was reaching into every corner of the reception room. It had stopped boiling up from the floor, but it didn't seem to be thinning at all, either. It was as Livaldi had said: the fog wasn't hurting them, but nor would it allow them to escape.

His eyes turned to the hole that Kyle had carved into the ceiling. A plan formed in his mind.

"We have to get above the fog," he croaked, hoping that the others could hear and understand him. "We need to go through the ceiling."

He heard a few groans from his companions, but no response. He tried again.

"We need...we need to get to the hole in the ceiling. Everyone come together!"

He started to crawl, dragging himself along the floor like a dying man across a stretch of barren desert. Every second he had to remind himself of what he was doing, and of the fact that the arms at the end of his shoulders belonged to him.

"Come on!" he shouted to the floor, half to himself and half to the others.

Finally he bumped into something. It was Rogan, who had been doggedly crawling in the other direction to meet him. Lugh looked up; the hole in the floor was directly above them.

Slowly, he climbed onto Rogan's back. His mind and body became clearer with every inch he rose above the fog. By the time he was sprawled across Rogan's broad back, he was panting like a drowning man enjoying his first gulps of air.

Meya was the next to arrive. Her face was pale and there were dark patches under her eyes; she looked like Nihs sometimes did when he used too much magic at once. Lugh grabbed her hands and pulled her up. But they were still much too far below the hole to be able to climb up.

Nihs. We need Nihs.

Lugh looked around wildly, but saw no sign of the tiny Kol. With a jolt he realized that even standing up, Nihs would be almost completely under the fog— and so almost certainly had fallen into unconsciousness.

"Nihs!" he shouted. "Where are you?"

Movement to his right. He looked and saw, to his immense joy, Saul shuffling toward him, carrying Nihs in his arms. Nihs was pale and his eyes were unfocused; his fingers and ears were twitching spasmodically.

Saul reached Rogan and presented Nihs to Lugh like an offering. Lugh took him, and he and Meya hoisted him above the fog. Within seconds Nihs' eyes had regained their spark.

"What...what manner of trap is this?" he said.

Saul was leaning against Rogan's flank, wheezing heavily. The blemishes on his face stood out against his pale skin. "This is...black soul containment," he said. "The same magic that was...in the bolt that struck Kyle. It puts your soul into conflict with itself, the...the more power you feed into it, the more tightly it binds you."

"I can't...believe...this is what Kyle was going through," Meya said.

Lugh nodded grimly. The feeling of having his soul twisted in on itself was unlike anything he had ever felt. He wouldn't forget it for the rest of his life.

With difficulty, he pointed straight up. "One of us...needs to get up there. They can help the rest."

Nihs nodded. "Boost me."

Lugh stretched up, and Meya held on to him to hold him steady. Nihs climbed up her back, then jumped to Lugh, moving with difficulty at first, then with growing confidence. He reached the tip of Lugh's hands; there was still a three-foot gap to cross.

"Don't...don't try to leap," Saul warned. "It will turn against you. Use your body only."

Nihs nodded, crouched low, and then flung himself upward, exerting all of the energy that his small body would allow. His claws scraped against the jagged edge of the hole; he curled his body and dug his feet into the plaster, then reached forward with his hands and found purchase. Soon he was in Livaldi's office; they heard him collapse against the floor, sighing with relief as his strength flowed back to him.

"Help...help us up!" Lugh called after him. "Throw us something!"

"I will!"

They heard him scuffling about upstairs. After what felt like an eternity, a thick fabric curtain drifted down through the hole. Saul recognized it as part of the curtain that had hung behind Livaldi's desk.

Using the curtain, Lugh pulled himself up. The first two feet were the hardest; but after that, his strength started to return to him, and he climbed the rest of the way easily. Nihs had knotted several lengths of curtain together, and affixed them to the heavy dresser that stood in the corner of Livaldi's office. Though neither of them knew it, it was the same dresser in which James had kept the black bolt that Lacaster had used to seal Kyle's soul sword.

With Lugh out of the fog, getting the rest of the party out was much easier. He pulled Meya up, then the two of them together helped Saul and Deriahm. Rogan was more difficult; he was much too heavy for any of them to lift, and the hole was barely big enough to fit him anyway. They solved the problem by the simple expedient of dropping Livaldi's desk into the hole; the extra height was enough to allow Rogan to push his torso into the office. Lugh grabbed him under one thick arm and Meya and Deriahm took the other and, somehow, they maneuvered his massive bulk up into the room.

They lay about resting for a while, letting the strength flow back into their bodies. For Lugh, it was like dipping into a warm bath after months of cold. The feeling of coming back to strength was sublime. After a few minutes, he rose to his feet, feeling as well as he ever had.

He wished he could say the same for his companions. Nihs was pale-faced and sickly, but worse yet was Saul. The old man was sitting on the ground, one arm propping him up, the other still clutching at his heart, as if he were worried it would leap from his chest. Meya was kneeling next to him, one hand on his chest, giving him magic. The look on her face was grim and reluctant; she obviously hadn't forgiven him for his role in all this.

Lugh hunkered down next to Saul, forearms resting on his thighs. "You going to be all right?" he asked.

It took Saul several seconds to answer. Lugh could see his thin chest rising and falling beneath Meya's hand.

"James…" he said finally.

Lugh nodded. "Do you have any idea where he could've taken Kyle?"

Saul shook his head miserably.

"Maida outposts…all over the world. But…James…I think he…" he shook his head again. "None of them. Somewhere…secret. Only trusts…himself."

Lugh had been thinking the same thing. With Livaldi the way he was now, he wasn't likely to share Kyle's existence with anyone else. The only question was, where could he have taken him?

Well, there was no time to be coy. They'd failed to keep Kyle away from Livaldi, but it wasn't too late to catch him up and take Kyle back.

He turned to Deriahm. "Do the Buors know where Livaldi is? They've been watching him for a while, haven't they?"

For a moment Lugh thought that Deriahm might deny it; then he said, "It is true that we have been closely following Doctor Livaldi's actions in recent months; however, I do not know the full extent of our intelligence."

"Now would be the time to use that lodestone and find out," Lugh said. "We're going to need all the help we can get if we're going to track him down."

Body, mind and spirit were the three pillars of the Being. Clerics such as Meya dedicated their lives to studying this trinity, understanding the relationship between the components and the necessity of each.

Without a mind, a body could not think; without a body, a mind could not act.

Without a soul, the mind and body could not feel; could not exist, could not *be*, could not give and take from the swirling, pulsating sea of energy that was the universe. But just as the mind and body needed a soul, so did a soul need a mind and body. A soul without mind and body was nothing more than a current of directionless magic, an eddy that would soon be subsumed into the greater universe around it. When Phundasa the Orc died—when his heart stopped beating and the flickering thundercloud that was his mind sparked its last thought—his soul was cut loose of its host, floating freely in the air before slowly dissolving into the atmosphere around it.

Kyle's soul, as James Livaldi had correctly explained, did not behave as Lorian souls did: the bonds that tethered it to Kyle's body and mind were indestructible. Though his body and mind could be brought to the brink of death, there was no force in the world strong enough to dislodge his soul from its bearings. By the slightest thread it would cling on; and slowly, surely, it would work to restore its host, rebuilding its fortress one cell at a time until it was ready to rejoin the world of the living.

The being was not aware of any of this.

All it knew was that it existed, and that somewhere in this vast grayness in which it found itself, something else did as well. Something else *must*, or else it would have no reason to remain here.

It had no eyes, no ears, no skin and no senses to speak of; all it had was a vague feeling, an *understanding*, that it was not alone in this universe, that there was an *other* as surely as there was a *this*. If Kyle had had the mental capacity to remember the experience as it had felt at the time, he might have described a single point of light, as small as a mote of dust, floating in an enormous cave that, for its vastness, might have been the blackness of outer space.

Tentatively, keenly aware of its own weakness and vulnerability, the last spark of Kyle's soul began to flit through the darkness, feeling into the empty crevasses and abandoned corridors that constituted its surroundings. It was not yet cognizant of what it was doing; it was merely an *it*, exploring the unending *not it*, the *zan*, in which it found itself.

There was no concept of time in this place, but eventually the mote came upon another like it. It was so faint that it could almost be said to not exist at all, but when the *it* drew close, the *other* was drawn into it and became a part of *it*, and the *it* felt itself grow larger by the smallest possible fraction that could be felt.

It floated on.

There was another *other*, and then another after that. Each time *it* found one, it brought it into itself, and each time *it* grew larger and stronger. Soon the dust mote had become a spark, then a candle flame. Relatively speaking, it was thousands of times its original size. It was now bright and intelligent enough to detect hints of its surroundings; it had a vague sense of where it was and what it was doing, but more than that, it now had a sense of *who* it was. It moved more purposefully, harvesting the fragments of itself that had been scattered among the gray crags. Now it was large enough to illuminate the edges of the landscape it had once thought of as endless; it saw patterns, impressions, imprints, channels, but as of yet could not divine their meaning or purpose.

Some of the *others* this *it* encountered were larger now. It realized that it was not the only one engaging in this coalescence, this rebuilding. Each of the *its* was searching for the others, and like drops of water that fell and became streams, they were all starting to run together.

The search, the *race* continued, accelerating faster and faster as more of the flames came together. The *it* merged with a massive flame that was nearly as big as itself, and suddenly understanding flowed in. It did not think in human concepts such as names (that was the brain's work), but it had now realized at its core a solid image of the human to which it belonged, to which it formed an integral part. To it, the inner parts of Kyle—his heart, his bones, the layout of the neurons in his brain—were as distinct and unique as the parts of him that were presented to the outside world: his black hair, blue eyes, and pale skin.

It wanted nothing more than to complete the image that it understood to be right and true; to billow outwards and inhabit the body and mind to which it belonged. But as soon as it had reached a certain size, it encountered a barrier that impeded all forward progress. The flame perceived it as a web of angry black ribbons trimmed with silver. The ribbons crisscrossed above and below it, squeezing painfully against the flame's presence. Whenever the flame came into contact with them, they lashed out at it, and part of it was painfully burned away.

The flame was distressed, but it was also still growing—more and more tiny motes were joining it with every second, and it could now no more control its own growth than it could understand what the ribbons were and why they were here. It grew and grew until it was straining against the barrier that caged it. It pressed harder and harder against the ribbons, and even though the ribbons lashed out in retaliation, it found it was growing bigger still.

There was a moment of exquisite pain as the ribbons cut deeply into the flame's swollen body; then, finally, they began to fray and tatter. A moment later, they burst, and suddenly a torrent of energy, released at last from its bindings, billowed outwards at a tremendous speed.

Energy gushed forth; the soul was no longer a speck of light or even a candle flame. Now it was a boiling river of vitality, a flood of power that moved with purpose and ever-growing force. It flowed through Kyle's body, at last understanding what it had been encountering all along. It discovered bones and ligaments, arteries and muscles. It plunged downward and discovered a pair of legs, then moved laterally and found a set of arms. Internal organs—heart, lungs, stomach—were all identified in turn, and though it was too early to engage them, the soul marked them nonetheless.

The soul then travelled upwards, and discovered Kyle's mind. It was almost completely dormant, a thundercloud reduced to a wisp of cirrus. The soul saw shocking complexity there, and decided to wait; this would have to be one of the last things switched on.

As the soul swelled ever outwards, it discovered parts of itself that were not entirely to its liking. They were natural and familiar, yes, but they were not a true reflection of the ideal vision that the soul had for its vessel. In the past, the soul had lacked the energy needed to sculpt them to its liking (the fact that the soul had not existed until a few months prior had not occurred to it). Now, however, it had more magic than it knew what to do with, and more was coming to it at an incredible rate. It decided to put it to good use.

It set to work.

James' eyes flickered to the control panel of his aircraft. One of the gauges was painted a gradient that ran through all the colors of the rainbow, from red up to violet. It was the atmospheric magic readout, meant to indicate how much magic was available to the Ephicer engine at any given time. In most skies over Centralia, the gauge never left the comfort of the green-blue zone. When flying over water, as James was now, the magic available was often less, usually sitting in green and sometimes flirting with the bright lime color that came underneath.

This was no cause for concern; most craft could maneuver perfectly well up until they fell into the orange or red.

And the needle had only dipped ever so slightly—it was now indicating a greenish yellow, like the skin of an unripe lemon. Livaldi decided to ignore it.

The Wyvern, with the orange stone inside it, was resting on the passenger seat next to him. James took one hand off the yoke and laid it on the gun's sleek golden body. Instant calm and clarity befell him. A smile crept onto his face.

He'd done it. He'd won. Nothing could stop him now.

In the back seat lay the corpse of Kyle Campbell. If Livaldi had turned around in his seat at that moment, he might have noticed that one of the fingers on Kyle's right hand was twitching.

Still the soul grew, and still the soul changed.

Muscles were tightened. Bones were reinforced. Scar tissue was regenerated. The body was optimized in a million infinitesimal ways, and whenever the soul thought its work might be done, it discovered a million more changes that it could make with the power available to it. Still it found that it couldn't make changes quickly enough; the more energy it spent, the more it had to spend.

Finally it could wait no longer. It set Kyle's heart to beating, and opened his collapsed lungs. He drew in a mighty gasping breath, and at that moment, his brain came alive. It instantly took charge, as brains tend to do, imposing a strict order on the radiant chaos that were Kyle's body and soul. It commanded the soul to stop bringing in energy for the time being, and the soul was happy to comply. It tested all of his muscles, tweaking them carefully, sparking in satisfaction at the soul's work. It regulated the beating of his heart and the expansion of his lungs; it set in motion the thousands of other processes necessary for the body to run smoothly.

Then it opened his eyes.

James watched the magic intake dial dip lower and lower. Soon it was in pure yellow, then began to tilt towards orange like a setting sun. For the first time he felt anxiety creep into his heart. He was in trouble if there was something wrong with his airship; he was miles from the nearest land.

Was it the sound or the light that he noticed first? Looking back, he thought that he must have noticed both of them some time ago, and chosen to ignore them. Nevertheless, now they both came to him at once: a soft blue-white light emanating from the back seat, and a persistent chiming sound not unlike the hum of an Ephicer engine.

He looked behind himself.

Kyle's corpse was glowing. It was wreathed in that silvery blue light, and sparks were dancing up and down its length. Livaldi didn't have to be told what was happening. Not only was Kyle reviving—he was *promoting*.

A kind of wild, exultant panic flooded Livaldi's mind. The power of the nuclear soul! Incredible! Despite the black soul container, despite its vessel being damaged nearly beyond repair not two hours ago, it had not only regenerated to its former power—it was surpassing it.

The airship's console gave off a warning beep. Livaldi looked down and saw that the needle had dropped into a deep, bruised orange. He looked back at Kyle.

Ah.

Kyle's mouth opened and he gasped a mighty breath. His eyes burst open, and they were glowing a blinding blue. A wave of force exploded outwards from him, and Livaldi felt it wash over him in a torrent of magic. At that exact moment, the needle plunged into the red and the airship fell in into an uncontrolled dive toward the sea below.

Kyle awoke confused, disoriented, frightened, and yet exhilarated. He felt fantastic, as if he'd just enjoyed the best night of sleep of his entire life. He was strong and clear-headed, and his senses were incredibly sharp. He picked out every detail of the small airship cabin in an instant: the cramped back seat, the passenger seat on which rested Livaldi's gun, and in the pilot seat, Livaldi himself, struggling madly with the airship's controls.

He realized that the airship's emergency alarm was going off, and red lights were blinking on the console. That, combined with the swooping feeling in his stomach, could only mean one thing: they were in a free fall.

He struggled into a seated position and thrust his body forward. Livaldi's hand snaked out, reaching for his gun, but Kyle had been expecting this. His reflexes were keener than they had ever been; his own right hand lashed out and he seized Livaldi's wrist. With his left, he reached around the driver's seat headrest and closed his fingers around James' neck.

"What's going on?" he growled.

James gurgled. It sounded like a laugh.

"What do you think? We're falling to our deaths—thanks to you, I might add. If you want to live, I suggest you let go."

"Funny," Kyle said, "I seem to remember a certain someone saying that I was invincible here in Loria. And it looks like that's true. So I think I'll take my chances. You, on the other hand…" he didn't bother to finish.

Now Livaldi gasped. "You heard me say that? Amazing!" His last word ended with a cough—Kyle felt his Adam's apple bobbing against his fingers.

"Seems like it," Kyle said. He was looking through the front window of the airship, watching the blue ocean below growing dangerously close. "Now where did you say my friends were again?"

"I'll tell you everything!" James gasped. "But if you don't let me go now I'll have little opportunity to!"

Kyle unclenched the hand that had been around Livaldi's neck and he drew in a shaky, rattling breath. Before releasing the hand that was around Livaldi's wrist, he reached over and pulled the Wyvern into the back seat with him. James, obviously sensing that this battle at least was lost, didn't protest, and instead gripped the airship's yoke with both hands. He flipped a lever on the control panel and the machine juddered horribly; then he pulled back on the yoke and turned their dive into a long, shallow glide.

They were still going tremendously fast when the airship finally collided with the ocean's surface. The bottom of its hull clipped the top of a breaker, and it instantly went into a vicious end-over-end roll. Kyle and James were thrown together, then apart, tumbling about inside the cockpit. Its doors were ripped free of their hinges, and a moment later they were sucked outside.

Water flooded Kyle's nostrils and boiled down his throat. There was a blossom of pain as something struck him solidly on the head, and he nearly fell into a daze. But he was still overflowing with the power from his promotion, and his injuries healed almost at once. He found himself suspended about fifteen feet underwater. He could see the outline of the airship above and off to his left. The water was full of debris, some of it floating toward the surface, most of it drifting down into the ocean's depths. Something directly in front of Kyle caught his eye: it was Livaldi's gun, the Wyvern, with the orange stone still set into its barrel. Kyle swam over—he couldn't believe how quickly he could move with his new body—and grabbed hold of it, careful not to touch the orange stone directly. He strapped it to his back, then looked up to the surface. His lungs were bursting, and it seemed dreadfully far away. But he felt a new power rising in his chest as he swam towards it. It was not completely unfamiliar; he'd felt it once before, when he'd woken from the prophetic dream that had revealed Vohrusien's tower to him.

You know how it's done, his soul told him. *You've done it once before. Go! Soar!*

A few seconds later, the surface of the water split open and Kyle came rocketing out, buoyed by his overflowing soul. His flight was slightly undisciplined; after breaching the surface, he listed dangerously to one side and he had to fight to keep himself from plunging back into the ocean. He felt as though a multitude of tiny beings were supporting him in the sky; to move in one direction or the other, he had to control their flow so they pushed where he wanted them to push. It was a bizarre experience, but within seconds he was starting to understand its rules.

He hovered twenty feet above the water's surface, arms outstretched for balance, looking like he was treading water himself. Below him was the body of the airship, half-submerged in water. One of its wings was nowhere to be found. The other was bobbing along on the far side of the ship. As Kyle watched, it drifted further away from the airship's body, and he noticed a bright purple shape holding on to it.

He went into a dive, instinctively leaning his front half forwards and pulling his arms back. He accelerated quickly, soaring down to where Livaldi was paddling through the water. James looked up at him with a strange blend of emotions on his face.

Carefully, Kyle floated down and landed on top of the wing. He pointed his right hand down at Livaldi and a cascade of sparks burst forth from the palm. Kyle's soul sword was more blindingly brilliant than ever before. It had grown to the size of a bastard sword, though it still weighed absolutely nothing. It hummed with terrific power, and sparks ran thick along its length, so jubilant that they occasionally jumped off the blade and earthed themselves in their surroundings

Kyle focused, and the blade extended even further, until it was not six inches from Livaldi's face. Of course, he had been able to do that all along; his soularm could be a sword, or a spear, or anything he wanted it to be. He just hadn't known it until now.

"I suppose you expect me to beg for my life, now," James said. His purple hair was plastered against his cheeks, and he'd been cut several times by the airship's glass. His smirk, however, was intact.

"My friends," Kyle said. "Where are they?"

"Back in Sky Tower. I left them stuck in a trap called a black soul fog. The same technology that sealed your sword—though I see now that it isn't quite as foolproof as I once thought. They're all fine," he added, in a soothing tone of voice. "They'll recover within minutes once the trap is turned off."

"Where are we?" Kyle asked then.

Livaldi grinned. "The middle of the ocean, of course."

Kyle squatted and grabbed him by the scruff of the neck. "I know that, you ass," he said. "*Which* ocean?"

"Centralia Bay. West of Reno. Now would you be so kind as to help me up?"

Kyle considered letting Livaldi squirm—it would be no better than he deserved—then decided it wasn't worth it. He retracted his sword, grabbed at Livaldi's belt, and dragged him onto the wing. Livaldi sprawled there for a moment, letting the moisture drain out of his waterlogged suit. He rose shaking to his knees and pulled his jacket off, then stood. He grinned viciously at Kyle.

"Well? You've managed to strand us. What now?"

Kyle shot him a nasty look. "*You're* the one who's stranded," he said. "I can leave any time."

"True—but you're not going to leave me here to die. It's not in your nature. In any case…" James pointed off to his right. "The southern coast of Elfland lies in that direction. If we mean to get back to land, that is our shortest route."

"I've got a better idea," Kyle said, and scooping James into his arms, he curled his body and began to gather energy. A moment later, he flexed his legs and burst into the sky.

He rocketed upwards at what must have been fifty miles an hour, eyes streaming as he headed for the low-hanging clouds above them. Livaldi was stiff in his arms; Kyle didn't know what it would feel like to be the passenger in this situation, but he hoped it was stomach-churning.

They broke free of the first layer of cloud and Kyle hovered, looking around. The sky was blue in all directions; the sun was so bright that Kyle's hair had already almost completely dried.

"What exactly are you doing?" James asked.

"Looking for a ship," Kyle said, spinning them on the spot.

"Then head either north or south. All of the main flight paths hug the coast."

Kyle didn't stop to question why Livaldi was being helpful; he reasoned that being held captive several hundred feet above the ocean's surface was reason enough to cooperate. He aimed himself south and soared off, figuring that if they didn't run into a ship, they would at least be heading back toward Reno city.

They flew for several minutes, and Kyle finally had the time to process the amazing transformation that he had just undergone. He felt like a new man in the literal sense of the phrase; his own body and mind were unfamiliar to him, as if he'd accidentally stepped into the life of someone else while unconscious. At the same time, he felt *good*—better than he ever had. His vision was clearer, his thoughts came quicker, and his body felt stronger. Soaring felt incredible, but natural at the same time; he might have learned how to soar at the same time he'd learned to walk for how easily it came to him.

He sped along, wind rushing in his ears, keeping an eye out for any airships passing by. Finally he saw one: a medium-sized vessel that looked slightly the worse for wear but serviceable for all that.

Kyle had no idea what the rules were for boarding unfamiliar airships, and didn't much care. He alighted on the deck and allowed James to spill from his arms. James immediately sprung to his feet and began fussing with his clothes; he was holding his beautiful purple jacket in a sopping ball under one arm.

"Hello!" Kyle called toward the ship's cabin. "Anyone there?"

The door to the inside of the ship swung open, and a town Selk stepped out. He was wearing a look of incredulity on his face. He greeted them with a traditional Selkic adage.

"Piss in me eyes," he said, eyes wide. "Where'd you come from?"

"I soared," Kyle said. "Listen, sorry for boarding your ship without permission, but it's kind of an emergency. My name's Kyle Campbell. Can I ask you to do me a favor?"

The Selk's eyes narrowed, and he glanced at Livaldi. The latter was keeping his head down, trying not to be recognized. "Why?" he asked. "What's goin' on, then?"

"I'm an adventurer," Kyle said. He took hold of James' upper arm. "This is my bounty. I need you to contact the Buorish police and tell them I've got him."

The eyes grew even wider, but the Selk seemed to believe him. Little wonder—Kyle was speaking with the absolute authority of one who had complete control over the situation at hand.

"Can you do that?" Kyle added, when the Selk showed no indication of moving.

That broke the spell. "O'course," the Selk said, backing away nervously. "Sure, sure. Hold tight a sec'."

And he disappeared inside the ship, leaving Kyle and James alone on the deck. James heaved a heavy sigh.

"Well," he said, "I suppose this means you win. How the fates can change in the blink of an instant."

"Shut up," Kyle said absently. He was thinking about how things were going to happen once the Buorish police got involved. He was willing to bet that every Buor in Loria would recognize his name by now. He could count on them to help—it was just a matter of getting Livaldi locked safely away, rescuing his friends, and then bringing the orange stone back to Vohrusien.

He reached for the gun strapped to his back and pulled it off. He wanted to look at the orange stone, break it free of the Wyvern so he could snap the gun over his knee. He had just brought the gun up to his face and realized that the stone's cradle was empty when a horrible pain struck him between the shoulder blades.

Livaldi, a look of savage terror on his face, had driven a knife into Kyle's back, and was twisting it deeper into his body. The knife's blade was black rimmed with a glossy white, and as soon as it came into contact with Kyle its edge began to burn angrily against him. Kyle fell to one knee, his balance shot and his sight wavering; the black soul container was doing its work, turning his own soul against him. His sight gave way completely, his other leg crumpled beneath him, and his head thudded against the ground.

Once Kyle had stopped moving, James twisted his wrist, and the end of the blade broke off into Kyle's back. He grinned so widely that a trickle of spit escaped from his mouth. *There! That ought to hold you, my flighty friend!*

He was resigned to the fact that he couldn't possibly bring Kyle with him as things stood; mister Campbell was far too powerful and volatile to be kept at bay by the tools James had at his disposal now. But given some time, and the power of the orange stone, James knew that he would be able to come up with something.

What was important now was making his escape while Kyle was still indisposed. He would commandeer this ship with the help of the Wyvern; all they needed to do was bring him to land, any land, and he would be able to disappear. He would have to abandon Sky Tower for now—vexing, but James had faced greater setbacks in his short life. He would discover some method of keeping Kyle's power in check, perhaps a more powerful version of the soul container, and then he would wait for Kyle to find him. It was a sure thing, after all: Kyle couldn't leave Loria while Livaldi still held the orange stone.

He unwrapped his salt-encrusted jacket and pulled out the orb. Kyle might be all-powerful, but he wasn't all-knowing. While he'd been busy playing the hero, James had removed the stone from the Wyvern. He hadn't been sure at the time if he would get a chance to use the black dagger; happily, Kyle had presented him with this opportunity, as well.

The orange stone felt like an electric fire in his hand. He'd only held it once before, when he'd first placed it in the Wyvern. Even in his current state, he recognized that this fire would destroy him if he held onto the stone for too long. He retrieved the Wyvern and had just slotted it back into place when the town Selk came back out on deck. His eyes nearly popped out of his head when he saw Kyle sprawled on the floor.

"What—" he began.

Livaldi pointed the gun at him. "I assume that you came back outside to let Kyle know that his salvation was coming. I, however, do not plan to spend the rest of my life rotting away in a Buorish prison. Disengage your flight path and climb into the clouds. Then, turn us northwards. I hope, for your sake, that..." but then he trailed off. Something on the deck had caught his eye.

The black dagger was growing out of Kyle's back.

As James watched, the blade fell out of the now-closed wound and fell to the deck with a *plunk*. Kyle began to gather his arms beneath him.

"You can't be serious," James said, and fired the Wyvern.

Kyle moved faster than Livaldi would have thought possible. His body twisted and his left hand shot out. A glittering shield of blue and white blossomed from his outstretched palm. The Wyvern's slug struck it with such force that the entire ship rocked, and the deck below Kyle splintered and warped. But Kyle didn't so much as flinch, and the bullet ricocheted off into the sky.

The soul shield was absorbed back into Kyle's arm, and Livaldi found himself looking directly into his eyes.

"That was a mistake," Kyle said.

He pointed a finger at Livaldi, and James felt a terrible intake of magic. Somewhere inside the airship's cabin, a warning alarm went off, as it had in James' ship during Kyle's promotion.

A bolt of white lightning exploded from Kyle's fingers and sizzled across the intervening space. It struck James full in the chest, and for one terrible moment his entire being was engulfed in pain, and he felt his heart stop beating. His soul shield fell in tatters around him, and he was blown off his feet. The Wyvern went flying, and clattered against the ground. James landed on his back, slid, and slammed into the guardrail that girt the ship's prow; had it not been for that, he would have tumbled off into the ocean.

Kyle stood. His eyes were blazing blue and crackling with lightning. He no longer seemed human at all. He raised his hand again, and magic began to gather once more. James had barely survived the first bolt; the second would have killed him as surely as a blast from the Wyvern would have killed a native Lorian.

"No! Stop!"

Kyle's focus wavered, and the magic dissipated. He shook his head to clear it, and some of the mad blue glow left his eyes.

There was another airship pulling up next to the one on which Kyle stood. It was sleek, black and red, like a scorpion flying through the sky. Emblazoned on the side was the Crest of Buoria, the symbol of King Azanhein. Standing on the deck were Kyle's friends and companions. Saul the magician was being supported by Lugh and Meya; it was he who had cried out, and now, as the Buorish ship was expertly maneuvered to run parallel to the other, he leapt from one to the other and fell heavily to the deck. He crawled over to James and lay across him, sobbing.

A loudspeaker on the Buorish ship was turned on and a commanding voice boomed forth. "This is the Buorish police! Relinquish all weapons and raise your arms above your head. Do not make any sudden movements. Do not attempt any magic. To do so will trigger the suspension of rights as well as our immediate retaliation."

Then, in very different tones, it added, "It is a pleasure to make your acquaintance once more, mister Campbell."

Things happened very quickly after that, and Kyle, in his state, was happy to let them happen. The ship was boarded by members of the Buorish police, who ushered Kyle and Livaldi onto their own ship and immediately began working to revive James. The Selk who had first spoken to Kyle and the other members of his crew were interrogated for a short while, then released once it was obvious that they had nothing else to tell.

Kyle was swarmed by his companions as soon as he was on board the police vessel. Meya hugged him and kissed his forehead, and Lugh pounded him on the shoulder. Rogan ruffled his hair, Nihs gave him a curt nod of approval, and Deriahm bowed almost reverentially.

"Hey," Lugh said, squinting. "There's something different about you. You didn't promote, did you?"

Kyle examined his hands. They were certainly his, but he still felt the slightest twinge of disconnect when he looked at them. A faint blue glow surrounded his fingers, and as he watched, a tiny spark jumped from his palm like a leaping fish.

"I think so," he said.

"How do you feel?" Meya asked him.

Kyle thought about this honestly. Dazed, yes. Overwhelmed, yes. But he looked at the faces of his friends and said, "Good. I feel really good."

A Buor approached their party, arms folded neatly behind his back. His armor was plain, and his sash was blue instead of the dark red used by members of the Buorish police. "Mister Campbell," he said, "it is good to see you in good health."

His tone of voice, so familiar, made Kyle pause. "Have we met?" he asked.

"We have, though we were never formally introduced." The Buor proffered his hand. "I am executor Sardassan, an agent of his majesty King Azanhein. Pleased to make your acquaintance."

Kyle took the hand. "An agent of King Azanhein?" he asked, but he was looking at Deriahm as he did.

Sardassan coughed politely. "Indeed. I am afraid, mister Campbell, that we have not been entirely forthcoming with you. You see—"

But Kyle shook his head. "Don't worry," he said. "I get it. You had this all planned out from the start, right? You and Azanhein and Deriahm. You knew that Livaldi had the orange stone and that I was going to try and take it from him. You couldn't interfere because you didn't have any proof, so you helped us under the table and waited for Livaldi to break the law so you could arrest him. And now…" he went on, the mental image growing to completeness in his mind, "you'll let me take the stone and disappear back to Earth, which will take care of both of us at once. Then everything can go back to normal. Is that about right?"

For a moment Sardassan said nothing, while Lugh grinned at him from over the Buor's shoulder.

Then Sardassan chuckled, merrily but briefly, and said, "An insightful summary to be sure, mister Campbell. But you give us too much credit—we engaged in this venture having our suspicions and our clues, but little else. It was you who discovered the secret of the orange stone and brought Livaldi's crimes to light. With, of course, the assistance of his manservant."

"Where is the man, anyway?" Rogan asked.

Sardassan dipped his head. "He is inside, tending to his master. You must not think too poorly of Saul, or of Livaldi himself, for that matter. The one was motivated by love for his charge, and the other was seduced by a magical artifact of incredible power. In fact, it is astonishing that James was able to resist the power of the orange stone for as long as he was."

"Speaking of which…" Kyle said. He looked directly at Sardassan. "If you've been following our quest all along, then you know that I need the orange stone to go home. Will you give it to me?"

There was the slightest moment of hesitation, and in that instant Kyle saw disaster stretching out before him. What would happen if the Buors refused to give the stone to him? What if they decided it wasn't safe for Kyle's hands, or that it was to be used as evidence in Livaldi's trial?

But then Sardassan said, "Of course, mister Campbell. Though it is wildly unconventional, the situation in which we find ourselves is unconventional as well." He turned to one of the policemen and nodded. They left, and returned with a heavy metal box. Sardassan took it delicately by the sides, and then offered it to Kyle.

"Take it," he said. "With the blessing of King Azanhein. Do you know where it needs to be brought?"

"Yeah," Kyle said, remembering what the Archsage had told him. "Northern Ar'ac. The place where I landed in Loria."

"I see. That is not far from here; do you wish for us to take you there now?"

Kyle looked up from the box. Sardassan's question, so innocuous, had sounded like a thunderclap in his head. The reality of his situation came rushing in, bowling him over like a seashell caught in a breaker.

Do you wish for us to take you there now?

Do you want to go home?

Do you want this all to end?

Kyle looked up at the blue brilliant sky and down at the blue brilliant ocean. He looked at the faces of his companions, marking them one after the other.

No, he thought. *No, I don't. Not yet. I'm not ready to leave yet. I haven't seen Elfland, or Okogan, or Nimelheim. I haven't said goodbye to King Azanhein, to Por Amam or Archmage Rosshku. I haven't met Rogan's wife or been invited to Mo.Ji.Ro, the floating island. I haven't seen what's at the bottom of Low Ocean, or flown around the world by soaring. I haven't seen Lugh and Nihs become famous adventurers.*

I can't go back. There's so much I still have to do.

"Yes," he said, gripping the metal box that held the orange stone. "Yes, please take me there."

Sardassan bowed and quietly melted away, promising to give them some time to themselves as the ship flew further south. Not two minutes later, however, he reappeared, with a white-and-red-sashed Buor in tow.

"Miss Ilduetyr?" he asked softly.

"Yes?" Meya said.

Sardassan stepped to one side, gesturing for his companion to speak. The other Buor bowed quickly, then said, "Despite our best efforts, Doctor Livaldi's condition is worsening. The blow that Kyle dealt caused him severe physical and magical trauma, and we fear that he may lose his life without proper treatment. Would you be willing to aid us in stabilizing his condition?"

Meya's red eyes shone, and her expression grew vicious. But Lugh put a hand on her shoulder, and she softened when she looked at him.

"Fine," she said, in tones of disgust. She brushed Lugh's hand off. "Fine. Let's go."

The white-and-red-sashed Buor said nothing, only bowed, and the two of them left in silence.

Most of the rest of the voyage passed in silence, as well. Kyle felt as though he should have a million things to say, but despite that—or perhaps because of that—he found he couldn't quite manage to say anything. He stood at the bow of the ship, leaning on the railing of the viewing platform, as he had done on the *SS Caribia* a lifetime ago. Lugh stood next to him, arms folded, Nihs perched on his shoulder. Rogan stood at his other side; Deriahm, for his part, was being debriefed by Sardassan's men.

Lugh heaved a heavy sigh. "Well," he said, "I guess this is really it, isn't it?"

Kyle nodded. The breeze played at his cheeks and pulled at the hem of his shirt.

Lugh looked at him sidelong. "Sure you don't want to stay here a little while longer?"

No, thought Kyle. "Yeah," he said.

Lugh nodded, gently enough that he might have been falling asleep. "Figured as much," he said. "Listen. We'll take things a little slower the next time you visit, all right?"

Kyle laughed out loud, but it in a way it had been a cruel joke. "I don't know if there's going to be a next time," he said.

Lugh shrugged. "It's a big universe out there," he said. "Besides, I've seen plenty of things lately that I would've thought were impossible a few months ago."

"Me, too," Kyle said, and it was Lugh's turn to laugh.

Meya emerged a few minutes later, looking tired and at least five years older. Lugh lifted one arm and she practically stumbled into it. He squeezed her close and she sighed against his chest.

"How'd it go?" Lugh asked her.

"He'll live," Meya said. "He doesn't deserve to, but he will."

"You did the right thing."

"We'll see."

"If it's any comfort," Nihs chimed in, "Livaldi is now at the mercy of the Buorish judiciary process. They are going to lock him away for quite some time—and even if they didn't, he would still lose his company, most of his fortune, and all of his credibility. His life is still, in many ways, very much over."

"This is dark talk for a group of friends sharing their last victory together," Rogan said.

"Hey, you're right," Lugh said. He clapped Kyle on the back. "Anything you want to do before you go?"

"There was something that I had in mind," Kyle answered.

Kyle stood on the railing of the police ship, clothes flapping in the wind. The northern coast of the Ar'ac was just beginning to emerge in the distance. He looked down at his companions.

"I'm jealous," Lugh said, sounding it.

"You'll learn sooner or later," Meya said, patting his back.

"Sure you don't want to come along?" Kyle asked.

Lugh shook his head. "I'll just slow you down. All right—get out of here. We'll still be here when you come back."

Kyle nodded, then tensed his body and leapt off the side of the ship. He spread his arms like he was floating in water, legs kicked out behind him. The magic propelled him forwards, and he soared, accelerating to an incredible speed. The wind was cold and ripped tears from his eyes as he flew, but he didn't care. He was jubilant and free. The world was his.

He stretched his arms above his head and dove toward the ocean below. Sunlight glinted off the waves as he skimmed along, mere feet above the surface. Already the coast ahead of him was growing larger and more defined.

He pulled up from the ocean's surface and shot upwards like a rocket. He broke through a layer of clouds, then another. Now there was nothing between him and the blazing sun; below him, the ocean's surface appeared mottled as the shadows of the clouds beneath marched across it.

Slowing his pace, he drifted lazily among the huge white formations that surrounded him. Moisture condensed on his arms and cheeks, forming tiny droplets of water that didn't quite get the chance to run together before the sun burned them away once more. He flew over rolling meadows and slalomed between cragged mountains of cloud. The coast was now quite close, so Kyle dove again, seeing how quickly he could bring it closer to him. He had no way of measuring his speed, of course, but it felt like he must be going well over a hundred miles an hour. His cheeks stung and his ears sang, but his heart pounded joyfully in his chest.

He hit the northern coast of the Ar'ac continent and followed it west for a time, watching the waves grow white and break against the rocky ground. He then turned inland over vibrant plains of lime-green grass and twisted, broad-leaved trees. He found a herd of bizarre bird-like monsters running through the grass, and followed them for a time, marking their peculiar long-legged gait. Perhaps these were gricks, the monsters whose eggs Kyle had eaten on more than one occasion.

Finally Kyle began to feel tired, and he alighted on an outcropping of rock that overlooked a gently sloping valley. He propped himself up with his arms and stretched his legs out, basking in the sun. In this moment, all of his worries were far behind him. His soul felt as light as a feather. He would never feel this free or this exuberant again in all of his life, but a part of this moment would remain with him for all moments to follow.

Kyle landed back on the deck of the police ship to find Rogan, Deriahm, and Nihs seated around a small table, playing a low-key game of mareek-check. Judging by the stack of multi-colored blocks sitting on the table in front of him, Deriahm was winning—as he always did.

Rogan looked up from their game and nodded in recognition. "Have a nice flight?"

"Yeah," Kyle said breathlessly. "Where're Lugh and Meya?"

"Meya's gone to tend to Livaldi again," Nihs said, setting one of his pieces down with a *clack*. "He had a slight relapse after you went. Lugh, if I'm not mistaken, is turning this ship inside out in search of food. Care to join us?"

"Don't mind if I do," Kyle said.

He would remember it as one of the happiest afternoons of his life; the simple pleasures of flying, eating, and playing meaningless games with his friends all blended into a sunny bliss that calmed his soul and filled him with a deep happiness.

An ashen-faced Saul made an appearance later that afternoon. He made directly for Kyle, and, taking one of Kyle's hands in both of his own, pressed it against his forehead.

"Thank you," he said, "for freeing the young master of his curse."

Livaldi himself, however, was nowhere to be seen; according to Sardassan, he had yet to awaken even after they were well beyond the Ar'ac's coast and less than an hour from their destination.

"Do not fear for him, mister Campbell," he said, seeing Kyle's expression. "We are confident that he will make a full recovery, particularly with miss Ilduetyr's assistance. And, in a way, it is a good thing that you struck him with that bolt of lightning. His soul had suffered a heavy degree of corruption by the hand of the orange stone; now, blasted down to its barest elements, it has received a chance to rebuild itself in a purer form."

Kyle didn't understand any of that, but he was happy to take Sardassan at his word, and happier yet that Livaldi was still unconscious. Somehow, he knew it would be simpler if he could slip out of Loria before James awoke.

They arrived at the crater just as the sun was setting. To Kyle, it looked the same as any other place they had flown over thus far. But Sardassan knew the exact coordinates of Kyle's landing place, and assured them this was the correct location.

The ship landed by the side of a small hill dotted with trees. The ramp was lowered, and Kyle and the others stepped out, flanked by Sardassan and several members of his crew.

The metal box in Kyle's arms began to hum as they circled the hill. Though the lid was shut nearly airtight, a thin ribbon of orange light began to escape from the box's lip.

Soon they found the crater itself; a depression in the side of the hill where Kyle had slammed into it with incredible force. The Buors had claimed that the crater was human-shaped, and perhaps at one point it had been; but the soil had eroded and the grass reclaimed it to the point that it was no longer possible to tell.

The box hummed more loudly still, and Kyle felt it vibrating ever so slightly. He set it on the ground and flipped the latch. Orange light flooded over them as soon as the lid was opened. The Ephicer was glowing so brightly that it looked like a miniature sun.

"Phew," Lugh said, stepping back as one would from a hot fire. "That's intense.

So what are we supposed to do with it now?"

"I'm not sure," Kyle said. He hesitated for a moment, then reached into the box and pulled the stone out. Powerful as he was, he felt a wave of magic emanate from the stone and attempt to climb his arm. His own soul fought off the stone's influence, but it was a near thing; it was no wonder Livaldi had been seduced by it.

He lifted the stone up to eye level, and as he did, he felt a subtle wind gathering about the hill. The sky grew a mite darker and the leaves of the nearby trees rustled in discontentment. Suddenly a voice, both distant and shockingly close, sounded in Kyle's ears.

You have done well.

Kyle looked at his companions and saw that they had all heard the voice, as well.

"It's the Archsage," he said softly. Lugh nodded silently.

Kyle felt the weight on his fingers lessen, and to his surprise the stone floated out of his hand and drifted over to the crater. It began to glow all the more brightly.

You have fulfilled your part of the bargain, and so will I fulfill mine. Behold: with the circle complete, a door to zan *can be opened. But your soul must first be stripped bare of all of its power; only then will you be able to pass through the gate. Are you ready?*

The stone's glow was by now so bright that the orb itself could not be seen at the center. The wind rose and rose, and began to twist around the stone, spinning it into a miniature orange galaxy. Kyle felt himself being drawn towards it.

"Wait," he said. "Not yet!"

I do not wait. Soon the gate will open, and you must enter the instant it does; the zan *must feed on you, or the world of Loria will be its surrogate. If you must make your goodbyes, do so in haste.*

Suddenly Lugh caught Kyle in a massive bear-hug from behind.

"I'm gonna miss you, kid!" Lugh shouted, squeezing Kyle so hard that he was lifted off his feet.

He found himself swarmed by his other companions, accepting handshakes and embraces from all directions.

"Goodbye, little one," Rogan said. "It's been a pleasure."

"Good luck, Kyle!" Meya said.

Kyle took her and Lugh's shoulders at the same time. "Take care of each other," he said.

"Don't worry," Meya said, "I will."

Kyle laughed, then unbuckled his belt. He handed his exquisite silver sword to Lugh.

"Here. Take it. I won't need it where I'm going."

Nihs and Deriahm were next.

"Good luck in your future endeavors, mister Campbell," Deriahm said, bowing. To say that his voice was thick with emotion would be an understatement; he sounded near tears. "It has been an honor to serve you."

"Goodbye, Kyle," Nihs said, rather more blandly. "You've managed to fairly shake things up here. I suspect that quite a few of our magical theories will soon need revising thanks to you."

Kyle reached out a single finger to shake Nihs' tiny hand. "That's me," he said. "Always causing trouble, wherever I am."

He was reminded of something else. He drew his clear-blue Iden card out of his pocket and handed it to Sardassan.

"Won't need this either," he said.

Sardassan laughed and accepted the card. "So hard-won, and now relinquished willingly. I will present this to his majesty. I am sure he will find it amusing."

The wind and light were now so intense that they had to shout to make themselves heard. Kyle shook hands with everyone again, then began to step toward the spinning vortex that the orange stone had become.

"Goodbye," he said for the last time. He didn't shout, only spoke the word in a low voice, half to himself, and yet he was sure that they could hear him. He marked each of their faces in turn. Lugh, sunny and laughing behind his glittering eyepatch; Meya, calm and beautiful; Nihs, aloof yet childish; Rogan, huge, gruff, and wise; Deriahm, poised and earnest. Even as he captured each face, they began to blur and swim together. The vortex was consuming him, and he felt it begin to eat away at the edges of his being, breaking him down into a form that could pass through the hole in the universe that Vohrusien had opened. Loria fell further and further away, the vibrant colors dimming, the thick atmosphere being blown away by a cold wind. His companions wavered, then vanished, like faces seen in the clouds.

"I'll never forget you," Kyle said, but this time he wasn't sure if anyone had heard. His reality was falling apart in tatters, revealing the empty gray void behind. He seemed to hear the Archsage's voice in his mind.

Zan, it said.

Zan.

Zan.

Zan…

Then all was white.

*K*yle awakens slowly, the way a man does after sleeping in on Saturday morning after a week *of all-nighters at work. His eyelids are heavy and filled with sand; his throat is hoarse, as if he's just run a marathon. But his body seems to be working fine, and after a minute he gathers his hands beneath him, flips onto his back, and opens his eyes.*

He's greeted by a warm summer sun, not unlike the one he just left behind. Its rays are warm against his skin. A slight breeze brushes his cheeks and raises goosebumps on his arms. It carries the faint smell of salt.

Memory begins to rush in. Suddenly Kyle sits up. His head swims, but he doesn't pay it any mind. He stands, staggers several feet to the left. He almost bumps into someone walking nearby. They glance in his direction, then hurry along their way.

Kyle presses his palm against his forehead—his head is pounding. But his heart is pounding harder, and he feels a wild excitement growing in his chest. Finally his head stops spinning and his eyes adjust to the light. He finds his balance, stands up straight, and looks around.

He's standing in the middle of a beach of yellow-white sand. Behind him is the depression in which he had been laying moments ago. To his left, a white wooden boardwalk, and directly ahead, a small dock juts out to sea. Moored at the dock is a dingy, medium-sized cruise ship.

He looks at the words picked out on the ship's flank. His eyes are blurry; he blinks several times and eventually the letters take on a readable form.

SS Caribia

For a moment Kyle just stands and stares. Then he starts to laugh. He laughs until his chest feels like it's been punched. He laughs until tears stream down his cheeks. He collapses to his knees in the sand, and still he laughs.

People are staring at him, but Kyle doesn't care. In this moment, he couldn't care less what anyone else in the world thinks.

He laughs until all of the pent-up laughter he has been denying these past twenty-six years is finally spent. By the time it dies down, Kyle is exhausted, and his throat hurts more than ever. But he is happy, and when he stands again, he feels as light as a feather. Light enough, in fact, that his feet are in danger of losing contact with the ground, and he in danger of simply flying—soaring—away into the beautiful blue sky.

He can't soar, not any more, but there are other ways to fly. Kyle fixes his gaze on the horizon, and a burning, ambitious joy takes him over, fueled by a single question:

What now?

Well…

His stomach gurgles. He places a hand on it and thinks, it's been ages since I've eaten a plain old cheeseburger.

He runs a hand through his matted, salt-encrusted hair and thinks, I could do with a wash, too.

And a shave, *he adds, scratching at his cheek.*

He looks around and thinks, But first I need to get off this beach, and as far away from that ship as possible.

More thoughts, more urges, jostle for attention, but Kyle waves them away. For now, he has enough to think about. After that…

He grins, in a manner more than a little reminiscent of someone with whom he has just parted ways. After that…

Well, it's a big world. How many adventures are out there, just waiting to be had? Enough to last a lifetime. Several lifetimes, in fact.

He'd better get a move on.

But first, food.

And then, some sleep. No, a wash.

Kyle laughs out loud again. Food, then wash, then sleep. Final offer.

He takes a step forward. Though he's taken many steps on Terra's soil before, this one is, in many ways, the first.